TO LOVE AGAIN

This is a work of fiction. Names, characters, places, and incidents are the products of the author's imagination or are used fictitiously. Any resemblance to actual events, locales, or persons, living or dead, is entirely coincidental.

TO LOVE AGAIN
by Margo A. Huizing
Copyright ©Margo A. Huizing
Cover Photo by iStock Photo.
Printed in the United States of America.
ISBN-13: 978-1725556935

ACKNOWLEDGEMENTS

Many people have encouraged me with kind words and
well-meant criticisms. Thank you to my friends, Barbara
Davidson and Winifred Morice, for the patient editing work,
loving me enough to be honest, and caring enough about
me to encourage me to keep writing. Another thank you to
Lola Torgerson for her editing help and her friendship. A
very special thanks to my friend, Graham Wilson, for putting
my book into print.

*June
2019*

*Dear Mary + Paul,
What a joy to meet you,
Can you imagine, we were
neighbors! Have a
wonderful trip and I am
sure we will see you in
Alaska!   Love
            Margo &
              Tony*

3

I would like to dedicate this book to my husband, Tony, for being the foremost inspiration in my life and for his support with every word and chapter. I would also like to acknowledge the never-ending support and encouragement of my daughter, Jill, who endlessly listened to rewrites and never complained. Thanks to my son, Tim, and daughter, Jen, for their help and encouragement. Margo A. Huizing

I

As the Southern Cross rose and fell on the midnight waves, it occurred to me that somewhere in the bowels of this dark night, the unrelenting, unforgiving loneliness of the sea had become my only companion, my friend, my confessional, my lover.

For months, wandering with aimless abandonment from port to port, I had hurried back to its arms, embracing its darkness. I buried my head in its shoulder and it accepted my tears without mocking me. My loneliness wrapped me in its blanket and encouraged me to feel. It absorbed my screams, my rants and raves at God for dealing me the deck of unfairness that He had bestowed upon me.

The loneliness shared itself with the darkness of the nights at sea and with the gentle sounds of the Southern Cross' hull gliding through the water. My companion created a sound, solid, nurturing environment for the depths of my despair to bury its strangling tentacles into the hollows of my mind.

My compass read due south and as I peered into its heading, the loneliness reached up to me and whispered, "I am here for you. Embrace me. I will never leave you." Once again, I succumbed to its charm. I could always count on it to fill the vast emptiness that Sadie had left in my soul.

I began, again, the inevitable recanting of my story. My friend listened intently. I told it of the pain, the ripping out of my guts, my reason for wanting to die, but before I could go there, I reminded the loneliness of the profound love Sadie and I shared, never completely finding the words to describe it.

Sadie and I had spent the better part of our lives together. I knew no one else. I never wanted to know anyone else. Our lives swayed in unison, like palm fronds in the wind, independently and separately, yet forming one melodic dance. We always laughed about being one person in two bodies.

After Sadie's death, life on land became unbearable. I saw her smile on every woman's face, tasted her lips in every friendly kiss and felt the warmth of her body in every human touch. No matter where I went, every ordinary scene of life held a memory of the astonishing love we shared.

On cue, loneliness yearned for me, embraced me in its blanket and warmed me from the chill air. It waited for my tears. My old friend, come to call.

As I sat at Southern Cross' helm, the wind bearing down, languishing in my own despair and anger, twinkling lights beckoned to me from the coast. I turned to port, suddenly in need of a human voice.

•••••

Almost to the day, thirty years prior, a ship entered this same port and altered the lives of the townspeople in this village, tearing them apart, and, at the same time, bringing them together.

Little did I know, I would have the same profound effect on their lives, leaving little doubt that fate weaves a continuous thread throughout time, past and present.

2

As I loosened the main halyard and the sail flaked downward into its cradle of lazy jacks, my old friend loosened its grip on me. A sense of weariness, beyond any man's imagination, took its place. It crept into the core of my body and mind and wrenched me into the present. The weariness transported me from my mental state to my physical one, of aches and pains that extended from the soles of my feet to the top of my head.

As I approached the lights, a small, time-worn marina appeared. Old fishing boats were cleated securely around a jutting pier, as smaller boats swayed in the anchorage.

The little town glittered against the sky and a dark, moonlit mountain towered beyond the lights. Extending from either side of the mountain, gentle cliffs fell into the sea, forming a peaceful, protected cove.

The moon's path created a glistening highway to the pier and I landed Southern Cross with ease. Tying her off, I noticed a fellow sitting in a rocking chair, hat over his face, all alone in the moon path, snoring, guarding his post. A shaggy dog slept next to him on the creaky boards of the old pier.

The dock tender began to stir as I secured my boat. His dog didn't. He lifted his hat and leaned forward, staring at his visitor, sleepy confusion on his face.

"May I stay the night," I asked, the sound of my own voice surprising me.

The man grunted. "Sesenta pesos."

"I only have American money."

"Okay, Senor, six dollars."

Deal completed, I handed him my money and finished tying down Southern Cross. The man replaced his hat and went back to his sleep. The dog never moved.

As I walked up the pier toward the village, I heard the dog emit a long, low growl. A smile crossed my face and I realized I hadn't talked, or smiled, in months. I needed a beer.

Climbing a small hill on a rocky, dirt road, the town lay in front of me. A long row of small, shanty buildings, closed for the night, lined the street. A few animals, including a goat, wandered around in the quiet darkness. At the far end of the street, a green sign hung on a wooden front porch, illuminated by the moon, announcing Tecate. Like a welcoming beacon, soft light filtered out onto the street through glass-less window frames.

On our few visits to Mexico, Sadie and I had managed to learn how to order a beer. We shared many laughs trying to figure out the road signs, the menus and words like "menudo."

I wondered, was anyplace devoid of her memory? How far will I have to go to recover? I hurried towards the green sign.

Two horses and a tired old mule were tied up to the porch rail. The dim bar, sawdust covering its wide-plank flooring, smelled like stale beer. Creaking ceiling fans, circulating the cigarette smoke-filled air, spun over dark, wooden tables. Each one hosted several men wearing cowboy hats and boots. Another shaggy dog slept near the front door.

"Cerveza, por favor," I muttered to the bartender.

As he put the beer on the bar, I sensed many pairs of eyes, even the dog's, watching my every move. Maybe no one here has seen an American, I thought. I drank the beer in one long swallow, quenching a deep thirst, and then ordered another, and another. Everyone still watched me and I noticed no one was drinking. The dog had lost interest and had gone back to sleep.

I had no idea how to ask for a room, but I didn't want to go back to the boat. I wanted a hot shower and a big bed. I wanted to sleep for a week.

The bartender approached me with what seemed to be apprehension. Breaking the silence in the room, he asked in labored English, "You want room, Senor?"

Every man stared at me, waiting for my answer. The dog awoke again.

"Si, Senor," pleased he had raised the question.

He pointed up the stairs. "Sixty pesos for room, ten for cerveza."

I paid up and he handed me a key with the number two written on it. I headed up the stairs and chose the one of two doors marked "two." I liked the system here.

I could hear the men in the bar talking now and I heard the dog emit a long, sleepy moan. For the second time today, I smiled.

The room looked clean. A medium-sized bed covered with a worn, colorful coverlet, sat against the wall. The gray walls and rusty shower gave the appearance of a prison cell. It matched my mood.

As I crossed the room to the window, my eye caught the image of a man next to me; a man I didn't recognize.

Startled, I turned towards him and saw a cracked mirror hanging on the wall. The face staring back scared me. It took a full moment to realize the returning image belonged to me.

My hair, caked with salt, stuck up all over my head, in crazy points. A heavy beard covered sun-baked skin. My clothes, hard with dried salt, had turned ragged. I kept staring at myself.

Not yet forty years old, I looked like an old man. What had happened to me? How had I not noticed that I looked like this? Had I lost my mind? Would I survive Sadie's death? No wonder everyone in the bar had stared at me.

Tears came like a flood and streaked the caked salt. Would I ever escape this hell? I lay down on the bed, too tired to move, too tired to go on.

I awoke to a confused array of sounds penetrating my head, children laughing, dogs yelping and people talking. Light shined through a window, warming my face.

A strange, shaggy dog slept on the floor by a chair.

I started to get up, keeping my eyes on the dog. She stirred, opened one of her eyes, and peered at me. I leaned down to her. "Come here, girl. Are you friendly?" She jumped up and started to bark. I fell back to the bed.

The door to the room opened and a woman stepped inside. "Good girl, you did a good job. Go to the kitchen and get a bone. Go now." The dog walked out of the room, stopping to kiss the woman's foot.

She turned to me. "So, Senor, you are alive. We were worried. We put the dog here to tell us when you wake up."

"How long have I been asleep?" I asked, confused.

"Two days. Take a shower, come downstairs, and get a good breakfast. I will cook for you." She smiled, turned and walked out of the room.

I hoped my appearance had been part of a terrible nightmare, but when I looked in the mirror, the strange man still stared back at me. I went to the shower. A razor and shaving cream lay on the sink. A comb, shampoo and soap were placed next to it. What a hospitable place, I thought.

The shower, hot and long, beat the salt from my body and the shave needed two razors to cut the hair from my face. I now recognized the man in the mirror. This time the returning image showed dark blond hair, although considerably longer than I kept it, blue eyes and tanned skin.

A white cotton shirt, matching trousers, underwear and a pair of leather moccasins had been placed on the bed in my absence.

I put on my new clothes and, standing tall, walked downstairs, feeling better than I had in months.

The woman stood waiting at the bottom of the steps. To my surprise, she patted me on the butt and said, "Angelina does good work, si? You clean up good, Senor. Come, eat. Breakfast is ready. Angelina will put some fat on your bones."

She pointed to a small table in the rear of the bar, instructing me to go and sit down. She disappeared behind the bar.

Quicker than the sleepy dog could open her eye, the food came. Plates of eggs, ham, tortillas, salsa and fried potatoes filled the table. I ate it all. A glass of cactus juice quenched my thirst. I couldn't help but remember my last meal on the boat; stale bread and a can of beans.

Angelina appeared again, as I put the last bite of food in my mouth. She had remarkable timing. She plunked herself down in the only other chair and grinned at the empty plates.

"I guess you like Angelina's cooking, si?"

The dog meandered over to her and lay down at her feet, placing her head on the woman's shoe.

"Best food I ever ate," I said, smiling at this amicable woman.

She smiled a great, huge smile. "I am happy you like your breakfast."

"You are an excellent cook, Angelina, and you speak good English."

"Many, many years ago, I fell in love with a man from America. He was an engineer on a ship which came to Puerto San Luis. He came back many times to see me.

He taught me English and I never forgot. It is a good language, my American, a good man."

"What happened to him, Angelina?" I asked.

"He was killed in a big storm at sea. I never saw him again, but I never stopped loving him."

"I am sorry, Angelina. It is a terrible thing to lose someone you love."

"I have a good life in this village. This bar belonged to my father and, when he died, I took it. I have many friends and family. And, I have many memories.

Now, tell me about you. How did you come here? Are you running from something? Maybe you are a criminal from America, si? Do you want to hide here?"

I laughed, surprising myself. She is charming, I thought. I could see why the American man loved her. I was willing to bet there were many lovers.

"My name is Peter Brentwood and I'm from San Diego. I've been at sea for months. I can assure you, I'm not nearly interesting enough to be a criminal. The only thing I have been running from is my wife's death.

I understand your loss, Angelina. I lost my will to live when Sadie died, she was my life. Now, I fear I've lost my mind.

In my quest to join her, I prayed for a storm at sea, one so violent that it would sink my small boat to the bottom of the ocean and leave me for dead, in the darkness of its depths. None came. Life is nothing without Sadie. I cannot escape her memory and I don't think I can go on without her.

As I spoke the words, I realized I had never spoken them before to anyone. I also remembered crying myself to sleep, the only time I had ever cried.

Angelina took my hand in hers. "The bartender, Pedro, told me you were here. He said you had a look of deep sadness in your face, under the sea salt. Now, I know where this sadness comes from.

Let me tell you this. I have had many years to think about my love. I knew I would never marry or have children. Even knowing this, my love for him has never ended. I learned to go on with my life, anyway. I found happiness with what I had left. It is not easy, but it is possible.

You must ask yourself this question. If your wife were alive, would she want you to be so sad? Would she want you to die? The answer is no. She loved you. She would want you to find happiness again. She is smiling at you from up above, knowing you are strong and will find a way to be whole again. Your love will keep her memory alive.

My love keeps Phillip's memory alive. And, I have found happiness. Only God chooses who will live and who will die. It is your job to go forward and then you will start to heal.

We've talked enough now. You will start your healing with your eyes. Look for the beauty around you. Look at the many different people in this village who have struggled too, in many different ways and yet, have all found happiness. When you heal your eyes, your soul will start to heal.

I walked out into the street, not wanting to leave this caring woman. She could be the only person I knew, on the face of the earth, who understood my pain. As soon as my foot touched the dirt road, I wanted to run back to her, sit at her table and never leave. I wanted her dog to sleep on my shoe.

I decided to check my boat. As I approached the pier, I could see the dock tender and his dog still sitting in his chair, sleeping in the sun. I wondered if either of them had moved at all since the night I sailed in.

The man stirred as I came close to him. The dog didn't.

He lifted his hat and said, "One hundred eighty pesos for three nights. Are you staying a long time? You look different. Did you meet Angelina? She is muy bonita, si?"

"I did meet Angelina. She is beautiful and an excellent cook. I feel much better."

He grinned and patted his dog's head. "You look muy better, too."

"Senor, may I leave my boat here? I would like to stay in your village for awhile."

"Si, you can stay as long as you want, sixty pesos a day.

Let me warn you about Angelina, Senor. You watch out for her. She likes American men. Do not anger her, but remember, she is the best cook in the village." Grinning, he tipped his hat and held out his hand.

"Thank you, Senor." I filled his hand with money. He sat back in his chair, thumbing the bills.

As I walked back up the dock, I heard a long, low growl from the sleepy dog.

3

Jilted by another lover, Megan sat alone in her apartment. Three men in five years. She had believed this one was going somewhere. Again, she found herself struggling with the familiar ending, tears and emptiness.

Her relationship with Michael seemed different than the others. So much so that she allowed herself to enjoy a type of security with this man. The vast holes left in her soul from her mother's death had begun to heal. This break-up hit harder than the other two. She had let her guard down and had begun to trust once more.

Trust; a funny word, she thought. A word used so freely and casually, its true meaning becomes taken for granted. Only when you lose someone you trust without doubt, do you begin to comprehend the meaning of the word. Until it's gone, you don't know you had it. Unlike love, anger or fear, it never identifies itself. It lives unquestioned in your soul and yet, it is the greatest gift you can give to, or receive from another person; because, it can only be earned.

Other than Michael, the only person she ever trusted had been her mother. She loved her father, but her mother had been the one to hold Megan's hand along the path of her life. Even when they were separated by physical miles, her mother led her and encouraged her in spirit. When all else went wrong, their relationship remained true. Megan wore that bond like a warm, comfortable pair of pajamas, taking it for granted.

Her mother always had a soft word, a kind hand and an unquestioned love for Megan. She knew when to offer a firm reprimand, yet never failed to be there to make the pain easier amid the inevitable realizations of life.

Megan trusted in her mother's love, trusted her not to let go of her hand, and trusted her with every detail of her life. She didn't think to trust her not to die.

She wasn't sure when the depression started. She wasn't sure it was depression. She just seemed to feel a sense of profound emptiness. Ultimately, that emptiness filled itself with sadness and an overwhelming loneliness.

The joy she had felt in her job as an art gallery curator dissipated into an apathetic lack of interest. She paced herself through the days with no particular thoughts of the future, no particular thoughts of the past. Her mind seemed to settle in purgatory, a place of nothingness. Conversations with fellow patrons of the arts caused her mind to wander into sketchy, non-definable areas.

The desire to sleep enveloped her and thoughts of daily life eluded her. Days turned to weeks, weeks to months and Megan didn't notice.

She sat in quiet darkness, lost in the solitude of her life, the aloneness a familiar feeling.

She felt tears on her cheeks and realized the sun had gone down. Somewhere in the distance, a baby cried. Lights shimmered like fireflies through her window. The city prepared for its night dance.

•••••

Megan had always loved the city. It seemed to move to its own beat. Rushing toward Broadway to see a play, buying vegetables for dinner at the market, hailing a cab, or riding an elevator, you unwittingly became one with it and one with the city, eagerly joining up with everyone else rushing to stay in time.

Nestled in the basement of her brownstone in Greenwich Village, Megan had to look up through the living room window to see the street. She and Michael had spent many Sundays sitting on her little yellow couch, sharing a bottle of wine, watching the feet pass by, and inventing lifestyles to match each set of shoes.

Every Sunday ended the same way. They fell together laughing and made warm passionate love as the feet of the city passed by the window.

One captivating year; learning to trust; learning to love. Learning to touch the part of their souls that no one else had dared touch; learning to experience the beat together.

Michael seemed to really care. His interest in Megan's life, her job, her feelings, her wants and desires were unending.

He wanted to know about her past and her dreams for the future. Their lovemaking led to many long nights of conversation, sharing intimate secrets and hopes and dreams, ending with daybreak sneaking through the window.

Megan believed in Michael, and his promises. He said he would never leave. He couldn't bear to think what life would be without her. He knew God Himself had put them together.

She allowed herself to feel, to love. She trusted Michael not to leave. And once again, the trust was shattered.

•••••

Megan fell into a deep, sad sleep, picturing again, Michael in his bed, lying next to his former wife. The same wife that decided their divorce had been a mistake and asked him to come back home to her and their son. Michael left Megan sitting on the yellow couch alone. She felt heaviness in her chest, knowing she would never see him again.

Megan woke to bright sunshine on her face. She dressed moving absentmindedly through the familiar routine.

Glancing at herself in the mirror, she wondered how she could go on without Michael and her mother. I can't, she decided. I don't even want to.

Drinking her orange juice, she glanced around her apartment, seeing the feet passing by her window. Feet she hoped never to see again.

Megan locked the front door, placed the key under the mat and walked out into the sunshine. Oblivious to the beat of the city, she stopped at the bank and withdrew money. She dropped a note off at the Post Office for her friend, Amy Gray, and boarded the subway to the airport.

Walking up and down the terminal, looking for a place to run, a place to hide, Megan decided on a flight to San Diego. Three thousand miles from her life seemed like a good, safe distance. It didn't really matter which flight she chose.

Boarding the plane, she did not look back. She fell asleep in her seat before the plane left the tarmac. Sleep, peaceful sleep. If only she could drift in sleep forever.

Megan awoke to the sound of a young girl's voice telling the passengers they were landing in San Diego, in a pleasant 82 degree temperature, in twenty minutes.

Standing in the exhaust-filled air of the airport, she hailed a cab.

"Welcome to our city, Senorita," the driver said, smiling.

She couldn't help but notice the friendliness in his face, her first conscious observation of another human being in days.

The cabdriver looked around, and seeing no suitcases, ventured to ask, "You have come to a wonderful city like this with no luggage?"

"I like to travel light," she said with irritation. "Please take me to any decent hotel with a view of the ocean."

"The Hilton is the closest thing we have to the water, Senorita. It is on the bay."

"That will be fine. Thank you." It didn't matter to Megan. She just wanted to sleep.

"Will you be in San Diego long?" he asked, as he started his car.

His voice droned in her ears and she wished he'd shut up. She wasn't interested in conversation.

"No, not long," she said and remained silent for the rest of the trip, although the talkative driver went on about his city non-stop.

Enduring his endless chatter, she glanced at the small medicine bottle in her purse, wondering just how much courage she had.

In her room, Megan stripped off her clothes, looked at the bay from the balcony window and lay down on the bed.

She wanted to join her mother. Although ready to take her fate into her own hands, it would be easier not to do it herself. She prayed for the Lord to take her in her sleep.

She held the small bottle in her hand and considered what her mother would think of her plan. Would she be happy to see her again, or would it be one of those rare moments when her mother became displeased with her?

Within minutes, she fell asleep.

4

Amy awoke with sunshine coming through her window, unusual for Manhattan, but it felt good on her face. She snuggled back into the warm sheets and tried to go back to sleep, but her troubles flooded into her head. She stood and walked to the window. The city of New York filled her senses.

She had come to see it as the smallest, big city in the world. The most crowded, yet sometimes loneliest place on earth. It could be your friend or your enemy and it always entwined you in a love-hate relationship.

She watched people below her on the street, bustling around like ants serving their queen. Cab-drivers pounded their horns and yelled obscenities at other drivers. Vendors hawking their wares, combined with the racket of shopkeepers rolling huge carts of Italian bread and cheeses into restaurants, permeated the inner-most chambers of her head, crowding out the previous day's events.

The noise of the city formed a never-ending music and the people, the cabs, the subways and, even the buildings, seemed to dance to it. She loved it and could not remember wanting to live anywhere else.

•••••

Arriving on a bus in New York with only her meager savings and one bag of possessions, Amy hailed a cab and gave the driver the address of the one person she knew in this immense city. Megan awaited her arrival.

They had grown up on Cape Cod, in a little village nestled by the sea. Adoring parents and a secure, comfortable world embraced their childhood.

They attended private school together and giggled over boyfriends while painting their nails bright red and watching their new breasts grow.

Their first dates were with twin brothers from a local boys' school. Amy and Megan wore each other's clothes and liked the same songs. They enjoyed the same parties and decided to attend the same college.

Amy's dreams of becoming a stockbroker were etched in her brain. She wanted to work on Wall Street. She wanted to be one of the movers and shakers. She wanted to make it in a man's world.

She even knew what her apartment, overlooking Central Park, would look like. She knew the doorman's name would be James.

Megan teased her all the time, but Amy knew her friend believed in her, and she loved Megan with all her heart.

Megan's dreams took her in a different direction. All she wanted was her mother's life. She wanted a child and a home. She wasn't interested in a career.

Throughout their lives Megan mimicked her mother, learning to cook, plant a garden and dabble in oil-painting.

She wanted to love a man, as her mother loved her father. She wanted to care for him, dress for him, live for him and have his children. She wanted the same look on her own face that her mother had when her father walked into a room.

Megan's father did not understand her pleas and insisted she go to college. This decision didn't make her happy, but she couldn't bear the thought of disappointing him, so as long as Amy was going, she would go, too. She decided to study art while she waited for the man of her dreams.

Although Amy studied a lot more than Megan did, their college lives were fun. Megan took art classes and painted flowers. She studied art history and flirted with her professors. She made fun of Amy and pouted when she wouldn't go to a party, choosing the library instead.

Everything continued this way until their senior year. Halfway through the year, their phone rang and Amy was told her father had been arrested. He had been accused of embezzlement. He admitted guilt right away to avoid the disgrace and public humiliation of a trial.

Astounded, Amy felt she had been thrown into a nightmare.

A court ordered everything they owned sold at auction and the same judge sentenced her father to twenty years in a white-collar prison.

Penniless and disgraced, Amy managed to finish college and graduate at the top of her class, but instead of New York, she headed home to Cape Cod to care for her mother.

As she put her dreams on hold, Megan secured a position in an art gallery in Greenwich Village and accepted a graduation present from her parents, a brownstone in the Village.

As Megan planted flowers in the window boxes and painted them on her canvases, Amy searched for a job and an apartment she could afford for herself and her mother in their hometown.

They kept in touch and both looked forward to Megan's frequent weekend visits to the Cape. But, over time, they each came to realize that Megan's successes and her own entrapment in a life she didn't want, made the visits painful for each of them.

Three years passed and her mother's divorce became final.

One fateful day, her mother announced she intended to marry a man from their old country club. Immediately following the wedding, Amy packed her clothes, called Megan and caught a bus to New York.

Megan welcomed her with tears and open arms. Amy felt a new beginning, a sense of hope and a way out of the nightmare.

She spent weeks walking up and down Wall Street, submitting resumes to receptionists in every brokerage house that had a front door. Not one phone call. Not one interview. Her money was low and her morale plummeted. She cried herself to sleep at night in Megan's small guestroom.

Then, one cold afternoon, the phone rang. A brokerage firm needed an assistant for one of the brokers. Amy dressed and fled to the interview as fast as she could. She landed the job, and danced for joy all the way home. It had been a long road, but she had made it. Her dreams, shelved for years, had at last come true.

She and Megan celebrated at a small Italian restaurant, with wine and huge plates of spaghetti, talking about the old days. Life was sweet.

Several weeks later, Megan came home grinning like a Cheshire cat. A friend needed to sublet his apartment while he worked in Europe. He would be gone two years.

"Oh my God, Megan, it would be perfect for me. I'd be close to my new job and to you. At last, I'd be on my own."

Two weeks later, Amy slept in her own sweet bedroom, overlooking the crowded streets of Little Italy. Happiness, for the first time in almost four years, overwhelmed her.

Her determination returned. She spent endless hours at work, proving herself among her peers, and within months she was offered a promotion to broker-in-training. She and Megan again celebrated at the Italian restaurant.

•••••

Standing at her window, breathing in the smells and letting the sounds of her beautiful city embrace her, Amy contemplated her current situation.

Her landlord wrote and told her he would be coming home within the month. He was sorry, but his job had not been successful and the project cancelled. She had to move.

The brokerage house informed her profits were down and there would be lay-offs, starting with the trainees. She didn't know where her name fell on the list. She had proven to be an excellent student and even made some profit for the company, but she didn't know if it would be enough. Where was her life going now?

She and Megan had all but lost touch over the last year. Megan's new love, Michael, kept her busy and up until now, Amy had been swamped at work. She missed Megan. She would call her later today and catch up.

In her pajamas and robe, Amy walked down to the lobby and opened her mailbox. A single letter fell out. She recognized the neat writing as Megan's. Why had she written a letter? What was the matter with the telephone? What could be wrong? Was Megan angry with her? I don't need this right now, she thought, anger gripping her.

She sat down on the chair near the door, with the doorman looking at her, and opened the letter.

Megan's writing seemed peculiar, stiff and tight, not her usual artist's flair. Its appearance scared her. She had trouble focusing on the words.

What she read caused disbelief.

My Dearest Amy,

I know this may come as a shock to you, but I have left New York. I need to go somewhere and be alone. I don't know where I am headed, as I don't have a plan at this moment.

I do not intend to return to New York, so, I would like you to have the brownstone and everything in it. I have signed the deed over to you and it is on the kitchen table. I have also left a sum of money, in a bank account, for you to take care of the house. My lawyer will see to all of the details. Please call him.

I love you, Amy. You have always been my only friend. Please do not worry about me. I will be fine and I will call you as soon as I am able. I just cannot take the pressures of the City any longer.

All my love, forever,

Megan

Tears filled Amy's eyes. What did this mean? Where had Megan gone? Why hadn't she talked to her? What had happened to Michael? No answers. No matter how many times she reread the letter, she found no answers.

"Are you alright, Miss Amy?" the doorman asked. "Can I help you? Please let me help you."

Amy looked at him through a flood of tears, bewildered and confused. Her friend was gone. She forgot she wasn't dressed.

She stood up. "No, James, I've had some bad news. I'll be all right. Thank you." She hurried to the elevator and stumbled to her apartment. She had to find Megan, but how?

5

I surveyed my boat and found its condition as deplorable as my own when I arrived. The Southern Cross had been a source of pride since the day I purchased her, never a rail unpolished, or a piece of teak weathered, and now she sat here in this ramshackle marina, in a complete state of disarray and filth. It embarrassed me to look at her.

I was even more appalled at the interior. Half-eaten food and empty beer bottles lay everywhere. A strong stench of soiled clothes, rotten food and stale beer saturated the cabin. I wondered how I had lived like this for so many months. I hadn't even noticed, let alone cared. I started to clean and began to think I would uncover bugs. I hoped not.

Opening a locker, my black medical bag jumped out at me. I hadn't seen it in months. I remembered stowing it when I left, because it occurred to me that I might get hurt.

I wanted to die, yet the irony of the situation must have escaped me; I'd put it on board anyway.

•••••

My earliest childhood memories pictured me sitting on my father's lap, his hand on mine, guiding the helm of our boat to stay on course.

I grew to know the California waterways better than most knew the roadways. There had never been a question that the sea was an integral part of my life, intertwined with boyhood, dating, college, medical school and Sadie.

When I met Sadie, she didn't know how to sail. Afraid of the water, she had never been on a boat. Her passions centered on art galleries, ballet, theater and nature. She had studied liberal arts in college and before meeting me, dreamt of living in a jungle in Africa, studying the lives of gorillas.

During our courtship, and after considerable pleading on my part, she agreed to go to the marina to see my boat. Unimpressed with all the possibilities it suggested, and the moving dock sending fear into her core, lunch interested her more.

I put my love for the sea and my boat on hold. My desire to sail paled by comparison to my desire for her. This shocked me because, up until that moment, the only true love I had was sailing.

I could never figure out how we got together to begin with. Our lives were so different that vast, empty canyons had to be crossed for us to have a conversation.

My friends were all members of the sailing community; from old salts to America's Cup racers and Sadie's friends were, in my opinion, stodgy, art buffs. She made fun of me and told me I led a sheltered life. I countered with her being stuffy and uptight.

A breakthrough came when she introduced me to an artist named Gauguin, an impressionist, acclaimed for his work in Tahiti. This happened to be one of my favorite places in the world, having sailed to its shores with my father.

My familiarity with the islands brought his work alive for Sadie, and she began to flirt with the idea of learning how to sail. The thought of going by boat to Gauguin's art gallery, in the middle of the South Pacific, appealed to her romantic side.

On a warm weekend, during the summer before my senior year in college, I again coaxed her onto my boat.

She made me promise I wouldn't go too far offshore and I wouldn't expect her to get in the water. At her own insistence, she wore a bright orange life-vest and sat unmoving in the cockpit, clenching her hands and frowning. Her blonde hair swirled gently around her face in the wind. The Southern Cross never looked more splendid.

I sailed with ease around San Diego Bay and when we anchored for lunch, Sadie began to relax.

Watching from the cockpit as I cleaned up the galley, she decided to come below and help me. Trembling, Sadie stood next to me, dishtowel in hand.

The huge vest overwhelmed her tiny frame. I smiled at her cuteness and then took her into my arms. At anchor, the Southern Cross rocking in the light current, we made love. I knew at that moment I would marry her and my life would be complete.

With time, Sadie learned to love the boat. I think she

understood that the boat and I were a package. So, as our life together began to unfold, I went with her to art galleries, tried to remember the names of birds and Sadie learned to sail.

As I scrubbed and cleaned, my mind drifted back to my college days.

My father had been my mentor, my disciplinarian, my worst and best critic. I, his only child, had been his one hope to have his name, and fame, live on.

As he laid down the bricks of my life for me to walk upon, I never once thought to question his wisdom. I would be a doctor. I would love the sea. I would follow in his footsteps. All of this went unsaid. It never needed to be spelled out.

His unyielding attitude molded my life. If I decided to learn something, I had to learn it to an expert degree, nothing less was considered acceptable. No margin for laziness, no boyhood shenanigans and no pubescent dalliances were ever allowed.

College opened new doors. For the first time in my life, I didn't live under his commanding eye. I discovered freedom. I also discovered parties, women, cigarettes and beer.

For the first time in my orchestrated life, my father's wrath raged. He threatened my funding, disownment, and sometimes, I thought, even my life. Filled with the arrogance of youth, I paid no attention. His condemnation fell on a deaf ear.

One fateful night, during my second year of college, on a short weekend trip to the Baja, his plane malfunctioned and crashed into the sea, killing both him and my mother.

The plane and the bodies were never found. All I had left of my parents' last moments was a taped, frantic call to the San Diego tower, screaming that their plane was going down. I also had an inheritance of ten million dollars and sole ownership of his practice.

The following months became unbearable. Guilt consumed me. Self-hatred personified me. I had caused him pain. I had failed him, me, his only son.

It took time, but I crawled out of my hole and dedicated my life to fulfilling my father's dream.

Spending all of my time in the classrooms or the library, I studied with an obsession, trying to live up to my father's reputation. I disciplined myself, as he had disciplined me. I vowed to honor his name. I vowed to make my mother proud.

I gave up the parties and my playboy lifestyle. My college buddies and my girlfriends gave up on me. I extended my classes into the summer, ignoring my boat and the impending sailing season.

My professors took a new interest in me. They gave me tougher and tougher assignments, as though to prove I couldn't live up to my father's name.

I worked harder and harder, plowing through textbooks, until my head pounded with fatigue. None of my efforts buried the pain of their deaths.

Late one night, well into my third year of school, my eyes bleary and my soul tired to its core, I reached for my hundredth cup of coffee. My eyes fell on the loveliest girl I had ever seen, sitting at the table next to me.

Long, silken, blonde hair cascaded down her back. Her head, tilted a little to the side, revealed a tiny, upturned nose and bright blue eyes. She chatted with another girl, her lips curving into a shy smile. I shook my head and tried to look at my book, but my eyes stayed on her face.

Every line I had ever used ran through my head, but none of them seemed appropriate for this magnificent girl. As I sat staring at her, she turned, looked at me and smiled.

The sun and moon came together; the world collided with them and bright stars shone all over the room. I felt as though I had been struck by lightning.

Embarrassed for having been caught staring; I blushed and stammered, "My name is Peter. I'm studying this book because I want to be a doctor." I heard myself and hated my mouth, but I couldn't stop it from talking. "I have coffee. Would you like some?"

Her friend got up, excused herself and left.

My mouth kept talking. "Do you come here often? I do because I'm studying to be a doctor like my father." Stupid, I had never sounded so stupid. Where had my finesse gone? I am a lady's man. Who is this girl? My mind went in one direction and my mouth in another. Something had to end this humiliating moment. She did.

She came and sat across from me. "I would like some of your

coffee," she said, in the most lilting voice I had ever heard.

After a small dissertation on how I prepared my coffee with milk and two teaspoons of sugar, my mouth stopped moving and I sat there feeling even more stupid.

Sometime later, months into our courtship, Sadie told me she had come to the library for three months, sat across from me every night and waited for me to notice her. She begged her friends to accompany her and when they wouldn't, she came alone. She was about to give up when I looked up and saw her.

One month after our graduation, we married in a sun-bathed ceremony on the ocean's edge.

My father would be proud. I graduated at the top of my class. My mother would be proud. I had found love.

•••••

A voice shook me out of my reverie.

"Senor, Senor, are you okay?"

I heard the question somewhere deep in my mind and it took a few seconds to realize someone was speaking to me.

"Hello," I called, popping my head up from the cabin. "Yes, I am okay, just trying to clean up down here."

The dock-master looked different standing up. Wrinkled, worn clothes did not hide the stockiness of his short frame. Jet-black hair and dark eyes, along with a three day beard, accentuated his tanned face. His bare feet looked in need of a bath.

"I am Enrique Pierre Santiago, he declared, extending his hand. What is your name?"

"Hello, Enrique. My name is Peter Brentwood and I am from San Diego."

His mouth formed a wide smile, exposing a shiny, gold tooth. "Many years ago my father took me there. A wonderful place," he proclaimed, nodding his head in approval, "many beautiful women there, si?"

Glancing at the Southern Cross, he asked me why I had come to Puerto San Luis.

"I lost my wife sometime ago. I decided to go to sea for a while and try to figure things out. The other night, I saw the lights of your village and decided to stop for a beer. Today, it seems all I have accomplished is a filthy boat."

"Senor Brentwood, I am sorry about your wife. I have many friends who, for a price, would be happy to clean your boat. The Mexican sun will kill you. Angelina has cold beer."

"Thank you, Enrique. That sounds like a good idea. Let's go."

Minutes later, Pedro sat two cold beers in front of us. Angelina was nowhere to be seen.

"My Angelina must be on siesta." Enrique's face shadowed.

Sipping our cerveza, letting the circulating fans cool our skin, we sat in silence.

"Did you say your name is Enrique Pierre Santiago?"

"Yes, Senor Peter. You have a question about Pierre, am I right?"

"Yes, only because it is a French name. How does a Mexican man, in a fishing village on the Baja, get a French middle name?"

"Many people have this question, Senor; you are not the first, so here is the story.

The French settled in Mexico many, many years ago in pursuit of the gold in our mountains. The French brought many new things to the Baja, but the Mexican men liked the French women the best.

My father's great-grandfather, the original Enrique, enjoyed roaming up and down the coast trail on his mule. On one adventure, he ran into a pretty little French girl, named Pasqual. He returned many times to see her and they fell in love.

Her wealthy and proper parents did not approve of his callings. They did much to discourage their daughter from seeing him, but she refused to obey them. Finally, locking her in her room, they forbid her to leave the house.

Their rebellious daughter escaped. Pledging their love for each other and under the cover of darkness, the young lovers ran away on his mule.

Before the parents realized she was gone, the couple disappeared high into the Mexican mountains, where Enrique knew no Frenchman could find them. He prided himself on his knowledge of the treacherous mountains, knowing not even another Mexican could track him.

While the girl's father and his friends searched for her, suffering many hardships in the unforgiving mountains, Pasqual's mother cried bitter tears at home.

Making their way back to Puerto San Luis, Enrique's family prepared a big wedding for the young couple.

In the end, her family scorned her for marrying a Mexican man. She had disgraced the good French name of their family. The girl's parents returned to France and disowned their daughter. They told their friends Pasqual had died from the Mexican water.

One year after that, she had their first son and, because she missed her homeland and parents, she named the baby Enrique Pierre Santiago. Pierre was her father's name and Enrique, her husband's.

Every son born to the Santiago family is given the middle name of Pierre to honor her and every first son is given the name of Enrique Pierre to honor the couple. I am the first son of my father."

"What an amazing story, Enrique".

He smiled. "I am proud of my name, Senor."

"You should be, Enrique. I am named after my father and I am proud of that, too. He was a good man."

Pedro placed two more beers in front of us.

"My father was also a good man, a man who loved this village more than anyone. Someday, I will tell you the story of our pier."

I followed his gaze towards the kitchen. Angelina's face smiled at us from the window.

I could see his interest in his father's story disappear.

6

Megan woke, startled and confused, to the muffled sound of a high-pitched scream. Her body jerked to an upright position.

Her mind, clouded like an undusted chalkboard, did not comprehend her surroundings, but it didn't take long for yesterday's events to seep into her consciousness. Her letter to Amy, the airport, the plane and the cab driver all marched through her mind. What had she done?

Walking to the window on unsure legs, she saw the bay and the screeching seagulls. She also saw her reflection in the glass, staring back at her.

Oh, my God, that can't be me. It can't be. What has happened to me?

A large mirror on the wall proclaimed the truth. Dark black circles reached down, touching her cheekbones. Her hair hung in pitiful strands, lying on the ashen, drawn skin of her face. She couldn't remember her last shower and had not noticed how thin her body had become. Rib bones protruded from her chest.

A chilling thought sliced through her brain. She had come here planning to end her life. Turning her gaze from the mirror to the nightstand, the small bottle stood menacingly in a ray of sunlight.

Have I had a nervous breakdown? My God, oh, my God; what's wrong with me?

She stumbled to the bathroom, afraid of herself, afraid of her own mind. She stood under the hot shower, praying she would come to her senses.

Returning to the bedroom, she found her clothes lying in a rumpled heap on a chair.

Hunger pangs overwhelmed her, but the thought of food made her sick. She sat for a while, looking out at the bay, trying to regain control, wishing this nightmare would end.

Her mind wandered to its familiar morning place, the death

of her mother. Every day, upon awakening, she replayed the events in her mind. They ran through her head like a play, and she, an outsider, watched it. She always knew the ending.

•••••

Late one night, her phone rang. Through tears, her Uncle said, "Meg, you must come home right away. Your mother has had a heart attack. Please, hurry".

Megan rushed to the airport, near hysteria, and flew the commuter jet to her hometown. She arrived too late. She would never see her mother again, never touch her again, and never hear her voice again. Within seconds, she passed from hysteria to shock. Her Uncle had her medicated and took care of arrangements. The funeral remained a blur in her mind.

She could not even think of going back to the coldness of the city. Megan arranged a leave of absence from the art gallery and took up residence in her old room. She wandered around the house for days, looking at her mother's life, realizing she had never seen it through her eyes. Everything looked different. She could see her mother walking through the rooms; feel her being in everything she touched. She spent hours sitting across the street at the ocean's edge, trying to figure out how to go on without her mother.

One afternoon, with the sun starting to set, she sat down at her mother's desk and noticed a small envelope addressed to her. The letter felt warm, as if her mother's hands were still on it and it carried the fragrance of her perfume. Breaking the little gold seal on the back of the envelope, she removed the small delicate paper it contained.

Dearest Megan, it began. I can assume if you are reading this, I am gone. Don't be sad for me. I have known for some time that I would soon be joining your beloved father. At last, I am where I have wanted to be for a long time. I am not complete without him.

You have always been the essence of my life. From the moment you were born, I was the happiest woman in the world. You were too perfect for me to have another child. I did not want to take any time away from you. Your father and I were complete.

For us, you were the sun that lights up the earth; the very meaning of life. Never forget my love for you. Take it with you wherever you go. It is yours for a lifetime. Someday, we will be together again. I love you.

Now, to business. Go to see our lawyer. We have left our estate to you. Enjoy the fruits of our labors. It is a small gift for the love and happiness you gave to us. - Your Loving Mother.

She stared at the letter with disbelief. Her mother knew she was going to die and hadn't told her? How long had she known? She said she loved her, and yet, never thought to say good-bye? Why? Grief-stricken, she put her head down on the desk and cried.

Sitting in the lawyer's office seemed surreal. She had never thought about her parent's money. She knew her father made a good living and they never wanted for anything. She decided it must be a small amount and didn't want it. The thought of spending her parent's money caused her stomach to heave. She stared at the lawyer.

Folding his arms across his chest, he coughed and began to fidget in his chair. When he spoke, his voice shook. "Megan, your mother has willed you her entire estate, including all properties. The cash value is a little over five million dollars in stocks and bonds and the properties will realize another five million.

Being the good business man that he was, your father set this up in a nice little package years ago to avoid inheritance tax. Presently, your net worth is more than ten million dollars."

Stunned, she sat in the chair and could not move. No thoughts came to her mind. No words came to her lips. She sat in shock unable to comprehend his words. The room just seemed to go black. As her senses returned, a feeling of bewilderment replaced the emptiness.

The lawyer had instructed his secretary to bring water, but in seeing the impact of this news on Megan, changed the order to brandy.

Muddled thoughts began to streak through her frozen brain. She jumped up from her chair, tense with sudden anger and paced back and forth in front of the desk.

"What are you talking about? Have you lost your mind? Ten million dollars? Ten million dollars?" The number sounded ridiculous to her ears.

Her outburst continued. "Where did they get that kind of money? Why didn't I know about it before now? What other secrets did they have?"

Mr. Clayton handed her a portfolio. "I think your questions will all be answered once you read this, Megan. I know this is a shock to you, but your parents enjoyed a wonderful life and they wanted to assure you were taken care of after their deaths. Their love for you was profound."

"Mr. Clayton, I have done a fine job of taking care of myself. If their love for me was profound, they would have told me about this themselves. I would have preferred that they had. I don't understand why they waited until now to reveal this. Did they think it would alleviate my pain? We were so close. How could they hide this from me? What else have they kept a secret?" Furious rage fueled her uncontrolled outburst.

Leaving the brandy untouched, Megan instructed the lawyer to leave every dime of the money where it was and arrange to sell the properties. She strode out of the office and told the secretary to call her a car. By the time she reached the pavement, it awaited her arrival.

She returned to her parent's home and sat, day after day, looking back at her life, revisiting her childhood, looking for any hint of this much wealth. Their life had seemed normal. They hadn't lived in extravagance. They had been comfortable. When had they started to deceive her? She found no answers.

Feeling betrayed and confused, she took great care going through the house gathering her mother's precious heirlooms. She packed them and sent the boxes to her brownstone. Calling a cab and going back to her life in the city closed the chapter on her life in Cape Cod.

•••••

The play had ended, again, for the millionth time. She stood up from the chair and walked across the room, trying to shake the despair from her mind. Once again she looked at herself in the mirror. The returning image invoked horror. She propped her hands on the dresser and stared at herself. Her eyes filled with tears.

"I need help. Oh, please God. I need help." Her hands trembling, her arms not strong enough to hold her up, she moved back to the window and sat down.

•••••

Her mind conjured up a little girl; herself, she realized. Long, shiny, chestnut-colored hair danced across her back as she swirled in circles, hands posed high above her head, around and around on the great front lawn of her parent's home. They stood, applauding her, as she pretended to be the graceful ballerina she had seen the night before. She bowed before them, reveling in their adoration.

The image changed to a tall, slender young girl, her skin possessing the color and softness of a gardenia petal in the early spring. Her eyes, the same color as her hair, glistened in the lights illuminating her college graduation podium. She could feel her father's pride; sense her mother's tears as she accepted her diploma.

Image after image of her youth floated through her mind like billowing white clouds on a warm summer day. Each one carried with it a sense of happiness, contentment, security and a warm, fulfilling love. Her emotions came alive with the goodness of her childhood, and then, as if her mind were on a wild roller coaster ride, it abruptly took a nosedive back into her depths of despair.

Lost in the deep caverns of her thoughts, hours passed. Darkness fell outside her window before she realized she hadn't left the chair all day. She moved, her muscles stiff, her head pounding, over to the bed.

She saw the small bottle, sitting on the nightstand. Rolling it between her fingers, she poured the pills into the palm of her hand. She thought about death. Eternal sleep. No more lost loves. No more betrayals. She could end her constant torment. Her mind and her soul would, once and for all, be calm.

But words Amy had said snuck their way into her thoughts. Her friend had told her, "Don't worry about me, Meg. I am a survivor. Life is too precious to give up. I will realize my dreams someday. Everything I want is out there; I just have to find it. I just have to keep trying. And, I know God is on my side."

Megan closed her hand around the pills and poured them back in the bottle.

She slept with dreams of Michael tormenting her subconscious. She woke in a fit of rage; mad at the man she had so loved, mad at her mother, furious with her father. She sat up, exhausted from the turmoil, her body aching with sadness. She hit the small bottle, sending it flying across the room.

The wheels in her head spun, spitting out question after question. Why had her mother never prepared her for the heartache of life? Everything had always been so perfect, so damn perfect. Why couldn't she find someone to love her? Why didn't she know how to pull herself out of this black hole?

The anger motivated her. Her mind changed gears. Okay, you left me to do it on my own, all of you, and now I'm going to do it.

Amy dealt with her problems and survived. She could too. She had avoided Amy, not knowing how to deal with her tragedy. She had run away that time, too, just like she did this time. I'm through running, she decided.

Strength filled her being, and then, fear replaced the strength. "Where do I begin?" she wondered. A new thought occurred to her. I will begin by stopping this self pity. Yes, yes, that will work. That's where I'll begin.

Feeling empowered, she decided to walk down to the beach. She did her best thinking to the rhythm of the waves. She dared not look in the mirror as she dressed. She knew how she looked.

As the elevator door opened, she smelled bacon and eggs. Hunger pains raced through her body. Well, that would be a place to start, she thought.

Devouring her breakfast and then ordering a muffin with her coffee, she couldn't help but notice the waitress' once-over.

Passing through the lobby, a small clothing shop caught her eye. A young salesgirl in the shop, seemingly motivated by her appearance, guided Megan's selections. Returning to her room, she showered and dressed again.

This time when she looked in the mirror, the image appeared more pleasant. I've made a good start, she thought. I have a long way to go, but I'll make it. I know I will. She headed for the beach.

As Megan walked along the water's edge, alone, young lovers holding hands passed her. Families laughed together and enjoyed picnic lunches on colorful blankets. Mothers sat on the beach playing with their daughters.

The scenes more than she could stand; the familiar depression filled her again and her eyes welled with tears. She had to get away from this beach, from these all too familiar scenes. She ran back up to the hotel.

Screams of rage formed in her throat. The only thing I know how to do is run. I am pathetic, her mind cried.

Filled with self-loathing, she ran through the lobby and out to the front of the hotel. A cab waited at the bottom of the steps.

As she approached the car, she recognized the driver as the same talkative one who had brought her from the airport. Oh no, she thought, not him. She didn't want to talk or feign friendliness. Looking around, she saw no other cab. Before she could run in another direction, the driver approached her.

"Hola," he said, smiling. "It is good to see you again. Are you feeling better? Maybe you are ready to take a ride around my extraordinary city?"

"Yes, yes I am," she said, regretting her decision to leave her hotel room. The minute she got into the car, anger consumed her again. She knew she had made a mistake the minute he started talking.

"What would you like to see today, Senorita?" His cheerfulness depressed her even more.

"I don't care. You decide. It doesn't matter to me. I just came out for some air," she lied, hoping he would shut up. It didn't take long to recognize an impossible dream.

"Let me introduce myself, Senorita, I am Francisco, the foremost authority on this fine city. Do you have a name I can call you?"

"Of course I have a name. I am Megan Summerfield. You may call me Miss Summerfield or Megan. I don't care which you choose." She thought her shortness would deter him from continuing the conversation. Wrong again.

"Have you come to our city to enjoy its beauty or are you here on business?"

She looked at him, sitting behind the wheel of his cab, deciding nothing would stop him. She assumed he had nothing better to do with his time then aggravate tourists and butt into their business. "I am here for a rest,"

As he drove along the ocean, past the bustling commercial ports, Francisco pointed out popular fish restaurants and declared them to be the best in the country; in spite of sawdust on the floors and the many swashbucklers that patronized them.

He drove her by the huge Naval Base, making sure that she knew the whole country remained safe because of the great job the sailors did from this one magnificent base.

He pointed out parks, one with a fine pipe organ on its lawn, which delighted the residents with free concerts. He showed her the zoo. "Biggest elephants in the country," he bragged. There seemed to be nothing he didn't know about this city and he never ran short of words.

Despite her aggravation with the man, she began to notice the quiet beauty of the city. She understood his pride for it.

Unlike New York, throngs of people were not hurrying up and down the streets. No horns blew. No steam rose from the grated sidewalks. The smell of bus fumes and subways didn't fill the air. A bright, blue sky laid over them like a canopy and sunshine warmed the interior of the car. Trees and flowers grew everywhere. The stark contrast between her home and this city impressed her.

His voice interrupted her reflections. "This is the heart around which my city was built, Senorita. This is Old Town San Diego.

Many, many years ago, only Indians lived here. The missionaries came to teach them Christianity and farming. A Franciscan Father came later and built the Mission.

Many more missions were built on the coast of California, along which is now called the El Camino Real, but we take much pride knowing ours is distinguished as the first one. You might enjoy a nice walk, and a margarita here."

"I think I'll do that, Francisco. Thank you for your time and the tour." Attempting to sound somewhat friendlier, she added, "I am now certain you are the foremost authority on the city."

"Here is my card, Senorita Megan. You can call me when you are ready. I would be happy to come back for you. You will enjoy Old Town." His dark eyes twinkling, he pulled away, smiling, leaving Megan on her own.

As he drove back into the city traffic, Megan watched him go. It must be wonderful to have a life as simple as a cab driver, she thought. No problems. No hassles. No heartbreak. Just endless conversations with strangers. He could afford to be happy. She would not miss his chattering.

She had sold many famous paintings of picturesque villages from around the world, but none prepared her for the sweetness of this tiny place.

Glistening in the sun, a brilliant, white stucco Mission stood at the far end of the square. Couples strolled, and children played in the tree-lined park that lay before it.

Cobblestone streets bordered the park, hosting colorful, open-air shops. Dancing sunlight accentuated the hand-embroidered clothing and delicate hand-crafted jewelry hanging in their arched doorways.

Cozy cantinas lent spicy aromas to the sweet smell of bountiful flowers.

Gentle Spanish music, gliding on the breeze, created a much different beat than the one she heard in the City.

Serenity encompassed her soul as she wandered around the town square.

She quenched her thirst with a margarita at one of the outdoor cantinas, finding herself swaying to the beat of the festive music and enjoying the sunshine on her face.

The lightness of the moment did not last. She noticed a young couple, across the room, sitting close together and sharing a margarita through one straw. The man reached over and touched the girl's face, placing a gentle kiss on her lips.

Visions of her and Michael rushed in to replace the pleasantness of the last couple of hours.

Her instinct to run away and isolate herself took over. Her mind fought back. Deal with this, it demanded. Don't run.

Instinct prevailed and she pushed her margarita away, disgusted with herself.

Her mood dark, the despair returning in spite of her effort, she walked to the curb. To her dismay, no cabs stood waiting.

She fumbled with Francisco's card in her pocket, not wanting to call him. As dark started to set over the city, she picked up the payphone on the corner and dialed his number.

Upon his return, and as she expected, he started to ask questions. "Did you have a good time, Senorita Megan? Did you have a margarita?" He persisted in endless, endless chatter.

She answered him in short, curt responses, Michael the only real thing on her mind.

In her room, she found that the maid had picked up her pills and placed them back on her nightstand.

She sat looking at them, feeling furious with herself, furious and ashamed. Once again, she gave in to the only thing that made sense. Sleep.

7

Sitting at the small kitchen table in Megan's apartment, Amy held the deed to the property in her hand. Just as Megan had said in the letter, it had been signed over to her. She couldn't believe her eyes. She still clung to her hope that this was some kind of sick joke.

Megan's lawyer had taken her call without hesitation, surprising her. Not waiting for her to ask any questions, he said, "I have been waiting for your call, Amy. Have you heard from Megan since you received the letter?"

"No, I haven't. Can you tell me anything at all about this? Where is she? Why did she leave? Is she okay? Did you talk to her before she left?" She fired questions at him until he interrupted her.

"Yes, I spoke to Megan. She would tell me nothing. I am concerned about her welfare and her state of mind. She sounded depressed and when I tried to question her, she rebuffed me with a short statement about the letter to you. She was emphatic about the brownstone being yours and instructed me to transfer a million dollars into an account in your name, with no stipulation as to how you used the money.

Megan told me a notarized letter with her instructions would arrive at my office taking care of any legal problems, and it did, that same afternoon.

Her plan seemed to be well thought out. She hung up and that is the last I have heard from her."

Amy sat stunned, trying to comprehend his words. The staggering amount of money paralyzed her already numb brain. She knew Megan had inherited a good deal of money, but Megan had never given her a figure and she had never seen her spend any of it.

Megan said her father had invested it and she wasn't interested in using it. She had joked about it being a nice inheritance for her children, if she ever had any. She laughed and said if she didn't have an heir, she would buy a dog and leave it to him.

Managing to find her voice, Amy spoke. "Do you have any idea how we can find her? Do you think we should call the police?"

"No, Amy, I don't know how to find her and I don't think we can call the police. Megan is not missing according to the law and a person has the right to go away for a while. Let's wait and see if she contacts either of us. I don't see what else we can do."

They chatted for a few minutes, each promising to call if they heard from her and then hung up.

Amy wandered around the apartment, trying to regain her senses.

She began to notice there was no sign of Michael in the apartment. No razors, no shaving cream, no toothbrush. She ran to the bedroom. No male clothes, only Megan's, all of them. She rushed to the kitchen. Michael's favorite box of Sugar Pops no longer stood in the cabinet. What had happened to him and why hadn't Megan called her? Where could she go with no clothes, no toothbrush? Amy felt sick to her stomach. Her head pounded like a jackhammer.

She noticed the answering machine flashing. A polite recording told her Megan had six unanswered messages. Four of them were the art gallery questioning her whereabouts. Each call became more concerned. The fourth message threatened to notify the police if she didn't return their call. The fifth one had come from her bank confirming her transfer had been received and the sixth one hung up. As she stood to leave the desk, she saw a small white envelope addressed to her.

Dear Amy, it began.

I'm fine and I swear I've not lost my mind. I just need some time to re-group. I know you don't understand and it's just too hard to try and explain.

Please don't be mad at me. I love you. I simply needed to get out of New York. I really don't have a plan, but I promise, when I figure things out, you'll be the first to know.

Live in the brownstone and love it as I did.

Do you think you could let my friends upstairs stay until they want to go? They're such nice, sweet people and I could never bear to ask them to leave. I'll be in touch soon. I do love you with all my heart. God bless.

Oh, could you throw the yellow couch out and replace it with a new one? Love you. Bye, bye." No. Megan was not going to do this. Her friend had stood by her through every minute of her troubles. Without Megan, she wouldn't have made it and she would repay that kind of kindness. Amy vowed to find her if it took every dime of the money.

Anger possessing her, she became aware of the yellow couch. Why did Megan want it thrown out? What part did it play in this? She had to think. She had to remain calm.

She kept looking at the couch. The only thing she could remember about it was the shoe game Megan and Michael had played on Sunday nights.

Megan had become obsessed with Michael and she had not seen much of her during the romance, but every time they did talk, Megan mentioned Sunday nights and the game. She loved it. She loved Michael.

Oh, my God, Amy thought. Michael. This was all about him. He must have broken up with her and she couldn't recover. Had she had run away because of the break-up? That would be stupid. Megan wasn't that stupid; or was she?

Every journey begins with the first step, she thought. Michael would be hers. She hunted down Megan's address book and found his work number. Dialing it, she wondered what she would say to him. Her sheer frustration spoke for her. "Michael, this is Amy. Where's Megan and what the hell is going on?"

"What do you mean where's Megan? What are you talking about? Is she all right?"

"No, she's not alright. She's missing and I figure you had something to do with it."

Hesitation, then, "Can we meet for lunch, Amy?"

"Just tell me what you know. I need to find her and I don't have time to waste on lunch with someone I figure broke her heart.

What else would cause her to leave town?"

"Please, Amy, this would all be so much easier in person."

"Fine, meet me at Dominica's in Little Italy at noon. I don't have a lot of time, so don't be late."

Her next call went to Megan's art gallery. No one knew anything. She seemed to have more information than anybody else. Her task promised to be difficult.

Before leaving to meet Michael, she went upstairs to speak to Megan's tenants. Finding out they also knew nothing made Amy realize Megan had confided in no one but her. And she had divulged almost nothing.

On her way to her meeting with Michael, Amy stopped at the bank and spoke to the bank president, again, nothing.

How could a woman just disappear with no trace? Someone in this huge city had to have seen her.

When Amy arrived at the restaurant, Michael already sat at a small table with a drink in front of him.

Although she hadn't seen him in some time, her first impression was that he looked terrible; tired, drawn and stressed. He attempted a smile, but it was not convincing. Her anger with him mellowed.

"Please, Michael, tell me what happened. I don't know why she left. I don't know where she went. I don't know where to start looking for her. Please, please try to help me." Her eyes filled with tears.

"I don't know much, Amy. I'm sorry. I did break up with her, but if you'll give me a moment, you'll understand why. It was not because I don't love her and she knew that."

"I knew it," Amy spit at him. "How could you break her heart? She loved you. She trusted you. She was sure you would ask her to marry you". She glared at him, hatred in her heart.

"Please, Amy, please listen to what happened. He looked at her and sighed. "I love Megan," he began. "I've never loved anyone more in my entire life. We were so happy. Every minute with her was complete and full. She understood me and touched parts of my mind and soul I thought had died years ago. She awakened senses in me I had forgotten. We seemed to have the same rhythm of life in our heads and moved together to it. She loved me as much as I loved her. I knew it and I was a fool anyway."

He glanced at Amy with an apologetic look and then continued. "My ex-wife, Christine, came to my office one day and asked to talk to me.

I thought she wanted money for our son. Instead, she told me she had made a mistake asking for a divorce and wanted to try again. She said she was sorry for her mistakes.

Sorry? I sat back in my chair, shrugged my shoulders and laughed. She was sorry. She had a lover for over a year and walked into my study to tell me she had never loved me and was leaving me for a real man.

I cried for a year. I gave up on life. Christine took my son away from me.

Now, Megan and I had fallen in love, my heart and my ego had healed and Christine wanted to try again? This had to be a joke and, if it wasn't, she could go to hell and I told her so. I got up to leave the room, furious and laughing at the same time.

Christine begged me to sit down and give her time to explain.

I stared at her in disbelief, but felt compelled to do as she asked. That was my mistake.

She told me how Jason cried himself to sleep every night since our divorce. She said he wouldn't go anywhere without a picture of me in his pocket.

She kept saying how wrong she was and how she didn't know what love was until she lost it and how she didn't realize what our break-up would do to Jason.

Christine thought that our son, in his own way, made her realize what a complete family we were.

She begged me to come back and try again, if not for her, for our son.

In the middle of all this, I heard the word Daddy. My little boy stood in the doorway of my office. He ran towards me and threw his arms around my neck.

Through his tears, he mumbled to his mother that he couldn't stay in the car.

He said to me, 'I wanted to ask you to come home myself, Daddy.'

He lay sobbing in my arms and I made the only decision I

could. I couldn't put my own happiness before my son's.

I tried to explain to Megan the best I could, and it turned into an argument.

She couldn't understand how I could go back to Christine. She hurled questions at me. If Jason was so unhappy why didn't Christine just give me custody? How could I go back to a woman who had prevented me from seeing Jason? Did I want to return to a woman who had tried to make my son accept her lover as his father? What had happened to her lover? Why did she want to come back now? Did I believe that, all of a sudden, out of nowhere, she loved me? What about her? What did I expect her to do with her love? Just forget it? Just get over it?

Every question Megan screamed at me made perfect sense. I had no answers, only the memory of my son begging. I tried to explain. I told her I felt compelled to put his world back together, that no sacrifice seemed too large. I told her we would both get over it. We were adults. We would survive. We could move on, but a six-year-old boy would never recover. My words sounded empty and meaningless.

She screamed at me to get out and threw the couch pillow at me. I left, torn and confused.

From the moment I moved into the house, Jason became my only joy. Christine seemed distant and cold, different from our encounters prior to the move and has remained so.

She still insists it will take time to readjust. She remains steadfast in her belief that this will prove to be best for Jason. I try to believe it will. We are living a quiet, routine life with no mention of re-marriage. I don't know where we're headed and I think about Megan every day.

I do know our son is much happier. His grades in school have improved and he is more social. He no longer cries at night, but he does ask me at bedtime, every night, if I am going to stay. I assure him I am, but I really don't know from one day to the next."

Amy sat stunned at Michael's candor, but nothing in his explanation led her any closer to knowing where her friend had gone.

"This is all interesting, and sad, Michael, but it doesn't help me at all. Do you know where Megan might have gone? Did she ever mention anywhere she wanted to go? I need your help, Michael, please think."

He assured her he didn't have any idea, but promised her he would do anything he could to help find her.

Amy looked at him for a long moment. "Well, I see that I have wasted my time here, Michael. Good luck with your decision." Feeling complete hopelessness, she got up and left the table, leaving him sitting there, lost in his own thoughts. She had no sympathy for a man who had hurt her friend like this.

Idiot, damn idiot. Why are all men idiots?

She walked home and called Megan's lawyer. He still had not heard from her and neither had the art gallery.

I have to find a way. There must be a way, she thought. She sat down on the yellow couch and drifted into a fitful sleep.

8

Megan woke early. Soft morning light filtered through the sheer curtain on the window. She dug deeper down into the covers, enjoying the coziness of the room.

Dozing in and out of a relaxed sleep, vague thoughts passed through her mind; the smiling women in Old Town, the bittersweet taste of the salted Margarita, the fragrant flowers, Francisco's persistent chattering and the young man and woman.

No. She would not let her mind go there. She sat up. Not today. I will not do this today, she demanded of herself. She saw the bottle sitting on the nightstand like a temptress.

She moved to the bathroom. Splashing cold water on her face, she looked up. Her face, drawn and tired yesterday, looked somewhat more rested today. The black circles could be erased with a little make-up. She decided looking better would help her mood. She vowed to fight off the despair, anyway she could.

Out of sheer habit, the familiar play started in her head. She almost gave in when an inner voice screamed at her - no, not today, move on, get out of this room. She obeyed the voice. Her mind would not win today.

Hurrying, running from the terrorist in her head, Megan showered, dressed and left the room.

Eating breakfast, Francisco edged once again into her thoughts. What a strange man; a simple, uncomplicated man, with an endearing love for his city, and a true gift of gab. She wondered if he had anyone in his life, or if strangers riding in his cab were the only thing filling his days. Megan found herself regretting her rudeness yesterday, even feeling a little sorry for the man.

The dark demons in her mind kept forcing their way into her thoughts. She pushed them back. Not today. Not even if she had to play-act all day.

Megan forced herself to think about anything other than her life in the City, but the minute New York came into her mind, the monster within grabbed the thought and threw in visuals of Michael. She tried, without success, to think of another subject.

Giving up, she left the restaurant and headed for the front door.

Standing next to his cab, the now familiar, smiling man bowed and waved her into his car. "Hola, Senorita Megan. Where are we off to today?"

"Good morning, Senor. I don't know. Do you have any suggestions?" This morning, she wanted to hear his chatter. She needed something to focus on to keep the monster at bay.

"No, wait. I do know what I'd like to see. Is it possible to see the Pacific Ocean from here? I've never been to the West Coast, but I have been told of the ocean's great beauty."

"No problem, Senorita. I can take you there. It is a long ride over to Coronado Island, but once we get on the backside, we can see the ocean."

"Let's get started then," Megan said, forcing a small smile, and giving her best effort to sound cheerful.

Francisco smiled, pleased with her choice and eased the cab into the traffic.

True to himself, Francisco chatted about every street and landmark they passed. Megan did her best to concentrate on his every word, staving off her demons. For once, she felt empowered.

Soon, she realized they were traveling over a huge bridge. It towered over the bay and she gasped at the sheer height of it. Megan knew bridges in New York, the George Washington and the Verrazano, among others, but she had never crossed anything this high. Francisco laughed at her gasp. He had a tale for the bridge, too.

"Would you like to hear a little story about this bridge, Senorita?"

Today she found his stories somewhat interesting and she needed him to keep talking. "Yes, Francisco, I would."

"The bridge had just been built, so new it was not open yet. A huge Navy ship, a cruiser, returning from active duty, entered the harbor. The sailors were all standing at parade-rest, in full dress, on the decks of the ship, as was their procedure when entering a port. The ship had been cleaned to its most magnificent beauty, showing off its powerfulness, its dignity and its honor. Someone made a slight error in judgment and the ship hit the bridge, knocking the Captain's private launch from the side of the ship and damaging the piling of the bridge. This incident caused much embarrassment to the Captain and to the Navy. It caused much laughter among the sailors."

Megan caught herself giggling at the devilishness in his voice as he finished his story. He really was a likable character.

As they drove across the island, they wove through narrow streets, lined with small houses.

It seemed as though, out of nowhere, the ocean appeared before her eyes. She became overwhelmed with a need to get closer, to stand at its edge. The crashing waves filled Megan with a sense of power, buried deep within its bosom. She felt its dark, foreboding, blue color hid secrets she would never know.

As the car stopped, she stripped off her sandals and ran towards it, trying to suppress the urge to dive head first into its water. A giant wave broke and tumbled onto her, soaking her skirt. For the briefest moment, she felt young and childlike.

She stood in the water looking out at the sea. Seagulls flew above her head, squawking and hunting for their breakfast. Sailboats, under full sail, heading for unknown destinations, maneuvered with ease in the light ocean breeze. Freighters, carrying heavy loads, waited to come into port. The magnificent blue sky glowed with sunshine, hindered only by light, fluffy white clouds.

On the beach, children laughed and played with sand buckets, their laughter intermingling with the noisy birds. The monsters were at bay.

Her moment of peace didn't last. Thoughts of her mother crept into her consciousness. Once again, sadness shadowed her face; the familiar heaviness enveloping her heart.

"Senorita, what troubles you? Why has your face turned so dark?"

"My mother loved the sea, Francisco. The memories of her and me on the beach in Cape Cod are too painful for me. I shouldn't have come here. I lost her and I don't know how to go on."

"Senorita, let's sit for awhile and enjoy the sea." She agreed.

"The first day I picked you up at the airport, I saw the great pain in your face, Senorita, Megan. I saw the heaviness in your shoulders. You must find your way out of your pain. I always turn to the sea when my heartache is stronger than my strength."

"I don't know, Francisco. I just don't know."

"Let me tell you about the sea, Senorita Megan. Maybe, when you understand its power, its understanding of survival, you will be able to draw what you need from it and find the strength and will to lift your own burdens."

Francisco gazed out across the water and started to speak in an almost reverent tone.

"Mexican men have a strong love and a profound respect for this ocean. We understand that the ocean itself demands this from us. We fear it deep in the essence of our souls and yet, we understand that we cannot exist without it.

Its waters are the deepest and the strongest. Its storms are the most violent.

It intensely protects its bounty with great waves, similar to the intensity of a mother protecting her children. It does not give us our food without a fight.

It changes its mood as a woman does, often and without remorse; enough to scare any man. Many lives have been lost to its unpredictable whims.

We sit unsuspecting on its shore. Like a temptress, it whispers, 'Come, sail on my waters. Come, fish my bounty. Come now. You can trust me.' The call is heard by every sailor, every fisherman. Romanced by its charm, we go, like men to a brothel, blinded and deaf, with no sense of reason, every time.

If we are lucky, if we respect her, we come back with fish, our lives and a deeper understanding of life. If we do not, it sucks us under its great waves and uses us for food for its own bounty. It is her destiny to take care of us. A mother must take care of her own and yet, she must also feed herself.

When you understand why, to ensure its own balance, the sea must so generously give of itself and at the same time, so selfishly take what it needs to survive, you will also understand the needs in your own life.

This sea holds the answers to all life's questions. If you wait long enough, if you trust her, if you listen, she will answer your questions. Be patient, Senorita, be patient and trust her."

As Megan listened, she hung on his every word. She had

never met a man who loved the sea like Francisco. Did her mother understand it, or love it as he did? Had she, herself, ever loved or understood anything with such intensity? She began to feel her whole life had been shallow. She wanted this kind of love in her life. Was it too late to form such an intense understanding of something?

This man had a simple life, but he was not a simple man. Francisco's only loves appeared to be challenging the sea and driving a cab and yet, he seemed to be the happiest person she had ever met. How did one find that kind of happiness? Where did one begin?

"I grew up sitting by the Atlantic Ocean with my mother. She loved the sea and spent every minute by its side, telling it her thoughts and figuring out life's problems. She shared her joys with it. She drowned her sorrows in it. She claimed the ocean as her church. She went there to pray, to confess her sins, to grieve, to thank God for everything good. She taught me to do the same. This ocean is so different from the Atlantic. I can't put my finger on it, but it seems so much deeper, so much bluer, and so much more powerful. She would have loved it here."

Francisco responded, "Senorita Megan, sit without words for a moment. Listen to the sea. Your mother is here with you. You have brought her in your heart. She gave you her love for the sea for a reason. She gave it to you so that you would always be together, no matter what happened. All you have to do is find the sea and sit and listen. You will feel your mother's being and her love. You will feel her kiss on your cheek. You will hear her voice. She gave you this gift. This powerful blue sea holds your mother's heart in its hands because she gave it the power to do so. All of our answers are in the sea. It was created by our God for that reason."

They sat in silence and listened.

Megan became filled with joy. Francisco's words were true. She could feel her mother. She felt as though she could reach out and touch her. Her demons were calm. Only the sweet memories of her mother filled her head.

As they sat, lost in their own thoughts, a dark, ominous looking ship appeared on the horizon. Megan noticed a shadow cross Francisco's face. "Francisco, did you always live in San Diego? Have you always been a cab driver?"

"No, Megan. I am from a small fishing village on the Mexican Baja and I have not always been a cab driver. I have a son and I had a wife. She died when my son was a baby."

"I am so sorry, Francisco."

"It is okay. It was a long time ago."

"Tell me about your life in Mexico, Francisco."

"Are you sure, Megan? I have not thought back to my younger years for a long time, but if you would like to hear about it, I will tell you."

Relaxed and smiling, Megan assured him she would.

"Okay. I am the son of Francisco and Louisa Gonzalez. My mother gave birth to me in a one-room house, really a fishing shack, in a small town at the southern end of the Mexican Baja, Puerto San Luis. I was the first of many children, eleven, I think. My father fished everyday of his life, my mother sewed his nets by hand and we always had plenty of food.

We had a simple life. The women and children collected wood from the mountains for heat and the cook stoves and grew gardens for food. While the men fished, the women took care of each other and the village.

The more children born to my parents, the more my father fished. He fed my mother and the babies first and then went up to the mountain in his old truck and sold the extra fish to the widows and old people.

As the babies grew, he managed to buy an old boat, so he could go further out to sea and catch bigger fish. We never wanted for anything, just our father to come home.

Being the oldest child, I became my mother's partner in worry. We watched every storm. We prayed at every dark sky. We watched the sea and waited, babies playing at our feet. He was a good, honest man. He loved his family. My childhood was happy. I kept my mother company and helped her with the little ones, while my father fished the sea. I did not have much time for school, but I didn't care. The most important thing to me was helping my father, as he had asked me to do.

I learned to fish at his knee. He taught me every mood of the sea and how to tell what every cloud was thinking.

He taught me to respect every woman because, 'a woman's

love is a gift from God.' He believed a man should humble himself in front of a woman because she could bear his children and this gift came from the Lord. He treated my mother like a queen.

He believed in the sea and in his wife. He needed nothing else to live. I have tried to live up to his image. It is a high goal to reach." Francisco ended his story with a warm smile and a tip of his hat.

"Your father sounds like he was a wonderful man, Francisco."

"I loved him more than life itself."

He did not seem to want to say anymore and Megan decided not to question him about the sadness on his face when the ship came into their view, but she was sure this sensitive, caring man had a much deeper story.

They lingered on the beach for awhile and when the wind kicked up, Francisco suggested they leave.

Back in her hotel, Megan enjoyed a quiet dinner in her room and fell into a peaceful sleep, thankful for a day she would remember and a man to whom she would always be grateful.

In the morning, she picked up the paper outside of her door and read a headline that sent her head spinning. "Oh, no, oh, no. Oh, God, not this," she cried out loud. She fell to the chair and reread the bold type. NEW YORK INVESTMENT FIRM CLOSED FOR EMBEZZLEMENT. Michael's picture stared up at her.

9

Motioning us to a table, Angelina carried a place-setting for Enrique. "I did not expect you for dinner, Enrique," she said with a sudden shyness.

Enrique, hanging his hat on the back of the chair, looked at her with softness in his face. "I always take the opportunity to see mi muy bonita woman in Puerto San Luis, Angelina. There can be no finer food in the world than what comes from your hands."

She stepped towards him and swatted him on the top of his head with a towel. "Don't speak your foolishness in front of Senor Peter. You embarrass me."

"My Angelina is a tough woman, si? She is a challenge. I love her anyway."

Angelina huffed away, mumbling things in Spanish I could not understand. Even with her back to me, I could sense the trace of a smile on her lips.

Mellowed from our afternoon beers, we lit smokes and settled back in our chairs.

"Your love for each other is obvious, Enrique."

"No, no, Senor Peter, Angelina does not love me. She is in love with a ghost, a man she lost to the sea many years ago. Her love is my curse. I have loved her all my life, ever since we were children."

"Angelina told me about this man, Enrique. I wondered, at the time, what she had given up in her life to continue to keep his memory alive. Now, I know. I am sorry for both of you."

"She has no room in her heart for Enrique. I have begged her to be my wife, many times, but mi muy bonita Angelina is a stubborn woman, I think more stubborn than me. I sit on the dock everyday and wait for her to come to me, but she does not.

My love for her pains me and I think, that maybe, it is a curse from God. Maybe He thinks Enrique is not a good man. I pray to Him to take the pain away, but so far, prayers for me do not work. Every morning, I wake up and my heart is still full with love. I know God is angry with me."

"Enrique, I've spent a lot of time cursing God for taking my wife away from me, but I realized it wasn't His fault.

I have also blamed myself for not protecting her as I should have. The truth is, we have no control over our destiny. We deal with it, in our own way, as it comes.

I think Angelina will come to her senses someday and accept your love. She is a wonderful woman, loving and caring. She has just chosen the wrong road. She will see her mistake and come to you."

"We will see, Senor Peter. I have nothing to do but wait."

She appeared again with three steaming bowls of fish stew.

"I made this just for you, Senor Peter, from our own Rock Cod." She snapped a napkin open and pushed it down into my shirt. "Eat now, while it is hot."

As we ate the spicy, thick stew, Enrique talked of his father.

"Every summer," he began, "my father followed the big fish up and down the coast of the Baja.

Standing on a wooden pier in some distant village, during my fifteenth year, his mind gave birth to a dream. He pictured his fishing boat tied to pilings in his own cove.

Returning home from the sea, he cut his first tree from the mountain and dragged it to the beach. Stripping the tree with his machete and then digging his first hole, the piling soon stood planted in the sand.

Many winter months passed. The sea fought him. The sand fought him. The men in town considered him loco.

He labored up and down the mountain, lugging, stripping, and digging. One young boy tried to help him, me. The local men watched from the hillside.

By early Spring, he pounded his last plank into place. Trudging far out into the water, he lassoed his fishing boat and dragged it to his pier. Turning to face his audience, he took a long low, bow. The Mexican men clapped and cheered."

I broke into uproarious laughter, picturing Enrique's father bowing to his audience. Enrique laughed with me and the other men in the bar joined us. We stood and bowed to the room.

Angelina joined us in the third chair, mumbling that we needed no more cervasas.

Her dog had joined us and lay with her head on Angelina's foot. Enrique's dog did the same, also laying his head on his master's foot and giving an occasional glance at Angelina's dog. She paid him no mind. It occurred to me that they seemed to mimic their owners.

"You like this fish, Senor Peter?" Angelina asked.

"I have never eaten a fish this good. I can taste the sea itself."

"Enrique caught it with his own hands," Angelina declared. "Enrique is the number one fisherman in this village."

Enrique glowed with pride, his humbleness taking a backseat to a compliment from his beloved Angelina.

Dipping the tortillas in the last of the broth, the bartender arrived with more full plates and bowls and fresh beers. We polished off the second round of food.

Enrique poked gentle fun at Angelina every chance he got and she rebuffed him at every turn, but I could feel an affection that went much deeper than just two old friends.

My belly full and my head warm and fuzzy, I excused myself, thanking my new friends for a wonderful evening, and went upstairs to bed. Enrique touched his lips to Angelina's cheek, bowed to his waist and left with his dog.

Angelina, smiling, instructed her dog to follow her to her room.

All had had a great night, new friendships had been formed and a new beginning to life had begun.

I awoke to someone pounding on my door. I looked out the window and saw only darkness. It took a minute to recognize Enrique's voice.

"Senor Peter, Senor Peter, get up, get up, right now. It is time to go fishing. The fish are running from the north. Get up."

Fishing? I thought. I didn't know I was going fishing. Do I like fishing? I opened the door and he pushed his way in.

"Hurry, you must hurry. We have waited months for the yellowtail to come from the north. They are jumping higher than the Mexican mountains. Dress, dress now, he demanded"

I did. As we ran through the bar, Angelina appeared and handed us coffees and brown paper bags. Even the dog hurried.

Angelina threw us a kiss and called, "Buena suerte." Little did

I know, at that point, just how much luck I would need.

We ran through the town, with the dog in hot pursuit. The coffee spilled all over me. Every man in town ran with us. At the dock, the men threw gear on rickety fishing boats at a frantic pace. The women added food to their gear. We boarded Enrique's boat along with two young boys I didn't know and the dog jumped on behind us.

As we pulled from the harbor, I saw Angelina waving good-bye to us from the pier. I imagined that for many generations this scene had been repeated and the women were born knowing how to wait for the return of their men.

As we went out further and further, I began to see the fish. They jumped high. The top of the water rippled with movement from the ones below. Too excited for conversation, Enrique manned his helm knowing exactly where he needed to be. The two young boys prepared huge nets. Boats surrounded us. Every man had a crew of young boys and the activity on each boat repeated itself.

As if he had a personal, reserved parking space on the sea, Enrique stopped his boat on a dime and raced to help the boys set the nets. They tossed them over the side of the boat with precise movements and, within minutes, they were heavy with the bounty of the sea. They dragged the nets back into the boats and dumped the catch onto the deck, covering them with wet tarps. The nets again were tossed over the side. I stood dumbfounded, but instinct told me to stay out of their way. I had no idea what to do. They had become a precision team and ignored me.

The scene repeated itself over and over. As if on cue, the fishing ended. The men stepped back, looked at their catch, their faces shining with sheer joy and slapped each other's backs. Bottles of beer seemed to appear out of nowhere and every man, including me, raised his in a toast to the fruitfulness of the sea. They bowed their heads and thanked God for the bounty they had received and then bantered back and forth in rapid fire Spanish. I had no idea what they were talking about, but a feeling of merriment filled the crisp ocean air. Even I, having done nothing but watch all day, felt the need to party with these men.

With the sun setting in the west, we sat together and drank hot mugs of coffee and ate tortillas filled with meat and beans.

Enrique and I talked as the young boys, Roberto and Juan, cleaned up the deck and attended to the fish and the tarps.

"Are we going in soon?" I asked Enrique.

He laughed, grabbing his stomach. "Oh no, Senor Peter, we are here for three days. The fish will keep for seventy-two hours under the wet tarps. The great fish only run from the north for a little while and we must catch them while they are here. We fish every day, sleep every night.

At the end of third day, we will take the fish to trucks waiting in the village and they hurry to take them to the cannery.

We make enough money to buy food and pay rent. Sometimes we have enough left for cervasas and fun, sometimes enough for a good woman. It is a good life, this being a fisherman. We want for nothing.

Tomorrow, you will learn to be a fisherman and when we get home, we will find you a good dog. You will be a content man like me and need nothing. You will see."

We sat together while I pondered this. For some strange reason, it didn't strike me as a bad idea. What could be wrong with being a fisherman?

Up until now, the only thing that had mattered was Sadie. I had resented my business. I had entered medicine to honor my father, maybe do some good and help some people and I ended up catering to a bunch of rich, spoiled women trying to stave off old age. Most of them had more money than brains and more ego than money. On top of that, I quickly learned that being a doctor, in my setting, was more politics than profession.

Sadie kept me going. She created fun and love, warmth and caring. She had been the reason to come home. She saved me from the parties, brunches and showy, ostentatious obligations of my profession. She lit fires and cooked steaks for two. She fed me tomatoes from her gardens and bought silk sheets. She lay next to me, made love to me and cradled in my arms until morning.

Yes, being a fisherman sounded like a good idea. I was surprised I was staying out here for three days. I hadn't even brought a change of underwear.

"Senor Peter, Senor Peter. Are you okay?" asked Enrique.

I realized I had been lost in thought and had not answered

him. "Yes, yes, I am, my friend. I don't know if I am worthy of being a fisherman. It takes a special kind of man to live by the sea alone. We'll see. After tomorrow, you may want to throw me over the side." After a few more beers, we retired below.

Before the sunrise, we were up, fed and ready to fish. Enrique gave me a spot on the nets, heavy gloves for my hands and a warning. "Don't let the fish win."

Choking on nervous anticipation, I said, "I am a strong man, Enrique, the fish will not win."

He translated for the boys and they all shared a laugh. Throwing the net out was easy. I looked at Ernesto and Juan. Sensing my smugness, they returned my look with a wide grin. The huge net became alive with hundreds of jumping and thrashing fish. I started to pull with the three fishermen and within a heartbeat, my legs flew up and out from under me and I ended up flat on my ass on the deck. The gloves were torn right through and blood rose to meet the fabric. For a moment, the sense was knocked out of me. The fisherman did not stop working. I sat up, dazed, and saw Ernesto and Juan laughing as they heaved in the nets. I joined in their laughter, humbled by my own inability. I got up in time to help them cast the nets once again. They patted me on the back, looking at my hands.

Enrique said, "Mi amigo, nice try. You will get it the second time. Use your arms, not your hands. Nets will pull your hands off and they will go to sea with the fish. Here are new gloves."

By the fourth attempt, I started to get it. Instead of seconds, I lasted two or three minutes on the nets before my ass connected with the deck. My clothes, soaking wet, smelled of fish. My hair hung in my eyes, dripping and caked with salt and fish scum. Maybe being a doctor, catering to rich, spoiled women, had not been a bad career choice after all. No, not a chance, I was having the best time of my life.

After the final pull, Enrique looked at me and said, "Good job, compadre, no hands in the sea at end of the day. The young boys think you are good. You keep trying, they like that. You will be a good fisherman."

As we had the previous night, we celebrated, thanked the sea, and God, for our plentiful bounty and ate tortillas and beans. Again, we washed them down with beer. The beer had gotten warm and the tortillas soggy, but it didn't seem to matter. The boat, heavy with its catch, rolled in the waves. The sun set and all seemed well with the world.

Ernesto and Juan retired early. Enrique and I sat on the deck; each lost in his own thoughts, watching the sun fall into the sea. The moon rose behind us, creating a path to our boat.

As a doctor, I was proud of my knowledge of anatomy. Tonight, as I sat here, I hurt in places even I could not identify. I had lived through a hellava day, but my body screamed like a woman being ravaged. I decided I would never recover when Enrique appeared next to me with two small glasses in his left hand and a bottle in his right. He poured me a drink.

"Here, compadre, this will take the ache away. Drink the tequila fast and then have another. Tomorrow your muscles will forgive you and they will be strong. You will see."

I swallowed the foul tasting liquor and extended my glass for another. The pain began to ease.

I raised the glass to Enrique. "Angelina is right, Enrique, you are a good fisherman."

"I have fished ever since I was a young boy. My grandfather took me to the sea as soon as I could walk. He would strap me into a seat with a leather belt, so I didn't fall in while he fished. At age six, he let me hold the fishing pole. Before that, I packed salt on cod, so it wouldn't go bad.

I asked him, "Grandfather, how do you know where the fish are?"

'I know this because when I was a young boy like you, I learned how to think like a fish. Fish are stupid. They only think with their bellies. They forget about any danger. When big fish see small fish, they eat.

The birds see the small fish, too, and join the big fish in the bounty. As the big fish eat, they cannot tell the difference between the small fish and my bait. So, you go where the birds are. If the birds eat, you eat. Remember that, young boy. You will never be hungry.'

My Grandfather watched the clouds and the moon. He could tell by the shape of a cloud which way the wind moved and which way the birds would fly in. He could look at the moon and know the weather for the next day. He was always right. He fished until he was seventy-five years old and died when he is ninety years old. I have never been hungry."

Trying my best to concentrate on his story, my eyes kept closing. My body had calmed down, but I feared moving any part of it.

Enrique looked at me and said, "I am sorry, Senor Peter. I ramble silly stories and you need sleep. I will help you to bed." Covering me as I lay down, he said, "Tomorrow, we fish again. Good, strong day. You will do good tomorrow, mi amigo. Goodnight."

By tomorrow night, I will be dead, I thought, pulling the damp blanket over my head.

The night brought fitful dreams of huge fish, dancing on their tailfins and frolicking on the deck of the boat. They pointed their dorsal fins at me and opened their mouths, exposing large, sharp teeth, and broke into laughter, mocking me. They tied me in ropes and fed me bait, large pieces of slimy, white stuff. I woke up, drenched in sweat; glad it was only a dream.

The snoring fisherman slept in their blankets. I fell back to sleep, praying the fish would not return and hoping the sweat would drown the stench of fish on my body.

Before the sun rose, we got ready for our third day of fishing. We ate hard biscuits and drank coffee as a cold, thick morning mist covered every inch of the boat and us. I was sure Enrique would call off fishing for today and we'd soon be on our way back. Wrong.

The nets were set within minutes of our last bite of food. It was so cold on deck that I believed the nets were unnecessary. The fish would probably be happy to jump on the boat and get under the tarps to keep warm.

I stayed back to clean up breakfast and lick my wounds. I needed to move about and see if all my parts were in the right places. I took inventory and decided I hadn't lost anything vital yesterday, except maybe my pride. My only redemption seemed to be to go up on deck and try again to be a fisherman.

The first nets were being hauled in. My new co-workers smiled at me and Enrique threw me my gloves. I jumped into yesterday's spot and all of a sudden, I was pulling and heaving right along with the other guys. It took a few minutes to realize I was not flat on my ass again. What a powerful feeling. I was fishing. I was throwing these nets like a pro. After the second set, the men hit me on the back, smiling and congratulating me. Excitement prevailed.

We fished all day, pulling our bounty from the sea, like the pros we were. After the last net was up, Enrique started the engine and we headed home, amidst jovial chatter and slimy fish. What a day.

As we pulled up to the pier, I noticed the scene had changed. The women stood waiting for us, armed with baskets of food and jugs of drink. They were a welcome sight.

Old trucks lined the waterway and large scales were placed next to the trucks. Men hustled about, pulling the fishing boats to shore, and the fish were weighed and moved to the trucks. Each fisherman received cash for his catch and, as the trucks filled, they pulled out and headed north on the old dirt road.

Enrique explained to me that the cannery up the coast cleaned the fish and shipped them north to America. Every part of the fish became a product, even the guts, which would ultimately be used for fertilizer. A perfect system, I thought.

As I ate the tortillas and drank the coffee, I thought about the fine restaurants I had eaten in. Fish had been one of my favorite entrees and I paid any price for a good piece. I never once wondered how it got to my plate. A fish dinner would never be the same again.

As I stood on the old pier, eating, reminiscing, and watching the village reap the rewards of its crop, I noticed Angelina and her dog, standing to one side watching Enrique and his crew unload their fish. She shuns Enrique, but I see a flicker in her eye every time she sees him, I thought. She turned and ambled up the hill to her tavern, her dog following close behind.

I took stock of myself and decided I needed a shower, a powerful hot shower, with lots of soap, and maybe, a disinfectant. I carried a three day beard, my clothes were thick with saltwater and I was rank with a sweaty, fishy smell that made my stomach turn. My soft, clean surgical hands were torn to bits and had started to form hard calluses. I headed towards town, seeking the refuge of my room. Overall, this had turned out to be the most rewarding day of my life, yesterday moving into second place.

I cleaned myself up and lay down on the bed to reflect on the last couple of months of my life. I had only gotten back as far as this morning when a knock came to the door. I got up and opened it to find Enrique, hat in hand, standing there smiling. His dog stood behind him. Both of them smelled as I had an hour ago. They came in. The dog placed himself next to the dresser, put his head down and went to sleep.

Enrique looked at me and said, "You still clean up nice, Senor Peter." He reached into his pocket and pulled out a roll of bills I recognized as pesos. He handed them to me. "This is your share of the fishing money for the good job you did. I worry that you will run out of money, so I wanted to bring your pay right away."

I looked at him, shocked. "No, Enrique. I don't want any money from you. I only want to thank you for the honor of taking me on your boat. You gave me the best time I have ever had. That is plenty. Here, please take this back."

Squaring his shoulders with stubbornness, Enrique shook his head. "No. You did a fine job on the boat. I made plenty of money, even enough for a good woman. You take this money so you can stay here with us for a longer time. You won't need to go back to work."

The dog raised his head at the sound of his master's voice and threw me a long, low growl. They were a tough team.

"Enrique, I don't need the money," I said, stuffing it back into his pocket.

He removed it and put it on the dresser. "You are a stubborn man with a great deal of pride. I like that. Every man needs money." He motioned to his dog, turned and they walked out the door. "I will see you for supper, compadre." He closed the door behind him.

I counted the pesos, all eight hundred of them, maybe worth fifty American dollars. Fifty dollars for three days work. Fifty dollars for the most back-breaking job I had ever done in my life.

The clothes I ruined cost ten times as much. Fifty dollars to add to the fortune I was already worth. My eyes filled with tears.

One hour of my work in San Diego netted thousands of dollars. One car accident and necessary reconstructive surgery could reap hundreds of thousands. Enrique had no idea. He thought I needed the money. He cared about me, really cared. No other bills I had ever held in my hand meant as much to me as these did.

10

Michael sat at the bistro table long after Amy left. He watched her walk down the street and knew his life had just turned to garbage.

Damn women, he thought, why can't they leave well enough alone? The truth be known, he was glad, no overjoyed, that Megan had disappeared. He'd thought he was rid of her, but this Amy could be a problem. He hadn't counted on her showing up, just as he hadn't counted on Megan falling in love with him.

All his life, women had screwed him up. If it weren't for a hellacious sex drive and a strong desire to be filthy rich, he wouldn't have anything to do with them at all.

Megan was different. His first perception of her had been that she was sweet and innocent. He liked this quality in women. It made them an easy mark. He soon discovered that Megan took these traits to a new level. He often wondered how she had survived this long in a city full of snakes.

Michael sensed right away that Megan had money available to her, along with a wealth of potential targets at her art gallery. Right up his alley.

It didn't take long to discover she was the kind of woman who needed a man in her life, needed a relationship. Another trait he liked to serve his own purposes. He was good at making women feel needier. A week or two into a relationship and they would do anything he wanted. In this respect, Megan was no different.

As perfect a mark as she seemed, Michael discovered a downside. She made him feel guilty, something he wasn't used to. He felt guilty about his lies, about leaving in the morning and about the way she loved him. The guilt scared him. He had never been in love that he knew of. He didn't know what it felt like. These strange sensations he felt for Megan caused him confusion. He ignored them at every turn. Michael's business didn't allow feelings of any kind. Feelings caused clouded thinking and that caused mistakes. Mistakes he couldn't afford.

•••••

Michael's mother, Anna, born in America and Juhn, his Philippine father, brought him to the United States when he was five years old.

His parents had met at a local movie house in the Philippines.

A whirlwind courtship ensued and they married after finding out Anna was pregnant.

Three years after his sister was born, Michael came screaming into the world.

Anna wanted to take her children to America and begged Juhn to accommodate her wishes. She relentlessly argued that he was a successful chef and could take his talent to the States and pursue his own restaurant. Tired of being badgered by his wife, he agreed and the family moved to California.

Before the furniture was arranged in their new house, Juhn noticed the pretty neighbor lady. With a charismatic personality, bordering on European charm and sensuous good looks, he had become a womanizer early in his life.

That his girlfriend had become pregnant, and his parents had insisted on an honorable marriage, only curbed Juhn's appetite for a short time. He loved the ladies and wined and dined them at every chance. It never took long to get invited to their bed.

As Michael grew up, it became apparent that he had inherited his father's elegant style, his lust for women and his sensuous looks.

It also became clear he had a quality his father did not. The ability to move past the romance and profit from his desires. He learned at a young age that women would give him almost anything.

Juhn admired this talent in his son, and often wondered why he himself hadn't achieved it. But as Michael matured into a young man, father and son became a team, a dynamic team. They scoured all the "in" bars in Los Angeles, reaping untold pleasures from the city's richest ladies and enjoying some of the most fabulous nights a man could imagine.

Michael tired of the boundaries of his life. He knew there were bigger fields to harvest and he wanted in on the action. He moved to New York, leaving his father to pluck the rest of the flowers in Los Angeles.

His time on the West Coast had not been wasted, as he managed to collect a wealth of names and numbers for some of the country's richest and loneliest women. Michael planned to put his smooth-talking, charismatic talents to work, and make himself a fortune.

Upon arriving in the City, he wasted no time. He rented opulent offices in the tallest tower in mid-town Manhattan and had them equipped with the finest surveillance equipment available. In his business, Michael would need to keep a sharp eye on the activities of everyone on his staff and anyone who wanted entry into his offices.

He furnished his offices with the most expensive furniture, artwork and adornments he could find. He needed to create an air of complete success and every dime would be worth the investment.

Michael's next step was to recruit a staff of secretaries and brokers. He needed dynamic sales people with less than perfect scruples. He needed men who could be bought and were willing to risk everything for the chance to be rich. His first call was to his father.

Michael soon realized it wasn't hard to find the people he needed. A short ad in the paper had men hungry for wealth flocking to his door. People amazed him. Dangle a carrot in front of their nose and they will inevitably take a bite. He could always count on the element of greed. No exception, his father arrived on the next flight.

Michael's plan was simple. He intended to bilk millions of dollars out of investors and open a swank chain of upscale restaurants in New York City.

He had tested the waters on a much smaller scale in Los Angeles and was amazed how easy it was to convince people to invest in him. The perfectly orchestrated failure of each business left his pockets lined with money, while his well-paid lawyers negotiated every contract to keep him from any liability. Now he was ready to try the big time.

Michael handpicked and personally trained each of his brokers, just as he would a baby parrot. In little time they were mimicking his every word, every behavior. And the money rolled in. At the end of two years, two restaurants were opened and successful, his father was the head chef and millions of dollars sat in fourteen accounts between New York and the Cayman Islands.

Michael owned thirteen cars, a Porsche, a Rolls Royce and a Ferrari to name a few. He rode in his private limo, driven by his bodyguard. He wore Rolex watches and gold rings. He owned lavish homes in the Hamptons and the Caymans.

Each client was, at one time or another, invited to New York, all expenses paid, and entertained in luxury by Michael and Juhn. Treated like the most important investor in the Company, they never failed to leave behind another hefty check to keep the Company successful. Ah, lonely women. A natural resource almost no one had tapped.

Michael expanded his company and took on other ventures, some involving shady characters. Some of them caused the Securities Exchange Commission to raise their eyebrows and threaten investigations. The danger excited him even more.

He had made only one mistake so far. His father had hired a little thing with long black hair to help with the office work. A new conquest called Kristine. Impressed with Michael's money and savvy, it didn't take long for them to meet on the couch in his private office. Before he could blink, she turned up pregnant.

Juhn was many things, many of them not good, but he did consider himself a man of honor. He had done the right thing in the same situation and expected his son to follow suit.

To his gut-wrenching disgust, he married her. Kristine gave birth to their son and Michael was trapped forever. He hated her and their life together and began to womanize even more. He came to realize no amount of money could correct this mistake.

Wandering around Greenwich Village one afternoon, he stepped into a small, but prestigious art gallery. Always on the lookout for new clients or contacts, he wandered through the well-appointed rooms.

As he stood feigning interest in one of the paintings, a young woman approached him. The mere sight of her excited him. Her long hair swayed from side to side and the air filled with a delicate scent of vanilla. A soft, silk blouse outlined full, sensuous breasts and her skirt hung gracefully over long, slim legs. He felt his mouth go dry and his mind go blank.

"May I answer any questions for you?" she purred with a slight smile.

Michael's mind said, how long will it take me to get you into my bed, but he heard his mouth saying, "Yes, I'd like to know something about this artist."

"Okay, but first let me introduce myself. I am Megan Summerfield and I'm the Head Curator of this collection. You are?" She extended her tiny hand and he took it.

At the sound of her name, his mind flashed through fields of green grass, white daisies and a canopy of brilliant sunshine. What a perfect name for such a splendid woman, he thought.

"How do you do, Megan Summerfield, Head Curator of this collection? I am Michael James, Head Curator of Nothingham," he said, his lips curling up at the corners.

Caressing the top of her hand with his thumb, he caught her eyes with his and applied a somewhat firmer grip to her hand. Her blush pleased him, as she withdrew her hand from his.

Megan returned his smile, but remained professional, with an air of challenge. "This is a particularly favorite artist of his time. You will notice the soft strokes, blended defiantly with bold colors, giving the impression of confusion in the artist's mind. He shows great turmoil in his emotions, cleverly manipulated through his brushes. Are you interested in owning this piece, Mr. James?"

"I am, Miss Summerfield. It is Miss, isn't it? I am also interested in having lunch with you, say tomorrow at one?"

"I would love to join you, Mr. James, but I have a policy of meeting with my clients only in the gallery. Thank you for the invitation though. Would you care to discuss a purchase?"

"The beauty of this painting pales only by its comparison to you, Miss Summerfield. I will return tomorrow with my decision and a fine lunch to enjoy with you in your gallery. Have a pleasant day." Michael turned on his heel and strode out of the gallery, but not without feeling her eyes upon his back.

The next day, as he promised, he walked into the gallery at one o'clock, followed by three men dressed in tuxedos, carrying silver domed trays containing a decadent lunch.

Day after day, he went back to her art gallery. He begged her to go to dinner. She refused. He invited her to a play. She refused.

He sent her flowers. She refused them. Tired of her rejection, he went to the gallery, prepared to argue with her.

As he walked towards her Megan said, "Okay. I suppose the only way to get rid of you is to join you for dinner."

Michael stared at her. Had he won? He didn't know.

He needed the connection to her clients. He knew they were wealthy. He didn't need her. Or did he? What was wrong with him? He hadn't been able to get her out of his mind. He hadn't been able to forget the delicate smell of her hair. Her sweet smile and innocence contradicted her professionalism, leaving the combination to weave its way into his soul like a gold thread through a fine carpet. Her constant rejection excited him more than any woman had ever been able to accomplish. He became obsessed with Megan.

Michael's limo pulled up in front of her brownstone and, what seemed to be on cue, her front door opened and Megan's delicate figure appeared, silhouetted in the doorway. Michael's driver opened the door and she slipped in next to him. Again, the air became infused with the scent of vanilla. His heart raced like a schoolboy. He had made love to many women in this car, but he sensed this one was not about to play.

The door was not closed before she turned to him and said, "Mr. James, I want you to understand right away that I am not interested in a romantic relationship with anyone. It has nothing to do with you. I am just not interested in romance. I would appreciate it if you would conduct yourself within the accordance of my wishes."

"I will give that my utmost consideration."

A good bottle of wine will change her wishes before dessert, he thought to himself.

Entering the Blackstone, the most famous old-world restaurant in Manhattan, eyes turned to look at Michael's date.

The Maitre d' approached and led them to a small room of the restaurant, where Michael's private table was prepared with flowers and a chilled bottle of wine. The art in this room equaled the value of anything in Megan's gallery and Michael couldn't help but notice she was impressed. Even in the dimly lit venue, he could see the flush in her cheeks.

"Mr. James, your choice of a restaurant is excellent. I have only heard of it. I have never been fortunate enough to dine here. Thank you so much for your choice."

"Please call me Michael. I would be pleased if you would allow me to call you Megan, if just for tonight." The wine steward poured a small amount of wine into his glass. He tasted it and decided it would do.

"I would be pleased to have you call me Megan, if just for tonight."

Before he could reply, a waiter appeared with a small plate of baby artichokes, filling the air with a fragrant smell of lemon.

"You are presumptuous to assume I like artichokes," she said, a small pout forming on her lips.

"If ordering artichokes will guarantee that look on your face, I will order them again and again."

By the second glass of wine, the waiter rolled Chateaubriand to the table on a silver cart.

"Do I have anything to say about this evening," she scolded, but in a much lighter tone of voice.

They chatted about each other's lives, staying only on the surface of details, but laughing often. She softened before his eyes and he wasn't sure if it was the wine or his award-winning personality. Michael hoped for the latter. At one point, their hands touched on the table and chills crossed through his body. He became more determined than ever to have this woman.

After a decadent dessert, the waiter appeared and handed her an exquisite rose. Turning to Michael he said, "As always, thank you Mr. James. We always enjoy your visits." Glancing at Megan, he turned and left.

Outside, Michael's limo waited. "Would you care to take a little walk before I take you home, Megan?"

"Yes I would, thank you."

He gave instructions to his driver, Louis, and arm in arm, Michael and Megan strolled through Central Park. He stopped close to a little bridge and pulled her towards him. She didn't resist and he kissed her in the moonlight. Through her long black evening coat he could feel the softness of her body and the firmness of her breasts. He wanted this woman.

Louis picked them up on the other side of the park.

In the car, Michael tried to put his arm around her, but Megan had become sullen and didn't speak the entire ride across town. She had pulled away from him.

Damn this woman, he thought. He didn't like rejection. Damn her and her clients. He didn't need either one of them. He had gotten this far without her and he wouldn't be made a fool of.

To his surprise, as they pulled up in front of her brownstone, she turned to him and touched his hand. "Michael, even though this is against my better judgment, would you like to come in for a drink?"

This night had started a year of Sundays. She understood that their time together was limited because of his business and she never plowed too far under the surface of his life. She accepted Michael for himself and didn't expect him to provide her with anything but him. He liked the feeling, but didn't trust it.

•••••

Now, after lying to Amy, Michael sat alone, waiting for either the SEC or the FBI to untangle his web of deceit and file charges against him.

He didn't have time to worry about Amy and what their meeting might mean. He needed to save himself. Things he had only worried about, up to this point, had now become reality.

11

Megan read and reread the news article. Inch by painful inch, despair started on the top of her head in a little circle, spinning, spinning, moving down, and consuming her entire being. It couldn't be true. Michael was the most honest, sincere man she had ever met. This had to be a mistake.

How could he be accused of being a con artist who bilked hundreds of women out of their money, or suspected of involvement in a murder with possible Mob affiliation? Not her Michael. It just couldn't be true.

A sound kept creeping into her head. Was she screaming? No, it was the phone. She stared at it. Michael, it was Michael. He had found her. He was calling to tell her it was all a lie. She tried to run to the phone, but her shaking body made movement almost impossible. She reached forward and lifted the receiver.

A man's voice said, "Miss Summerfield, your driver is here."

Francisco. She had forgotten Francisco. Last night, having seen a brochure in the hotel lobby, she had asked him to take her to Julian, a little town in the mountains famous for its apples.

"Please, please tell him I am not feeling well today. Tell him I am sorry."

Several times during the day she reached for the phone. She so wanted to call Michael, to hear his voice, to hear him tell her it was all lies. She drew her hand back every time, afraid. Afraid he wouldn't talk to her and afraid if he did, he'd tell her it was true.

She relived the feel of his arms around her, their Sundays on the yellow couch, his smile, and his promises. Lies, it had all been lies. She doubted he had ever loved her. No, she knew he did. She had given him money. He had returned it. Oh, Michael, I'll never stop loving you.

Pacing around the room, trying to make sense of a senseless situation, hours passed. She finally lay down, exhausted, on the bed.

She woke late in the evening, the demons alive and well in her thoughts. They took her back in time, back to other failed loves, other broken promises and other broken trusts.

•••••

Megan had met Paul, a tall, dark-haired actor, with a devilish personality, in a neighboring coffee shop. His many friends were artists, of one kind or another, and they spent endless hours involved in great philosophical conversations trying to imagine how starving artists survive.

Paul played on Broadway, when he could get a part, and introduced her to her first backstage party. The carefree group and their artsy lifestyle kept life interesting and exciting. They roamed the streets of New York, eating hot dogs and slices of pizza. They swiped oranges and bananas from the open markets when the merchants weren't looking. They explored every nook and cranny of the art galleries and libraries, picnicked in Central Park and roller-skated around the lake.

Megan and Paul lived on her income from the art gallery, and she subsidized his friends at times, not wanting them to go hungry.

Megan fell in love with Paul; head-over heels in love. He never spoke a harsh word to her, adored everything she did and always made her laugh. After many silly, flirtatious relationships in college, she had finally found someone just like her father.

With the winter approaching, she dropped by Macy's to buy Paul some sweaters she knew he couldn't afford. Happy and smiling, Megan decided to walk down Broadway, foregoing a cab, to enjoy the brisk fall day.

As she approached the theater district, she saw him and a cute little blond sitting on the steps of a building. He had one arm around her and, with the other hand, held her face while he kissed her. Megan hid behind a pole and watched their romance play out. They stood up, turned and walked, arm in arm, down the street.

She threw the sweaters in the trashcan, hailed a cab home and cried for a week. She didn't let Paul explain, even though he tried several times. It was over. It would be impossible to turn back.

According to Paul's friends, he had been using Megan because she had a job. He had been seeing the girl, a fellow actor, for some time. They admitted he laughed behind her back at what an easy mark Megan was. Tears led to anger and anger led to resolve. Her father could not be replicated.

Megan concentrated on her job at the art gallery and earned a promotion to Head Curator. Her parents were proud of her and the three of them celebrated over dinner in her favorite Italian restaurant.

Many months later, she met Dave at an art premier. Somehow, love blinded her like a truck smashing headfirst into a brick wall. The minute she met him her head began to spin. Her impression of worlds colliding couldn't have been more accurate.

Dave swept Megan off her feet, dancing her around Manhattan, dining in fabulous restaurants, buying her expensive gifts and making love to her as though she were the only woman in the world.

She found herself caught up in a whirlwind and couldn't get out, nor did she want to.

Dave adored her, worshipped her; he marveled at her beauty as she woke up in the morning. She heard him say all the things her father said to her mother. Megan had finally found her father's counterpart.

One Monday morning, after a glorious weekend with Dave, she sat in her office trying to concentrate on paperwork, feeling light-headed and giddy.

All of a sudden, she heard commotion in the front office and her secretary saying, "I'm sorry, I don't care who you are, you can't go in there." Her door flew open and an obviously hysterical woman pushed her way past the secretary. Two crying children followed.

With the frustrated secretary in hot pursuit, the angry woman marched up to her and slapped Megan across the face.

As the woman accused Megan of being the slut her husband spent his time with in New York, the police arrived. They dragged the screaming, crying woman out of the office, onto the street and Megan stood still, her face stinging, her heart breaking

The phone rang. Picking it up, she heard Dave's voice say, "I'm sorry, Megan, I'm sorry. I didn't want you to find out. Please forgive me."

Megan laid the phone down on the desk and walked out of the office. On her way out, the police asked if she wanted to file charges. She shook her head "no" and glanced at the woman, now sitting on the curb.

She saw the frightened children sitting next to her, trying to console their mother. The smallest one, tears streaming down his face, kept repeating, "Don't cry, Mommy. We still love you."

She muttered, "I'm so sorry. I didn't know," and walked away.

She didn't know how long she walked, but Megan found herself on a train, going home; going home to her parents. Going home to the only security she knew. Going home to the only honest relationship she had.

Two years went by. Megan's father died after a short, sudden illness and she and her mother grieved. She worked and worked at the art gallery. Nothing else seemed to matter. She traveled to Europe to buy art, wheeling and dealing at auctions and estate closings. She dated several men, enjoying dinner and conversation, but nothing else.

Megan liked being away from the city. She had time to think and try to figure out why she always chose the wrong man, although she never came up with an answer. She decided she had lost the ability to trust anyone except her mother.

Megan added up the pluses in her life. She had been blessed with a wonderful, secure childhood. She had the greatest parents a girl could have. She was college educated with an outstanding career. She lived in and owned a prestigious brownstone. She had experienced love not once, but twice.

Deciding there wasn't much more a person could ask from life, she declared a state of peace with herself and made a commitment to be happy alone. Megan didn't need to be married or have children. She was okay.

And then came Michael; pushing his way into her life like a puppy nuzzles his nose into a warm neck. She didn't need him. She didn't want him. She wanted him to go away. He did. And then he came back, over and over and over again. She gave in, but just to have dinner, just to have enough time to explain that she didn't want him or a relationship. As he left the next morning, she tried to explain again. The words seemed to have gotten lost somewhere in her head.

Megan had never been with a man like Michael. He oozed sex. His voice melted her soul. He had touched her hand during dinner and her body begged for more. As his words put footprints on her heart, she convinced herself that this time she'd be the one to be in it for sex alone. No man would ever use her again. In the end, which would be inevitable, she would hail herself as the best user ever. She would declare justice had been done for all women throughout time, for every poor woman who had ever been betrayed by a man.

So Megan had invited him to her house. Let the games begin. Her plan fell right into place. Stupid men, she thought. They are so easy. He couldn't wait to get her clothes off. She couldn't wait for him to do so. Instead of him ravaging her, she ravaged him. All night. She would make him beg her to stop. He didn't. Light fell on the bedroom. She asked him to leave and as he went, she said, "I'll call you sometime." He looked surprised, but he left. She congratulated herself as he walked out the door. She waited until nine o'clock that morning before she called him.

The games had begun all right; the same old games. Within the time frame of a shooting star, Megan found herself in love. Michael had a magnetism, drawing her to him. She couldn't get enough of him. He was an adventurous, sensitive, explorative lover. His conversation followed suit. He had a profound interest in her career and attended every function he could at the art gallery.

Michael charmed her clients with his charismatic personality. He served them wine, with the undivided attention of a master wine steward. He complimented their exquisite clothes and fine jewelry; their wonderful ability to put together such a sophisticated look. He acknowledged their ability to recognize fine art. At times, he personally delivered their purchases.

Megan enjoyed watching them flourish under his attention. Her sales increased tri-fold. He said his only goal was to see her succeed at the career she so loved. He told her life was a game. There were haves and have-nots. He enjoyed being able to flip the switch to see them change roles.

Michael's business as a Financial Broker consumed most of his time and energy, and he said they would only have a limited time together. He didn't volunteer much information about his company and she didn't pressure him.

Her career also demanded a lot of her time, but it didn't matter. The lasting effect of their relationship carried her on air for days.

Michael had told Megan in the beginning of their relationship about his wife and son and how he despised her. He resented that she had taken his son away from him and was raising him with another man. He saw little of the boy because of the divorce. She made it difficult for him to visit and even told his son that he didn't love either one of them.

Megan's heart ached for Michael, to the point that she would have been happy to have a child to ease his pain.

He explained his business as 'high-risk'. A lot of money was made and lost in minutes and he loved the excitement.

Michael traveled to the islands often, particularly the Caymans. He said he had many clients there and unless he wined and dined them, he would lose good money.

He liked Atlantic City and they often went there and lived the high life. He gambled large amounts of money and was well respected at the hotels. Michael was the most dynamic, debonair man she had ever encountered.

A part of him seemed secretive and maybe a little dark, but she attributed this to his wife and son. A man like Michael didn't like to lose at anything.

When they were in Manhattan, they spent every Sunday in her Brownstone. Michael didn't like to go out in the city. Megan didn't know why he preferred to stay in, but she was content to eat in and just spend quiet time together. She had her job, and him, and she needed nothing else. She was happier than she had ever been.

One afternoon, he came to the art gallery distraught and visibly upset. They went into her office and she poured him a glass of wine. He sat down on the couch and put his head in his hands. She went to him.

He grabbed her in his arms and said, "Oh, Megan, I don't know what I am going to do. I've lost so much money on a bad deal that I don't know if I can pull my company out of the hell I've put it in. So many people depend on me. I don't know what else to do. I didn't know where else to go. I'm sorry to lay this on you Megan. I'm so sorry. Just hold me for a few minutes. I need you to just hold me."

She knew she had to do something. She could not stand to see Michael like this. She offered to mortgage her brownstone and give him the money she'd saved. Over his protests, Megan convinced him to let her help. He finally conceded. She didn't see that he had a choice.

After they put together her money, he said it would help, but it wouldn't be nearly enough to save him. He needed more clients to invest in him, but he was afraid he had run the well dry in Manhattan. He didn't know what he was going to do.

She had a brilliant idea. Her clients were wealthy. Maybe some of them would invest in Michael. She hurried to get her client list.

Overcome with gratefulness, Michael declared them a team and suggested they seal the deal by getting married. She couldn't have been happier.

Within weeks, he was back on his feet and flying to the Caymans again. His investors stopped into the art gallery and thanked her for putting them together with "such a wonderful young man."

Everything was perfect. Michael paid her back a lot of the money and they talked almost daily about marriage. After they were married, she would tell him about her parent's money, maybe even invest it in his company for a wedding present. He would be so surprised. Megan's parents would have been so happy to see their money invested wisely. They also would have been proud to know their daughter had become savvy in the business world. Her father had always joked about his 'girl' not knowing a thing about money.

Months flew by. Megan and Michael were so busy with their jobs that the wedding plans were put on the back burner.

A couple of times, Michael, being so stressed for time, arranged short business meetings at her house. The fellows he met with seemed kind of shady, but she attributed it to the nature of his business. New York is made up of all kinds of people, she thought.

One Sunday, she sat in her apartment waiting for Michael to arrive. When he let himself in, Megan could see by the look on his face, he was troubled. He asked her to sit down and paced in front of her.

He explained his wife had contacted him and wanted him to come back for his son's sake. She said the boy was inconsolable and failing at school. The child no longer played with his friends and his mood was always sullen and angry. He had given it a lot of thought and decided he only had one choice. They had a terrible argument and he left.

•••••

Megan came out of her reverie with the morning light shining on her face. She had sat here all night reliving her failed relationships. Her shoulders hurt. Her face felt swollen.

Out of nowhere, it occurred to her the one common thread which kept coming up all night had been her father. That was it! Up until this moment, the only thing she had done with her life was to try and find a man just like him. Anger consumed her and turned to rage. How dare they? How dare her parents set this kind of a goal? Why didn't they have a normal marriage? Why did he forgive her mother for all of her shortcomings? Why didn't they ever fight? What secret did they have to a perfect relationship? Why had they never shared it with her? Why had they died and taken it to their graves? Her mind ranted and raved, as she paced around the room. Selfish! They were selfish, that was it! They were the most selfish people she could think of. They must have intended to ruin her life on purpose.

A knock at the door interrupted her tirade. Megan stood stock still, staring at the door. The knock came again. Her mind screamed, Michael. He's found me. She ran to the door and swung it open.

Francisco stood, hat in hand, smiling at her. "Good morning, Miss Megan. I thought I'd stop by to see if you are okay. I got worried when you cancelled our trip. Please forgive me for bothering you, but I started to worry." His smile turned to a look of fear as he began to comprehend her appearance.

She stood staring at him, her eyes wild with anger.

"Get out," she yelled at him. "Who do you think you are coming here? I don't need you to worry about me. You could never understand my problems. You're just a cab driver." She almost spit the word into his face. "Go away and leave me alone. I don't need an immigrant from Mexico to worry about me. What makes you think you could help me? Get out." She slammed the door in his face.

Francisco stood outside the door, stung by her words. He replaced his hat and walked down the hallway towards the elevator, too stunned to feel any emotion.

12

After her meeting with Michael, Amy spent weeks trying to find any clue as to where Megan had gone.

Her first problem had been Michael's story. It didn't make sense. Instinct told her he was lying. Logic pointed in the same direction.

She called him several times, but his answers to her questions were vague and of no help. He seemed annoyed with her. Was that a logical reaction for someone who professed a profound love for Megan? One would think he would want to help find her. Amy's last call to him resulted in a taped recording announcing the line had been disconnected.

A trip to his offices proved futile. They were abandoned. No one in the building had a forwarding address for the missing company and everyone she talked to seemed reluctant to discuss Michael, or his business.

Amy managed to find his home address in Megan's office at the art gallery and drove out there. A 'For Sale' sign graced the front of the vacant house. The neighbors had no clue what had happened to him or his family. Sitting in front of his house, Amy laid her head on the steering wheel and prayed. Please God, please help me.

Driving back to the city, she began to wonder if Michael had disappeared from the face of the earth, had gone to meet Megan on some distant island, or if paranoia had taken control of her mind. Clenching her hands on the steering wheel, Amy tried to regain her composure.

Could Michael have involved her in something illegal? Could she be afraid and running? Megan loved him so much; she would have believed anything he told her.

Amy knew her friend so well. Kind and trusting to a fault, Megan had always been an easy mark for anyone. She never doubted anyone's credibility or motive and her compassion and heartfelt love for people exceeded anything ordinary.

Even though her parents were wonderful, Amy thought they

had never taught Megan to manage in the real world. To the best of Amy's knowledge, in Megan's entire life, she had never had a real problem to solve.

In New York, Megan gave a dollar to every beggar she saw. Her heart broke for each one of them. She didn't care how they intended to use the money; she felt the need to help. No matter how many times she'd see one of them a few minutes later with a new bottle of beer, she never stopped caring!

The thing Amy loved most about Megan was the fact that she never stopped caring. The thing she hated the most about her friend was that she never stopped caring.

Amy knew that someday her naiveté would lead her into trouble, but no matter how much Amy talked to her, Megan insisted she was right in her feelings.

A visit to the police resulted in their refusal to take a missing person's report because of the letters. They wouldn't even listen to her explanation that neither one sounded like her friend. Crying didn't help either.

Desperation led her to Megan's lawyer's office for the second time.

"Amy, you know that by law I cannot talk to you about Megan."

She knew he knew more, but couldn't convince him to talk. "Fine, take that road if you want to, but know that I will not stop looking for her, and I will find her." She started for the door, frustration consuming her.

Calling for her to wait, he walked over and closed his door. "Okay, look Amy. I am worried about Megan, too."

"Please talk to me, Mr. Clayton. I am begging you. I'm at my wits end with worry,"

Her worst fears were about to come true. She knew in her soul Megan was in trouble and braced herself for what she was about to hear.

The lawyer looked at her over his glasses and he began, "A friend of mine at the bank called me the other day and told me the FBI had done an investigation on her accounts. I don't know what it means and I don't know what she's involved in, but I think she's in trouble. We have to find her, Amy."

Bile rose in Amy's throat and panic set in. She sat down. Funny things had been happening. Things she had tried to ignore. She decided to tell this man. His concern now seemed to equal her own.

"Men have been sitting in cars outside the brownstone. They are not always there and they are not always the same men. They are dressed in suits and although they don't look at me, I know they are watching me. I have seen cars, similar to the ones at the house, following me. I've seen men on the subway glance at me over the edge of their newspaper.

The other day, when I went to the art gallery, Megan's co-worker told me two men had come in and requested to see her office. They wouldn't say why and the co-worker refused. They told her they would be back. This incident convinced me to come and see you again.

At first, I thought it was just paranoia, especially after Michael's disappearance, but the art gallery thing convinced me I am not paranoid. I don't know what to do. I don't know how to find her. Do you have any suggestions?"

"I have a friend who might be able to check for a money trail, credit cards or something. Maybe we can hunt down an airline or a bus ticket. I'll call him. Is the number still the same at the house?"

"Yes, it is, but don't call me there. I don't know if the phones are tapped. I don't know if I'm just acting crazy. I'll call you. When would be a good time?"

"I'll call the house as soon as I know something and say, "Hi, Megan. This is Uncle Bill. Give me a call when you get in."

"Okay. Thank you so much for your help. I didn't know where else to turn. Thank you again. I'll be waiting for my message." She hugged him and left the office. For the first time, Amy felt hope and not so alone.

As she left his office building, she noticed a man standing on the corner dressed in a trench coat and lighting a cigarette. He seemed to watch her leave. When she reached the corner she turned just in time to see him enter the building. Amy hurried home.

13

Returning home from the bistro, Michael picked up a small white envelope that lay inside his door. What now? Michael thought. He only wanted to turn back time and walk out of his nightmare. He took a long hot shower and, wrapped in a towel, decided he should face whatever message the envelope held.

Michael, call me at this number from a payphone, 647-4688; don't waste any time. Jack.

He dressed and hurried downtown to find a phone. Dialing the number with shaking hands, he caught himself looking over his shoulder.

Lehman, his lawyer, answered on the first ring. "Michael, the FBI knows more than you think they know. I've heard from a good source that they are on their way to pick you up. Find a hiding place. Don't go back to the house or offices. Hide the car and walk from now on. Appear to be broke. I'll contact you as soon as I have more information."

Michael rented a room in a fleabag hotel in lower Manhattan. He hated it. The room was dirty and cold. It stunk of cigarettes and stale old men. A rust-stained sink hung from one wall, roaches parading across its top like little soldiers. A cracked mirror hung from a nail above it. A rusted, iron bed protruded from another wall, complete with threadbare sheets and a worn, thin blanket. It was impossible to tell what color any of the linens had been. Ragged curtains hung from the only window, which overlooked an alley laden with old bums. A beat up, three-drawer dresser held a copy of the Gideon's bible. The bathroom contained a leaking, stained toilet and a shower to match, completing the décor.

Michael sat on the side of the bed and put his head in his hands. He couldn't stand to look at his surroundings. God only knew how long he would have to stay here. Damn his life. Damn his luck. Three days had passed since his call from Lehman. He had plenty of time to think.

•••••

Everything Michael touched had been successful. Investors threw money at him hand over fist. He opened restaurants. They succeeded. He bought a private island in the Caribbean and planned to build a huge resort, catering only to the rich.

Everyone around him prospered. His brokers, his parents, his office staff, his lawyer, everyone. He did it all on other people's money and took a generous share for himself. He gambled like a drunk on a binge. He spent money like a madman. No one cared.

The investors just kept giving him more. They begged him to spend it. They were all convinced he could turn their investments into fortunes. He did and he kept most of it. Every month he sent them a small stipend and called it interest. They loved it. They knew their money was secure in his hands.

One stupid, greedy broker spoiled it all. Michael had picked Richard up off the street after the jerk ran himself into bankruptcy with bad deals.

Next to himself, Richard, an old friend, was the smoothest talker Michael had ever met. He could sell shoes to a man with no feet. With a desk and a phone, this man could make magic.

And make magic, he did. Richard closed deal after deal. He made the twenty other brokers in the office look like amateurs. Money rolled in. Michael and Richard were a dynamic team. They worked together two years. High fiving each other after every deal, they thanked God for the mother-lode of vulnerable women in this fine country.

Then, out of nowhere, Richard became sullen. He slacked on deals. He picked fights with the other brokers and with Michael. He disappeared for days, showing up out of nowhere and claiming he was away entertaining clients. His expense accounts became unreasonable.

Michael figured it was time to do some investigating. When working on the perimeter of the law and carefully hiding the deviancies from it, a tight community is formed. His Company involved interstate fraud, but no one had ever been able to prove it because the terminology in the sales pitches was legal.

All brokers in the industry knew each other and nothing

could really be kept a secret, except their lists. Each firm had a list of clients and protected it at all costs. Lives were lost when a broker went bad and shared his firm's list.

It only took a few phone calls; a few favors repaid, to find out that Richard had hooked up with his old partner, Paul. They were partnering a deal that involved a gambling ship off the coast of the Florida Keys.

It didn't take Michael long to figure out that Richard had used many of his clients to obtain money for his own venture.

As deadly a move as this could be in their industry; Michael knew what would bring him the most trouble. It was common knowledge that the mob controlled all gaming aspects of Florida.

Because Richard was a broker in Michael's firm, it wouldn't take the FBI long to form a link to him. He had spent years resisting the mob's pressure to "co-operate." He had even suffered occasional strong-arming. Anything was better than being indebted to their agency. Michael liked calling the shots and did not want to answer to anyone, particularly the "Family."

Michael confronted Richard at the first opportunity. "I took you off the street, you bum. What the hell do you think you're doing? I'll have your ass killed."

Richard screamed, "I'm tired of playing second fiddle to such a pompous ass. I want the gold ring. You've had it long enough, you scumbag." Rage streaked his face.

"How can you stand there and tell me you are stealing my clients and my money and think you are justified." As the word justified came out of his mouth, his right fist rose and hit Richard square in the face.

Richard was too smart to come back at him. He knew Michael could kill him with his bare hands. Michael was huge and had the temper of a wild bear. "You bastard" he screamed.

"You're fired you son of a bitch. Get out of my office before I kill you right here." Muscles pulsed in Michael's face.

"I'll get even with you. You'll be sorry you ever met me, you punk," Richard spat at him, throwing more insults over his shoulder as he left the office.

Michael promised him a violent death if he ever came near him again.

Richard slammed the door as he left.

Michael spent the rest of the day in his office, trying to figure out how much trouble Richard could cause him if he set his mind to it. He had trusted him with information no one else knew. It had been a mistake. It would prove to be a bigger mistake than even he realized. It was the beginning of his hell.

In a matter of days, things changed. Odd people called the secretaries in the office asking off the wall questions. The IRS scheduled an audit. The SEC wrote a letter requesting copies of the broker's licenses. The State Labor Board showed up to audit his payroll. For weeks, every day brought a new agency and a new suspicion.

Michael's nasty little wife paid a visit to his office. "Why don't you tell me about your little piece of ass?" "I'll divorce you, you son of a bitch" she threatened. I'll own this friggin' company and live a high life on your money. You'll never see your son again. I'll tell him you're dead. I'll expose this whole scam to the Commission and the FBI, too.

But first, I'm going to pay a little visit to your whore. She'll know who I am when I'm finished. The whole world will know who I am when I'm finished, you bum."

She stood toe-to-toe with him, her face contorted with rage. As she screamed at him, bits of spit flew from her mouth, hitting his face. He became enraged.

Grabbing her flailing wrist, he twisted her arm backwards and pushed her to her knees.

"You won't do any such thing, you slut" You'll live the rest of your life out quietly, spending my money and raising my son and you'll be a respectful wife."

From her knees, his body towering over her, pain shooting through her body, she said, "I'll see you dead first."

Getting down on his knees and pulling her face up by her hair, he looked into her eyes, smiling menacingly. "No, you won't and do you know why?"

He had waited years to play his trump card with her and his moment had finally arrived. His emotions surged with the triumph.

"If I ever hear anything again from your nasty mouth, other than 'Yes, sir', your illegal immigrant mother will be deported before you can say your name and your criminal father will be in the most ruthless, savage prison I can find. He'll die wishing they had caught him for his crimes in Mexico."

She stared up at him in utter disbelief; her face took on a sickening ashen color.

"That's right. Understand what I'm telling you. You didn't think anyone knew your secret did you? Well, Sweetheart, it's always been my job to know people's secrets." He released her and stood up. The fight was gone from her body.

He moved from in front of her, over to his desk, and began silently stacking papers. Without looking up, he said quietly, "Get out."

As his office door closed, his secretary buzzed him on the intercom. "A man, who won't identify himself, is on line one. He said it is urgent and he needs to talk to you about a matter of life and death."

Michael picked up the phone. A voice said, "You are in trouble. Richard's partner, Paul has been found dead on a boat in the Keys. One shot through the head. Looks like a mob hit, clean and quick. The FBI is trying to connect you. It won't be hard to do. Be careful. Richard has caused you trouble. He talked to your wife, too." The line went dead.

It only took seconds for him to make a decision. Michael went down to the lobby of the office building and made a quick phone call. He arranged a meeting at Megan's house for that evening. After two more meetings, the time, finances and details were worked out. Richard would no longer be a problem.

Two nights later, as Richard got into his Lincoln Continental in his garage, a man sat up from the back seat. As the car rolled out of the garage, one shot entered the back of his head and he slumped over the wheel. The car rolled across the street and hit a tree. By the time his wife got outside, no one was around. She started to scream. The police said it looked like a mob hit.

Things quieted down at the office. The agencies couldn't seem to find anything wrong. Michael figured they had given up. He went about business as usual.

A newspaper article broke about a company similar to his that had been busted by the SEC. Soon after, another and then another.

The news stations started covering investment companies based in New York and alerting people to their scams. They warned people about cold callers asking for money to be invested in a great deal. Michael's brokers were having a hard time getting people to listen to their pitches. Funds stopped coming in.

Within a month of Richard's death, Michael's business began to collapse. Sitting at his desk one morning, his doors burst open; the FBI rushed in and confiscated everything. They raided his home at the same time.

He went to Megan and laid lies on top of the hundreds of other lies he had told her. He even cried as he walked away from her. In some circles, he would have been awarded an Academy Award. Everything had turned to shit and he couldn't change it.

The Feds harassed him, but couldn't hold him until their investigation was complete. They had taken his passport and told him to stay in town.

"Big shots," he sneered. "They can't get anything on me."

The women he had deceived called his private lines every day, begging him to return their calls. They pleaded with him, explaining that they still had faith in him and would stand by him. Stupid women. Didn't they know they were all broke? As far as anyone knew, all the money was gone.

It was gone alright, gone to banks in the Caymans. He had been moving it for months. Michael, his father, his lawyer and Louis would be fixed for life. At first chance, he was out of this country forever.

The conversation with his father caused pain he did not think he was capable of. "Papa, you and Mom must return to the Philippines for your own safety. Christine, my son and her parents will go with you. I would not want any of you to be subject to questioning by these agencies. It is too dangerous. I will join you as soon as I can."

His parents cried, but after discussing their options, they realized they would do more harm to him if they stayed. Armed with a million in cash, they took the next flight out. Christine and her family almost ran to the airport with them, another cool million lining her purse. Michael had never felt so alone.

•••••

A small sound broke his reverie. He watched as a white paper slid under his door. Picking it up, a one-line message read, Call Lehman, he needs to talk to you now.

Michael trusted three people in the entire world, his lawyer, Jack, his bodyguard, Louis, and his father. Their greed matched his own. If he knew anything about people, he knew that greed was a stronger bond than cement. His life had been based on it. His life had prospered on it and so had theirs. Michael knew Louis had gotten the note to him.

He put on his pants and T-shirt and walked out to the dark, gray hallway. The stench overwhelmed him. He checked to see if anyone was around and then, feeling sure he was alone, picked up the sticky receiver to the payphone. His bare feet stuck to the linoleum and his stomach turned sick. In his hurry, he had forgotten his shoes. He listened to the phone ring on the other end and cursed at his feet. Lehman answered. He must have been expecting the call.

Michael pictured him sitting at his grandiose desk, swinging around in his custom leather chair, to gaze out his window and stare down at mid-town Manhattan while he talked. A steaming hot cup of coffee was being held in his free hand and he was being careful not to spill it on his custom-made, three-piece suit or his shiny Italian leather shoes.

He had moved way up in the world after their dealings. Michael had found Lehman in a shabby one-room office, wishing he had enough money for a pack of cigarettes. The hundred thousand-dollar retainer he had placed on his desk in one hundred-dollar bills bought the lawyer's loyalty and a lot of unscrupulous law practices. People were so easy.

"I got your message," Michael said, cupping the receiver with his free hand.

An old woman in a filthy dress appeared in the hallway. Michael turned his back to her and bent over the phone. She disappeared down the hallway, talking to herself. She hadn't even noticed him.

"Find Megan," Lehman barked. "Get rid of her right away. A

subpoena has been issued for her. The FBI thinks she is the only one who can tie you into the murder. They know you met with the hit men in her house. If you remember, I told you it was stupid, at the time. They want her to identify them. You know she can.

They also think you moved the money in her name. They know her personal accounts alone are worth ten million. She is the link they need. Do what you have to do. You have a lot at stake to lose over a piece of ass." He hung up.

Shocked by this news and stunned by the amount of money Megan was worth, he started to retch. Prison scared him more than anything in the world. Returning to his room, he vomited until nothing was left but bile.

Anger exploded in his brain. Where had that bitch come up with ten million? She had only given him a half million and said it was all she had and he had been stupid enough to pay her back. Maybe she had been conning him all along. It would be easy to get rid of her. He needed to think.

One or two more deaths didn't matter. All he had to do was find Megan. He would get rid of that pest Amy, too. She had called him several times asking more stupid questions. She was annoying, like a gnat at a picnic. Thank God she couldn't reach him anymore.

Yes, he could arrange it. They could only burn him once anyway. Just another little mess to clean up, he mused.

14

After a solid night's sleep, I wandered downstairs. I felt like a new man. The night before, I had placed my hard-earned pesos in a back compartment of my wallet, making a vow never to spend them. A sense of pride overwhelmed me and I fell asleep wanting to show my partners, my parents and Sadie my eight hundred pesos.

Angelina sat at one of the small tables holding a cup of coffee. Her dog lay next to her foot. She grinned as I approached her and motioned for Pedro to bring me a cup of coffee.

The dog opened one eye and looked at me as I sat down. I don't think I had ever seen her with two eyes open at the same time.

"Do you want breakfast, mi amigo? How was your fishing trip? Did you help with the nets? Did Enrique share his good tequila? Did you like Angelina's food?" She had a devilish grin on her face.

By the time I finished answering her questions; Pedro delivered a giant plate of food and a cup of coffee. The delicious aroma of the food filled my nose. I dug into it.

While I ate, we discussed the events of the fishing trip and laughed at my lack of knowledge, and clumsiness, on the boat.

"Angelina, you must understand that the closest I have ever come to fishing would be deciding which fish to order in a restaurant."

She didn't pick up on the humor in my statement. It seemed unthinkable to her that a man did not know how to fish and she pondered over it for a long moment.

Checking my damaged hands, laced with cuts and bruises, she informed me I would live. She clucked her tongue a couple of times and assured me that after a few more trips with Enrique, the best fisherman in the world, I would also be considered a fisherman. I doubted it, but she did help to soften the blow to my bruised ego.

"Angelina, I want to give the money back to Enrique, but he won't take it. I don't deserve it. I did nothing."

"You will not do that, Peter." Her eyes turned dark. "Do not insult Enrique. He is a proud man and you will insult his honor to refuse what he thinks you deserve. Mexicans are proud people. The men in this town work hard. They take care of the women and children. They take care of the horses and mules. They provide food and shelter. They take nothing from anyone."

As fast as her temper flared, her face softened and her voice lost its tension.

"Let me tell you about Enrique, Peter." She leaned forward in her chair, resting her arms on the table.

"When Enrique was a young man, a big ship came to our harbor. The Captain of the ship made an offer to the fathers in our village that they could not refuse. He offered their sons a life in America. He promised they would have a good life, with many chances to prosper. It is every father's dream for his son to have a better life and the fathers took no time to make a decision.

The Captain picked the boys he wanted for his ranch and everyone celebrated this proud, promising day.

On the day the boys boarded the ship, their fathers cried tears of happiness, their mothers cried tears of pain, and their brothers and sisters cried tears of sadness, but all understood that it was good for the boys to go. It was a chance for them to have a good life and a better future than they could have in this village.

The Captain did not choose Enrique. He remained on the beach, knowing that he was not strong enough, that he was not big enough and also knowing he would never have the chance to prosper.

He watched with sadness as his two friends, Carlos and Francisco, and many others, left with the Captain. Enrique, left alone to take care of the village for the aging fathers, realized his fate.

He spent his life fishing, making sure the women and families had enough food. He taught the younger boys to fish and provide for their families, a job their brothers should have done. He took care of the widows, helping with their gardens and working on their houses. All by himself, he kept this village going.

The younger boys made fun of him because he was not chosen by the Captain, but, over time, saw the work that Enrique did and grew a deep respect for him.

In the end, he proved to be the strongest one of all. He is a man of great honor and great pride. We consider him our Delegado, our chosen leader.

The sad part is that I hurt Enrique more than the young boys could ever have done with their mocking and taunting. I hurt him more than even the Captain did."

"Tell me about that, Angelina."

Her eyes clouded with emotion. She took a deep breath and lowered her eyes to the table.

"Enrique has always loved me, from the time I was a small girl. He told his father that when I grew up, he would marry me and give him grand-children.

I grew from a child into a pretty young woman with long black hair, a soft face and a good body. Every boy in town wanted me and Enrique fought them all. He declared me as his woman.

Then, the ship came.

The Captain came to shore and walked to town. All the boys followed him. The young girls followed him, too, but not me. I stayed behind and watched a good-looking man walk behind the Captain. I smiled at him, as sweet as I knew how. He smiled at me. He looked at my body and I could see that he liked what he saw. I swayed my hips and smiled a sweeter smile. He came closer and asked my name. I stood close to him, swung my hair over my shoulder and said, "I am Angelina."

She stopped and mimicked the move she made with her hair, a faraway look in her eyes. Obviously reliving the moment, her voice softened and a shy, girlish grin crossed her face as she continued her story.

"He looked into my eyes, with the bluest eyes I had ever seen."

"I am Phillip," he said. "I am the engineer on this ship. You are a stunning girl. Will you walk with me?"

"I looked around. No one was on the street. I said yes and we walked towards the other end of town.

I snuck to my mother's house and got us food and cervezas. We sat on a pile of horse's hay in the barn, at the end of the road, and ate and drank.

He kissed me. Gentle, sweet kisses, then, long, hard kisses. My body was on fire deep inside. We made love. I knew, from this minute, I would never want another man.

Many days passed and when I finally told Enrique that I had fallen in love with Phillip, he cried, and then he begged. He said, Angelina, I waited my entire life for you. I love you more than anything else. This man is no good for you. I am good for you. No one could love you more than me.

Then he got a crazy look in his eye. He yelled. He stomped. No, I am wrong. I am no good for you. I was not good enough for the Captain of the ship. Everybody ridicules me. He walked away from me, and no matter how hard I tried, he would not speak to me for a long time.

Phillip came to see me every time he could. He told me it would be impossible for him to take me to America because he is always on the ship. He said he would be a bad husband. He told me he could not bear to think of me sitting all alone in America, waiting for him.

He brought me many presents, bows for my hair, candy, jewelry. He told me how much he loved me and how much he wanted to marry me, but couldn't. I waited and I waited. I knew someday I would be his wife, have his children and it was alright with me to wait forever.

Then, he got killed in a big storm at sea. The Captain of the ship brought me the news.

Enrique heard of his death and came to console me. He said now is his time. He still loves me and still wants me for his wife. I told him no, I will never stop loving Phillip. He said he will wait for me forever. He said someday I will see that he is right.

I look now at Enrique and think about the life we could have had, the children we could have had and I think, maybe I made a mistake. But then I think of Phillip and know I made the right choice. I still love him. I wait for us to be together again. I know we will.

I love Enrique, too, but at the same time, I cannot dishonor my love for Phillip. I must honor my vow to him. I never told Enrique how I feel about him. It would only make his pain greater."

Her story finished, she looked up at me, her eyes pleading for understanding.

I did understand her love. And, I understood her vow, but somehow, in this moment, a sense of clarity enveloped me. I felt the realization of truth land like a bomb in my consciousness. Even though my instinct wanted to tell her that she was right, that her vow should take precedence over everything else, my mind fought me. Under the spinning fan, in the quietness of the room, light bulbs went off in my head as if I were a cartoon character.

"Angelina, when I first came here you told me my wife would not want me to be so sad. You said she would not want me to die.

The next day, as I cleaned my boat, I thought about your words. I decided you were right.

I thought about the laughter Sadie and I had shared. She used to say to me, Peter; I love the way you laugh. Your handsome face softens like a child. I always love you most when you are laughing.

We spent our lives trying to make each other happy.

So, your words struck my heart like no others. Sadie would want me to be happy again, she would want me to laugh again.

But, unfortunately, those words were hard to hold on to. I fell back to Sadie's love being the only thing I could cling to.

But now, hearing your story, those words are back. They are the truth that I pushed aside, the truth I have to accept. I owe that realization to you. I want to be happy again, because Sadie would want me to be."

I cupped her face in my hands. Tears streamed down her cheeks and slid into the hollows of my palms. "Do your words not apply to you, too? Do you think Phillip would want you to be happy? Do you think he would have wanted you to spend the rest of your life thinking of death so you can rejoin him? Angelina, don't be foolish. Don't waste the rest of your life alone. Go to Enrique. Let him make you happy. Phillip would want you to love again."

Angelina, sighed, got up from the table, reached over and kissed me on my cheek. She walked away from the table, shoulders bent.

Her dog followed her and stopped for a moment to look back at me. Her woeful glance seemed to say, I've been trying to tell her that for years.

My eyes followed the two of them and my heart broke for the

years Angelina and Enrique could have shared, the children they could have had and the puppies that could have been born. I vowed to put the four of them together before I left this village. I knew Phillip and Sadie would be proud of me.

15

Cars continued to be parked outside Amy's work and her house. The phone made a funny little noise every time she picked up the receiver. The mail in the mailbox didn't sit right. It always looked handled.

Somehow her paranoia had turned into her own reality. The sense of being spied on often went unnoticed. Amy hadn't done anything wrong and didn't know any more or less than anyone else. Let them watch, she thought.

This attitude changed with the ransacking of her house. Now they were getting serious. About what she had no idea.

She had come home from work and found the brownstone broken into. Every drawer had been emptied, every cabinet ripped apart. Rugs were turned over and cushions tossed to the floor. Although nothing seemed to be missing, she called the police. They told her there was nothing they could do but take a report. They left her standing in the middle of the living room without offering any advice, comfort or suggestions for her safety. New York's finest!

Her boss called her into his office and asked her to sit down. She didn't like the look on his face. Here it comes, the final blow, the end of her job, she thought.

He started, "Amy, you are an exceptional broker. We know you are dedicated to the company. Everyone here has a great deal of respect for you. We would like you to know if you are in some kind of trouble, we are here to help you. We are your friends". He folded his arms across his chest and leaned back in his chair. "You look puzzled. I assure you that all we want to do is help you. To this end, you will need to confide in us".

"Mr. Dunbar, I appreciate your concern, but I don't have any idea what you are talking about. I am not in any trouble. Quite to the contrary, my friend, Megan, has just given me her brownstone, in the village, because she decided to leave New York. She left me enough money to take care of it. I love my job and am happy in my life." Not knowing what this was about, Amy surely wasn't going to tell him everything else that was going on. Not now anyway.

Her boss stared at her for a long minute and then took a deep breath. He uncrossed his arms and leaned forward on the desk. "Amy, it is odd that you mention your friend Megan. Two men from the FBI visited us yesterday evening. They also mentioned your friend. They suggested we allow them to go through your desk and accounts. They also suggested we allow them to tap the phone line into your office. They are trying hard to locate your friend because they think she is involved in interstate fraud and a murder."

Murder? Interstate fraud? The words hit her in the face like a thrown brick, soaked in gasoline and flaming. What was he talking about? Surely not Megan. Surely not herself. This screamed insanity.

"It is interesting that she has left you money, enough to take care of her house. They think she helped move a lot of money to the Caymans. They did not want me to tell you about their visit.

We had a meeting and decided it was only fair to you to let you tell your side. You can understand our concern, being a brokerage house." He paused long enough for effect, giving her time to catch her breath.

She tried to stand up. Her legs seemed to be paralyzed. Her mouth seemed to form words, but she could not hear them. Her next clear vision came from a prone position, looking up at Mr. Dunbar and his secretary. All of a sudden, she started to choke. Foul smelling ammonia filled her nose. She didn't know where she was. She felt them lift her to a chair and realized she had fainted.

She heard Mr. Dunbar telling the woman to get a doctor. "No, no", she protested, "I'm all right. Please, I'm all right."

Regaining her senses, Amy said, "Mr. Dunbar, I have no idea what you are talking about. Please, please believe me. I don't know why Megan left. She didn't tell me. I have spent weeks trying to find a clue. I've seen the men following and watching me, but I don't know why. Megan sent me a letter and also left me a note in the brownstone." Reaching into her purse, she said, "I can show them to you."

He read Megan's words. He rubbed his hand over his eyes and looked across the desk at her. "Amy, what can we do to help? You tell me. I will advise the Board that we will not co-operate with the FBI.

Of course, we will have to look at your accounts, just to erase any lingering doubt. I hope you understand."

She left his office blinded with fear. It consumed her, not only for Megan, but also for herself. Her mind raced. She needed a place to think. Could she go back to the brownstone? Oh, God, please let this nightmare end, she cried almost out loud. Please let me find Megan and figure out what the hell is going on.

As she wandered the streets of Manhattan, hours passed. Exhausted, Amy sat down on the patio of a small coffee shop. Holding her face in her hands, she heard a voice speak. Looking up, a waitress stood over her.

"Are you alright, honey?" she asked.

"Yes. No. I don't know. Would you get me a cup of coffee, please? Thank you." The girl hurried away.

Before the waitress reached the doorway, Amy noticed a man on the street corner; same familiar garb, trench coat and cigarette, and she jumped up and started running.

She raced through the streets, her feet barely touching the ground. She tore into her front door, slammed it shut and leaned back against it to catch her breath. Her eyes focused on the red light blinking on her answering machine. Megan, it must be Megan, her mind screamed. She ran to the phone.

Pushing the button, she heard the words she had been waiting for. "Megan, this is your Uncle Bill. Please call me."

Looking out the front window, she didn't see anyone around. She opened the door and climbed the steps to her upstairs neighbor's apartment. Knocking on the door, she kept an eye on the street. It remained clear.

She explained to her neighbor that her phone was not working for some reason and asked permission to make a call. The woman welcomed her in, taking a long look at her. She offered her a cup of tea.

"No thank you," she managed to say. "I'm in a bit of a hurry, maybe next time." The woman directed her to the phone and she dialed Mr. Clayton's phone number. He answered right away.

"I must see you right away, Amy. Can you meet me at Mario's on Tenth in half an hour?"

"Yes, yes. I'll be there." She hung up wondering how she

would get there without being followed.

Thanking her neighbor, she went downstairs, only to see the familiar car parked on the corner. Not looking at the driver, she turned the corner, started to run and ducked into an alleyway. A minute later, the car drove down the street in pursuit of her and kept going. He did not see her behind the trashcan. Seconds later, she ran and headed in the other direction. She had tricked them. She ran non-stop to Mario's. Bursting through the door, the Maître-d looked at her disheveled appearance with disapproval. She stammered Mr. Clayton's name and, with obvious skepticism, he led her to his table.

As she sat catching her breath, the lawyer asked, "Were you followed?"

"I don't think so. I tricked them. Who are they?"

"It could be anyone. Apparently, there are a lot of people looking for Megan and her boyfriend, Michael. It could be the FBI, the mob, his investors and God only knows who else. It seems as though everyone thinks you know where they are."

"Mr. Clayton, I don't know anything, nothing at all. The FBI came to my office and told my boss Megan is under investigation for interstate fraud and murder. Someone ransacked my house and the police can't help me. Cars are still in front of my house and men are still standing on street corners, wherever I am. Have you found out anything about Megan's whereabouts?"

"The people I know have been able to find out nothing that can help us. She took fifty thousand dollars from her account the day she left. The bank manager said she seemed distraught, carried no bags and looked as though she had been crying. He remembers her because she wanted the money in one hundred-dollar bills and, when he questioned her about the safety of carrying around that much cash, she said, I don't have a choice. He had considered calling the police, but didn't. He didn't feel the bank should get involved in such a good customer's personal life.

I found no record of a plane or bus ticket in her name and there were too many cash purchases that day to narrow anything down.

No credit card purchases have been made and no calling card usage, either. This appears to be a young lady who does not want to be found.

Since I saw you last, the FBI came to my office also. I declared attorney privilege and they left without a word.

One more odd thing happened. Just before I left my office to meet you, my phone rang. A man, claiming to be a friend of Megan's family, called inquiring about her. He said he wanted to talk to me about some personal matters and asked to meet me tomorrow. I agreed. He gave his name as Mr. Rodriquez. I am meeting him at two-o'clock. I don't know what to make of it."

Amy stared at him. How could Megan disappear without a trace? What was she involved in? Was Megan's life in danger? How about her own? Questions raced through her mind so fast she couldn't keep up with them.

They parted with a promise of another meeting. Amy walked home, too exhausted to care who might be following her.

In the questionable safety of the brownstone, the red light flashed on the answering machine. This time it was a man's voice, Spanish accent, introducing himself as Mr. Rodriquez. He would like to speak to her about Megan and would call again tomorrow. Rodriquez? Who was this man? Mr. Clayton had agreed to meet with him. Why would he call her? She double checked the locks and fell into her bed, too confused and tired to cry herself to sleep.

16

I learned to while. Although I had heard of people wiling away the hours, it had always been ingrained in me that time should be well-spent.

I slept until I felt like getting up. I began taking each day for granted, enjoying cold cervezas with Enrique and his friends or chatting with Angelina. I looked forward to pulling my hat over my eyes and participating in the fine tradition of siestas.

I had met most of the people in this small fishing village and now felt a profound closeness to all of them. I moved about the town as though I were a long-time resident, my newfound friends tipping their hats and smiling great, broad smiles.

I spent many mornings exploring the village streets and little shops, or as locally known, tiendas, in town.

My knowledge of Spanish had become adequate and I, in turn, taught a lot of English. We shared many cervezas and laughs trying to pronounce each other's words.

I enjoyed catching a glimpse of myself in the mirror in my room. Remembering the first morning I woke up crusted with salt, the new image pleased me.

I now looked clean and relaxed, more so than I ever remembered. My skin glowed with a fine tan, the result of the constant Mexican sun. Thanks to my many recent fishing trips, my arms bulged with muscles I previously didn't know I had. I did have to admit, my belly had grown somewhat from the cervezas.

Most days, I had to remind myself of my life in San Diego. It became easier and easier to forget, to feel no pain. I no longer felt guilty for feeling good.

As I sat one morning in an old rocking chair in front of Angelina's bar, watching the rain and reflecting on why I hadn't left with Sadie ten years earlier and walked away from our life in the city, I heard a frantic voice calling my name.

A young man, running up the street, called to me. "Senor Peter, Senor Peter. "You come help me. Come help my daughter. Come now. Por favor, Senor Peter," he begged.

I recognized him as Enrique's friend, Jose. He lived on the mountain with his wife and two small girls.

"Por favor, Por favor, come now." My daughter needs a doctor. She has the fever."

I grabbed his shoulders. "Jose, Jose, calm down. What fever? Tell me what's wrong."

"I think my daughter is dying. The same fever killed her brother. We need you now."

Angelina came running from the bar, dishtowel in hand, and stopped dead in front of us, a look of horror on her face. A small crowd grew.

Jose pulled at my arm, begging me to follow him.

"Wait, wait. Someone tell me what's going on. What is Jose talking about? What fever?" I asked again.

Angelina spoke. "Two years before now, the fever came to the village. The nearest doctor is many, many hours away. Lupita, our curandera, our healer, had gone to visit her dying sister. We were alone, with no help.

We tried all we knew to save the children, and many of their parents, but we did not do enough. Many children died and so did their parents.

The fever moved fast. We could not move fast enough. The women burned sheets and towels. We boiled everything in the village. We thought maybe the fish brought the fever. The men burned every one we had.

When the fever had taken every life it wanted, it disappeared. We buried our dead and tried to go on. We could not bury the pain."

My mind raced with the speed of a lightning bolt. I am a plastic surgeon, I thought, a lousy plastic surgeon, catering to the rich. What do I know of a fever in a small fishing village? My life had been dedicated to pompous, conceited women and their money. My precious, respected hands had never been dirty. A small, sick child had never entered my office. I had never treated a real sick person. These humble, sweet people were about to find out the truth about me.

Angelina interrupted my thoughts. "Please, Senor Peter. Help us. Please, help us. Do not let the children die."

"I must go to my boat for my bag. Hurry, follow me, then lead me to your house."

I wondered what I was going to do when faced with the child. "God help me," I prayed.

We climbed the muddied streets on the side of the mountain. Rainwater ran down the dirt road in rivulets. We held onto each other as the unrelenting rain pelted us.

Goats, chickens and dogs wandered around looking for shelter, while baying mules remained tied to trees. Little groups of children played in the rain puddles, having as much fun as children in a heated swimming pool in Beverly Hills.

The mountain took on a different feeling than the village. In the short time I had been here, I had learned much about the culture of the people on this mountain. They were poor; gut-wrenching poor.

The houses were no more than ramshackle shacks. They plowed the desert earth into poor gardens and slaughtered their own meat. Sanitation was, at best, a hole in the ground; everything poured onto the earth's surface. No law prevailed and none was needed. One man was too poor to steal from the next.

The people from the mountain did not come to the village often. Once in a while, one such as Jose, looking to feed his family a little better, tried his hand at fishing and befriended the village men.

For the most part, the men stayed on the mountain and lived hand to mouth, surviving any way they could. The women sold vegetables to the village merchants and sometimes eggs if they could spare enough. Strawberries in the summer provided more cash. They lived from the land and did without everything else.

The small group approached Jose's house, with Angelina at the front of the pack. The front door hung open, swinging in the wind. The house stood alone, a few old trees gracing the right side of the property. Chickens scurried at our arrival. An old dog slept on the front porch, raindrops sliding from the top of his head, down between his eyes, along his nose, and falling to the top step of the porch. He didn't stir as we passed him.

The house was cold. An old couch and torn chair sat on bare wood floors. A wooden table and chairs formed a small cooking area. Two small rooms to the right of the living room held beds and single dressers, just enough to live. No adornments. No toys. No curtains. No bathroom. Clean as a hospital.

A pretty young woman with long, black, shiny hair and piercing dark eyes sat on the side of the bed in the smaller room and leaned over her daughter. The child's dark, damp hair hung around her pale face. The child's sister stood next to her mother, holding the little one's hand. The mother looked up at us, her eyes drowned in agony and pleading for my help.

Everyone looked at me. As I walked to the bed, I prayed, for the millionth time today, God, help me, please.

From behind me, I heard Angelina take charge of the room. "Out! Men out! Give Senor Peter room. He does not need to be crowded by fools. Go get boiled water. Go sit on the porch. Out!" The men, hats in hand, backed out of the small room.

The rain beat against the walls of the house, the sound pounding in my brain. The air in the room carried a damp chill. The child, covered by mounds of heavy blankets, appeared to be sleeping.

Except for the rain, the room was silent. The two women and the older child stood to one side, staring at me. Looking down at the little girl, I froze with fear. I could not move.

All of a sudden, the child lurched up and started vomiting. Everyone ran to her, except me. No part of me would co-operate. The child began to cry. Angelina tried to clean the bed, while the mother held her baby in her arms, rocking her and purring little nothings in her ear. Her sister stood nearby sobbing in silence. Angelina stared at me.

It seemed like hours passed. From somewhere deep in my brain, I heard the word cholera. Oh my God, that's it, this child has cholera.

I reached over and stripped the blankets from her. Her legs were cramped and her skin felt clammy and cold. Signs of diarrhea stained her diaper.

Years and years before, my father had insisted that I go to Columbia with him to volunteer medical services to the needy. The one disease we fought most often was cholera. We stood side-by-side, re-routing sanitation ditches through the mud and burning contaminated gardens. We fought the cholera with antibiotics and shovels. I had almost forgotten about the trips. They had gotten lost in my pretentious lifestyle. Thank God for my father.

As Angelina translated, I questioned the mother. Yes, the child was thirsty all the time, but she threw it up right away. Yes, she had a small fever. She had been sick for a couple of days. Yes, she liked to sit in the garden and eat strawberries. The mother had scolded her because they were not quite ripe. No, no one in the house has eaten the berries. No, she didn't know if any of the other children had eaten them, but they played with her in the yard.

I told Angelina to bring my bag. I had kept it well stocked in case anything happened to Sadie or me when we were at sea. She made fun of me for the things I carried. She joked that I could save a small country with it. Good fortune saw to it that we never had to use it. Laugh now, Sadie, my dear.

Having been used to the finest medical equipment money could buy in my private surgery unit; I had no idea how to hang up an IV in a ramshackle house, built on a dirt road, on the side of a mountain in Mexico.

"Angelina, call Enrique,"

I gave the problem to him and within seconds, someone produced a nail and a rusty hammer. They pounded the nail into the wall above the bed and placed the hook on the bag over the nail. Death from cholera was caused by dehydration.

I prepared the IV bag with boiled water and the antibiotic I had in my medical bag and inserted the needle into the child's arm. The bag began to drip fluid into the small body.

Instructing the mother to give her as much cooled, boiled water as possible, I walked to the porch covered with sweat, hiding my shaking hands.

To my surprise, three young mothers, their faces white with fear, waited for me at the bottom of the steps. Upon seeing me, each woman, held her child up to me.

Enrique spoke for them. "Their children are sick like Jose's, Senor Peter. Can you help them? They need a doctor's medicine, too."

The rain had stopped. The sky had cleared. Mud ran down every hill. The dog still slept. No one spoke.

I told the mothers to wait and motioned for Enrique to follow me. We trudged through the mud to the back of the house. The strawberry patch sat in the middle of the mud, dirty and half-buried.

"This is the problem, Enrique," I began, "the strawberries, and probably the whole garden, are contaminated with feces. This causes a disease called cholera. This is what the children have. I think we have caught it in time, but it is a fast moving disease and can kill right away. I only have a little medicine. We need more and we need it fast. Where can we get medicine?"

"I have an old truck in the barn. We have to cross the mountain on a bad dirt road to get to the main road and travel north, maybe one hundred kilometers, to a big town called Puerto Santiago."

"How long are we talking, Enrique?"

"If the truck doesn't get stuck in the mud on the mountain, or stopped by a dead cow on the road, maybe it is a one and half day trip, a hard trip."

"We have one more problem, Senor Peter," he said humbly. No one here has money to buy medicine." Enrique lowered his head, feeling shame for not having what was necessary to take care of his people.

"I will stay with these children. You go and get the truck. We will make it, Enrique. I have money and we will push the truck if we have to. Better bring one more man to help us. Go now. Go fast."

Enrique and Jose left for the truck and I stayed behind to give the children what medicine I had. I instructed the women and remaining men to boil the water and to destroy the strawberries.

Enrique and Jose returned covered with mud. They drove the oldest, most rusted pick-up truck I had ever seen. Had the need for it not been so great, I would have laughed. Instead, I jumped in and we took off.

The mountain road wove through the high desert like a snake on its belly. Climbing higher and higher, the truck slipped and slid on every bend. It hit pothole after pothole, bouncing high off the road and returning with a thud. Every mile or so, the three of us got out and pushed it either out of, or over, a rut.

Stubborn livestock; cows, chickens and mules stood in the center of the muddy road. With each encounter, we got out of the truck and coaxed, and sometimes pushed, them to the side.

Dark fell upon us before we reached the summit.

Our clothes caked with mud and our tongues parched with thirst, our bellies screamed for food.

Enrique reached under the seat of the old truck and came up with three warm cervezas. Another reach produced a sack of tortillas. He pulled the truck to the side of the road and we sat on the tailgate and dined under the stars. It had to be one of the finest dinners I had ever eaten.

Halfway into the tortillas, Enrique asked, "Are you a rich doctor in San Diego, Senor Peter?"

I thought for a long minute before answering him. "I always thought I was, Enrique. I know now that I am not rich at all. I have learned a lot from you and your friends. I realize I have pursued the wrong things. I am a poor man. I have nothing of any value.

You are the rich man. You have friends and values. You have something to show for your life. You have a whole town that respects and loves you. I have nothing. I don't even have a dog that loves me."

"I am not a rich man, Senor Peter. I do not have Angelina. A rich man has the woman he loves. He has the children she bears for him. Enrique only has a dog."

"Then in the end, my friend, we will both die poor men."

As they got back in the truck, I asked Enrique if I could drive.

He enjoyed a deep, belly laugh. "You think a city boy can drive good old Mexican truck?" He stepped to the side and let me get into the driver's seat.

It didn't exactly compare to my Porsche. It rode a little rougher and was not quite as close to the ground. The stereo was missing, but Enrique made up for that by breaking into a Spanish song I didn't recognize. Jose joined him. The old truck rattled and rolled through the dark, avoiding the livestock and taking the potholes like a trooper.

My two passengers fell asleep, hats over their faces and snoring, leaving me to my own thoughts. The darkness on the mountain provided the most spectacular starlit sky I had ever seen. I wondered if these millions of stars shone over San Diego. I had never seen so many in my life.

My mind wandered to my mother and father. They had loved me so much. They had provided everything I ever needed. I wondered if they had ever sat under the stars. I wondered if the night their plane crashed they had been headed into them.

I thought about Sadie and the warmth of her body against mine, the way her hair fell across the pillow and the gentle, little bites on my bottom lip when we made love. Why had I never shown her these stars?

I wondered if I would be able to save these children. Would I ever be able to be a plastic surgeon again? I wondered where the rest of my life would be spent.

Fatigue consumed me. Dawn broke on the horizon and Enrique stirred. He sat straight up, trying to figure out where he was. He glanced at Jose and then me, his face breaking into a smile.

"Let me drive, mi amigo. We have a long way to go and you need sleep.

The dawn brought dry, hot desert air and a blazing sun. It had taken us all night to cross the treacherous mountain, but to my unbelievable happiness, I could see the paved road ahead of us, at the bottom of the last slippery hill. As far as I could see, there was nothing but desert terrain and not one sign of life.

I dozed, in and out of sleep, next to my two compadres, anxious to return to Puerto San Luis with the medicine. A strange feeling possessed me. I felt needed. I tried to remember ever having the feeling before. Nothing entered my mind. It was just a barren wasteland of feelings, except for my love for Sadie. I clung to her in my sleep.

I awoke to the truck stopping. Enrique and Jose jumped out and Enrique started kicking the tire, in a fit of rage. I scrambled to his side, trying to figure out the problem. We were still in the middle of the desert and I felt a brief fear of rattlesnakes. Scorpions wandered through my mind following the snakes.

"What's wrong, Enrique?" I asked. "Calm down."

"The truck, Senor Peter, she is out of gas. We go no further." He continued to angrily carry on in Spanish. I could only guess at what he was saying.

"How far are we from a town?" I asked, dreading the answer.
"Many miles, Senor, many miles."

The three of us set out walking, not sharing another word. The sun blazed down.

After what seemed like an endless journey, Jose spotted something moving in the desert. It was coming directly towards us. We stopped to watch. Nothing in this desert was high enough to provide shelter, so we stood at the mercy of the sun.

I prepared for death. I couldn't look up from the ground at the sun. My eyes burned, my skin baked and my tongue felt as though it were a hot brick in my mouth. I positioned myself in the center of the road to avoid one possibility of death, snakebite.

The moving object took the shape of a tractor. Moments later, we could see a man driving it. Waving our hats high in the air and whooping and hollering, the tractor continued towards us.

The old man climbed down from the decrepit machine and he and Enrique spoke at length, both shooting looks at me. Jose interjected his own thoughts whenever he could get a word in edgewise. The man kept staring at me as if I were holding his two compadres hostage.

He walked back to his tractor and returned with a rusty cooler. We drank his water, quenching the unbearable thirst, with the man still keeping an eye on me.

The three of us jumped onto the tractor and we headed back towards the truck. What had seemed like an all day journey took less than an hour to return. The man unstrapped a rusted red gas can from the back of the tractor, poured its contents into our gas tank and with a broad grin, bid us farewell and rode back into the desert.

As we got into the truck, my friends started to laugh. They chatted in their language, laughing until tears formed in their eyes.

"What's so funny? I demanded.

Enrique tried to explain to me what had just happened.

"The old Mexican man does not trust Americans. He wanted to save us from you. He thought we were criminals and you are a U.S. Marshall. He thought that you have a gun and are taking us back to the United States to jail.

Jose tried to tell him you are a doctor and trying to save his bambina, but the kind stranger man did not believe us. He said no doctor looks like you. Doctors are rich and clean. He wanted to run you over with his tractor, leave you in the desert for hawk food, and let us escape. If we didn't like that plan, he offered us his shotgun.

After much talk, he finally said he would help us, but if the American made one bad move, he would take care of you.

We saved your life, amigo. He wanted to make snake food out of you." My friends, once again, burst into laughter.

I was just glad they had convinced him. To think, I had only been worried about snakebites and scorpions.

After many hours of traveling, a small, hand-painted sign directed us to a town. Enrique turned the truck off the paved road, right onto another dirt road. It led us to the center of a town, much larger than Puerto San Luis. Enrique parked the truck in front of a building with a sign that said, "Farmacia".

I tried to explain to the pharmacist that I needed tetracycline, lots of it. No one in the pharmacy spoke English, so Enrique took over. Rapid fire Spanish ensued. The pharmacist looked at me with suspicion. More rapid fire Spanish. I now understood enough of the language to know they were talking about money, a lot of it.

I opened my wallet and produced the money I had. "Enrique, tell him I have more in the bank. I can get whatever he wants."

Enrique stared at the money with a look of disbelief, but instead of speaking to me, he turned to the pharmacist and gave him my message.

A small crowd had formed outside. The pharmacist moved to the back of his counter and brought out a box with one hundred vials of the antibiotic. He turned and walked to the far back of his shop, motioning Enrique to follow him. They returned with three cases of saline IVs. Not enough, but better than nothing.

I asked him if he had a telephone. He led me to a small office, picked up the phone and said to an operator, "Hola, Senorita, Americano cobro revertido."

Smiling at the clever pharmacist, I wondered if my office would accept a collect call.

To my sheer joy, they did. I asked my surprised receptionist to get my partner, Frank, on the phone right away.

"Where the hell are you, Peter?" he yelled into the phone. "Everyone here is frantic. They think you killed yourself. What do you mean you're in Mexico? Where the hell in Mexico? You missed the annual convention. Explain yourself, Peter."

"I don't have time to explain anything. You wouldn't understand anyway. Shut up and listen to me.

I need you to send me as much tetracycline as possible, enough for at least five hundred people. I need saline IVs. Oh, and I need as much cholera vaccine as you can put together. Pay for it from my account and send it as fast as possible. Tell everyone I'm fine, that I've never been better. This is an emergency, Frank.

I need you to believe me and do this as fast as possible. I have no time to waste. And, no, I won't be back anytime soon. I may never be back. You can carry on without me."

"Have you gone mad, Peter? Because if you've gone mad, I'm going to lock up your accounts," Frank answered with sincere concern in his voice.

"No, Frank, I haven't gone mad. For the first time in my life I am needed for something really important. I feel alive. I want to go on. Please, please do as I ask.

Oh, and one more thing Frank. Go to Sadie's grave and my parent's, too. Take flowers and tell all of them that I am happy and I am, at last, doing something worth doing. Tell my father that now I understand why he went to Columbia every year. Do that, Frank. Please."

I gave him the address of the Farmacia and realized that Enrique had been translating my entire conversation to the pharmacist and the small crowd. When I turned to look at them, they all stared at me, some with tears in their eyes.

The pharmacist moved to the back of his store again and came forward with bags of things he thought I might need, including a case of vaccine. He shook my hand and said, "Gratis, Senor Doctor, mi amigo. Gracias. Vaya con Dios."

Free. He had given me these things for free. I choked up and hugged him.

We took what we had and hurried to the truck. Several women stood next to it with bags of tortillas and bowls of beans and rice. Someone handed us several jugs of water. One of the people had filled the truck with gasoline and put two cans in the back. Enrique started the engine and we began our long journey back to Puerto San Luis. The young people ran with the truck to the edge of town yelling, "Buena suerte." "Good luck" in English.

By early next morning, we stood on Jose's front porch. The return trip had been much easier due to the same blazing sun that had tried to kill us. The roads had dried up and many of the ruts had filled up from the flowing mud. Even the livestock from the night before had disappeared from the road. The three of us said a small prayer and thanked God for watching out for us.

Our little patients seemed to be doing much better. My two compadres and I, now a team united in a common cause, set up a make-shift hospital in the front room of the little house and started inoculating the people on the mountain and issuing doses of the antibiotic.

I instructed each family on sanitation and the importance of cleanliness, with Enrique and Jose translating.

Enrique had taken on an air of authority, running our little operation like a military assignment. He made the people stand in line and wait their turn. He cared for the children first, comforting their fears. He declared Angelina his nurse and, with an air of dignity, she accommodated him. Jose became his right hand man, carrying out his every command.

Enrique came up with a plan for better sanitation and had each man dig a deeper hole, lined with desert rocks to dispose of sewage. He had them corral the animals away from the gardens.

Within the week, he had every man in town following instructions. He wore his authority like a badge of honor and every man in town obeyed him with the greatest respect.

I also caught Angelina looking at Enrique with the soft look a woman gets when she is in love. The three dogs slept together on the front porch.

The following week, we returned to Puerto Santiago and, to my sheer amazement, found that Frank had followed my instructions to the letter. I had enough medicine for every single person in Puerto San Luis.

One of the boxes contained a small white envelope addressed to me. It held a hand written letter from Frank.

Dear Peter,

I don't pretend to understand what you are doing. You have the perfect life here. You are a rich man with many assets. Why you would want to live in a Third World country and fight diseases from the dirt, I will never understand. You don't even speak the language. What does a prominent, well-respected Plastic Surgeon know about real medicine anyway? I know Sadie's death was a traumatic shock to you, but don't you think you are going to extremes?

Look, old fellow, we want to help you. Tell us where you are. You are going to miss your life in San Diego. What about your Porsche? What about your house? Your standing in the community? Theater? Ballet? Opera?

Of course, we will stand by any decision you make, but come to your senses, man. You are an American. You have a great life. What can Mexico possibly offer you? Think about what you are doing. Wrap up this nonsense and come home. You cannot save the world.

I will come down there if necessary and beat some sense into you.

Regards, your sane partner, Frank.

P.S. I visited the graves as you asked and I took flowers. I felt all three of them roll over. Come home.

I read the letter twice. Yes, I suppose my parents would roll over, but not Sadie. She would understand. She would stand by my side, roll up her sleeves and help me. I knew she would. No, I didn't intend to save the world, only this small part of it. If I wrote Frank twenty pages explaining why I was doing what I was doing, he wouldn't understand. I threw his letter away and continued giving inoculations.

One night, I wandered along the main street and came to the big barn. I had seen it a hundred times before, but tonight, it looked different. Staring up at it, I had a vision, or was it a dream? I didn't remember ever having a dream, only wants and desires.

I certainly had the means to call in a team of engineers and construction companies and have a beautiful hospital built in this village. I could also raise enough money from my well-heeled friends to not use one dime of my own money.

However, my dream consisted only of me and my new friends building it with our bare hands. I vowed to myself that I would accomplish my dream.

17

All day, as Francisco drove his cab around San Diego, Megan's words scratched at his heart and reverberated in his head. He drove in a daze, thankful he could do his job on instinct.

His moods swung between anger, humiliation, confusion and worry. What did this girl know about him? How could she call him those names? A battle raged in his head.

It had troubled him from the beginning that he could not deny his interest in this young woman. She reminded him of his long ago, beautiful bride, Consuela.

His wife came alive in the way Megan's hair framed her face and with the sad, but pretty, pout on her lips. She came alive in the way Megan's eyes clouded with sadness, and again today, in the way they shone with fiery anger. Consuela had taught him all the moods of a woman and he had learned his lessons well.

Francisco dared not let his mind go back to the black depths of his past for fear he would not return to the present ever again. It had been a long, struggling climb back to life, but he had made it and wanted to stay. Ah, but tonight, alone in his tiny apartment, he could not stop his mind from traveling to the past, letting it climb down into the dark abyss, inch by painful inch.

•••••

In the small fishing village on the mountainous, remote coast of the Mexican Baja, the day that would alter their lives forever had started the same as all others before it.

Weather-worn fisherman and their wives sat on the pure white sand beach, repairing their fishing nets, torn by some great fish not willing to be caught. Their hands worked sharp needles pushing the huge ropes back into place. Their children splashed in the waves or collected firewood from the mountain. The hot sun baked their bodies.

Gazing out to sea, they saw a giant white ship pull across their cove and throw anchor. A small tender, lowered from the side of the ship, brought two men across the pristine water and landed them on the small pier.

As the younger of the two men secured his tender, the older man stepped off the boat, nodded to the stunned fisherman and walked towards the village. The young villagers, hats in hand, followed him. The older people stayed on the beach.

The man entered the bar and ordered a beer. He turned and looked at the curious men and began to speak in perfect Spanish. "I am Senor Brisbane. I am the Captain of a great fishing boat. I own a large horse ranch in America, in a city called San Diego. Many men work for me. I provide housing and money. They have a good life. I need more men to work on my boat and at my ranch. Are any of you willing to go with me to America for a better life?"

The men began to speak among themselves. Francisco did not. He could not leave his family. It was not a question.

Several of the men stepped forward, including his friends, Carlos and Enrique. "Take me, Senor," they all pleaded at once.

The Captain looked at him and asked, "What about you, Senor? Why have you not stepped forward?"

With head bowed, he placed his hat over his chest and tried to explain to this great man why he could not leave his family. "My mother has many children and my father is at sea all the time. I am responsible for my family, Senor."

"Where is your father now," he asked.

"He is at the beach until the sunset."

Without answering the other young men, he put his arm around Francisco's shoulder and said, "Take me to him."

He felt dread in the pit of his belly. He didn't want to leave his parents. He wanted only to love a woman and the sea. He wanted to be like his father. He wanted a life with a woman like his mother. He wanted his children to play on this beach. He wanted to run away to the mountain and hide. Why did this man want him? He knew he was strong. He knew his back was thick with muscles. He hated him and his boat.

And, he knew what his father would say. It had always been his dream for one of his children to go to America and have a better life. He had told them stories of this place and all its gold. Life was easy in America. Hard workers were welcome to this country and they were rewarded well. There was much money there and you could have it if you worked hard. Francisco knew his father would not let him say no to this man.

Senor Brisbane approached his parents with an air of dignity. His father stood up and placed his hat over his chest. The man towered over him. His father didn't look up. Brisbane extended his hand and his father took it.

"Buenos tardes, Senor. I am Senor Charles Brisbane the Third, from San Diego.

"Buenos tardes, Senor Brisbane, I am Francisco Antonio Gonzales, Senior and it is my pleasure to meet you. Is there something I can help you with?"

"I have come here for men to work for me in America. I provide housing and good pay. Life is good for my men. They are happy. They send money home to their families. I like your son. He is young and strong. He has intelligent eyes. But most importantly, he has responsibility to his family. I respect a man with that quality. I can make a man like him a foreman on my ranch. I can teach him to raise my horses and pay him good money. Will you let him go with me, Senor?"

Francisco watched his father's face. He seemed to stand taller in front of this man. His mother stood behind him, her eyes focusing on the sand below her feet.

His father looked up at the Captain. He studied his face and looked into his eyes for a long moment. He looked from the Captain's eyes to Francisco's and back to the Captain. Sensing the greatness of this man, but not intimidated by it, he squared his shoulders and spoke to the Captain with an air of dignity.

"Senor Brisbane. I am honored for you to like my son. Francisco is a good boy and a good son. He has taken care of his mother and his brothers and sisters while I fish for our food. He carries many burdens for a young man. He has no time for himself, not even for girls. He has learned to fish well and has always made me proud. My one wish for my children is to go to America for a better life.

I am a simple man Senor Brisbane. I know the sea and I know the fish. We have great respect for each other. I can look into a fish's eye, as he dies in my net, and know what he is thinking. He tells me, 'you have won, great fisherman. I have lost, but my children are still in the sea, and the next time they will win. They will pull you from your boat and bring you into the sea.'

I can read the sea and tell you what mood she is in and I can see a storm in a fluffy white cloud, as it tries to trick me with its beauty.

I can also see in your eyes you are a good, honest man. I feel you will take good care of my son. Francisco will go with you. You will give him a better life. It is the best choice a father can make for his son. Tomorrow morning he will be ready."

The two men shook hands. Tears fell from Francisco's eyes.

At home, he pleaded with his father. Forgetting his manhood, he begged and cried, like a young girl. It was no use. His father sat with him all night, trying to make him understand this was best for all of them. It was a chance not many young men got. He would have a better life and so would his children.

In the morning, he kissed his brothers and sisters good-bye as they slept. He held his mother in his arms and cried.

His father walked him to the boat and at the last moment, took him in his arms and whispered, "Goodbye my wonderful son. I love you and someday we will all be together again." His father took his face in his hands, kissed his cheek, patted his back, bowed his head and put his hat across his chest.

As he boarded the boat, one small, tattered suitcase in hand, he watched as his father turned, his shoulders slumped and walked back to their house. He would never see him again. He drowned at sea in a sudden violent hurricane that crashed his boat onto the rocks, tore it apart into little pieces and tossed him, uncaring, into his beloved sea.

Reaching San Diego after weeks of sailing, Senor Brisbane took him to his horse ranch, along with his friend, Carlos, and several other select men. He had not chosen their third friend, Enrique. The men guessed it was because of his small body. It was painful to leave him standing on the beach waving good-bye. They had been friends since they were small boys.

He worked hard for Senor Brisbane, in honor of his father's dream. He made him foreman, as he had promised. He paid him well. For two years, Francisco sent as much money as he could back to his family.

Senor Brisbane received word that Francisco's father died, and sent for his mother and family. Three of his brothers chose to stay and remain fisherman, in honor of their father. Two of his sisters were married to local men and stayed in their village. His mother came to America with the smallest children and became Senor Brisbane's cook and housekeeper. He took good care of them.

The children grew up over the years and went to school. Senor Brisbane would have nothing less. He also insisted Francisco go to school. Francisco's mother died in a peaceful sleep, fulfilling her dream to rejoin her husband. The children made lives for themselves and lived in different places in California.

In his early twenties, Francisco met a sensuous Mexican girl named Consuela. She had the longest, blackest hair he had ever seen. She possessed the smallest and sweetest body a man could imagine. She moved to the rhythm of the wind, creating longings deep inside the soul. When Francisco took Consuela into his arms, his heart felt as though it had lost its holdings in his chest. At the sight of her, his mind lost its bearings.

Knowing he was not good enough for her and that she would never agree to marry a man like him, he asked her anyway. When she agreed, he could not believe his ears. He asked her to repeat her answer. Shocked by his own good fortune, he wondered what he had done in his life to so please God that He would send him this perfect woman. Francisco knew that any man in his right mind, and some that were loco, would give their life to have his good fortune. He made plans for their wedding before Consuela could come to her senses and change her mind.

They were married in the mission in San Diego on a bright Saturday afternoon. Senor Brisbane attended the ceremony. Francisco felt proud to stand before such a successful man.

He wept as Consuela walked down the aisle towards him. He turned to the altar and thanked the Lord for her.

Senor Brisbane held their reception at his ranch, his gift to them. Every man at the party wanted to dance with Consuela, including their host.

In the wee hours of the morning, Francisco became tired. He asked Consuela to leave and go to their home. She refused. She would meet him later. Senor Brisbane would be kind enough to see her home, she told him. Thinking not to upset her, he left and went home.

He awoke many hours later and his new wife lay by his side, sleeping. His bed looked different, graced by this woman's beauty. He awoke her with gentle caresses, and cradled her in his arms. His need for her was great. They became man and wife on this morning.

In time, he began to realize Consuela did not like to stay home. She went out every day and if he asked where she had gone, her face formed a pretty pout and she said, "What's the matter my strong, handsome husband? You do not trust little Consuela? Every night I show you how I love you. Why do you care what I do during the day? It is of no concern to you. It is better to have a good wife at night than one bored from staying home all day, si?"

Francisco had no choice but to accept her answer and soon stopped asking.

Returning from work one day, he found Consuela sitting on the side of the bed, crying. He went to her side. "What's the matter, my sweet Consuela? Why do you cry?"

She looked up at him and said, "I am pregnant, Francisco. I am going to have your child."

His heart burst in his chest. He grabbed her in his arms and lifted her into the air, swinging her around. "You have made me the happiest man on this earth, Consuela. I love you with all my heart."

"Put me down, you idiot," she scolded.

As the pregnancy progressed, Consuela became sullen. The more her body grew with his child, the more sullen she became. She no longer went out during the day. Sullenness turned to anger. She pouted and shouted at him. Everything he did made her angry. She refused to clean the house or cook meals. She stayed in bed all day. Consuela screamed at him, "I hate this baby and you for putting it there."

He tried to understand her anger. He did everything to make her more comfortable. Everything he did just made her angrier.

The day of the birth came. He looked forward to having his wife return to the happy woman he'd married, and to have a child to hold.

After many hours of labor and screaming, the midwife Senor

Brisbane hired came to him with a baby boy. He held him in his arms and brought him to his cheek. His smell was one of love. He was a creation of two people joined by love. The baby would reunite him and Consuela. He hurried to see his wife. She lay on their bed, tired, fragile and pale. A faint smile crossed her lips. He kissed her forehead.

"He is perfect, Consuela. Only you could create such a handsome child, only you. We will name him Francisco Antonio Gonzales. We will call him Antonio in honor of him being the first Gonzalez to be born in America. I love you, my precious, sweet wife. Now sleep. I will join you later."

The following morning, he went to his wife with juice and eggs. She sat up in bed and asked about their son.

"He sleeps in his bunting. My mother will see to him until you feel strong again. He is the image of you, Consuela. Everyone has said so. We must have many children so your beauty can spread throughout the world."

"Francisco, he is the only baby we will have. I will not spend my life with children tugging at my skirts, making me old and ugly. Look at my body. You and that baby have ruined my beauty. There will be no more, ever. There will be no discussion of this ever again. And I don't care if you and your mother keep this one to yourselves."

He reeled from the sting of her words. Consuela will get over these feelings. She is tired. No, she is exhausted. These words cannot be true. He would give her time.

Consuela demanded he leave the room at once. Too stunned to argue, he walked from the room, hat in hand. He drove to the ocean and sat for a long time watching the sea crash to the shore. He prayed for strength and he prayed for Consuela. He prayed for their son.

After much time went by, he made a decision. He had enough love for many, many children and now, he would just give it all to his only son. Together, Consuela and little Antonio would be enough to erase any desires he had to have more children.

He went home to his new family, thankful to his beloved sea for once again providing him with the strength he needed. He would show Consuela how easy he would make it to just love them. No mention of more children would ever be made. He would see to it.

Many months passed and Consuela showed no interest in their son. She went out again, with more passion than ever before and continued to show him her love at night. He became sure that time would bring her to love their little Antonio. His mother cared for the baby and he provided the money.

No one was sure what Consuela did all day, or where she spent her time.

Every morning, she dressed in her finest clothes and jewelry, put her hair in a tight bun on the back of her head, painted her tiny face with colorful make-up and rode away on the stallion Senor Brisbane had given her for a wedding present.

Consuela returned late at night and crawled into Francisco's arms, to satisfy every need a man could have or imagine. He waited every night.

One hot summer afternoon, as he groomed Senor Brisbane's favorite stallion, a young, handsome man entered the stable. Francisco felt his presence before he saw him. Feeling eyes staring into his back, he turned to see the stranger standing in the doorway. "Buenos tardes, Senor," he said. "Can I help you?"

"You are Francisco Gonzales, si?" he asked, as he started towards him.

"Yes, I am. What can I do for you?" The man looked angry and Francisco wondered who he was. The stranger came closer and closer until only inches remained between the two men.

He said, "I am here as one man to another to ask you to give up your wife. She does not love you. She loves me."

"What? Who are you? What are you doing here? My Consuela does not know you. She is my wife and she loves me. You are loco. Get out or I will get a gun," he yelled at the stranger.

"I am not mistaken, Senor. I am Vincente Rosario and I am your wife's lover. I have been for a long time. We share a love and a passion you cannot begin to understand.

Where do you think she goes every day? She comes to me. Who do you think she dresses for? She dresses for me. Have you never smelled my body on hers? She does not love you, or your child. I come here to ask you as a gentleman to let go of her. She wants me and only me. I will give you time to talk to Consuela and then I will return for your answer." He turned and left before

Francisco, too overcome with shock and disbelief, could run after him and beat him to death.

That night, he waited for Consuela with his pants on.

The front door opened earlier than usual. Consuela appeared in the bedroom doorway, looking timid and afraid. He watched from their bed as she approached him. Moonlight coming through the window fell on her tear-stained face. Her hands trembled. Her lips tried to speak, but no sound came.

He motioned for her to sit down next to him. "Is it true, Consuela? Do you see him every day? Do you love only him? Is your body scented from his?" She stared down at the floor. "Answer me, Consuela. At least pay me that respect."

The calm in his voice belied the raging anger in his head, but his white knuckles and trembling, rock hard muscles did not.

"Yes, it is true, but please Francisco, let me try to explain. When we married, I wanted to be only your wife. Love only you. My plan did not work. I could not stop loving Vincente. I have known him for a long time. Before you, even.

We were great lovers, but he was married. He could not leave his wife and I could not have him. She became pregnant before their marriage, from just a fling, and his family forced them to marry. They forbid him to leave her, or the child.

You were the answer to my problem. You were easy to love and you were so in love with me. I thought my feelings for Vincente would die with time. I soon found out I had never been so wrong.

In the beginning, I only met him once in a while. The meetings became more frequent. Then I became pregnant with our child. I know he is your child Francisco, because Vincente and I are careful and, as you know, you and I are not. I have been in love with two men.

Vincente is now free of his wife. She has left him and taken their child with her. He now wants me to come to him.

I begged him not to come to you. I knew the minute he told me he planned to speak to you that it was you I loved more. I could not bear the hurt you were going to feel. You are a wonderful husband. I knew I had no right to do to you what I did. It took this for me to realize how much I love you. I do not want to leave you and I do not want to go with Vincente.

Please believe me, Francisco. It is you I love. I know that now. Please forgive me. I will never see him or speak to him again. I beg you. Forgive me."

"What about our son?" he asked.

"I will learn to love him. I will take care of him, and you, for the rest of my life. I promise."

He stared at her and felt his passion rise. She had said the words he wanted to hear. He made love to her as never before, believing in the future. It takes a man a long time to realize he is a fool.

Time passed, his wounds healed and he had no reason to believe Consuela was not living up to her promise. She took care of Antonio, and expressed her love for him. She took good care of him and continued to be a passionate lover. Vincente finally left town.

After Francisco's mother died, Consuela filled her position with Senor Brisbane. She spent long days in his great home, preparing his meals and managing his staff. Francisco protested her working for Senor Brisbane, but she insisted she needed something to do during the long hours he worked. Antonio had started school and she said she had too much time to do nothing.

Early one evening as he sat reading to Antonio, Senor Brisbane appeared on the front porch. Consuela stood by his side. He looked at the two of them and felt dread in the pit of his belly. He sent Antonio to his room.

Senor Brisbane spoke first. "Francisco, you know I love you like a son. You have been with me a long time. I have something to tell you that you will not like. I am sorry to do this to you, but I don't have a choice. I can no longer keep it a secret."

He sat staring at Brisbane in disbelief. Francisco didn't need to hear his words. He knew what Brisbane needed to tell him.

Brisbane continued to speak, his words falling on deaf ears. "I have been in love with Consuela since the first day you brought her to meet me. I cannot resist her. I made love to her on your wedding night.

I concocted the Vincente story to try and make you go away. Consuela could not bear to hurt you that way and my plan fell apart. I tell you now that I want your wife to be mine. We have been together all these years and I no longer can tolerate our arrangement. I want you to leave and take Antonio with you".

Senor Brisbane took Consuela's arm, turned and together they walked back to the house.

Francisco sat frozen in his chair. Questions raced through his head. Vincente, a set-up? Her words that night were lies? Her lovemaking, a joke? How could he have been so blind? How could he have been such a fool?

He packed up his son that night and left. He wandered through life for a long time, only making enough money to feed and house him and his son, not caring if he ever loved again. He never did.

Several years later, Francisco's friend Carlos, who stayed on at the ranch after he left, told him the rest of the story over beers in a local bar. Consuela had never loved him. The baby had been a mistake. She had married him to get next to Senor Brisbane and his money from the beginning. He fell in love with her sooner than even she expected and the baby just complicated her plan. They were afraid his mother would find out about their affair and, during a lull in their relationship, she met Vincente, an old lover, in town. Brisbane caught them in a cheap hotel and tried to kill her new lover. It was then that he came up with his plan to get him out of the picture. He traded Vincente his life for the lie.

Consuela had a sudden attack of conscience and the plan fell through. Brisbane became furious with her, but continued their affair.

Sometime later, Consuela found out Vincente had returned to town and she started to see him again.

Brisbane caught them for the second time, in the house where Francisco and Consuela had lived. This time he went for his gun and shot them both as they lay in bed together. The bodies were buried on the ranch and the Mexican workers never spoke of the incident. Brisbane continued to live in his house, alone and bitter. He sold his horses and fired the men. No one ever saw him again.

Antonio became Francisco's salvation. As he grew taller and stronger, the little boy gave him a purpose to live. He found a steady job as a cabdriver and a nice place for him to grow up. Not wanting him to know the truth about his mother, he told his young son she died of a female disease soon after his birth. Because of that simple lie, his son decided to become a doctor. Francisco worked longer and harder to help his son with his dream, eating only enough food to stay alive, and buying only enough clothes to go to work. He saved every extra coin he could manage. His reward came when his son earned a scholarship to a fine school in Los Angeles and he realized he had saved enough money to help with the rest of the costs.

Francisco stared out into the darkness from his window.

The old familiar pain ate at Francisco's soul. His mind lifted from its depths and he willed away the dark memories.

•••••

He wasn't just a Mexican immigrant cabdriver and he knew with absolute certainty that he could understand someone's problems.

His thoughts turned back to the young woman at the Hilton. He would forgive her anger. He would go back to the hotel and try once again to extend his hand in friendship. Someone had to help her.

The following morning, Megan opened the door to persistent knocking. She faced Francisco once more, his hat again placed across his chest.

"I told you to go away yesterday. Nothing has changed. Please leave me alone," Megan said, not looking up at him.

"Senorita Megan, I know something is wrong with you. I spent a great deal of time last night thinking about you and my own life. You are wrong to assume no one can help you with your problem. A long time ago, I, too, had a problem, a big problem. I, too, thought no one could help me and I considered for a long time about ending my life."

Megan's head shot up to face him and a small, guttural sound escaped from her throat.

Francisco knew he had hit a nerve and continued to talk. "Please, Senorita Megan, let me try to help you. If my story does not help you, I will leave and you can do as you like with your life. I know despair and heartache. I can help you."

Megan stepped aside and allowed Francisco to enter her room.

The room, strewn with clothes, newspapers and a few half-eaten plates of food, confirmed Francisco's fears. He noticed a small vial of pills on the nightstand with the lid still on. Maybe he had made the right decision, he thought.

One lonely chair sat in front of the window, positioned to view the bay. Placing his hat on the dresser and dragging another chair to the window, he asked Megan to join him.

Looking like a frightened child, she sat down across from him.

She spoke first. "I am okay, Francisco. This is entirely my mother's fault. She left me all alone, but the worst thing she did was to not prepare me for the realities of life. I will be okay. I don't want to trouble anyone with my problems and that is why I ran away from New York. I am sorry for the way I spoke to you yesterday and I am sorry you are worried about me."

Francisco placed his hand under her chin and lifted her face to look at him. "Senorita Megan, you are a lovely, young woman who has lost her way. I will help you find it. Please listen to my story and then, maybe you will feel like telling me yours."

Megan only stared at him, her eyes blank, her hands folded in her lap. He began his tale.

Morning turned to afternoon as Francisco talked.

Megan said nothing, but listened to his every word. Several times her eyes had come alive, once or twice with anger and again with sadness,

As Francisco finished his story, Megan said her first words. "Where is Antonio now, Francisco?

"My son is the finest accomplishment of my life. I have worked and saved since his birth and managed, with the help of scholarships, to send him to a fine medical school. He will finish his internship this year. My father was right. Anything is possible in America."

"I can only tell you how sorry I am for my angry words yesterday. I didn't know what an amazing man you are. Please forgive me for my selfish and stupid behavior, Francisco, I am very sorry."

"I will accept your apology if you will now confide in me. Let me help you."

Megan felt a strong desire to talk to this kind man. She realized she hadn't spoken to anyone at all since the day Michael walked out of her brownstone. She decided it was time and started with her mother's death.

The afternoon passed uninterrupted as she told Francisco about her parents, her bad love affairs and Michael. At the end, she showed him the newspapers and told him of her desire, and fear, to call Michael.

As the sun set over the bay, casting shadows into the room, the newfound friends agreed the day had been well spent. They ordered dinner from room service and continued to talk about their lives.

Francisco reminded Megan of her request to go Julian, and again, holding his hat in his hand, asked her if she would join him for a piece of the town's famous apple pie and a buffalo burger. To his amazement, she agreed. They bid each other goodnight, both in a much better frame of mind than they were ten hours ago.

As Megan showered, she thought about Francisco's life and wondered if she would have survived his problems.

Francisco drove his cab to his tiny apartment with only one thought on his mind. His instinct told him Megan was in more trouble than even she imagined.

He tried to put together the facts he knew about Michael. He was a thief. He doubted the guy ever loved Megan. She had been used again; only this time she didn't know it. She still believed he loved her and that he was only a victim of his own circumstances.

There was one thing Francisco loved about being a Mexican. It meant that no matter where you ended up in this huge country, you were part of a brotherhood. All one had to do was make a phone call and help was on its way.

Francisco had a friend in New York. Carlos had migrated to the City to become a cop. He would call on his friend to find out everything he could about Michael. Maybe he could save Senorita Megan some future trouble from this man. He would try.

Early the next morning, Francisco made two phone calls.

The first was to his son. He needed to hear his voice. He needed to know he was all right. He felt shaken by Megan's story. He knew his son would advise him with care. They were close and he could count on him to keep a secret. They both understood it was dangerous business to involve the Mexican Mafia in anything.

Antonio listened to his father's story. He also felt the woman was in some kind of danger. He didn't know why. It was just a feeling in the pit of his stomach. He advised his father to call Carlos and to do it right away.

His son's feelings unnerved Francisco even more. He hung up and dialed his friend's number. Carlos answered on the third ring.

18

Francisco never called just to say hello, so Carlos knew something was wrong as soon as he heard his voice. He and his old friend had a long history.

At different times in their service to Brisbane, and for different reasons, they had struck out on their own. He headed for New York and Francisco chose San Diego.

They took with them secrets they would carry forever. They did not want to cross a rich, powerful landowner in his own country, so with the honor of a servant to his master, they kept their mouths shut and buried their tale deep in the hollows of their minds.

At first, the two men chatted in their native tongue. Not having called for small talk, Francisco came to his reason for calling at the first break in their conversation.

"Carlos, I need your help. I have met a lovely, young lady from New York."

Carlos laughed out loud, a sly laugh shared and understood only between men. A kind of congratulations, you're getting some laugh. He said, "My friend, I am glad you have moved on. I never thought you would get over Consuela. I am happy for you."

Francisco felt his face flush with embarrassment. "No, no, my friend, not like that. I think she is in some kind of trouble. I'm not sure, that's why I called you. I need you to do some research for me, but you must be careful. The FBI and others are involved. I slipped her address book from her purse and I have names and addresses I think will help you."

He told Carlos everything he knew about Megan and her relationship with Michael. He told him about the brownstone and Amy, her parents, the art gallery and her reason for coming to San Diego. He had found a lawyer's number in the book and gave him that, too.

"Please help me, Carlos. She is alone and scared and I am scared for her. Shadows are following her and she doesn't realize the possibilities. I am sure of this, so is my son."

"I will do everything I can, Francisco. We are part of the

brotherhood and if something is out there, I'll find it for you. I know people who can get me the information we need". He thought a minute and then added, "Do you know if this Michael has any affiliation with the Family?"

"I don't know, my friend. This is my problem. I just don't know."

They said good-byes and Carlos promised to call as soon as he had something.

Carlos sat in his chair for a long time. It was too late tonight to do anything, but first thing in the morning he would start with a couple of calls.

He had many friends willing to help him in matters like this. His brothers in New York were a tight community, some of them in high places. They called on him often and asked for favors, some of which sat on the sharp edge of the law. He had always co-operated and had always been protected. Now he could call in a couple of those favors. Not unlike his boyhood village, his compadres in this city knew him for his temper, his stubbornness, but most of all, for his loyalty. His friends would be more than willing to help him find the information Francisco needed.

·····

His mind drifted to his friend. Carlos had never had anything in common with him and yet; they had become best friends as young boys. Francisco and another boy, Enrique, were friends before he became involved with them.

They were two years younger than he was and much smaller. The older boys in town loved to taunt Francisco and Enrique, and he never shied away from a good fight.

He hadn't cared about them; it just gave him a chance to show off for the girls. Carlos had huge arms and flexed his muscles at every chance, to the delight of every pretty young thing in town.

His heroic tactics towards the young boys endeared the pretty girls to Carlos and he bedded everyone he could. It was easy. There wasn't much entertainment in Puerto San Luis and he took advantage of this. Most of the girls fought over who would be next. Many a night he spent on the hay, in the big old barn at the end of

136

town, rolling around with his newest conquest.

The two boys followed Carlos around like tails on a dog's ass and he loved being their hero. He taught them the ropes, told them what women like to hear and what they like men to do. They hung on his every word and giggled like silly schoolgirls.

As soon as he thought they were ready, Carlos took his students to the barn, along with a couple of girls and they put into practice what he had taught them. They were forever grateful. They were just starting to grow beards.

It wasn't long before their world changed. The ship came. The ship that would take two of them away from the only world they knew and leave one to hold the village together; the ship that would make men out of all three of them.

Senor Brisbane took them on a voyage to "The Promised Land." In the daylight, they tried to act like men, but at night, in their bunks, they cried like small children. They wanted their mothers. The young men held onto each other, overwhelmed with fear. They became brothers. A bond was formed that no one would ever change. Brisbane became the only father they knew. He weaned them from their mothers.

On their arrival at the ranch, Carlos buried himself in caring for the horses. He brushed them and shined their hooves. He spoke to them and caressed their ears. He saved parts of his supper and slipped them treats. At night, he sneaked out to the barn and slept with them on their hay. He was used to hay anyway. They rewarded him by letting him mount them and ride. They seemed to understand his loneliness. They were his salvation.

The men on the ranch were a different story. Carlos got into a fistfight every time they opened their stupid mouths. They began avoiding him like the plague and he spent most of his time with the animals. Francisco remained his only friend, and the only visitor to the stables. He liked it that way.

A servant called Carlos into the big house one day, directing him into an office at the end of a long entrance hallway. Hat in hand, head down, he entered the huge room. Brisbane sat at a hand-carved, oak desk in the center of the room, exuding the confidence of a man who has everything.

Not many men intimidated Carlos, but this one did. Beads of

sweat popped out on his forehead. He dared not look up. He knew he smelled like the horses and wore their feces in the cracks of his shoes. He wished he were back in Puerto San Luis, flexing his muscles for the girls. He wondered why he had been called here. Damn my temper; damn my stupidity, he thought. Muscles flexed in his cheek.

As he stood there, Brisbane's stare piercing the lowered brim of his hat, his mind wandered, something that always happened when he was nervous.

A voluptuous girl he had in the barn appeared in his head. He could feel her body in his hands, her breath on his neck and hear her moans, as he made love to her. He remembered her smile as he picked strands of hay from her naked, wet body. He hadn't had a woman since he came to this ranch. Carlo's mind snapped back when Brisbane stood up.

His boss moved towards a small table. He picked up a crystal bottle filled with an amber liquid. "May I offer you a drink, Carlos?"

Stunned, he kept his head down. "Si, Senor Brisbane".

The great man poured two drinks and handed one to him.

"Sit down, my friend. I have been watching you, Carlos. You are a feisty, young man, but you must stop beating up my ranch hands". With this, he chuckled and his face softened. "They are only trying to do a job. They miss their families, also. They are not as angry as you and they are not as strong. You are like a young bull, proving your manhood, staking out your territory.

I understand you had many women in your village. I want you to go to town, for the weekend, and satisfy your needs. Satisfy them many times. When you come back, you will be in charge of my stables, and my horses. You are a good man. Horses only love good men. My driver will take you to town. Come home on Sunday night, not so angry."

He did as he was told; and he did as he was told every weekend, from that day forward. He still picked fights for fun, but not as often.

The problems started when Francisco met Consuela. From the beginning Carlos knew what she was, but her beauty blinded his friend. Francisco had always been simple-minded when it came to women. He believed in love. He talked all the time about his mother and father and how they loved each other. It was all he wanted for his own life. Francisco thought Consuela filled the bill.

Many times, Carlos saw her and Brisbane together in town. They never saw him. Sometimes he followed them to a big hotel and saw them walk in together. He watched as Brisbane rented a suite and then he watched as they climbed the twisting staircase in the lobby, hand in hand, like young lovers. A man he feared and respected became a man he hated.

He considered telling his friend, but he knew Francisco would not listen. His eyes, and his heart, were blinded by love. Carlos didn't want to have to beat sense into him and he knew it would come to that. They had been friends too long. He had to let it play itself out. It did, and it left both men with scars too deep to heal in one lifetime.

In the end, long after Francisco left the ranch, Carlos was fired along with the rest of the men. It was then that he headed for New York.

When he arrived it took no time to get connected with the Mexican community. He wanted to be a cop. He wanted to carry a gun. It was arranged for him and put him in debt to his native brothers. He didn't care. He acquired a tough guy reputation out on the street and no one bothered, nor questioned him. Carlos called his own shots and became the one every one feared and respected. He no longer held his head down or carried his hat in his hand. He did favors when needed and went about his business the rest of the time. He liked his life. It was easy for a man to make money here. Women were plentiful and ripe for the picking. They would do anything for a man with power and money. And he saw to it that they did.

Yes, he would help Francisco. He owed him that much.

19

Two quick knocks woke Carlos from a sound sleep. Looking through the peephole, he saw no one. Opening the door, he reached down and picked up a heavy, white envelope. A quick glance assured him the hallway was empty. He closed the door.

He poured himself a glass of the same amber liquid Brisbane had served him long ago, lit an expensive, and also illegal, Cuban cigar and sat down in his favorite leather armchair. The small lamp on his end table provided the only light in the room.

The curtains on the window swayed in the cool breeze. His chair faced the front door and his cocked gun lay on the table beside him. One never knew what to expect in his line of work.

The city below him had settled down for the night and the familiar night sounds permeated the room. He liked the city late at night. A man could move through the streets, never being seen, if he so desired. After midnight, the people changed, especially the women, the rules changed and the attitudes changed. No suits, no theater-goers, no tourists, no pompous Wall Street asses, just his kind of people. People he understood.

Inhaling his cigar deeply and taking a pull on his drink, he settled in. The envelope contained a file at least three inches thick. He prepared for a long night.

•••••

The morning after Francisco's phone call, Carlos made two calls from a payphone. He didn't like traceable calls. He never used the phone in his apartment and only a few people had the number to call in. He didn't like phone calls anyway. He wasn't much of a talker and really didn't care how anyone was. If he wanted to talk to people, he chose to look in their face. A man's face told you more than any words could say.

While he waited for the information he needed, he decided to start with Megan's friend Amy and her lawyer, Clayton. Chances were they didn't know anything, but it was worth a try.

He reached the lawyer and made an appointment. He hated lawyers. The pasty little jerks, always afraid to talk to anyone, disgusted him. The idiots studied law for eight years and then used it to protect themselves. Every time one of them said the words Attorney-Client privilege, he wanted to punch them square in the face. Most of them made their money chasing ambulances or protecting criminals. They drove around in their big cars, screwed in their big houses and lived the high life because they set criminals free. As far as he was concerned, they should eat swine and drink pig piss.

He entered the eighteenth floor office and faced a museum quality interior. A bookish, staid woman sat behind her polished desk and looked at him over her glasses.

"What can I do to help you?' she said, in a tone that made him feel as though a slug had just crawled in.

He could play her game. "Mr. Rodriquez here to see Mr. Clayton," he feigned an air of indignation.

"Have a seat and I'll announce you," she said, as she got up from her desk and disappeared behind two huge mahogany doors.

Who the hell did she think her boss was, a king? Announce him? Why did people act like they didn't shit in a toilet like the rest of the world? Nice ass, though; probably not a bad roll.

"Mr. Clayton will see you now. May I get you a cup of coffee?" she asked, the words falling from her mouth with a practiced politeness.

With equal politeness and, maybe with a little sarcasm, he said, "No thank you."

The lawyer sat behind his grand desk, twice as polished and twice the size of his secretary's. As Carlos expected, he wore a three-piece Brooks Brothers suit and sported a gold watch chain. Cut crystal decanters, probably holding the oldest Scotch in the world, sat behind him, on a polished mahogany cabinet.

Rich, affluent shysters, he thought.

As he approached the desk, the lawyer stood up and extended his hand. "What can I do to help you, Mr. Rodriquez?"

Just as he would have expected, the soft, lily-white, bony little hand with polished nails, caused revulsion in the pit of his stomach. I hate these slimy, little worms, his mind screamed while his mouth said, "I am Carlos Rodriquez and I'm here trying to help a friend of mine, Mr. Clayton." It felt like he spit the word Mister at this little sleaze ball and he wished he hadn't.

He continued, trying to hide his contempt. "An old friend of mine called me to say he is involved with a client of yours. He thinks she may be in some kind of trouble and has asked me to find out what I can do to help her. He gave me your name."

The lawyer studied him. He sat down in his chair and leaned back.

Carlos's mind moved towards rage. The punk is deciding if I can afford to talk to him or not. Maybe I should put a couple of grand on the desk. Money talks and these guys only talk for money. Maybe I'll just punch him in his ugly little face and walk out, his mind ranted.

"Who would this friend be, Mr. Rodriquez?"

"Megan Summerfield."

"I am not at liberty to say anything about Miss Summerfield, Mr. Rodriquez."

Uncontrolled rage, at the answer he expected, filled his face. Carlos put both hands on the lawyer's desk, leaning on them, making his muscles almost break through the shirt he wore. He looked into the lawyer's face, his eyes no farther than an inch away from the frightened lawyer's eyes.

"Look you little asshole. I have information that leads me to believe Megan is in serious trouble and it's also possible her life is in grave danger. Her life being in danger puts my friend's life in danger, and, if anything happens to him, the word torture will have to be redefined in the dictionary when I'm through with you. Now, shove your Attorney-Client privilege up your ass and help me to help her. This girl doesn't even know she is in trouble. She is at the mercy of everything that moves."

Carlos glared at Mr. Clayton, his face red and muscles bulging in his cheeks. The muscles in his arms bulged and his knuckles turned white. He'd love one excuse to beat the shit out of this guy.

To his mind-boggling surprise, the lawyer put his face in his hands and shook his head. This guy thinks I'm going to kill him, he thought. The little chicken-shit. Maybe I will.

What he didn't know, at the time, was that Mr. Clayton was

making a decision. He had watched Megan grow up, had participated in all the milestones in her life. He loved her like a daughter, but he loved her father even more. Brad Summerfield had been one of his best friends. Brad had helped him through all the bad shit in his life. He had been there when his son was killed. He had held him together through his wife's cancer. He had bailed him out of bankruptcy. Brad would expect him to help his daughter. No, he would demand he help his daughter.

He had resolved important matters for Brad, some bordering on the edge of legal, like the Cayman Island deal. Brad had an associate in the islands that had brought the three of them close together, by way of some bad banking. His own clever legal maneuvers had saved the day for both men and left favors being owed. It was the closest he ever came to going to jail, but it had turned out well. A considerable amount of money had been made for all three men.

Yes, he would co-operate with this guy. He really didn't have a choice. Everyone involved with Brad owed him something.

"Sit down, Mr. Rodriguez, and calm down. I can assure you, I do not need to be strong-armed. I owe the Summerfield's. I am in their debt. I know Megan's father would want me to help you.

Mr. Summerfield's, Brad's, life centered on his wife and Megan. He treated his wife, Audrey, and Megan as if they were the only two people in the world.

He amassed a fortune in his business dealings and left it all to Audrey, who in turn left it all to Megan. She has spent little, and I do mean little, of it. She never knew they had it and the mere thought of it made her feel betrayed by her parents.

I can tell you that I do not know where Megan is. I know the FBI and the New York Police, and God only knows what other agencies, are looking for her because of her involvement with a man named Michael James. They say they only want to see her for questioning, but murder and interstate fraud are involved. They have investigated her bank accounts, her friends and her job.

Megan deeded her brownstone to her friend, Amy Gray, and left her enough money to take care of it.

I have searched credit cards and telephone calls through friends of mine, to no avail. I cannot find any airplane tickets or record of any other method of transportation. It seems as though Megan does not want to be found.

Her friend Amy is near hysteria all the time and her life has become a hell. FBI agents, we think, follow her on a daily basis and have visited her work. Her phones are tapped, as are mine.

Right now, Mr. Rodriquez, neither Amy, nor I, know what Megan is involved in. We can presume innocence because we both want to, but we do not know for sure.

You came here to ask me for help. Now, I am asking you for help. Do you know where she is? Do you know any more than we do?"

Carlos sat with his jaw slack. The rage disappeared. His first inclination had been to punch the little bastard out when he told him to calm down, but he sat down instead. As soon as the man started to talk, he had his attention and he did calm down. Now he sat here confused and shocked.

Instinct told him to call Francisco and get rid of this woman. His life had already been destroyed by a little tramp and he didn't need another one taking advantage of him and putting him in danger again.

Something in the back of his mind nagged him. It felt like a spider nibbling at the nape of his neck. Something Francisco had said. What was it? The thought wouldn't come.

Carlos decided not to tell Clayton Megan's whereabouts. He didn't know who to trust and he wasn't starting with this guy.

It seemed to him that the man was happy to hand the problem off to him. Thanking him for his help, he stood up to leave. "I'll get back to you as soon as I have more information. You've helped me more than you know. Would you mind if I met with Amy?"

"Please, Mr. Rodriquez, I beg you not to follow her around or frighten her any more than everyone else has already done. I will have Amy contact you. It is easier that way and, I venture to say, safer."

Carlos agreed and decided not to tell Clayton he had already called her.

He left the posh offices and walked down the streets of New York. He passed bums, sleeping in alleyways and on museum steps. Hordes of self-important people rushed to nowhere. Hotdog vendors sold hotdogs. Women clad in mink coats brushed past prostitutes standing on corners. Just another typical day in the City.

He let his mind wander back to Puerto San Luis, the quiet, sweet little village he loved. He could have stayed. He could have been a fisherman. He really needed a drink.

Opening his door, Carlos saw the red light flashing. The drinks had quieted his nerves. He thought about ignoring the light. Sitting down in his chair, laying his head back on the headrest and closing his eyes, he reached over and pushed the button.

A pretty female voice said, "Mr. Rodriquez, my name is Amy Gray. I have talked to Mr. Clayton. Tomorrow I will be at Mario's at seven o'clock. I will be wearing a pink blouse and my hair will be in a ponytail tied with a pink ribbon. If you cannot make it, I will return the following night, at the same time. Please do not call me again." Click.

He would be there. Not opening his eyes, he fell asleep remembering the young, eager, well-endowed girls in the barn. In his sleep, his fingers moved on the arm of the chair, still feeling the warm, wet, tight places on their bodies, eager for his touch and his manhood.

Carlos woke up with the thought that had been eluding him. It shocked him into awareness. Megan had told Francisco the men Michael had brought to her house looked shabby and their appearance had surprised her, but New York was made up of all kinds of people and she hadn't thought any more about it.

He might be naïve, but a guilty person would not admit that her lover had brought his partners-in-crime to her house. Not to anyone. This girl is innocent. He knew it. He'd stake his career on it.

Promptly at seven o'clock, he walked into Mario's. One quick glance around the restaurant and he spotted Amy. The sight of her almost stopped his heart.

He stood looking at her, forgetting why he had come. Probably in her early thirties, her face looked as though an angel had given it to her. No makeup; none needed. Her blond hair was tied up in a ponytail and the shorter strands framed her face. Intense blue eyes glanced nervously around the room and small pink lips pouted like a spoiled child. Her tiny hands rested around a glass of white wine and she emitted the aura of a delicate sunrise.

He tightened his stomach muscles, squared his shoulders and walked over to her, not aware of anyone else in the room.

She saw him coming and a frightened look penetrated her face. Her hand involuntarily jerked, sending her wineglass into a small dance on the table. She steadied it and tried to stand. She looked ready to run, like a cornered, frightened, wild animal.

"I am Carlos Rodriquez and I'm trying to help your friend, Megan," he said, extending his trembling hand.

"Please, Mr. Rodriquez, please tell me where Megan is. I am begging you. She is in trouble and I need to talk to her."

"Sit down, Amy. We will talk." He needed to sit down. His knees felt like a bucking mule had kicked them.

They sat and a waitress appeared. He ordered a beer, two orders of spaghetti and another wine for her.

He could not take his eyes from her. His palms were wet. The skin under his collar felt damp. What the hell was wrong with him? He had bagged hundreds of women. He never acted like this.

She wasn't beautiful anyway. Not actress, model-type beautiful. It was some other kind, some kind that touched your eyes and made you blind.

All the things he felt sure of, his good looks, his pride in his muscles, his sureness in himself, were gone. He felt naked in her presence. He couldn't think of anything to say and he had no idea why he ordered two orders of spaghetti. Finally, the beer came.

She spoke again. "Are you alright, Mr. Rodriquez?"

Her words went into his head; sounding like music he had heard once at a symphony, but nothing came out of his mouth. Carlos took a long pull on the beer and tried to look cool. Maybe if his mouth were wet, it would talk. "I'm fine," he mumbled. "Why wouldn't I be fine?"

Amy stared at him. He finished the beer in one long drink.

"Mr. Rodriquez, Mr. Clayton told me you know where Megan is. I want to know where she is and if you don't tell me, I'm leaving. I don't have time to waste with you. I am scared to death for my life and hers. Talk or I'm gone."

"Amy, please call me Carlos. I am a New York City cop and I have a friend named Francisco. He called me and asked me to find out what I can about Michael. I'm trying to do that and I now think Megan is only guilty of being naïve, but she is in some kind of danger stemming from her involvement with a guy named Michael. I can't tell you where she is, for her safety and yours, and you must tell no one that I know where she is. I promise you that the minute I can, I will personally take you to her. I need you to tell me everything you know about Michael, anything that will help me. The smallest detail may be important."

The spaghetti came and Amy ate without questioning his order. She talked about her meetings with Michael, her subsequent search for him, the ever-present men watching her, the ransacking of her house, her disturbed mail and everything else she could think of. He listened, although distracted by the woman herself. Every detail matched the lawyer's story.

They lingered over dinner, with him using every tactic he could think of to avoid ending the meeting.

After several more drinks, they decided to meet again at the restaurant later in the week. Neither one of them thought it a good idea for him to walk her home, so she left first, but not before she hugged him good-bye, pressing her small body into his, kissing him gently on the cheek. He sat down, trying to regain his composure and summon up his arrogant personality.

Carlos limped out of the restaurant feeling half the angry, tough cop he was when he walked in. He had just had his first full encounter with a human being where he hadn't felt like punching someone. Once again, he felt naked.

Outside, the cold wind stung his cheeks. Hunching his shoulders and raising his collar, he walked directly into it. In the darkness of the night, he felt safe. The streets belonged to him. His cocky attitude returned to his walk, but his brain felt like hot cereal, mucked up by a child's spoon.

He lay awake in his bed trying to figure out the strange sensations Amy had aroused in him. Carlos didn't recognize them.

He had sat with this girl for four hours and hadn't thought about sex once. He hadn't even checked out her ass. He couldn't remember if she had tits or not.

And yet, he had never desired a woman as much as he desired her. Amy's kiss lingered on his cheek and he found himself reaching up to touch it. He fell asleep only to have her face haunt his dreams all night.

•••••

Carlos sat in his chair, smoking his cigar, reading Michael's folder. If Clayton and Amy knew the extent of Michael's crimes, they hadn't let on. Their knowledge of his antics was limited to what the FBI had let them know. They had no idea how dangerous this man could be. He had to call Francisco, but it was too late in San Diego. He'd call first thing in the morning. There was only one place to hide Megan from Michael.

20

Megan took extra care to dress on this evening. Francisco had called and invited her to dinner at El Cajon, one of his favorite restaurants. He seemed excited and told her he had a surprise for her.

They had spent a sunshine-filled day in Julian and now she found herself looking forward to a good dinner.

The loneliness of her room, the newspaper article, and the little bottle of pills, tormented her nights, but her time with Francisco allowed her to keep her demons at bay.

At seven o'clock, as she entered the hotel lobby, Francisco and a strange man stood waiting for her.

Stopping in her tracks, her mood became dark and sullen. Megan hoped he was not trying to "fix her up." She did not want anyone in her life and she had no intention of being cordial to a potential suitor, picked out by "The Foremost Authority on San Diego."

Damn him, she thought. Why do men always screw things up? She turned on her heel, anger consuming her, starting back to the elevator.

"Megan, we're over here," he called.

"No. No thank you. I feel ill. I'll call you later," she lied.

"Megan, wait; wait just a moment. I want you to meet someone."

Before she could escape, the two men stood next to her. The second man looked like a young version of Francisco.

"Oh, my God, you are Antonio. I am so embarrassed."

"Please don't be," the young man said. "I am happy to meet you. My father has told me so much about you."

"Oh, Francisco, why didn't you tell me he was coming home? I'm so sorry."

"Never mind, Megan, I know what you thought. Do you think I would do that to you? I am not a foolish man." He smiled, but she could see his feelings had been hurt.

Feeling reprimanded and foolish for her own self-centeredness, she turned her attention to Antonio. "When did you get in town?"

Before Antonio could speak, Francisco said, "I wanted to surprise you and Antonio agreed. He doesn't get much time off from school and he is only in town for the weekend. I never thought that you would...," his voice trailed off. "I can only apologize for my stupidity."

"Francisco, please forgive me for my assumptions. I am the foolish one, not you." She kissed him on his cheek. "I want to enjoy this beautiful night with you and your son."

Antonio interrupted their apologies. "I can't think of anything more charming than a woman blushing and a man trying to take responsibility for it. Suppose we go to dinner?"

Francisco's face beamed with pride.

Antonio stood somewhat taller than his father and had a slimmer build. Francisco attributed his height to the American food he preferred. His son also appeared more Americanized than his father. He had no accent and, by way of dress and listening preferences, this was the first time Megan heard an English-speaking station on the radio, she guessed he led an American life-style.

She could not have been more wrong. Over dinner, Antonio explained his intentions upon graduating from medical school.

"I would like to return to my father's country to practice medicine," he said. "Most of my friends don't understand my thinking and disagree with me. I believe every person is born with an intended purpose.

Fate forced my father to leave his country, the village and the land he loved. My grand-father made the most painful decision a man could ever have to make, so that my father might have a better life.

I believe in the greater realm of things. I believe fate played its hand so that my father could help his own country.

He instilled in me the need for education. He worked sixteen hours a day to send me to school. He has produced a doctor with his efforts.

I believe this is the purpose of his life, to create someone who can help his country. I am destined to return to Mexico and help his people, my people. It is the natural order of things.

Someday, with my help, my children will help my father's

homeland. Mexico needs everything; doctors, educators, money, food, and clean water. Every generation will have its work cut out for it."

Megan listened to his every word, amazed by this young man. Overwhelming admiration misted her eyes.

The evening turned out to be the finest she had spent in San Diego. They parted in front of the hotel with plans to meet early in the morning for a trip to Tijuana.

She fell asleep trying to think if she had ever had a plan, a purpose or a cause for living. She couldn't come up with one thing.

If Old Town painted a perfect picture of serene Mexican history, the next morning, Tijuana painted its own picture of modern day.

A rollicking, bustling town laid before them, filled with endless cabs, vendors hawking gold jewelry, and peasant children offering Chiclets, while their mothers reached up from blankets to offer trinkets and statues.

Fish tacos, hot cinnamon churros, and cold beer were all offered from open-air stands, their exotic smell filling the air and mingling with raucous Mariachi music. Bars lined the streets, proclaiming to have the best margaritas in town. Colorfully dressed burros stood on corners, posing for pictures.

Enjoying lunch in an upstairs cantina, overlooking the commotion on the street below them, Megan remembered the beat of her own city. This one had its own special beat and everything moved to it.

"We have one more surprise for you, Megan," Francisco announced as they returned to his car. "On our way home, we are stopping in San Diego to introduce you to Antonio's aunt, Tia Juanita.

She is looking forward to meeting you. She is my aunt and helped me to take care of Antonio. Without her, I don't know what we would have done."

"That is a wonderful surprise, Francisco. I didn't know you had any other family in San Diego."

"She is our only other relative here. She is also a sly woman, so be careful of her sense of humor."

A tiny, matronly woman, gray hair tied in a knot at the base of her neck, flew into Antonio's arms, as he stepped out of the car. He lifted her to his height. Kissing and caressing him, she talked non-stop in rapid Spanish.

With open arms, she quieted, and turned to Megan. "Let me look at you. I have heard all about you and I am pleased to meet you."

She took Megan in her arms and kissed both cheeks. Wrapping her arm through Megan's, she said, "Come, let's eat. I have made much food. The only good meal these two get is when they come to mi casa, si?"

For several hours, long into the night, they ate, laughed and talked. The love between Megan's three friends overwhelmed the night.

Amongst kisses and promises to see each other soon, Francisco, Antonio and Megan left, exhilarated and tired, having had a day to be remembered.

Back at the hotel, the two men kissed her on her cheek and promised to see her tomorrow.

Once in the car, Antonio asked his father if he had heard from Carlos.

"He called me only once and told me things did not look good for Megan. He suggested I keep an eye on her, at all times. He needed more time to be sure his information was correct. I am worried, Antonio. I don't know what the problem is."

"Is she aware of the problem, Dad?"

"No, I don't think she has any idea."

21

The rain hit the town with a vengeance. Mud slid down the mountain, forming rivers along its path. It carried the gardens and personal belongings across the pristine beach to meet huge waves crashing on the shore. As the waves returned to sea, it carried everything back with them. The dirt roads flooded and rose to meet the storefronts.

On the second day of the storm, I woke up to noise, loud noise. I jumped up to look out the window and saw the villagers running towards the pier.

By the time I got dressed and rushed through the bar, the street scene changed. The people were trudging back up the street, through the mud, following a man I recognized.

His head down, trying to avoid the pounding rain, he half ran, half leaped his way along the street. His expensive clothes hung from his lithe body like rags, running with mud and rain. It was the saddest, and yet, the funniest scene I had ever seen.

Jumping from the porch, into ankle deep mud to try and help my friend, I tried to control my laughter.

"Frank, Frank, what are you doing here?" I yelled over the rain to him.

Mud ran from his face in little streams and his eyes were wild.

"I don't know what the hell I'm doing here. I am now certain you are not worth this. Have you gone mad? The question is, what the hell are you doing here?" he screamed at me.

I grabbed his arm and led him to Angelina's. My new friends followed behind us, clamoring, "Senor Peter, man have a big plane. It is on the beach. Senor Peter, man come to see you."

I began to understand. I hadn't thought about Frank's seaplane. He had come down here to take me home.

Angelina appeared at the door of the bar with towels.

Frank grabbed them from her like an enraged animal stealing raw meat.

Wiping the mud from his face, he turned his rage on me.

"You bastard. You stupid son of a bitch. Look at me. Just

look at me." he screamed.

He turned and looked at the men watching us. With all the dignity he could muster, he squared his shoulders, lowered his voice and said, "Excuse me, which one of you brought my bag?"

I lost all composure and laughed out of control. Enrique stepped forward and handed my poor, embarrassed friend his bag, tipping his hat.

Frank glared at me as I tried to stop laughing. I knew my sanity was no longer a question in his mind.

I took him by the arm and led him to my room.

Once inside, he didn't speak. He went to the shower and spent the next hour trying to pull himself together. I in turn, left the room, trying to pull myself together.

The bar had two inches of water on the floor and it continued to flow in the front door. The men were trying to block the water and Angelina was busy preparing fish stew for everyone.

"Your friend is okay, Senor Peter?" Enrique asked.

"He will be fine, Enrique. His pride is wounded, but he will recover. I don't think he has ever been dirty in his entire life. He is my partner from San Diego and I think he has come here to take me home."

The men stopped working, fixing their stare on me. Angelina walked around from the bar and the room went silent.

Enrique, self appointed spokesman for the group, stepped forward. "Will you go, Senor Peter?"

As they waited for my answer, the looks on their faces, the silence in the room and the realization that they did not want me to go, cleared my mind as it had never been cleared before. They cared about me, not my business, not my money, not my ability to make more, only me. If I had any doubt about not going home, it disappeared into the sound of the rain.

"No, Enrique. I will not be leaving." I stated with certainty.

The men started to smile and Angelina marched back behind the bar, waving her finger at them. "Of course, he is not leaving, you stupid men. Now get back to work and stop this water from coming in or I will not feed you." The deafening silence was over.

I rolled up my sleeves and my pants legs and joined the men in their work. Happy chatter filled the air along with the wonderful smell of Angelina's stew. We would survive this storm.

Steps sounded on the staircase and all looked up.

Frank looked like his old self. I realized I preferred him covered with mud.

"Feel better, old boy?" I asked.

"I am fine and I would like to thank all of you for helping me land the plane and reach this tavern. I am in your debt."

Embarrassed by his intended sophistication, I tried to soften his arrogant attitude. "He'll stop talking like that after he's here for a couple of days. I promise." We all shared a smile, except for Frank.

"Frank, I'd like you to meet my friends. This is Enrique. He is my friend and the town Delegado, our leader."

Enrique stepped forward and took his hand, tipping his hat for a second time.

Frank returned his handshake. "It is my pleasure, sir."

I smiled over his shoulder at Enrique and mouthed, "I promise he will." Enrique returned my smile.

The formal procedure repeated itself through every introduction, each of my friends tipping their hats and stepping backwards to their original place. Frank looked tired and disgusted, but I could see that his pompous air of superiority remained intact.

Angelina had come out from her kitchen near the end of the introductions.

"Frank, I've saved the best for last. This is our Angelina and she is the one who has helped me see the error of my ways."

Frank stepped back and took a long look at her. "So, you are the reason Peter has gone mad?" With an uncharacteristic rudeness, he said, "I would have thought it would have taken a much younger woman."

Before I could react, Angelina stepped towards Frank. "Senor Peter is not leaving Puerto San Luis, and now I understand why not."

The two squared off for a battle. I interrupted. "Frank, if you came here to insult my friends, we will take you back to your plane. These are wonderful people and I will not tolerate you being rude. Make your choice."

Frank's face turned red. He looked around the room at the silent men, all poised to defend Angelina. A long minute followed.

"Angelina, please forgive me. I can only offer lame excuses for my behavior. I have had a long trip, I am tired and I don't understand what Peter is doing. I beg your forgiveness."

Angelina thought for a moment, glaring into the stranger's eyes. "If you are a friend of Senor Peter's, there must be some good in your soul. I will find it. I will forgive you. You almost did not get any of Angelina's famous fish stew. Now, you and Senor Peter sit down and enjoy my cooking." She looked past us and said to the men, "Get back to work or I will give your food to our new friend." She paraded back to the kitchen, confident she had her flock under control.

Frank stood there, his three hundred-dollar shoes soaking in the rising water, and watched her walk to the kitchen. He looked like he wasn't sure what just happened.

"How about a cold one, old man?" I said.

Frank looked grateful and sat down at the nearest table. The men went back to work. Pedro delivered two cervezas.

"What the hell are you doing, Peter?"

"You first, Frank. How did you find me? Why are you here and how did you fly through this storm?"

He sighed, his anger depleted.

"After you called, I sat at my desk for a long time. I thought about the practice and how it would be without you. You know, you are the one with the reputation.

I thought about the tragedy of your parent's death. You seemed to gain strength and an insight into your life from it.

I thought about Sadie and how the suddenness of her death must have eaten away at you.

"I began to think you probably deserved a nervous breakdown.

I decided to follow your instructions and then come down here and bring you home to heal, home to your proper life, your social circle. Home to the security of the only world you know.

I cancelled all appointments for a couple of weeks. I called the pharmacist and he gladly told me which village you were trying to save. I figured I would help you finish up here, do our bit for humanity and then we would fly home together, get you well and send someone for your boat.

On the way down, I hit this storm. The plane sounded as if

it might break up into tiny pieces. I thought I was going to die. I vowed that if I lived, I would kill you when I got here.

I came in on instrument and as I cleared the cloud layer, to my amazement, I saw the men standing on the beach, ready to help me. They pulled the plane onshore, dragged me out and started towards the village. They had no idea who I was, but were braving the storm to help me. No one has ever done that for me before, Peter." He took a long pull on his beer.

Clearing his throat of obvious unwanted emotion, he continued. "I want you to come home, Peter. We will take care of these children first, but for your own good, you must come home. For the sake of the business, you must come home. This is no place for a man of your talent and resources. Peter, you must listen to reason."

I looked at him. Not once had he said I must come home because I am his friend.

Angelina delivered two steaming bowls of hot stew and a basket of freshly baked bread.

"You will love our Rock Cod, Senor Frank. It is Senor Peter's favorite. Do you see how healthy he is? When he got here, he was skinny and bad looking. Angelina made him good again. You will see. In a couple of days, you will be healthy, too. American men do not eat enough. You eat now, then go to room number one and sleep until tomorrow. No more serious talk today. You need rest. Never before have we had two guests at the same time. I will get your room ready."

I smiled at Angelina. It wasn't a good idea not to follow her instructions. It looked as though Frank had completed his first lesson in Angelinaville. Right after an encore of stew, he headed upstairs for the night.

In the morning, I came downstairs to find Angelina and Frank sitting at my usual table, enjoying a cup of coffee and smiling. A tinge of jealousy crawled across my brain. "Well, don't you two look cozy," I sniped, the jealousy leaping from my head to my mouth.

"Good morning, old man. You didn't tell me how lovely the mornings are here."

"Sorry, I didn't think of it while I was fighting cholera." I said, my voice singed with sarcasm.

Angelina stood up and moved to the kitchen to get me a cup of coffee. I turned a chair around and sat backwards, glaring at my partner.

"Don't mess with these people, Frank. Don't sit around here thinking you are better than they are. I appreciate you coming down here, but you don't understand why I am here or know anything about these people.

They are nothing like our so-called social circle in San Diego. They want nothing from life, just good fishing and enough food to eat. And, oh yes, they really know how to love. Don't underestimate them. What they have is stronger than anything you and I know because they have learned to survive with nothing. All they have is each other and the sea. Don't think that your money and your education mean anything to them, because they don't. The villagers here welcomed me before they knew I was a doctor, and they still don't know I have money.

If I sat here for twenty years, I couldn't explain to you what these people mean to me, what they have taught me or what they have made me feel." I stopped to take a breath, surprised at my own anger.

"Are you finished, Peter?"

"Let's just understand each other, Frank. Your callous and inappropriate behavior last night embarrassed me.

I have not lost my mind and I do not intend to go home. I do not intend to listen to any lectures from you or anyone else. I do intend to stay here and build a hospital, even if I have to use all of my resources and the rest of my life to accomplish it.

Let me explain something to you. When Sadie died, as you well know, hundreds of people came to her funeral. Hundreds of cards came to my house. As of one week after the funeral, not one person from my "social circle" contacted me or tried to help me through my grief. No one mentioned Sadie's name. No invitations came for parties or lunch or dinner. How much did these people care for me?

I grieved alone. Is that what friends do, Frank? Do they politely leave you alone to heal? Do you know how many times I wished I had someone to put their arms around me and tell me it was okay to cry? Everyone politely avoided me.

I went to work every day with my mind in its own world. I got sick of the pathetic looks from people who couldn't find it in their heart to mention her name. No one asked me how I was because they were afraid I'd tell them. This is what social status and breeding do for a person. We live in a pretentious, fake, screwed up world, afraid someone will think that we are failures if our life doesn't look perfect. We cheat ourselves of feelings except in the darkness of our bedrooms. We spend our time making money. The more we make, the more we are accepted into our circle. I hate it all, Frank and I can't go back.

I arrived here after three months in my boat, half dead, covered with salt and dying to hear a human voice. I slept for two days and Angelina took care of me. Within ten minutes of sitting with her, I told her about Sadie and she really cared. These people have done nothing but care about me and I realized it was for all the right reasons." I stopped for a minute to catch my breath.

Frank tried to speak and I cut him off. "No, Frank. Don't sit here with your pompous attitude thinking you are better than they are. I won't tolerate it. Are you starting to understand me?"

Frank sat back in his chair, staring at me. I stared back.

"May I speak, Peter?"

"I'm sorry, old man," I said with a sudden calmness. I didn't realize how strongly I felt about this until I saw you sitting with Angelina. I am serious about this, Frank."

"I can see that you are, Peter, but let me tell you this."

Again, anger raged in my mind and contorted my face.

"Will you get off your high horse, Peter? I no longer intend to try and talk you into going home. I also know you do not want me here interfering with your life. But, as you know, I am here for the time being and I am going to talk to you. Don't raise your eyebrows at me. I am not your keeper, or your father, and I have no intention of telling you what to do. I do know you can't hide down here forever, whether you like it or not.

If you, for one minute, think that I am not your friend and I only like you for your money, you've been crazy much longer than I thought. I will admit, that maybe, I didn't help you enough with Sadie's death and I didn't realize how much you needed someone, but don't insult me by telling me I don't care about you and don't dare jump to conclusions about our friends.

Did you expect me to ask you if you wanted me to hold your hand, or maybe hold you in my arms, while you cried? Did you just once come to me and say you needed help? I would have held you if I knew you needed it. How was I to know? I'm not a mind reader. I didn't know what to do anymore than anyone else did.

Our recollections seem to be light-years apart. You retreated into your own mind and stayed there. You spoke to no one and hid in your house at night. You are the one who put yourself in self-exile.

You are wrong about the invitations. As I remember it, we invited you to everything, trying to get you back into life. Do you remember refusing us, or could it be you didn't even hear us?

We tried to find you for almost four months. We called the Coast Guard. They couldn't locate you. No one dreamed you came down here. We issued an APB with the police. You are still considered a missing person. We protected your assets and mowed your lawn.

While you were floating around at sea, licking your wounds, we were busy trying to figure out what the hell you were doing. We didn't know if you were dead or alive.

How dare you say we didn't care about you? Your mind was locked in your grief. You are the one who went into hiding long before you left on your boat, Peter, not us. Your body was present, but your mind wasn't.

And by the way, my pompous attitude was fine with you before Sadie died. You sported quite an attitude yourself, so don't sit there all high and mighty, thinking you are now better than I am.

You are like a person who finds God. You think no one else believes. Well, my friend, I know pain. I know real love. I know what it's like to do without. Have you forgotten how poor my parents were and how I worked my way through college. Just who do you think you are judging me, you pompous, conceited, self-centered ass?"

I stared at him in disbelief. "I'm so sorry, Frank, I'm so sorry. I had no idea what I put everyone through. You're right, I've been lost."

A flood of memories filled my mind, things I hadn't thought about since the first days of my departure from San Diego.

"Let me try to explain, Frank. After the funeral, I was in a daze. I don't remember thinking about anything. I felt that Sadie was watching me and I wanted to be perfect for her. I dressed in clothes she loved, wore the cologne she bought me, cleaned the kitchen up after myself. She hated that I left the bathroom a mess, so I made sure it was immaculate before I walked out. I don't know why, but I felt her eyes. I felt them everywhere.

I didn't move her make-up from the vanity, or pick up her slippers from the side of the bed. I put fresh fruit in her fruit dish and placed bouquets of daisies right next to it. When they rotted, I replaced them. I kept the kitchen full of her favorite foods and only ate the things she liked. I no longer craved French fries or milk shakes. I think I thought that if I kept everything perfect for her she would come home.

It got worse, Frank. I'd hear her footsteps in the hallway. I'd jump up and look, and she'd disappear down the stairs. I'd open her closet door and her scent would overwhelm me. I'd wake up in the morning and hear her humming and frying eggs. When I'd get to the kitchen, she'd be gone, along with the eggs. I'd see her jogging in the park, run to her, and again, gone. I'd wake up in the morning and see her watching the birds from our window. The list is endless.

In our surgery unit, I'd be performing an operation and the air would fill with her scent. I'd look up and see her face behind a green surgical mask. The scalpel became an extension of my finger caressing her lips. Do you know how many women now live in San Diego with a nose shaped like Sadie's?

I woke up one night, soaked in sweat. My bed felt like a bathtub. I bolted up and she was standing at the foot of my bed. I blinked my eyes and she disappeared again. The word crazy ran through my head for the first time.

I waited for the trial and made my plan. I saw the drunken bastard go to jail, and without any more thought, boarded my boat and left. I left with the intention of my boat sinking in the deepest part of the ocean I could find. Somewhere along the way, I turned my anger towards you and our friends. I think it became easier to blame you for abandoning me, than to think about my own blame for her death. I think the transition of thought may have saved my life.

When I landed here, half-dead, Angelina and Enrique took me in and helped me to start healing. This intensified my anger with you and my life. The crawl out of my self-hatred and self-pity has been slow, but they have been there every minute. I have grown to love all of them.

I am sorry, Frank."

We sat for several long moments, neither of us speaking.

"Peter, we all loved Sadie. We all love you. None of us knew what to do. You are quite an actor, my friend. I never would have guessed all of that was going on. It answers a lot of questions. Is there anything I can do now?"

"Yes. Let's get out of here and I'll show you my new home."

We stood up and Frank took one step forward and put his arms around me. He pulled me tight to his chest and muttered, "I'm sorry, Peter. God knows how sorry I am. If I had one wish, Sadie would be alive today."

"Frank, I'm okay. I can't tell you how it makes me feel that you came down here for me. All this time I thought I had no friends. Grief takes you to the brink of madness and, just in time, life brings you back."

We released our grip, turning our heads to shield each other from our tears, and walked out into the warm sunshine.

22

Amy walked into the hotel and approached the desk. "Sir, can you tell me if a Miss Megan Summerfield is registered here?"

"Let me check for you, Madam,"

Amy, exhausted and near tears, looked around the hotel lobby. They were all beginning to look the same. This was the fourteenth hotel she had checked for her friend since she arrived, all to no avail. There were only fifteen more high-end hotels in town, and then, she would start on the smaller ones.

"I'm sorry, Madam, but no one by that name is registered here."

She glared at him for a second, turned and walked towards the front door. Spotting a coffee shop, she changed direction and headed towards it. She needed to sit down and reorganize her thoughts, but most of all; she needed to regain her self-control.

Sipping her coffee, she re-checked the list of hotels she had made on the airplane. Where would Megan choose?

•••••

As Carlos had promised at their first meeting, he called one week to the day and asked for a second meeting. They arranged a time at a small, but upscale restaurant uptown. He said he thought they would be safer there.

Something about this man attracted her and she found herself dressing up a little more than necessary. She dabbed her favorite cologne behind her ears and on her wrists and chose her delicate diamond earrings. She checked her basic black dress several more times in the mirror than she needed to and decided to wear her three inch pumps with the little rhinestone clasps. She fussed with her hair, hating the silly, childish curls framing her face.

Enduring the long cab ride uptown, it occurred to her she hadn't once thought of Megan as she dressed. What is going on, she thought. Who is this man and why can I not get him out of my mind? I have to be focused on Megan, she scolded herself. To spite her own demands, her mind kept creeping back to Carlos.

Entering the restaurant, she spotted him right away. He looked up and smiled. A strange look for this intense man, she thought.

He stood as she approached the table, lifting his big frame from the small chair. To her he looked like a giant of a man sporting an uncustomary silly grin. Her heart fluttered. Once again she reminded herself of the purpose of this evening.

As she took the chair he offered, she opened the conversation with, "Have you found Megan, Carlos? The gravity of her situation returned with a vengeance. She now felt foolish for her appearance. The thought of her dress and the smell of her cologne sickened her.

"I know that this is inappropriate, but you look beautiful tonight. I am glad to see you again." His own words embarrassed him, but he seemed to have no control over his mouth.

He continued. "Let's order a bottle of wine and then I'll update you on our situation. In the back of his head, his mind screamed at him. What the hell are you doing? You don't wine and dine women. This is business. Keep your mind on business. His mouth said, "You smell lovely, kinda like a flower." He blushed.

Amy stared at him and felt her body relax. This man made her feel weak and at his command. She liked the feeling.

"Do you like Merlot, Carlos?"

He didn't even know what the hell Merlot was. He wanted a beer, a large cold one, in a frozen glass, and a cigarette. He wanted his palms to stop sweating. "Yes, Merlot will be fine."

As the Wine Steward prepared the tasting glass, Carlos looked at it. Thank God, he remembered seeing this ritual somewhere on television. He picked up the glass, sipped it and placed it back on the table.

Shooting for a tone of sophistication, he said, "I think we'd prefer it cold."

The Steward stared at him icily and stepped away from the table.

Amy held her breath to refrain from giggling. They drank the Merlot with ice.

The wine, the candles and the soft violin music pushed Amy's thoughts farther and farther away from Megan and her own frame of mind. The musky, masculine smell of Carlos didn't help either. She listened to his voice, hearing melody from his Spanish accent, combined with hardness from his New York City life. She watched the small muscles in his jaw flex as he talked. She admired his thick, black wavy hair, forbidding herself from reaching out and brushing it from his forehead.

Their conversation remained light until their steaks came. She hadn't been surprised that he ordered his rare, but was delighted that he ordered hers medium-well. He seemed to know what she liked.

She found him to be suave, kind, independent, arrogant and obnoxious.

It also occurred to her, as she studied him, that he had a dark shadow over his life, one he tried hard to mask. It could be seen in his eyes.

As he pressed his knife into his meat, his face changed. Shadows crossed his eyes and his breathing deepened. With his fork suspended in mid-air, holding a piece of the steak in its tines, he said, "As much as I am enjoying this night, we need to talk."

"Please, Carlos. I don't care what Megan has done. I am her friend and she needs me. If you know where she is, please tell me now."

He put his fork down on the table, sat up straight and took a long minute to light a cigarette. Inhaling deeply and releasing the smoke slowly through his lips, he locked his eyes onto hers. "I'm not a man who is good with words, Amy."

His voice had changed. It sounded almost threatening, the words coming from some unknown place deep in his mind. "I am a cop. I am good at stalking strangers at night. I am good at working with the underground. I don't see much daylight and I'm not comfortable with it anyway. I don't like phones and I don't like people. I don't like feelings and I don't like to care.

That said, an old friend of mine from San Diego, a man who I would die for, asked me into this Megan thing. I wouldn't be involved otherwise. I don't like this situation and I don't like that I care about you.

Your eyes look deep inside me and I don't like that either. Nothing good can be seen inside me.

I haven't been able to get you out of my head and I don't like it. My life is what I want it to be and I don't want it to change.

To that end, I am going to call my friend with the information he needs to save this woman's life and then I am going to forget I was ever involved. I won't tell you where Megan is because the danger is too great. I don't want you to get hurt. My friend and I know people who will help us. Megan will be safe and when she is ready, she will call you. Now, let's eat our dinner and call it a night."

Amy dropped her knife and fork on the table. Rage contorted her face and her eyes shown like bright blue projectiles. "How dare you decide anything for me? Who the hell do you think you are? I don't need you. I don't need this steak and I surely don't give a shit if you care about me or not. I want to know where Megan is. You made one mistake, buddy. You already told me your friend is from San Diego. That's all I need to know. Screw you, you bastard." She jumped up and flew across the restaurant, hailed a cab and jumped in before Carlos could reach the front door.

Returning to her brownstone, she told the driver to wait, threw a bag together and got back into his car. "Take me to the airport," she demanded.

Carlos reached her house fifteen minutes later, in a state of shock. How could he have made such a mistake? At what point had he told her where Francisco was from? Damn that woman, he thought. Damn her.

•••••

The waitress brought Amy her third refill as she sat staring at the picture behind the counter in the coffee shop.

As the waitress stepped aside, bringing the print back into view, a thought hit her like a thunderbolt. It was a picture of a beach in Hawaii.

Where would Megan go if she were in trouble? She had sat for months on the beach when her Mother died. She and her Mother had spent their lives sitting on the beach. When she and Megan were young girls they took all their problems to the beach for contemplation. My God, oh my God, she thought. There has

166

to be a hotel on the beach.

Running into the lobby, she found the Concierge. Breathless, she asked him what hotels were on the beach.

"There are only two, Madam; the Hilton and the Majestic. May I call a cab for you?"

"No, no thank you," she said, bolting to the front door and jumping in the first cab she saw.

"Take me to the Hilton and please hurry," she begged the driver.

As the car moved away from the curb, the driver turned to look at her and said, "How do you do, young lady. I am Francisco, the world's foremost authority on San Diego. Can I tell you anything about our fair city?"

23

Frank stayed more days than he had anticipated. He languished around Angelina's bar and slept afternoons away on the front porch, a borrowed hat pulled down over his eyes. He appeared first at Angelina's table and ended each meal sitting back in his chair, like a stuffed Buddha, enjoying a fat Cuban cigar from his personal supply. Endearing himself to my friends, he shared the cigars and taught each one of them to use his gold cigar cutter. They were willing students.

Raucous laughter and many beers were shared as the local men entertained Frank with stories of life in their village.

Frank's favorite, of course, was the story of my fishing adventure. He checked my hands to see the calluses and laughed so hard he couldn't swallow his beer.

Enrique explained to Frank his love of the sea and the teachings of his father. He entertained him with our trip over the mountains to get medicine. He continued with his own favorite story; that of his French name. He told Frank of his love for Angelina and she hit him with the dishtowel.

Angelina shared her story of my pitiful arrival and my heroics on the mountain with their children.

I walked Frank around the town and up onto the mountain. I introduced him to the children who had suffered from cholera and showed him the new drainage techniques and the new gardens. He hugged the little children and, at one point, he hid tears, overwhelmed at the simple life and simple desires of these people.

We ended our tour with a look at the old barn.

"I know why you brought me here," Frank said. "You are planning to build your hospital in this building, aren't you?"

"Yes, I am, Frank. It has become the strongest desire I've ever had."

The change in Frank was remarkable. He didn't get angry. He didn't start to argue. He didn't start a speech about going home.

Instead, he asked only one question. "Where will you get the supplies to do this?"

"Enrique's father built a pier out of the trees on the mountain by himself. He hewed them with his bare hands. He accomplished his dream with only an axe and determination. I will figure it out."

"You know, old man, when I came down here, I was sure you had lost your mind. Now I think you have found it, for the first time in your life.

I've begun to doubt my own convictions and have found myself wondering if my own motivations have benefited me. I don't think anything will ever look the same to me again and, for that, I thank you and your new friends."

He put his arms around me and hugged me. This time I welled up.

At a loss for words, I mumbled, "Let's go get a beer, Frank,"

Several days later, deciding he could no longer postpone his departure, Frank prepared to leave first thing in the morning. We partied the night away.

The following morning, Angelina served us steaming bowls of menudo, a rich soup, made with beef bellies as its main ingredient. She assured us it was the only cure for the prevailing hangovers. We ate with gusto, and it worked.

All of the villagers followed us to the beach. As we cleared the hill, we stopped dead in our tracks. Frank's plane sat on the beach, glistening in the sun. We turned to look at our friends and they stood grinning, hats in hand, obviously proud of themselves.

They had spent the previous day washing and polishing Frank's plane. The inside was stocked with food, beer and a blanket, "Just in case he got cold," they explained.

"I am not the kind of man who is ever at a loss for words, but I find myself unable to tell you how thankful I am for your kindness. You have showed me what true friends are and I will never forget you. I am sure my life will never be the same. Thank you all so much."

Angelina hugged him good-bye. Enrique removed his hat and shook his hand. One by one, the rest of the men approached him, removed their hats and also shook his hand.

A hush fell over the small gathering as Enrique said, "Senor Frank, I speak for all the people in Puerto San Luis. We wish you to return to our village and stay here with us. You and Senor Peter are good friends and now we are, too. We invite you to be part of our life here. We have not much to offer great men like you and Senor Peter, maybe only our friendship, but we wish you to come back. We are honored in your presence."

Frank looked stunned. "Enrique, you and your friends are not the ones who should be honored to be in my presence. I am the one to feel honor in yours. You have much to offer a man like me.

You've made me remember a long ago life with my parents. I haven't felt the warmth and love of that relationship in a long time. Not until now. You have given me a great gift.

I've also learned to laugh again. I've learned to relax.

I will consider your offer to return with the intensity of a huge fish trying to free itself from your hook. I will see you again soon, no matter what it takes.

Frank stepped towards me and put his arms around me. "I have no words to thank you for this, Peter. God speed, my good friend. I love you."

With that, he turned and climbed into his plane. The engines started, blowing sand up into the air. It rolled down the beach, lifting itself just as the waves crossed its nose, sending spiraling plumes of water high into the air. The plane became immersed in water and then bounded from the sea, picking up momentum and soaring across the ocean like a giant bird catching a thermal. It banked to the north with elegance and disappeared behind the mountain. We stood, watching the plane go, waving to Frank. It was time for a beer.

Days passed and everyone seemed to go back to their normal routine. The men fished, the women cooked, the children played and the dogs slept.

Parents brought their children to me for fevers and scrapes and bruises. Women came to me with headaches and various other aches and pains and even some of the men brought their problems to me.

I spent my idle time working on my boat and enjoying an occasional sail with some of the men. I also spent my time concentrating on my hospital, a task that appeared impossible at times. The one thing I didn't think about was going home.

One day, as I idled up the street, returning to my room to

prepare for dinner, a strange woman approached me, her walk intense and determined.

She looked to be in a bad mood. A burlap bag, slung around her neck and over her shoulder, hung down to her waist. She wore an old dress, heavy shoes and bangles on her arms. A scarf covered her head, strands of gray hair pushing their way out. Her face, weathered and wrinkled, wore a stern grimace.

I wondered why I hadn't seen her before and where she was headed at such a furious pace.

Within seconds, she stood in front of me, her crooked finger pointed in my face.

"You are a bad man. You are a bad man," she screamed at me.

A little frightened, I asked, "Who are you?"

"I am Lupita. I am the curanderas. I take care of the people in this village. Lupita does not need you to fix my people. You leave my people alone. You do bad things. You are a bad man. I warn you. Leave Lupita's people alone. You will be sorry. Lupita will get rid of you with mal puesto."

She removed her finger from my face, turned on her heel and stomped down the street, mumbling things I could not understand.

I hurried to Angelina's.

Before I could call to the kitchen, Angelina raced towards me, waving her arms and spewing incoherent sentences in both our languages.

"Angelina, Angelina, calm down. I can't understand you. Calm down," I demanded.

Her eyes wild, she stopped and stood still. With trembling hands, she took hold of mine. "You have met our Lupita, si? She is angry with us. We did not call her for the sick children. She is disgraced in front of the village. This is bad. We are in big trouble. She has strong powers."

"I don't understand, Angelina. Explain to me what is going on. What have we done? Who is she? I could not understand her."

"She is our curanderas, our healer. She has el Don, the gift of healing. She has cured us from sickness with her herbs and her gift. She has delivered our children and protected them from the evil. When we die it is because God has taken over the power of our curanderas and he wants us back.

At some point in college, I remembered studying folk healing and I knew not to tell Angelina the foolishness of their beliefs. I decided it would be better to know more about this woman.

"Tell me more about Lupita, Angelina. I am interested to know about her."

She wiped her hands in her apron, yelled to Pedro to bring two beers and sat down at a table, still trembling.

"She is a woman not to be angered, Peter," she began. "Lupita and her ancestors have taken care of us for many generations. She is at the right hand of God, as was her mother and many generations before her. They all followed His commands.

When she was born, her mother saw in her tiny eyes that she would follow in her footsteps. She was the seventh born and the only child with the grace of God in her eyes. Her mother named her Guadalupe after the patroness saint, Our Lady of Guadalupe. If you know the history, Our Lady had the image of God in her eye and was also a healer.

Guadalupe or, Lupita as her mother nicknamed her, lives high on the mountain and keeps her gardens growing with seeds she received from her mother, which were, in turn, passed down from her Grand-mother and all the other healers before them. The trees are medicine trees, and only the healers have the power to make them grow.

Lupita gave birth to a child without the sanction of marriage. She angered her mother and believes she angered God. Lupita has kept her daughter sheltered on the mountain, fearful that the villagers would not accept her. Lupita knows she must soon introduce her to the village. She is our next curanderas.

There is still another reason she is afraid she has displeased our Lord. Many years ago, the fever came to this village and she was not here to save the children.

She had a sister in a village a long way from here and this sister sent word to Lupita that soon she would die. Lupita packed her mule and went on the long journey to see her sister, the last of her family still alive. Soon after Lupita left, the fever came. No one could get word to her. When she returned, many children lay dead, many parents, too. Lupita begged God for forgiveness, but she has never forgiven herself. She has never left the village again.

She has helped us with every sickness that has befallen us and she is angry that she was not called with this cholera. No one went to get her. By the time the word got to her high mountain, it was too late for her to help us. You had taken care of the sickness. It has taken her this long to come down to find you. She is disgraced and afraid she has angered God for the second time. She thinks He took her powers because she did not know her people were sick.

Lupita has many powers. She has threatened to curse you with mal puesto, evil spirits that will make you sick, maybe die. Enrique has followed her up the mountain to try to talk reason. We must wait. We must pray for her forgiveness."

"What can I do to fix this, Angelina?"

"Nothing, Senor Peter, nothing. She is angry with everyone and we can only wait to see if she will talk to Enrique. Enrique fixes everything in this village. Lupita knows he is a strong man and important to us. She thinks he has his own powers to take care of us. Many years, many conflicts. Many times they lock horns like two bucks in the forest and fight almost to the death. They are always jealous of each other, but neither one can do what the other can, so they always come to some agreement.

Maybe this time, Enrique can talk sense to her, or maybe she will curse all of us." Angelina crossed herself, touching her fingers to her forehead, her heart and both sides of her chest. She lowered her head in prayer.

I sat in amazement, at the intensity of her beliefs. I watched her pray and wondered if I had ever prayed. I was a man of science. I had never had time to explore a belief in God. I knew I believed, but had never paid much attention to it. I did know I didn't believe in folk healing. Powers? Nonsense. Curses? Nonsense. Was it uneducated, medieval ignorance? Absolutely. Medicine was black and white to me.

I touched Angelina's hand. "Everything will be alright. I will go and see her. I'll help Enrique to fix this. Don't worry, Angelina." I kissed her forehead and went to my room. I needed to make sense of this, if I could.

I fell into a restless sleep. A crooked finger kept wandering around my face in my dreams. I woke to Enrique standing over my bed.

"Senor Peter, wake up. We must go to the mountain. Lupita will talk to you."

"What happened, Enrique?"

"It took me many hours. We fought until the sun went down, and we are still fighting when the sun comes up. She is more stubborn than my Angelina. She is like an angry bull. Mean woman. She threw things at me. She hit me with her broom. She pushed me out door. She kicked my legs. Ugly woman.

But I won because I am also a stubborn man. I told her you have new herbs and medicine from America and if she is a stupid woman she will not learn. She hit me again with a stick. I told her she is not the only one with powers. You have powers, too. She spit at me. I asked her how she knows you are not sent from God. I asked her why she does not talk to you. I told her maybe she slaps God in the face by cursing you. She cried. I win. She wants to talk to you."

"What will I say to her, Enrique?"

"You will tell her you believe in her herbs and her powers. You will ask her questions about her many potions and bottles. You will look at her gardens and her trees. If she throws things, you will duck down, cover your face. She is a mean woman."

"Let's go, Enrique."

"Put on your coat, Senor Peter, it is cold on the mountain top."

We trudged our way up the mountain on the muddy dirt road, slipping on wet rocks and holding onto branches to steady ourselves. At points, the brush, cacti and trees grew across the road, making it almost impassable.

I almost laughed at the absurdity of my situation. Had anyone ever told me I would be climbing a mountain to go to see a folk healer to prevent a curse from being put on an entire village, I would have called them insane. My colleagues would certainly not believe this. I didn't think Sadie would believe it either.

I could no longer see the village. I had only looked at the height of these mountains from the beach. I never dreamt I would someday climb to the top. My legs cramped in pain, I feared my lungs might explode and my feet felt like lead weights hanging from my ankles. When I became so uncomfortable I thought I would rather die than make amends with Lupita, the road took a sharp turn to the right and leveled off. We were at the summit and I had lived.

A ramshackle house stood in front of us, huge trees surrounding it, touching the roof, as if they were one with it. The entire summit had been plowed and gardens grew everywhere. An old dog slept on the porch, next to a rocking chair. A giant cat hung from the seat of the chair, swatting at the dog.

Jugs and jars, bottles, wooden barrels and rusted shovels, rakes and, God only knew what else, where strewn all over the place. Old farm equipment littered the yard. Chickens wandered around, pecking at the dirt, avoiding the goats, chewing on rusted cans. A giant black crow cawed from a tree branch. A face stared at us from a curtain-less window.

The still air, stagnated by an old, stale and musty stench, lay on the scene like a blanket.

Like a ray of sunshine on the Summit of Death, a monument, to what I assumed to be Our Lady of Guadalupe, stood next to the porch.

A dome, adorned with fresh flowers, held a white granite statue of a woman, her delicate face tilted towards the sun. Her hands folded in prayer held a tiny rosary and a cloth, carved into folds, draped over her hair and down her shoulders caressing her body.

As I gazed at the statue, I felt she knew all the secrets of the world.

With reluctance to leave her knowing face, I followed Enrique up the stairs. They wobbled and groaned as we walked to the door. The chickens clucked. The goats rattled their cans. The door opened as we approached it. No one stood behind it.

My skin was cold. I couldn't feel my heart. My shirt and jacket were soaked with sweat and my pants were covered with mud. Scratches, from the trees on the road, covered my hands and face. Fear racked my body.

Lupita appeared in the doorway, an eerie light framing her from behind. My body jerked backwards and I almost fell down the steps. I caught myself on a rickety post sticking up from the porch floor and stepped on the dog's foot. He jumped up from his sleep and ran off howling. The cat screeched and ran off in pursuit of him.

Frenzied commotion took over the scene. The rocking chair thumped like a drum on the floorboards. The crow took off, cawing and beating his wings in hot pursuit of the highest place he could find. The goats raced to shelter. The clucking chickens, wings flapping, scrambled around the yard and ran into the gardens.

"You don't look like you have powers," she scowled, pointing her wicked finger at me for the second time.

Without her scarf, her hair stood out in crazy points. She still had the burlap bag slung over her breasts. Her feet were bare, the toenails twisted and yellow. Strange potent odors from the house assaulted my senses.

"You look like a dirty peasant. Get out." She slammed the door and closed the curtain.

"Lupita, open the door. Open the door, right now," Enrique demanded. "You promised to talk to Senor Peter. Open the door or I will kick it down."

She opened it and we stepped in. She moved backwards, behind the door. Not prepared for the sight, I gasped at the large room, illuminated only by candlelight. The walls were lined to the ceiling with shelves that were filled with hundreds and hundreds of cobweb-covered bottles in every size, shape and color imaginable.

Several tables stood around the room. A giant mortar and pestle sat on one of them, surrounded by various cutting tools, and jars of seeds, berries and other plant life. Every flat surface held dried bunches of flowers, herbs and piles of tree bark. In a corner to the right side of the room, a mattress covered with blankets lay on the floor. A mirror and washstand stood to its left. A small table, covered with dishes, bowls, utensils and old rags sat to the left of that. A zinc sink hung from the wall, a hand water pump perched on its side.

A clay stove, its chimney sticking into the ceiling, stood towards the front of the room, a pile of wood leaning against it.

The one exceptional thing in the room, an intricately designed, hand-carved cross, hung above a small statue like the one outside, complete with flowers at her feet.

I heard the rusted hinges on the door start to move and I

turned to see Lupita step from behind the door into the dimly lit room. It grew darker as the door swung shut.

Enrique glared at her, his shoulders squared and his jaw protruding. I stood silent, my forehead breaking out in sweat. I realized I was saying a prayer.

"You tell me what powers you have and then you get out," she said, looking me straight in the eye.

Enrique translated her words into English for me.

"I have no powers. I am a Doctor of medicine, but I would like to know more about your healing powers. I didn't know you when the cholera broke out or I would have called you for help. I worked so fast with the disease; no one had time to come to you. I am sorry. You know your people better than I do and I respect that. It is my fault you were not called. Please forgive me for insulting you, I meant no harm. I saw a problem and jumped in to solve it. Again, I am sorry." I prayed nothing was lost in Enrique's translation.

For a moment, the woman was silent. Enrique waited for her reaction. I held my breath and every tiny sound in the room reverberated like a thunderstorm in my ears.

Lupita glared at Enrique. He waited, with a defiant look on his face, not backing down.

She yelled. She screamed. Enrique did not change his expression and he didn't change the look on his face.

She grabbed for her broom, swinging it at Enrique.

He grabbed the broom mid-air and returned her anger, yelling at her and throwing the broom across the room.

"Let's go, Senor Peter," he demanded. He stomped towards the door and I followed, assuming I was cursed and would die on the way down the mountain.

We walked halfway home in silence. I kept watching the sky for thunderbolts and the ground for poisonous snakes. I half-expected fire-breathing demons to storm from the woods and devour me with long green tongues.

Enrique stopped and perched himself on a large rock. He removed his hat and wiped his brow with his sleeve.

"She likes you," he stated, frankly.

"What?" I yelled at him.

"She said she likes you, but you must not know. She said you show her proper respect for her great position in the eyes of her people. She said you must do something great to restore her from disgrace in front of her people.

She told me to keep yelling so you would think she would not forgive you. She wants you to save her face. She wants you to not be able to heal someone and call her to help. She will settle for nothing less. She has great interest in your medicine and wants to ask you to show her how doctors heal people without her herbs and spells. She threw the broom at me to scare you."

I started to laugh and Enrique joined me.

"She is the devil herself," I said. "It was all an act? I can't believe it."

"Lupita is a great healer, but she is still a woman. She is sly like a fox. She will not let a man win. She is curious like a puppy exploring its mama's teat. No woman is ever different. They are all just like my Angelina."

We enjoyed our walk home, discussing our plan.

24

As Amy entered the cab, Carlos stepped off the airplane in San Diego. He ran to the terminal and found a phone.

Francisco's dispatcher unwillingly patched him through to his cab. Why did he always have to threaten everybody?

"Francisco, I'm at the airport. Go and get Megan right away. Michael's put a hit on her and as close as I can tell, his men are only a few hours ahead of me. I think her friend Amy is in town looking for her, too. I'll fill you in later."

Francisco, terrified, his foot hitting the gas, said, "Do you remember where my Tia Juanita lives?"

"I think so."

"Tell the cabbie to take you to the old warehouse district, pick up Tenth Street and take it to 1142. I'm on my way."

Carlos gave his driver the instructions and sat back for the ride. He wondered what the hell he was doing in San Diego. He gazed out the window, puffing on his fiftieth cigarette and watched how the city had changed.

I vowed never to come back here, he thought, and here I am again. He knew the root of his motivation, knew it from the moment he went to the airport in New York. Amy had taken over any sense of reason he possessed. His mind reeled with the possibility of her getting hurt.

He knew Francisco could get Megan to safety. It would have only taken a phone call on his part and he could have been home, sitting in his room, reading his girlie magazines, drinking his brandy. But no, he had to be her hero. Carlos could feel her pulling his strings, and he found himself completely incapable of stopping her.

"Hurry up, cabbie. I haven't got all day while you pick your nose. I have important business to see to. Step on the damn gas pedal. You know, the one on the right. The cabbies in New York would eat this guy alive," he mumbled, lighting another cigarette.

This city had bad memories. He hated the memories.

He leaned over the front seat and yelled at the cabdriver, "Can't you go any faster? You drive like a damn woman. Stop this car and get out. Let me drive. I'll show you how we drive cabs in New York. I haven't got all friggin' day."

"We are almost there, Senor," the driver pleaded. "Calm down, Senor, the policia are very tough in this city. I will lose my license if I don't obey the law."

"You're going to lose more than your license if you don't get me where I'm going. I'm a New York City cop, a real cop, and I don't give a shit about your pansy policia in this town. Now step on the gas. A woman's life is at stake here."

•••••

While Carlos fought with his driver, Francisco raced his cab to the Hilton. To his surprise, as he pulled up in front of the hotel, Megan came running down the stairs and jumped into the car. He took off, swerving around the other cabs and entered the street, cutting off traffic to get in a lane.

Megan, hysteria contorting her face, didn't notice his passenger. "Someone ransacked my room," she cried. "All of my things are thrown all over. What is going on, Francisco? How did you know?"

Francisco started to tell her about Carlos, when a wild voice from the back of the cab yelled, "Megan, Oh my God, Megan."

Megan and Francisco turned around, reacting to the voice at the same time. Francisco avoided a collision with a car in the opposite lane. Tires screeched. Horns blew. In his haste, he had forgotten all about his passenger.

"Amy!" Megan yelled, almost jumping over the seat to embrace her friend. "What are you doing here? How do you know Francisco?"

Swerving away from another car, Francisco blurted out in disbelief, "This is Amy?"

"I can't believe I've found you, Amy cried. "Are you all right? How do you know my cabdriver?"

No one answered anyone's questions. They all talked at once.

"Wait, wait," Francisco said, trying to calm down and get some order. "Let's start at the beginning. I will talk first."

The women looked at him and stopped talking.

"Megan, I called my friend, Carlos, in New York. After you told me of Michael, I started to think there could be more to him than you know. I followed my instincts. Carlos is the only person I know with the connections to find out the information I needed. He has done a lot of leg-work on this and has kept in touch with me, updating me on everything he found out.

Today he called to tell me Michael has put out a hit on you and the two men he hired are in San Diego, along with some Federal agents, who also want to talk to you.

I don't have any more information, but we will soon have all the facts. We are on our way to Tia Juanita's."

Amy interrupted Francisco. "Carlos is an asshole, Megan. He wouldn't tell me where you were. He had forgotten that he told me Francisco lived in San Diego. He is a stupid man."

"Amy, Carlos is my friend. I asked him not to tell anyone Megan came here, for her own safety. We knew she was in trouble, but it took time to find out how much."

"I'm sorry, Francisco. I didn't mean to insult your friend." Amy peppered the apology with sarcasm.

The conversation started and stopped for Megan with the words "Michael put a hit on you." Why? What had she done? Fear, hatred and anger consumed her. Succumbing to the rage, she cried.

Amy and Francisco stopped bickering and looked at Megan.

"Oh Megan, please don't cry. Michael is the asshole." Amy leaned forward and hugged her friend's neck. "I'm so glad I found you. I've been so worried."

"Don't cry, Megan. You will understand all of this when we get to Tia Juanita's. We are meeting Carlos there. He is on his way as we speak. You will be safe there for now." Trying to console his friend, he reached across for her hand.

"Why did he come here? We don't need him," Amy argued.

The nasty, relentless woman in the back seat would not stop. He could do without her, Francisco thought.

Consumed with his anger at Michael, and fueled by his contempt for Amy, he lashed out at her.

"Why do you care? It is Megan that Carlos and I are worried about and we plan to protect her. I don't know why he came here, but if he thinks he's needed, then I think he's needed, period, end of subject. Carlos does not give of himself easily and this is not about you anyway."

He didn't like this woman. She wasn't sweet like Megan, but worst of all, she had insulted his friend.

Amy lashed back. "What do you mean why do I care? That would be none of your business. You just drove me across this town, at a hundred miles an hour, not even bothering to explain why, ignoring me when I questioned you, and now you want me to like your friend, Carlos? Who do you think you are? Are you crazy? Megan is my friend. I care about everything that concerns her and you and Carlos can go to hell."

Anger raging, Megan screamed at them. "Shut up. I almost killed myself over this asshole. What a fool I am. Take me to the police. I'll bury him if I have to lie."

As the car swung onto Tenth Street, Francisco saw Carlos's cab up the street. Thank God. Maybe he can explain this to these two women.

Carlos stepped out of his cab, handing the driver a fifty-dollar bill. "I'm sorry, buddy," he said. "Buy yourself dinner and a beer on me." Turning away from the car, he saw Francisco's cab coming up the street. He walked to the curb, checking everything around him.

Tia Juanita appeared on the front steps of the walk-up, just as Carlos got out of his cab. "Hola, Carlos, Hola, she called down to him, smiling, like a mother who had found her lost child. She ran down the steps and threw her arms around him. "I thought I would never see you again. Welcome home."

Francisco pulled up, seconds later, and she let go of Carlos and ran to him. "I never thought I would see you and Carlos together again. I am so happy. Where is Megan?"

As she spoke, she saw Megan get out of the car. Releasing Francisco, she ran to her. "Mi niña bonita, it is so good to see you again. She hugged her with all her might. "Mija, what is wrong? You are like a limp rag. Why are you crying?"

As Francisco's Aunt hustled Megan into her house, the two old friends turned to look at each other. This was a reunion neither of them had expected.

Francisco took Carlos into his arms. "It is so good to see you again, my friend. It has been many years. You look good. I try not to think about our old days, but I always think about you."

Carlos, not noticing Amy step out of the car, returned Francisco's hug. "I miss you most of all in the middle of the night when I sit in my chair and let my mind wander. I wonder how you are doing. It is good to see you, my friend. It takes me back many years." As he finished his sentence, he caught a glimpse of Amy coming towards them.

"Amy," he stammered, not believing his eyes. "How did you find Megan?"

"I told you I didn't need your help. Why are you here? We don't need you now either." She turned her nose up and her face away.

"You don't understand the grave danger your friend is in. I came to help because of Francisco. I also came to find you. You are a bull-headed woman. You are headstrong and will not listen to reason. I came to protect you from yourself."

She lifted herself up on her toes and slapped him. I don't need you to protect me. Now I understand why you are friends with Francisco. You are both arrogant, conceited fools. You are a perfect pair. I am going to get Megan and get us out of here. Neither one of us needs big shot men."

"We will protect Megan and you won't do any such thing. Don't ever hit me again, do you understand?"

"I won't have the opportunity, because as soon as I get Megan out of here, I'll never see you again. Maybe I'll slap you again, just for the sheer pleasure of it." She raised her hand and he caught it.

At that moment, Tia Juanita appeared on the porch, in her apron, waving a dishtowel. "Come to dinner, mi amigos, it is on the table."

The three of them glared at each other. Carlos released Amy's hand.

"For Megan's sake, let's put this aside and try to help her. She needs us," Francisco pleaded.

They turned and walked up the stairs, not speaking.

After she introduced herself to Amy and kissed Carlos one more time, Tia Juanita took Francisco by the hand and led him into another room. "We will return en un momento," she told her guests.

"Francisco, Megan is in the bathroom. She will not come out. You must tell me what is wrong. She will not speak."

"I will, Tia Juanita, I will, but not yet. I will send Amy to her. She will listen to her friend. They are stubborn women. Right now, I think they need each other."

As they spoke in the hallway, Carlos and Amy sat in silence, not talking to each other. Carlos reached across the table and covered Amy's hand with his. She is so pretty, he thought. She didn't remove her hand, which gave him courage to speak.

"Amy, I didn't come here to help Francisco. I came here to find you. I can't get you out of my head and when I realized you would be in danger here, I caught the first flight out of New York. I have never been in love and I don't know what it feels like, but if this is it, I like it. I know this is fast, but when something feels right, it is right. Do you think you could forgive me"?

He hesitated, searching her eyes for any sign that she planned to slap him again. "Please don't laugh, Amy. I am not used to any of this. I just know that since I met you, I cannot get my head together. I know I am not much to look at and I am not friendly and, oh yeah, I don't like people or phones, but maybe we could have something together. Would you give me a chance?"

Amy stared at him, caught completely off-guard. No one had ever said anything that sweet to her in her whole life.

He took her hesitation as rejection.

"Okay, just forget it. I shouldn't have said anything. I embarrassed you. You're right. I'm a conceited, arrogant fool to think a woman like you could want me. Let's just forget it and not fight any more". He removed his hand, his face red; sweat beading up on his forehead. The tiny muscles in his jaw twitched.

Amy reached across the table and touched the twitching muscles with her fingertips.

"Let me tell you this, Carlos. I don't really think you are an arrogant, conceited fool. I am frightened and angry. I have been sick over Megan and terrified of the men following me. I am tired of the dead ends I've been running into. You were just one more. I had to do something. I had to find Megan, so I went with the only clue I had.

You're right. I probably am a danger to myself. I don't think things through enough, but I will tell you what I have thought through. I can't get you out of my head either. I've wondered about us, too".

"Oh, Amy," Carlos muttered, as they leaned across the table for their first real kiss.

Francisco and Tia Juanita chose that moment to walk into the room.

Francisco coughed. Tia Juanita stood silent, not sure about this new twist.

"Amy, I am sorry to interrupt, as confused as I am, but Megan is in the bathroom and she won't come out. Would you go and talk to her? I think she needs you."

"Oh my God, how could we forget Megan?" She jumped up and ran to the bathroom.

Francisco stared at his friend. Tia Juanita stared, too.

"We were just talking", Carlos said, clearing his throat.

"I will get dinner. You two talk," Tia Juanita declared and left the room.

"Francisco, I'm not a man to fall in love. As a matter of fact, I haven't ever been in love. I like one-night stands. I'm good at them. Amy makes me feel something I don't recognize. It scares me."

"When did this happen, my friend," Francisco asked, as he sat down. By the way, that silly grin is uncharacteristic of you".

"The first time I saw her. I called her during my investigation to find out what she knew. You gave me her number. When I met her at the restaurant, her eyes burned themselves into my brain and I haven't been able to think of anyone else. I didn't know she felt the same way until just now."

"You are somewhat older than she is and she has a fiery temper."

"I don't think she cares, and in fact she may need a spirited temper to put up with me."

Francisco frowned. "If you can forget your love life for a minute, I want to talk about Megan."

"You know, Francisco, in all the confusion, I don't think you introduced us."

"No, I guess I didn't. She went from the car to Tia Juanita's arms and I haven't seen her since."

With an air of authority, Carlos declared, "I think we should take Megan to Puerto San Luis. We can keep her safe there and the authorities should be able to take care of this side of it."

"I agree, but tell me this. The men were in her room. They ransacked it and scared her to death. Tell me why Michael is so afraid of her," Francisco asked.

"He is suspected in the murder of another broker and they know he met with the hit men in her house. She is the only one who can identify them.

Along with that, the Feds suspect there had to be a lot of pillow talk. There always is with a lover. They also think she could be hiding money for him. Michael has to be afraid Megan will be able to put him in jail. They are all looking for her. It appears obvious that Michael's men found her first."

Francisco took a minute to contemplate this information. "Do you think she is involved in any of this, Carlos?"

"No, but what I think doesn't matter. Everyone else involved in this does. We have to get her out of here until we figure out what to do, or at least before the Feds make their case some other way.

They already have what they need for embezzlement charges, but the Feds want him on the murder. He has nothing to lose and he's running scared. Nobody has been able to find him.

His money is secured in a bank in the Caymans, so that's not a consideration. He will do what he has to do to save himself."

"I can't identify them. I was in my room doing research on an art purchase when they were there."

Francisco and Carlos jumped at the sound of Megan's voice. Both women were standing in the room. They had heard the whole conversation. Tia Juanita appeared from behind the kitchen door and they knew she had also been listening.

Carlos spoke first. "That's not important right now, Megan.

Our most serious concern is getting you out of San Diego. Michael's men are already here. They are the ones that ransacked your room. The Feds wouldn't be bothered with that. I don't know how they missed you."

"Yesterday, I took a train ride up the coast. This morning, I went to breakfast. When I returned, my room had been ransacked.

How did they find me?"

"The only way they could track you is if you used a credit card. Did you?

"I had to make the train reservation on my card."

"Then the Feds know where you are, too." Carlos sighed and leaned back in his chair.

Francisco sat with his hands folded on the table, chewing on his bottom lip. Quiet engulfed the room. The women stood in silence, lost in their own thoughts and Tia Juanita watched the two men, sure they would make the right decision.

Francisco looked at Carlos. "I think Puerto San Luis is the only answer, my friend."

"And where would that be?" Amy asked.

"Carlos and I were born in a small village on the Baja of Mexico. We haven't been there in many, many years, so it would be good to go back. We have friends there and we will be safe. I will need to call my son."

Megan asked, "How will we get there?"

"We will drive. I have been told the road is better now. I have a van in my garage. We will all fit."

"I am going," said Tia Juanita. "I do not want to stay here and be afraid I will be asked questions. If these people are following you, you have led them to my front door. I will not be safe here, and, I, too, would like to see our village again."

Francisco took charge. "It is settled, then. Carlos, you and I will go to Megan's room and get her things. Amy's are in my trunk. Tia Juanita, go pack. We'll be back in an hour. Don't open the doors or answer the phone. Keep the lights out and the curtains drawn. Don't leave this house. Do you understand?"

The women nodded.

"Let's go, Carlos."

"Wait, Francisco," Megan said. "We will need money. I have to go to the bank."

"We will take care of that when we get back, Megan, once we know we are safe."

Twenty minutes later, the two men walked into the hotel lobby. Carlos spotted them right away. They sat in chairs, near the elevators, reading newspapers. Carlos and Francisco walked by them, sporting a casual air and talking in Spanish. They got on the elevator and the men did not move.

Fifteen minutes later, Francisco and Carlos waited as the elevator doors opened. They walked past the men carrying Megan's suitcases. They were clear.

Carlos stopped walking. "Wait a minute, Francisco."

He turned and walked over to the men.

"Excuse me, Sir. Do you have a light?"

One of the men reached into his breast pocket and handed Carlos a pack of matches. Carlos placed Megan's suitcase next to the man's foot, lit his cigarette, inhaled deeply and released the smoke from his mouth in a long, slow plume. It swirled around the man's head.

"Thank you, Sir." He handed back the matches and picked up the suitcase.

"You're welcome."

Both men watched them as they walked out of the hotel. Carlos knew they would.

Once outside in the safety of his cab, Francisco looked at his friend. With a grin, he said, "So, in all these years, you haven't changed one bit."

"No, I haven't," Carlos said, enjoying his own arrogance.

25

Leaving before the sun rose, like thieves in the night, their car crossed the border and entered México.

Carlos and Francisco saw the black car at the same time. A sidelong glance between the two men confirmed each other's fears.

Megan sat in silence, staring out the window. She had made two phone calls before they left, making sure no one could hear her conversation. At her request, the group stopped at a bank. She insisted on going in alone.

"We are being followed," Carlos said, his words shattering the silence in the car.

Francisco watched the car. The driver stayed several cars behind them, but he could see him in his rear view mirror and he knew it was the same guy from the hotel. They hadn't been so smart, it turned out. These guys must have caught on and followed them.

Megan spoke for the first time since getting into the car. "I've put all of you in danger. Francisco, turn this car around and take us back to San Diego. This is not your problem and I won't put your lives in danger. I don't understand what I did or why Michael wants to hurt me, but I will find out and stop this craziness."

Francisco glared at her. "I'm sorry, Megan. I won't turn this car around. If anybody wants out, I'll stop and they can get a bus back, but you are staying with me and I am taking you to safety. Does anyone want to go back?"

Amy said, "I'm staying. I didn't come this far to lose you now, Megan."

Carlos glanced at Amy. "No way am I leaving. How many men get to defend three gorgeous women at the same time?"

Tia Juanita laughed out loud. "Yesterday, I was a bored, old woman making soup out of bones. Today I am an adventurous woman running from two New York hit men and wanted by the FBI. I have never even seen New York. I never want to see soup bones again. Drive faster, Francisco. Let's outrun the banditos."

Megan ignored them and continued her plea. "Neither one

of you can protect us from them. They are probably armed and we are defenseless. Please go back. What is wrong with all of you? I didn't do anything to Michael. I don't know anything. I'll go to the police. This has gotten out of control." Anger burned in her eyes.

Carlos turned to face Megan, his black eyes piercing her own. With a frightening chill in is voice and an attempt to control his temper, he explained Megan's situation to her.

"Don't you understand, Megan? These men are cold-blooded killers. They work for money and have no personal attachment. If Michael wants you dead and has enough money, these men will see to it that you are. They will walk away and not look back.

And one more thing, Megan, I will stake my life on the undisputable fact that I can protect us."

Amy put her arms around Megan. "We're in this together, Megan, no matter what happens. I will die protecting you."

"Count me in on that," Francisco added.

Carlos nodded in agreement.

"We should name our gang," Tia Juanita suggested.

The mood lightened and Megan managed a smile.

Francisco noticed the car had moved up one car length.

"I want to stop for a margarita," Carlos announced.

"Are you crazy?" Francisco said, staring at him in disbelief.

"Drive to Avenue de Revolucion and stop. I want a drink and I want to make a call," Carlos demanded.

Hoping his crazy friend knew what he was doing, Francisco followed his orders. When he turned, the black car turned.

Driving up the Avenue, Carlos pointed to a parking spot. "Stop here."

As Francisco parked the van on the busy street, Carlos instructed everyone to walk into the bar and not look around.

"I don't want them to think we've seen them. Sit down and act casual. They won't do anything here. Tijuana is too full of people to make a move. Francisco, sit facing the door."

Once they were seated and the frosted drinks were on the table, Carlos left to make his call.

Megan ignored her drink and began to talk.

"I think that as long as we seem to all be in this together, I should clarify some things for you.

I don't remember what those men looked like. I thought they were just business associates of Michael's and I didn't pay any attention to them.

Michael and I didn't share any pillow talk that would help convict anybody.

I don't know about any murder and I would never have thought Michael was capable of such a plot. Of course, I've been wrong before.

My money is mine. My mother and father left it to me and every dime of it sits in investments and banks.

I never dreamt Michael was a con artist or a thief. I, myself, willingly gave him money because he told me he would have to declare bankruptcy. I had to beg him to take it.

I contacted my clients and gave him their information, thinking he ran a legitimate business. I had no reason not to believe in him.

This whole situation is ridiculous and I want to call the FBI and tell them so. I don't have any trouble telling these other two idiots the same thing. I'll call Michael if I have to."

"You won't do any such thing, Megan. From now on, you'll do as we tell you to do. This is a dangerous situation. We will handle it and when it's over, you can tell the FBI anything you want to. They are the least of our worries and I don't think they would follow us into Mexico. The men behind us are cold-blooded killers and Carlos is the only one here with experience, so we will listen to him."

The tone in Francisco's voice sent chills down Megan's spine. She had never known him to be so stern and it scared her. The other two women just stared at him and downed their second margaritas, at the same time.

Carlos's approach to the table stopped any further conversation. "We are going to sit here and drink and talk for another fifteen minutes and then we are going to walk to our van like nothing is going on and get back on the road. Now, talk about something."

Tia Juanita broke the silence. "So do you want to name our gang?" How about the Misfits? I saw a movie with that name once."

To an ordinary eye, they just looked like a bunch of friends out for the day.

Carlos checked his watch. "It's time."

The black car sat two cars behind them and as they pulled out, it pulled out. About five minutes later, red lights flashed behind their follower and the two gangsters had no choice but to pull over.

"Step on it, Francisco."

"What just happened, Carlos?" Francisco asked, accelerating the van.

"I had a buddy on the force in New York. His only dream was to return to Tijuana and he said if I ever came to town, to give him a call, so I did.

He's going to delay them awhile to give us time to get out of here. With any luck, they'll give him a hard time and they'll spend the night in jail. No rules down here. Sometimes a simple 'hello' pisses them off.

Nothing I know of compares to a Mexican jail. The law down here treats you to a nice dirt floor and cold slop for dinner. Mouthing off earns you a couple of punches to your gut. A day can turn into a year just because they don't like the look on your face. If you ask me, it's one mighty fine system."

He turned and smiled at Amy, enjoying a chance to show off his connections.

"We should buy a gun," Tia Juanita offered. "The Misfits should have a gun."

Francisco decided Tia Juanita's margaritas would have to be monitored. They all agreed it would be some ride for the Misfits, if she had anything to say.

Carlos fingered the holster under his jacket, smiling to himself.

26

Monsoon season moved in quietly behind the summer season and the weather turned cooler.

Occasional, violent rainsqualls quelled the constant dust in the small port.

The sea swelled up without any warning and harsh waves beat the small beach to a pulp. Within the blink of an eye it receded to a flat gray sea, shining like a brilliant mirror in the sun.

The mingled smells of summer; hot dry air, the scent of cactus flowers, freshly caught fish and playful wet pups, changed to that of sea spray, clean ocean breeze and wet earth.

During the day the sky shone a crisp blue, dotted by fleeting white clouds. At night, winter constellations glistened in the crisp, cool night air, creating a brilliant blanket over the village.

In my mind, a more peaceful place never existed.

I no longer thought about the day I would leave Puerto San Luis. I anticipated and welcomed each new day. I looked forward to my day's work.

I woke up every morning, my nostrils alive with the smell of bacon frying and Angelina's voice filling the air with sweet songs. She sang with the softness of a mother to a child, but in the quietness of this little village, her songs drifted through the rafters like feathers on the lightest breeze.

After breakfast, it had become my habit to wander down to the end of the village, visiting with my friends along the way. At the end of the road, I always enjoyed stopping to look at the old barn before going in. It looked more like a hospital every day.

After Frank left, I spent days drawing pictures of hospital rooms on scraps of paper, making lists of things I'd need and wandering around the barn, measuring and marking off planned walls in the dirt floor. Enrique, my constant companion, hailed my ideas or explained why he thought I was crazy.

"Senor Peter, do you know how much money this will cost? You are a loco man. Puerto San Luis has no money. We have fish. We have beer. We have sunshine. We have no money."

"Don't worry, mi amigo. We have money now."

"Senor Peter, you are a loco man. You can't spend your money on a hospital for us. We can never pay you back. We don't know how to run a hospital. Lupita will put a curse on it anyway."

"Enrique, you have already paid me back. You and your friends have given me my life back. I will run this hospital. And, as for Lupita, I am going to make her the Chief Consultant for the hospital and build her an office, with shelves for all of her herbs and medicines, right over here." I pointed to the far corner of the barn. "I'll build her a window, on that wall over there, so she can see her mountain. She'll be happy."

Every day, one way or another, we had this conversation.

The sounds of hammers pounding nails and handsaws chewing through old beams became familiar sounds in the barn.

Every man and boy insisted on participating in the building of the hospital. They woke at sunrise and hurried to the barn, working until the last ray of light slipped into the sea.

The older, more experienced men assumed leadership and teaching roles with unspoken words. The younger workers treated them with the utmost respect, a quality instilled in them from birth.

Some men whistled, some sang. All admired each other's work and shook hands with pride at the completion of a project.

I took joy in rolling up my sleeves and learning the intricacies of a hammer and saw. My fishing calluses grew rounder and deeper. I learned to whistle. My pride swelled.

Every so often, Frank paid a visit, his plane laden with supplies for the hospital. He brought bags of cookies for the children, bolts of fabric for the women and plenty of beer for the men. Everyone in town hurried to help drag the plane onshore.

He had established a little ritual, which seemed to amuse him to no end. He'd wait for the children and the men to empty the plane and then, pretending to be a confused and befuddled, he'd climb into the plane, scramble around, making lots of noise, and then return with a great look of sadness on his face, empty handed.

"I'm sorry, my good friends, I must have forgotten the cookies and beer." After moans of disappointment from the children, he'd scratch his head and say, "Well, let me look in one more place" and hop back into the plane, only to return with his gifts.

As everyone caught onto his little game, the moans became louder and louder with each visit. The louder the moans became, the more Frank beamed. He reveled in his newfound fame.

On this morning, I awoke to silence, the air devoid of aroma. No smells of bacon and eggs permeated my nose. No sweet songs filled the air. I could not find Angelina. The streets were empty and there were no men in the barn.

As I pondered the possible reasons, an excited Enrique came running into the barn. "Senor Peter, come with me. You must leave your hospital today. We have something to show you. Come now. We are going to take you on an adventure."

If my stay here had taught me anything, it would be to do as Enrique said. He never had any intention of letting me say no.

I followed Enrique down to the beach, only to see every man, woman and child jumping into their pangas and heading out to sea. Their excited chattering filled the air with contagious anticipation.

•••••

Enrique and his friends had invited me to help build one of these boats and I, in the process, realized I had no idea how my own boat had been built and had never cared. I had taken it for granted, as I had everything else.

These men held great pride and satisfaction in their pangas. Every man had built himself one, at some point in his lifetime. They were considered a rite of passage, from boyhood to manhood.

The long, strong wooden boats handled every chore necessary for these born and bred fisherman.

Scouts took their pangas out to check the sky for storms and squalls and look for signs of running fish. The boats taxied the men out to their fishing boats and hauled their catch to shore. When the fish weren't running, the men raced the pangas around the bay, while the women cheered their men on from the shore.

The elders guided the young man's hands on every new boat. The process started by searching high on the mountain for the perfect tree and then, cutting long narrow slats of wood from its sweet part, the wood closet to the core. With the hands of artists, they water-cured the wood, bent it to precision angles and cut it to form the ribs of the boat. Carefully constructed, with hand-hewn wooden dowels, made from the flesh of young saplings, the skeleton of the boat took shape. More slats were cut and cured to cover the ribs. Three wooden planks were positioned across the width of the hull, creating evenly spaced seats and providing proper weight distribution of cargo for speed across the water.

Handled with long, strong oars, the boats glide through ocean waves and cross strong currents with ease.

A man's pride in his panga passes from generation to generation. A young man's status in town grows with his ability to maneuver his boat in high seas. A young girl's attention is his prize.

•••••

"Hurry, Senor Peter, hurry. It is the Day of the Whale."

I thought I had heard every possible legend over beers at Angelina's. This was a new one, but I had caught the infectious anticipation in the air and ran headstrong into the cold water, jumping into Enrique's panga, without a question.

As he rowed hard over the breakers, the salt-water spray soaking us and cutting a bone-chilling wetness into my soul, I wondered about my sanity and then, realized I no longer cared.

Enrique didn't speak until we were out of the harbor.

Laughing, he asked, "Did I tell you about the whales, mi Amigo?" I assumed he was laughing at the pitiful sight of me.

"No, Enrique, although, it might have been a good idea."

He rowed his boat with ease, the strong water pushing us along at a rapid clip.

Enrique began to speak, his voice low and reverent.

"Many generations ago, a mucho terrible storm came in from the sea, sending grand waves crashing on the village and crushing it to splinters.

Terrified screaming people tried to run to safety. They had nowhere to go. Many people died. Many people wish they had died. The storm destroyed everything, the houses, the gardens and the animals. It contaminated all of the food and water.

It rained for days. Mud slid down from the mountain and covered the ruins. The ones that survived lived in the mud, starving.

Rainwater kept them from dying of thirst. They ate mud-soaked plants and dead animal carcasses. They found no fish in the sea. The storm had washed them out to deeper water.

The villagers fell to their knees and prayed to God to help them.

After the rain stopped, the people did not know what to do. They tried to gather things to rebuild their village, but they were starving and weak. They tried to fish, but there were no fish. They prayed harder.

Many days and weeks went by. One man went down to the beach, early in the morning. He saw, with his weak eyes, a whale in the sand. The night had brought it. He ran up to the huge animal and looked in its eye and found the image of God staring back at him. As the man stared at the whale's eye, the big fish closed it and died. He knew he witnessed a miracle. No whale had ever been in the waters of Puerto San Luis. The man knew God sent the whale to save the people.

The villagers ran to the beach. They knew God had answered their prayers. They cut the whale up and ate the flesh. They dried the blood and boiled the bones to make soup. They used the whales heart and organs to make stew. They dried the skin to make blankets and shelter. They used the oil from its blubber to light their lamps. Lupita's ancestor took some bones and ground them to a fine powder to put in her medicine. They survived. They rebuilt the village.

Every year since that time, whales swim by our village to have their babies in the cove below us. They dance in the water and raise their mighty tails in the air to let the people know they are here. Men in the village watch the whales, from their pangas, to see when the first baby is born. The whales know we come. They wait for us.

You, mi amigo, will see the ceremony today. You are the first American ever to be here, Senor Peter. We are honored."

Resting his oar in its lock, Enrique lowered his head and tipped his hat to me.

I sat, wet to the bone, the wind whipping at me in ferocious gusts and did not feel the slightest sensation of cold. Only awe gripped my consciousness. No words in the English language could

197

describe my admiration for these people.

"We are here, Senor Peter," Enrique said, in a hushed voice.

I turned to see a serene cove, surrounded by mountain. The pangas were positioned in a large circle, in the middle of the cove, their bows and sterns touching to keep the circle complete. Enrique artfully took his place in the circle.

I sat in amazement. At first, not a sound could be heard from the people. As if by magic, by some unspoken signal, a quiet, steady hum arose from the circle, growing louder with every passing minute.

The circle of boats sat on a still sea, the water glittering blue, its color matching the cloudless sky that met it at the horizon.

From a boat, somewhere on the other side of the circle, a voice rose, a melodic, high-pitched voice that sounded like a prayer being chanted. I could not understand the words, but they were God-like.

A woman, dressed in long, flowing white robes, stood and raised her arms to the sky. The sun, appearing as though it had burned a hole in the otherwise solid blue sky, shone down on her like a spotlight.

I realized it was Lupita.

As she chanted, I looked around. Not a person moved. Not a boat moved. The humming increased in volume and the chanting grew mystical.

Lupita seemed to be in a trance. The people stared at the center of the circle. Nothing I had learned in college, or in life, had prepared me for what happened next.

In a split second, the ocean opened up in the center of the circle and a giant whale sprang into the air, like an atom bomb exploding under water. Rivers of water, illuminated from the sun, fell from her body back to the surface of the sea. Her huge body gleamed, almost blinding the naked eye. Her tail flipped up, as her nose dove back into the water.

Simultaneously, her calf catapulted from the water, as if on cue, flipping its tiny tail, in conjunction with its mother's. They both seemed to glance at their audience, mid-air and then dove deep into the sea.

The baby whale had been introduced to his adoring fans.

The water calmed as if it had never been disturbed. The people broke into screams of joy.

The ceremony had ended.

The circle of pangas broke rank and the villagers rowed toward the open sea, heading home, their mission complete. Their respect and honor to the whale had been duly paid for another year. Their thankfulness to God had, once again, been given and hopefully, received.

The ensuing celebration would last long into the night.

I watched them celebrate, pondering with admiration, their intense traditions, their pride, their love of their village and each other. I wished they would help me build a panga, and I knew, with the gratefulness of a man having been reborn, that I only needed to ask.

27

As the blood left his face and his knees went weak, Michael's throat made a guttural sound that mimicked a death rattle. His arms instinctively tore the payphone from the wall, and, with the strength of a wild boar stuck with a hot spear, he threw the phone down the stairs. It flailed wildly, hitting the steps, bouncing, echoing through the stairway, crashing at the bottom, and sending pieces flying out the front door of the ramshackle building.

Back in his room, blinded with a hot white rage, Michael broke up every piece of filthy furniture in his room. He heaved it through the dirty window, crashing it on the city below him. Driving his fists into the walls, blood splattered on the ugly gray paint. Kicking the bathroom door into splinters, he ran cold water on his hands, caught a glimpse of himself in the mirror and punched it, shattering the mirror into shards of splintered glass. Looking at his bleeding hands, he knew he had reached his end.

The call had come from the two idiots he had hired to find and kill Megan. Not once, but twice, working on the last dime he could muster, they lost track of the little bitch and she got away. Now they were stranded someplace in Mexico and wanted more money to finish the job. He'd find and kill the two bastards with his bare hands.

For what seemed like a lifetime, he had lived in this hellhole, fighting off roaches and roaming the city only at night so he wouldn't be found.

He ate cold cans of beans and sometimes slept with one of the hallway drug addicts to appease his animal lust. He couldn't go any lower.

His life, his son, all his available money and most of all, every tiny sliver of dignity he had were gone. For all he knew, he could be dying of some horrible sex disease. The thought of prison caused him uncontrollable vomiting.

In all his misery, he heard pounding, hard persistent pounding, on the door.

The door burst open and the slumlord barged in, glaring at him.

He grabbed the one possession he had left, punched the fat, old man in the face, sending him sprawling to the floor and walked from the room.

His hands bleeding, his clothes filthy, he raised his head high and walked out of the flophouse, gingerly avoiding the ruins of his rage scattered on the street. He hurried along, his head down, cupping his prize, solid gold watch in his pocket.

Four blocks down, he walked into a pawnshop and left, a few minutes later, with twenty thousand dollars in his pocket. His gold watch, with its exacting Swiss movement, sat in a dusty showcase.

Walking another two blocks, he entered a sunless, dark alley and halfway up, pounded on a warehouse door. One hour later, he walked out with eighteen thousand dollars in his pocket and a brand-new Passport, in the name of James Shockley. Michael had picked the name himself.

After a brief stop to buy some clean clothes and a suitcase, he walked towards the tunnel that would take him out of the city. He walked past Megan's apartment, her art gallery and his old offices. He walked out of his past, looking for his future.

He found it, as he thumbed a ride, from an old guy in a truck who picked him up.

"Where you headed, buddy?"

"Florida," Michael mumbled.

"I'm only going as far as Jersey, but I can drop you off somewhere along the way."

"Good enough."

"Some bandages in the glove box for your hands, if you want 'em.

"Thanks." He did.

The rest of the ride, neither man spoke a word.

The pick-up stopped at a shabby diner about two hours later.

The old man spoke. "End of the line, buddy, but if you wait here awhile, a guy named Jerry will pass by. He's got a big, long, red beard and an ugly scar over his left eye. Got it from some broad he wanted to nail. She hit him with her spiked heel. Laid him open like a gutted fish and once she had control, she screwed 'im. He's a trucker and picks up oranges in Florida. Mention my name and he'll likely give you a ride. Be glad for the company, he will."

Michael handed him a fifty dollar bill and growled, "Thanks for your time and trouble, Mister. Now forget you ever saw me."

"No problem, buddy. I ain't ever laid eyes on the likes of ya." The old man sauntered into the diner, shoving the bill into his back pocket, never looking back.

Two hours later and a promise of five hundred bucks, Michael sat in the cab of a beat up tractor-trailer, looking at Jerry's scar. "How'd you get that scar on your face?"

"Well, I tell my buddies some ugly broad laid me open with the heel of her shoe because I wanted to bang her, but the truth is, I cut myself shaving.

Now, if you want to stay in this truck, shut the hell up and don't ask anymore stupid questions. I ain't gonna tell you nothing about myself and I don't wanna know nothing about you either, so shut your trap."

The accommodations suited him and he fell asleep.

He woke up, sunshine beating in his face, every muscle in his body screaming pain and glanced at his wrist to check the time. All he saw were black hairs and no watch. It took a minute of panic to come completely awake. Consciousness exploded in his head.

He realized the truck had stopped and mumbled, "Where are we?"

"Gotta piss," the driver said, as he opened the door and got out.

They were in a parking lot, in front of a dumpy restaurant. He got a cup of coffee and pissed into a dirty toilet and crawled back into the truck.

The incessant whining of the truck's tires wore ridges in Michael's brain for two grueling days.

During the heat of the day, the cab of the truck burned like a furnace. At night, the air turned to a chilling cold.

The chain-smoking, foul smelling driver insisted on the windows rolled down, so his day-time, sweat soaked clothes laid on his skin like ice-cold cloths at night. Michael found himself cursing his mother for giving birth to him.

Out of nowhere, a sign appeared declaring, "Welcome to the Sunshine State."

Hundreds of miles of trees, swamps and orange groves later,

the truck labored into a mile long, dirt driveway and stopped in front of a small metal building.

Jerry pulled up the big hand brake and said, "Well, here we are Mister, good old Florida. Give me my money and get out."

"You could have dropped me up on the road, you asshole," Michael said, as he counted out the bills.

"I guess so. Too bad. Probably should of thought of it." He snickered and walked up to the building.

Michael headed back up the road and put his thumb out when he reached the highway. The heat enveloped him like a heavy winter parka. His shoes filled with sweat.

His mind traveled back to his limousine and his driver, Louis. He pictured the restaurants he had frequented, the waiters catering to his every need and serving him the world's finest foods. He thought about the extravagantly expensive wines he drank. He pictured the diamond necklaces he gave to the ladies he entertained. He thought about the stupid women he had cheated out of their money. He thought about the bank in the Caymans.

He walked up the highway for miles, dripping sweat, swatting huge black flies and cursing Megan, the two idiots in Mexico waiting for his call, the SEC and once again, his mother and father for giving birth to him.

The suitcase pulled at his arm, the sun blinded him and the sparse traffic passed him by. He didn't even know the time of day. Soon, someone will pay for this, he thought.

He remained sane by picturing the fate, at his hands, of everyone he hated. He put them in order; first, the two idiots that had lost Megan, next, that little twit, Amy and finally, the piece de resistance, Megan. Being the only one that could send him to jail, the pleasure would be all his. He regretted not handling it himself from the beginning.

Three bummed rides later, he found himself standing at the mouth of the Miami River. He figured about four or five days had passed. No one had followed him. Chances were good no one even missed him.

He breathed deeply, enjoying a sense of freedom. Now, if he could hitch a ride on a boat, in a couple more days, his money would be his again.

He had made it back and his hope renewed. He raised his head up high and walked up the banks of the river, looking for a ride to the Caymans, but first he needed a beer, a long, cold beer.

In his wildest dreams, Michael never could have imagined the adventure that lay before him. His life so far had been pampered, self-centered and one of complete self-absorption. If he thought his life had turned upside down, up to this point, he would soon find out how wrong a man could be.

As he walked the dock along the narrow, deep river in search of his beer, he felt as though he had arrived in a different century. On either side of the river, old warehouse buildings spoke of years past. Ancient, rusted Bahamian ships, destined for some faraway island in the Caribbean, seemed to squeak and whine to each other about their impending heavy journeys.

Baking under the tropical sun, sweat-soaked black men, muscles bulging from their bare chests and arms, formed human chains from the loading docks to the ships. They worked rhythmically while chanting their native island songs, passing heavy wooden crates from one man to the next and stacking them high on the worn teak decks or sending them deep into the bowels of the ships holding areas.

The river itself cut the city in half and meandered down to the ocean to spill its warm waters from its mouth and integrate the city with the sea.

The air, thick with salt and the smell of fish and sweat, sickened Michael. The choking humidity filled his lungs.

He stopped in front of a man barking orders at the black men.

"Excuse me," Michael said.

Without looking up, the man spit words into the air. "If you're from Customs, we ain't breaking any laws, and if you're not, move on. You're in our way."

"Look, Mister, I'm not from Customs. Do I look like I'm from friggin' Customs? I just want to know where I can get a beer."

The man looked at him and his face relaxed. He spit his wad of tobacco at Michael's foot. "Up river, a ways. Joe's. You can't miss it."

"Thanks. Any jobs around here? I need to work my way over to the Caymans."

"Caymans, huh?" he spat again.

Michael's stomach rolled. "Yeah."

"What can you do? Under that hair, you look like a pretty boy."

Michael reached up and ran his fingers through his hair and moved them down through the beard he hadn't realized he'd grown. He glanced down at his clothes, not surprised at how crummy he looked. He didn't feel like a pretty boy, but it pleased him that this guy saw through the filth.

"I can do anything it takes to hitch a ride and I ain't no pretty boy." He flexed his muscles a couple of times and tightened his face a little.

"Go past Joe's to a tramp steamer named Crystal Lee and see Captain Phil Smith. He's always looking for somebody to call First Mate." He chuckled, and resumed barking orders to the workers.

Knocking back two cold beers, Michael took a look around the bar. The place looked like it had seen years of sweaty, rough-hewn men. The floor, covered with dirty sawdust and littered with cigarette butts, hadn't been swept in years. Men, whose appearance mirrored his own, sat in small groups talking amongst themselves. The air smelled of boiled crabs and stale smoke. Michael's stomach turned. He got up and went in search of the Captain, not sure what his future held, but willing to do anything to end this nightmare.

It wasn't hard to find the Crystal Lee. As bad as the other boats were, it stood out like a sore thumb. It looked like a rusted, old garbage scow with way too many years of neglect. Michael wasn't even sure of its seaworthiness.

Captain Smith stood on the dilapidated dock, glaring at the men working for him. He was old, maybe as old as the boat.

A long, white, mangled beard, stained with nicotine, hung from his face and a navy blue flannel hat, worn-out from years of salt and seawater, sat on the top of bushy, white hair.

He stood, long and lean, in a thread-bare, cable knit sweater and wore a pair of jeans that should have been retired ten years ago.

His face, etched with deep lines and folds, proclaimed his many years in the sun and wind. Michael wasn't sure he looked seaworthy either.

"Captain Smith?"

"Who's askin?" the Captain snarled, without an iota of friendliness.

"I'm looking to work my way over to the Caymans. A guy down the way said you might be hiring on help."

The Captain looked him up and down. "Under the filth you're wearing, you look like a Customs asshole. Those pretty hands give you away. You ain't dealing with no fool. Get going. We ain't doing nothing wrong."

"Look. I'm not from Customs, which I already told the other guy. I can do anything you need done. I can load this boat, cook potatoes or wash your friggin' decks.

I need to get to the Caymans and I ain't screwing around. My hands are none of your friggin' business. I need to get over there and I'll do anything you need."

The Captain took another long look at him. The scowl on his face pissed Michael off and he wanted to hit the guy square in his face. While he considered the consequences of this, the Captain squared his shoulders.

"Okay, pansy-ass. I'll take you to the Caymans, but I'm gonna call you pansy-ass until I see those lily-white hands bleed from the work you're gonna do.

Nobody will call you pansy-ass after I'm done with you, and I ain't gonna pay you nothing either.

I'll feed you twice a day, but you'll cook it for all of us and if I don't like you're cookin; I'll throw your ass overboard.

We'll be out there with five black workers and it'll take us a week to get there. You sleep when I tell you to, and that goes for pissin, too. Like the terms?"

"When do I start?"

The Captain grinned and pointed to the gangway. "Throw your stuff down below. Last cabin on the right. Find the galley and make something I like. The loadin will be finished in an hour and we'll be underway.

By the way, some of the fools around here call me Crazy Captain Phil Smith. Well, I ain't crazy, and if I start thinking you think I am, you'll be shark bait, so watch your step every minute you're on board the Crystal Lee."

Michael turned and walked up the plank. Well, chances are

good I'll be shark bait, he chided himself.

He threw his clothes on the dirty bunk, puked in the bucket next to his bed, wiped his mouth clean on his sleeve and went in search of the galley. Finally, I'm safe. He thought.

28

Tia Juanita kept the conversation jovial with her ideas for their gang. "The Misfits will need a plan. I saw a movie once and the banditos caught up with the good guys.

When the banditos catch up with us, and they will, we will need a plan. Francisco, where does the gang intend to 'hole up' when the banditos catch up? Do you know?"

Francisco chuckled at his Aunt's ramblings. "Tia Juanita, I am glad you came with us to point out these things. Yes, you know I have a plan. I am taking all of us to our old village. We will be safe there and I don't want you to worry about it."

"Well, how long will it take The Misfits to get there? Is it a one-day drive? Because I don't think a one-day drive will be far enough away. It took more than one day for me to come to America from Puerto San Luis, but of course, The Misfits have a fast van, much faster than the boat I came on. How long will it take, Francisco?"

"I don't know, Tia Juanita. You remember, I came by boat, too, long before you, and I have never been back. We will stay someplace, if it is more than one day.

I promise The Misfits will be safe. After all, we have Carlos and he is the experienced gunman in the gang."

Everyone laughed, except Carlos. He liked this image in front of Amy. Truth be known, he had long been an experienced gunman, an accomplishment he revered. His unquestioned confidence in himself never wavered.

They passed through the many small towns south of the border, stopping only once for fuel, always keeping a vigilant eye out for the black car.

Abruptly, at the end of the last town, the two lane road reached far out into the desert, as far as the eye could see, wandering like a ribbon. It touched the horizon, and disappeared into the brilliant blue sky.

Distant chalk-colored mountains, cacti and jumbled rocks lined either side of the road.

Wandering tumbleweed pelted the sides of the rumbling van and potholes, too many to count, consumed the tires. Their speed decreased to almost a crawl. As far as their collective eyes could see, there appeared to be no sign of life. Not even a rattlesnake.

By late afternoon, the blazing sun had heated up the van to sweltering temperatures.

"Can't you go faster, Francisco? This van is going slower than the boat I left the village on. We need a cold margarita. We need a bathroom. You are a terrible driver," Tia Juanita complained.

"A real gang would have brought a map," she continued. "I have to go to the bathroom. Megan, Amy, do you have to go, too?"

Francisco pulled the van off to the side of the road, next to a giant formation of rocks. "This is the best I have to offer Tia Juanita. Help yourself."

Megan and Amy visited the rocks and quickly returned to the car. "The ground is burning my feet," Amy said.

"Mine, too," added Megan. "Where is Tia Juanita?"

"She went over to that pile of rocks," Carlos said, pointing to the other side of the road.

Just then, Tia Juanita appeared from behind the rocks, running, as if to save her life, pulling down her skirts as she ran.

"Rattlesnake, rattlesnake", she yelled in a state of hysteria.

Her companions' uproarious laughter pierced the silence of the desert like a sonic boom in still, dead air. They doubled over at the sight of her scrambling to get in the van.

"Stop laughing, you fools. It crawled right under me. I turned around when I heard the hissing and it looked right at me, spitting its forked tongue at me. Start the van, Francisco, start the van. Get out of here and don't stop again."

Their momentary laughter lightened the mood in the old van, but soon, the setting sun sent chills through Francisco's soul. He could see ahead of him that the road led up into a mountain range and he knew the mountains in Mexico.

They were treacherous and maneuvered with a great deal of trouble, even by the mules in his village. He didn't want to attempt driving through this range in the dark. Tia Juanita had been right. He needed a better plan. It occurred to him that just driving Megan to Puerto San Luis did not constitute a complete plan on his part.

The oppressive desert heat had turned to a chill air. Francisco remembered how he had liked the evenings in Puerto San Luis. They meant the end of a long, hard day.

They meant a cold beer on the porch of Angelina's mother's bar and flirting with the young girls.

He remembered, with a smile, as the young men flaunted their muscles in staged fights in the middle of the street, to impress those girls. He remembered the big barn, at the end of the road.

He wondered if Angelina had ever married Enrique, or if the villagers would even remember him. He wondered why he had never gone back.

Lost in his reverie, he almost missed a small, wooden sign stuck in the sand at the edge of the mountain pass. "Ulpima Oporpunidad Hotel y Barra," it proclaimed. "Last Chance Hotel and Bar." An arrow pointed to the right. His glance followed the arrow and he caught a glimpse of a narrow, dirt road leading to a couple of buildings built at the base of the mountain, about a half-mile in.

He made a quick right and the van swerved, almost upsetting itself. Francisco regained control of the van, looked to see if everyone had survived, only to hear Tia Juanita say, "Finally, somewhere to get a margarita. After we get the drink, The Misfits will camp in the mountains. The banditos will not find us there."

Francisco pulled into the long driveway of the complex. Three long, low, white buildings with red tile roofs, sat at the mountains edge.

Chickens, a boney mule and a ragged, white dog graced the property. Several desert palm trees stood behind the buildings and a battered truck sat in front of the main house.

A woman, smiling and waving her arms, stood on the front porch. She appeared as old as the truck and as dry as the desert. Her bright, colorful dress swung around her full body as she waved.

"Hola, you have come to spend the night at Maria's? Good idea, the mountain is bad at night. Mountain lions will eat you if your car breaks down. Come in. Get a cold drink. Mucho grande long ride across desert. Come." She waved her skirts, did a little dance-like turn and disappeared into the house.

Tia Juanita jumped out of the van like a woman on fire and

ran towards the house chanting, "Maria, Maria, donde esta el bano y los margaritas?"

Even with her limited Spanish, Megan started laughing. "I wonder how long she has needed the bathroom again."

Her laughter became infectious and the rest of the Misfits stood in the middle of the desert, making fun of their gang. Carlos placed his arm around Amy's shoulders, Francisco took Megan's hand and, together, they walked into the friendly woman's house, forgetting, for the moment, the danger they were in.

They had no way of knowing the men in the black car had just been released from the jail.

Maria met them at the door and led them through the house to a huge dining room, telling them to sit. She hurried to the kitchen and returned with large pitchers of Sangria for the women and placed tall, blue shot glasses of tequila in front of Francisco and Carlos.

"Drink up," she told them. "If you hombres are anything like my late husband, the loco fool, you don't ruin your tequila."

Both women smiled at the two men and lifted their glasses. Before Francisco could down his drink, Tia Juanita appeared next to him, took the glass from his hand, and swallowed his tequila in one long gulp. Laughter erupted again.

Maria had found a friend. She returned to the kitchen and brought back two more glasses, poured shots and the two women shared a drink together.

"I have had no one to drink with since my husband died and left me alone to run this place. Not that anyone ever stops here. It is good to see people.

I am old and I'm tired of that mule. I don't like the chickens, either, but their eggs are good. The dog is useless. No reason in the world to keep him around here, but he won't go away.

My husband built this place forty years ago and he thought we would be rich. I told him no one travels on this dirt road and he said he considered himself a man before his time. He thought that the road would become traveled someday. I called him a loco fool, he died poor and the road just got older, like him.

I thought about leaving this place, but the truck doesn't run and nobody would want the mule, or the useless dog. Somebody would probably take the chickens, as long as they lay eggs. At least they have a purpose, not like that stupid mule. So what brings you by here?"

Tia Juanita jumped in before anyone else could speak. "We are a gang called The Misfits and we are from America. We are running from some men that want to murder us because Megan has information that the FBI can use to put a friend of hers in jail, forever. The Banditos are following us in a black car and they have guns."

Maria put her glass down and looked at the men. She stopped smiling.

Francisco cut Tia Juanita off, afraid that Maria would throw them out into the night. "My Tia, you have had too much tequila. Maria, please forgive my aunt. She has exaggerated our problem. We are headed to Puerto San Luis, where I am from. My aunt and Carlos are from the same village.

It is true that some men were following us, but we lost them at the border and have not seen them since. We are perfectly fine and are delighted to find your great hotel. Please allow us to stay for the night."

"Do not hush your aunt. Show some respect. I can tell you that I know she is a woman I can trust. I can tell this by the way she drinks her tequila." She smiled at Tia Juanita and refilled her glass.

Francisco's aunt sent him a scathing glance.

"Now let me ask you this. Do you know that these men are not following you now? One lone road goes south. It will be easy to find you. We will have to hide your van in the barn. You cannot travel the road at night. I will go to the end of the road and remove the old sign. I will ride the mule. He will, at last, earn his food. We will not have light, except for a small candle. They will not be able to see the hotel from the road in the dark and they will get eaten by mountain lions on the mountain, if the black car breaks down."

Tia Juanita whooped with joy. "We have a plan. We have a place for the gang to hole up. I will go with you to remove the sign. Can the mule carry two women?"

Megan and Amy laughed at the sight of it and Francisco and Carlos became indignant at the thought of it.

"We are the men and we will go to remove the sign," Francisco insisted.

Carlos stood up from his seat, his face red, his shoulders squared and veins popping from the side of his neck. "I won't listen to anymore of this nonsense. We don't need women to protect us. We do the protecting. You will all stay here and cook food. We are hungry. And, we will not ride the mule." He pummeled his fist to the table. "I would rather take my chances on the mountain, than be insulted by a woman," he raged.

"You are a fool, like my late husband," countered Maria. "But, like that fool, if you need to prove your manhood by removing the sign, be my guest. I don't like riding the mule anyway."

She waved at Megan and Amy and the three women walked to the kitchen, agreeing men are fools to their egos and enjoyed a shot of un-ruined tequila together.

An hour later, the two men returned, sign in hand, van hidden, and the group settled down to a feast of beans and rice, topped with fresh eggs and laced with tequila, just for flavor, Maria insisted.

After dinner, Maria escorted them out to the hotel rooms. Megan, Amy and Tia Juanita shared the biggest room they had ever seen.

Three beds sat lined against the wall. Huge piles of blankets cured the cold night air. No electricity and the tequila led to silly laughter long into the night. Not one of the women brought up the gravity of their situation.

Carlos and Francisco shared the only other room. The mood did not match that of the women. The two men sat down at a small table. Carlos lit a smoke and watched the flame light up the room. He studied the smoke from his cigarette, as it rose to the ceiling. He liked the night.

"Your crazy aunt is driving me nuts with her shit," Carlos complained as he glanced out of the window behind him. "We should leave her here with that other crazy woman."

"She is harmless, Carlos, and she keeps the mood light. She takes Megan's mind off Michael with her crazy gang stuff. We need her."

"What are we going to do when we get to Puerto San Luis, Francisco? Have you thought about it? You know as well as I do that these guys are coming after them. I don't think we should go any further. Let's end it now. We'll leave the women here and go up to the mountain by ourselves." Carlos spoke in a hushed voice, not wanting to take any chance that he would be overheard.

"What are you saying, Carlos? You intend to kill them?"

"Why not? They intend to kill Megan. Do you think they'll just let us go? Don't be naïve. It'll come to this anyway. Why drag it into a village we haven't seen since we were young boys. I wouldn't call that a happy homecoming, would you?"

"Carlos, I don't intend to be involved in murder. I don't know what I intend to do once I get to Puerto San Luis, but it won't involve murder. My only goal is to protect Megan until this thing gets sorted out. They aren't going to kill her and I'm not going to kill anyone either. If you can't agree with that, you'd better borrow the old lady's mule and ride it home."

Carlos laughed. "You know, old friend, a lot of years have passed since we last saw each other. A lot of water has gone under the bridge. Our lives went in different directions, but now I remember you well.

You were the one avoiding the street fights to impress the young senoritas. You were the one that never made a second visit to the barn. You were the one who brought the girl flowers and told her you were sorry for what you did to her.

You also were the one that tried to impress the young pretty things with fancy, sweet words and little gifts. You never learned anything. You are still the same. You think life's problems can be fixed with nice words.

I can see that I am going to have to stay with you and these women so that you can all live."

"Your choice, Carlos, but we'll do it without cold-blooded murder. I've protected Megan so far and I'll keep doing that until I know she is safe, my way.

And by the way, you'd be surprised what sweet words will do. You should try it sometime. Maybe with Amy? Good night, old friend. I'm going to bed."

Carlos stayed by the window, lighting another cigarette and watching the smoke drift towards the ceiling. He and Amy had not mentioned the conversation at the table. They had barely looked at each other again. He wondered if they ever would.

A loud screeching sound burst into Megan's head and she jumped up in the bed. Morning light streamed through the window and hurt her eyes. Her next sensation was her head pounding. Oh my God, she thought. Where am I?

Reality crept into her brain. A rooster, that's what it is, a rooster.

She heard a voice that sounded as if it was coming from outer space. "Nothing like a tequila hang-over," the voice said.

Rooster? Roosters talk? Moving her pounding head to the side, she saw Tia Juanita sitting up in her bed.

Amy, on the other hand, remained buried under the mountain of blankets, completely undisturbed by the rooster's call to get up.

"What are you talking about, Tia Juanita? I've never had a hang-over." The sound of her voice pulsed in her head and felt as though it bounced off the walls of her skull. I'm going to die, she thought, fearing any more use of her own voice.

The door of the room opened and Maria stood there, carrying a pitcher and three glasses. She ceremoniously poured the liquid into the glasses. "I knew you'd wake up sick. Drink this. You'll feel better."

Megan looked at the glass. It contained a slimy, green liquid that smelled like a wet cat. "I can't," Megan whined, beginning to wretch.

"I'm not leaving until you do and I'm going to stand right here talking to you. I'm not going to stop. I know my words will bounce off of the inside of your head until you go crazy, so drink this now.

I already had mine and I feel great. I told you, my husband, the fool, died many years ago and I have had no one to talk to, except the mule and the useless dog. I have plenty to say, so I can talk forever, believe me."

"Okay, okay, I'll drink it." Megan closed her eyes, held her breath and downed the foul smelling liquid. Within seconds, she felt better. "My God, Maria, what is that? I feel great."

"Cactus juice and special herbs I grow in my garden. I have only given it to Mexican men. It works every time, but maybe too strong for woman. It makes me happy that you did not die. Wake your friend; make her drink hers and come to breakfast. Juanita, come with me. We have to collect eggs and feed the useless dog."

Megan watched Maria leave the room and decided her husband died to get away from her.

Looking at Amy, Megan's eyes welled with tears. She put the covers over her head and buried her face in the pillows. She could not admit to anyone how scared she was. Terror filled her soul. What would her mother do? What would her father do? Should she try to escape and hide from her friends so they wouldn't get hurt?

She felt the covers lift from her head and her friend take her into her arms.

Breaking into tears, she cried, "I'm so scared, Amy. Oh, God, I'm so scared. I'm scared for all of us and I don't know what to do.

I shouldn't have let all of you get involved in this. Amy, what are we going to do? Where are we running to? Why is Michael doing this?" Question after question fell from her mouth.

Amy held her in her arms and stroked her hair. This is what she had been waiting for. She needed her friend to face the truth. She needed her to remember what she heard, what really happened. Then and only then, could they deal with this problem.

"Shush, Megan. Listen to me." She rocked Megan back and forth. Amy spoke in a hushed, mother-like voice. "No one needs to know how afraid you are. We are all afraid, except maybe Carlos.

Your mother and father would face the reality of this. You have to as well.

The only thing that is going to help us is if you try and remember all the details of your love affair with Michael. You have to push the good memories aside and objectively go over your conversations with him. He said or did something in front of you that is the key to all of this.

What you have to believe is that Michael remembers it; otherwise we wouldn't be here, being chased by two men with guns. He is in a lot of trouble and a man in trouble will do anything to save himself. If you truly are the only person who can put him in jail, he will find you, one way or the other. You must remember, Megan. We all could die if you don't."

"I have gone over and over every minute we spent together

for days. I've tried to remember where this could have started. If he is a con-man, he played me from the beginning and he took his good, sweet time. I offered him the money. I offered him my list of clients. What about them, Amy? How many lives did I ruin? He never asked once, for anything. Who did he have killed? What part did I play in it? And why? I have more money than I can ever spend. I would have given him every dime. I never wanted it anyway. I just wanted to help him. I just wanted to love him. I just wanted him to love me." The words tumbled out, mixed with heart-breaking emotion."

"Good Megan. I'm happy to know you are thinking about it. I have been afraid that you are locked in your own mind, not allowing yourself to believe anything. Thank God, you are okay. Now we can start to work on this.

The men have us on the run, trying to protect you. I don't know where Tia Juanita is coming from, but she has made you smile.

You and I are left to figure out the why. We are the ones who need to find the key. It will, at least, give us bargaining power, maybe for our lives. Get up and get dressed. When you calm down, you will be able to think clearly."

She decided to take a giant leap. She cleared her throat and toughened up her voice. "Stop feeling sorry for yourself and get down to the facts. We don't have any more time for self-pity. You are the center of this, now help us. Forget your 'why doesn't anything work out for me?' attitude and take charge of your own life." She knew her words stung Megan, but someone had to shock her into reality. She only hoped it didn't cost them their friendship."

As she prepared herself for Megan's wrath, her friend looked up at her. For a brief moment, anger crossed her face and then she got up and walked to the bathroom. Amy dressed in silence and left the room for breakfast.

The cold water in the shower pelted Megan like ice bullets. Her body started to shake. She had forgotten about the lack of electricity in this place. She vaguely remembered Maria saying something about her generator only running in the evening for light. It wouldn't come on again until dark. How does someone live like this, she asked herself, jumping from the shower and toweling off.

And, who does Amy think she is? Who is she to say I am full of self-pity? Who is she to accuse me of feeling sorry for myself? Since when have I had a 'nothing works out for me attitude'? Who does she think she is, my mother?

Oh my God, my mother. What would my mother do? She would do exactly what Amy did. She would set the facts straight for me. She always did. Her head cleared as if her mother's hand touched it. Throwing on her clothes, she ran to find her friend.

She found her standing next to the van, smoking. "Amy, I didn't know you smoked."

"Picked up the habit after my mother died. If you came over here to tell me off, Megan, go ahead, but I meant what I said and I won't apologize. Our lives are at stake here and you need to realize it." She took a long pull from the cigarette, inhaled it deep into her lungs and stared into Megan's eyes.

"No, I don't intend to tell you off. Actually, you are right, as usual. I have been wallowing in self-pity ever since the day Michael left me. I thought death would end my pain, but Francisco foiled that plan. I just wanted to join my parents. They were the only ones who ever loved me.

You did exactly what my mother would have done. You set me straight with the truth. I can help us now. I'm sorry for being such an idiot, Amy."

Watching the smoke from her cigarette rise into the sky, her eyes blazing with anger, Amy lashed out at her friend. "How can you possibly stand there with your grandiose attitude and tell me your parents were the only ones who ever loved you? You fool. What about me? I searched the entire country for you. I buried your parents with you. I nursed you through your grief, not only at their funerals, but at every other single instance of heartbreak in your life.

Ask yourself who held you during all the break-ups with boyfriends and puppies dying and everything else in your life. I listened to all your silly foolishness about how great the world is. Who do you think you are? Just because you were raised in a lily-white world, doesn't make you any better than me. We stood together through our entire lives, good and bad, and you have the audacity to say only your parents loved you?

Well, Miss Priss, I have always loved you and you're too blind to see it. You're too blind to see anything you don't want to see. That's why we're all in this mess."

"Amy, I know you love me. I guess I take it for granted, because it is so comfortable. I'm sorry. I'm sorry for everything. I love you more than anything. I just never think about it. You're right about everything. Please forgive me." She took Amy in her arms and the two friends held each other.

"I'm starving," Amy said.

"Let's go," Megan said, wiping Amy's tears away with her sleeve.

Maria had prepared a breakfast of eggs, fried beans with goat cheese and toast. Megan wondered where the goat cheese came from. "How do you survive here, Maria? Where did you get the cheese? I didn't see a goat."

Maria's face softened. "I have a friend who lives on the mountain. He comes to see me in his truck. We share milk from his goat and other things, if you know what I mean. It got lonely after my husband died. A woman does what she has to do."

The men looked shocked, Amy and Tia Juanita seemed amused, but Maria's words burned an instant hole in Megan's brain. A woman does what she has to do. She would do what she had to do, starting now.

As they stood by the van preparing to leave, Megan paid Maria for her hospitality and hugged the woman good-bye.

The others followed suit, except Carlos. He stood at the rear of the van, finishing his smoke. Maria walked over to him to say good-bye and offer a last word of advice. "You are the strong one here. You are not shadowed by emotion. It is your job to protect them. Do not let them down."

Carlos glared at her, threw his smoke to the ground and kissed her cheek. Thank you for everything, Maria. Don't worry about me. I know what my job is."

One day later, the black car pulled into the complex. Maria told them nothing. She insisted she hadn't seen anybody in all the years since her husband, the fool, died.

As they walked to their car, one man reached down to the ground and picked up the butt. "An American cigarette. Well, what do you think? Not so old, huh?" He looked at his partner and let out a chuckle. "They were here alright. One of them was smoking in the hotel in San Diego. He asked me for matches. What a wise-ass. We're on the right trail.

We'll get our money. We'll contact Michael's lawyer and tell him we're close. We'll get her this time." He glanced back at Maria, still smirking, rolling the butt between his fingers. "And she calls her dead husband a fool. Maybe someday I'll come back to take care of the live fool."

From her porch, Maria watched them go. She said a small prayer as she crossed herself.

29

Moonlight and a blanket of glittering stars illuminated the beach. The tranquil sea, lit by the serene light, glistened in the background, lapping gentle waves to the shoreline.

Silhouetted dolphins jumped high from the sea and then dove deeply back into its depths. Seals and seabirds played amongst them, creating a sea ballet of intriguing beauty.

Barefooted men and women danced in the sand, holding each other closely, swaying to the rhythmic sounds of guitars, maracas and small drums.

The women wore long, white, ruffled cotton skirts and tops, their waists adorned with colorful scarves. Long black hair, brushed until it shone with natural oils, and then tied into a small knot at the back of their neck, held bright, fragrant summer flowers. Sun-bronzed skin contrasted with the whiteness of their clothes and finalized the beauty of the look.

Around midnight, Angelina and Enrique raised their arms in the air and the people quieted.

Enrique stepped forward. "On this, our most reverent day, it is time to pray to God for our debt and gratitude to His whale. It is with His grace that the whale gave his life to save our people and our village."

The villagers fell to their knees and bowed their heads. I followed suit, in awe of this ceremony.

A moment of silence followed and as I looked up, Lupita appeared in a long, flowing white dress, her long, salt and pepper hair gracing the edges of the neckline, her feet encircled by flickering candles. Her piercing black eyes stared, unblinking, into the moonlit night. She raised her arms above her head and stood motionless, assuming a trancelike appearance.

The silent congregation remained on their knees, but now, watched Lupita intently.

She, once again, chanted prayers in her own tongue, as she had done earlier on the sea. Only this time, the moonlight became her spotlight. She raised her head and closed her eyes. She continued to chant and the villagers wept. Someone in the back tapped gently on a drum. Her arms and head fell simultaneously and her body dropped to its knees. The villagers cheered. God, and the whale, had been thanked again.

Everyone rose and Lupita disappeared into the night. The music resumed and the beer flowed once again.

I lit a smoke and watched the young girls dancing, swaying and flirting with the young men. I had smoked in college and given it up for Sadie. Odd, I thought, that I felt a need to smoke now. A sense of sadness overcame me. No, wait, I thought, not sadness, but longing. I longed to dance with Sadie in the sand. I longed to share this day with her. I longed to see the pearl color of her skin and touch the softness of her hair. I longed to see her smile. As tears welled in my eyes, a voice, from behind me, interrupted my thoughts.

"Many mountains lie between our lives and our medicine. Mountains are treacherous to cross alone. I bring you this drink to begin our journey of understanding."

I whirled around to see Lupita glaring at my back, her eyes now piercing only my soul.

"Do you know you are alive because of me? Do you know that your medicine could not save you, so I did? Did anyone tell you?"

I threw down my smoke and crushed it with my foot. "No, I did not," I said, not sure I wanted to confront her with this many beers under my belt. She intimidated me and she knew it, but I was not up to games. Sadie's image was still in my head.

"The day after you came here, Enrique came to the mountain to get me. I came to help you. I put my medicine in your mouth as you slept. I put my medicine on your forehead and your burned body. I tended to you for two days. My medicine and my herbs saved you." She turned, and again, disappeared into the night, before I could collect my thoughts enough to speak another word.

I stood sipping the unusual tasting drink and watched her go. A possible peace offering? I wondered.

The thought of Sadie and Lupita both in my head at the same time made me laugh. It must be the beer, I chuckled to myself. As I lit another smoke, my head ran rampant with images of Sadie and

I, in bed, discussing Lupita. Enrique appeared by my side, glaring at me.

"You are Okay, Senor Peter?"

"I'm fine, Enrique, but I need to ask you a question. Did Lupita save my life when I came here?"

As I asked the question, I noticed one of the village girls standing alone, smoking a cigarette. My eyes fell on her face and she smiled. The moon enhanced her beauty. "Never mind, Enrique. I'll talk to you tomorrow."

Enrique followed my eyes, saw the girl and grinned. "Good luck, Amigo," he whispered, as he turned and walked back to the beach.

I walked over to her and she lowered her eyes. Her lips curled into a sheepish smile. I wanted to touch her and attempted to move my hand. It remained motionless at my side. I felt a longing in my fingers to touch the softness of her skin, to run my fingers across her cheek, to draw her into my arms.

"I am Isabella. I live on the mountain. You are Peter, the doctor. I have heard about you and how you saved the children." She spoke in a lilting voice, almost a whisper.

"Yes, I'm Peter. You are beautiful."

"Thank you, Senor. So is the night."

"Yes, the moon has created a paradise and you make the paradise complete."

"I would like to know you, Senor, but my mother does not like you and I am afraid she would disapprove of me speaking to you."

"Who is your mother, Isabella?"

She looked up at me, sparkling black eyes staring into mine, and whispered, "Lupita."

I reached out and placed her chin in my hand. My other hand caressed her cheek. My body felt alive.

"I am sorry, Senor." She turned and walked away from me.

I went to my room and lay across my bed. Not one time, in too many years to remember, did I once long for another woman. Tonight that changed.

I remember awakening in the middle of the night. My head pounded and my body shook with cold. My hands were trembling.

I couldn't get out of bed and fell back into sleep.

My next conscious memory was of a woman standing over me, chanting. Again, I fell back to sleep. Dreams of Sadie, a whale and a girl swirled around in my head at a blurred speed, all mixed with a great sense of pain. Thoughts of death and dying laced the dream like a winding road in a desert.

I moved in and out of consciousness, sometimes aware of pain, sometimes chanting, sometimes nothing. My body seemed coated with stickiness, but I couldn't move to tell.

I finally awoke with awareness. The moon shone in the window, penetrating the darkness. A shadow sat in a chair on the far side of the room. As my eyes focused, I thought I was still in the grips of the nightmare. The shadow took definition. Lupita. Fear enveloped my soul. I tried to sit up. What had she done to me? I remembered her daughter. I took stock of my body and it seemed to be intact. I stayed still, afraid to move for fear she'd find out I was awake.

She rose from the chair and walked towards me. I closed my eyes.

"Senor, Peter? You are awake? Senor Peter, wake up."

I opened my eyes. "Where is Angelina?"

"You will be Okay, Senor Peter. You have been sick. Go back to sleep. I will take care of you."

"No, no more sleep. What has happened? Where are Angelina and Enrique? Where am I?"

"You are in your hospital. Enrique brought you here. You have been sick many days with mal puesto. You will live, but only because of Lupita and her medicine. Not your doctor's medicine, but mine. Lupita is all this village needs. She saved the big doctor, again. Lupita does not need any help to make people better. People know this now." She turned and stormed from the room.

Enrique and Angelina appeared in the doorway. "Senor Peter, you are okay" Enrique cried. "We thought you would die. Thank God you are okay."

Angelina busied herself straightening the bed and the room, not looking at me.

"I will go and make you food. You will need food to get strong." She left the room, but I saw her tears.

"What happened to me, Enrique?"

"We don't know. You are the only one to get sick. Your body burned with fever, but it shook with cold. Your belly rose like a balloon, into a hard rock.

We called Lupita and she brought her medicine. We do not know what Lupita does. We trust her.

She didn't leave your room and she refused to let us come in. We watched you from the outside. We all prayed."

"Does my sickness have anything to do with me speaking with her daughter, Enrique? Why does she keep that beautiful girl hidden on the mountain?"

"There are many village secrets, Senor Peter." "As a young girl, Lupita took a lover and became pregnant.

Ashamed and fearing God's anger for her daughter's sins, Lupita's mother forced her daughter's lover to leave the village. She has great power and a fierce temper. No one ever heard from him again.

While Lupita carried the baby, her mother practiced many rituals and ceremonies asking God for forgiveness for her daughter's sins and for Him to end the pregnancy. He did not.

The baby was born in the night, with only the full moon for light. Lupita's mother birthed the baby and as the child took its first breath, she took it outside and held it up to the Lord and asked him to take it back. The moon went dark and the skies thundered. Lightening struck the ground. Rain pounded on the grandmother and the baby, convincing the woman of God's wrath.

She took the baby back and laid it on Lupita's chest. The mother walked away from her daughter, vowing to disown a baby born in lust and sin. She would never look at the child again.

Lupita built a small house on the mountain, with her bare hands, and raised the baby by herself, ashamed of her sins and knowing she had angered God forever. Her own shame never died, but her mother did.

As the child grew, Lupita realized her daughter had inherited her, and her mother's, powers. She knew her daughter could take her place in the village when she, herself, died. She has put aside her shame to allow her daughter to come to the village in preparation for her rightful position amongst our people. This is why she is so afraid of you. She is afraid the village will never accept her daughter if you are here, but she struggles with her great interest in your knowledge."

"The funny thing is, Enrique, I have realized that I am afraid of her."

"You are afraid of Lupita, Senor Peter? Why?"

"I am a doctor, Enrique. I think with a scientist's mind. When a man like me encounters something we cannot explain or we think is foolishness, it frightens us. It does not fit into our training. People have come a long way away from herbal medicine and witchcraft. I am beginning to believe I have a lot to learn. Ignorance creates fear and I have been afraid."

"We have talked long enough, mi amigo. Go to sleep now and soon you will be strong enough to go fishing again."

"No, my friend, I think first, I'll teach you to sail."

I fell asleep wondering about the girl and worrying that my longing for her would take me away from Sadie.

30

Fatigue and weakness plagued me. The excruciating headaches were gone, along with the fever and chills, but I continued to sleep most of the day and night. Enrique and Angelina saw to my few needs when I woke up.

Angelina insisted I drink a foul tasting, foul smelling, bitter, hot liquid, three times a day. A tougher nurse never lived.

"Senor Peter, you will drink this tea or I will call Enrique and he will make you drink it. Sit up so you don't spill it. I do not want to be the one to tell Lupita you won't take your medicine. Now sit up." I obeyed, too weak to argue with her.

Lupita did not make an appearance at my bedside and when I awoke, I wondered why.

The men in the village continued to work in the hospital, stepping up their pace in anticipation of the upcoming fishing season.

Rooms were taking shape. Hand-hewn beams braced the ceiling and windows, cut roughly in the walls, let the warm sun into the building. Wooden shelves lined walls and the floor was covered with wide planks.

The mountain held the resources they needed and, what they couldn't find there, they got from Frank's endless supply of materials.

As I slept, the sound of saws and hammers became a rhythm in my dreams. A smiling Sadie, wearing a soft, white dress flowing gently around her hips, swayed to the sawing. Moving her arms and hands as if caressing the air, she kept time with the beat of the hammers. Her hair shone in the sunlight.

Angelina moved around her, keeping to the beat. "The tea, the tea, drink the tea," she chanted to the music.

I moved in and out of sleep. I couldn't stay awake.

Early one afternoon, I woke to the sound of propellers. The villagers dropped their tools, abandoned their projects and ran from the hospital.

"Senor Frank is here." they yelled, running to the beach.

Great, I thought, just what I need, another lecture. I sat up in bed, tried to straighten my hair and my clothes and became consumed with dizziness. My mouth tasted rotten.

Frank appeared in the door, frantic with concern.

"I'm alright, Frank. Don't panic."

"My God, Peter, what happened? The men said you almost died."

"I don't know what happened. We had a party for the Day of the Whale; I went to bed and didn't wake up for days. Lupita doctored me with her herbs. I've been down for quite a while, but now I'm just weak and tired."

"What? What did she do? What were your symptoms?" He grabbed my arm and started to take my pulse. With his other hand, he checked my forehead for fever.

I pulled away from him. "Leave me alone, Frank. They've taken good care of me. They saved my life. I don't need a doctor."

"You've finally gone mad. I knew it. You should have come home when I told you to. Get up. I'm flying you home to a hospital. Get up right now." His face turned from concern to fury.

The men stood, hats in hand, silently behind him. They understood his fury more than his words.

With all the energy I could muster, I told him, in slow precise English, so the men would understand me, "I am in a hospital. My hospital. Their hospital." I pointed to the group of men. "Shut up, Frank."

He turned to see the men, and must have realized he offended them. He turned back to me, his face white.

"I'm sorry, Peter. Of course, you are in a hospital. Of course, you are okay."

"I'm sorry mi amigos," he directed towards the men. "I was just scared and worried about my old friend. Please forgive my foolishness. Why don't you go out to the plane and see if I remembered the beer. Don't forget the cookies for the children."

The tension broken in the room, the men left for the beach.

Ever the gentleman, I thought.

"Okay, Peter. Your friends are gone. Now tell me what witchcraft she used on you. Tell me what symptoms you had."

"First of all, I don't think she uses witchcraft."

Frank scoffed.

"Let me finish, you stubborn fool."

Frank scoffed, again.

I continued with a tone of sarcasm. "As far as I can tell, without any scientific evidence, I suffered from chills, then fever and then sweats, in that order. Being the great plastic surgeon that you are and never seeing a case of actual sickness, I'm willing to bet you don't know what those symptoms mean."

"Well, since you are a betting man, I hope you bet a lot, because I would be happy to relieve you of your money. My money would be on malaria."

"And you would be right. What is the cure for malaria, Frank?"

"High doses of quinine."

"Right again. And here is where your witchcraft theory falls apart, my friend. Quinine comes from the bark of a tree. Lupita put thin, wet slices of bark, from her mountain, on my body and covered me in cloth to hold the medicine in. She forced small, ground bits of the tree pulp and water down my throat.

The only thing she doesn't have, that we do, is a factory to manufacture her cure in. She produces her own in her garden.

She has had Angelina pump cups of hot quinine tea down my throat, day after day. The bits of tree bark almost choked me to death. The bitterness of the liquid has killed my last taste bud.

Is she any less of a doctor than we are, Frank? Where do you think our profession got its humble beginnings? I've had time to think about this and as a trained, modern doctor, I think we've been taught to ignore our own beginnings. We are conceited, pompous asses who think the only way is our way."

"Are you finished, Peter? Can you throw away all these years of training and experience and go back to treating diseases with tree bark and voodoo? Can you tell, without modern technology, if your organs have been damaged? Can you tell, without blood-work, if you really had malaria? Can you trust your life to guesses? You are a man of science, education and the wisdom of thousands of doctors and researchers before you. Can you really throw that all away to use tree bark and guesses? What has gotten into you, Peter?"

"No, of course not, Frank, but I am beginning to believe that it can all be incorporated. I believe I can better this village and not have it lose its own culture. I believe I can blend the two worlds and that's exactly what I intend to do, with or without your help."

My friend of so many years took a long pause and stared at the floor. Apparently, deciding this argument could not be won, he continued with an air of defeat.

"I have supported you this long. That's not to say I haven't questioned your sanity. I guess I can keep it up. Can you get up?"

"Not yet. I have bouts of dizziness."

"Does Lupita have a magic tree for that?"

"Stop it, Frank."

"Only kidding. Go back to sleep. You look terrible. I'm going down to the plane."

I saw him a couple more times in the next few days. I let him take a blood sample, but only so he would leave me alone. Angelina let him help give me the tea. He wouldn't leave until I could stand up and walk with him. A good friend, I decided, once again.

I began to feel better. I knew that because I had enough energy to fight Angelina on the tea. I also wanted a bath and a shave. I looked almost as bad as I did when I arrived in the village. Enrique took over and assured Angelina I would drink the tea. She stopped coming by.

Early one morning, feeling like a new man, I got up, dressed and left the hospital for the mountain, leaving a note for Enrique on the pillow. I convinced myself it was Lupita I wanted to see.

The morning sun felt good as I walked the trail. The mountain trees, wet with glistening dew, smelled fresh and clean.

I picked up a walking stick and thoughts of Isabella drifted through my mind. I envisioned her hair, her smile, the softness of her face and the lilt of her body. I recognized the internal struggle over Sadie. I tried to ignore the bad thoughts. I didn't need both of them in my head. Sadie would know she wasn't alone.

I forced myself to think about Lupita and not get lost on the mountain. Mountain goats gazed at me from rock formations high above the trees. Hawks circled in the air, looking for prey. Villagers' rancheros appeared along the way. Men and women smiled and waved at me, dogs and cows co-mingling on their property.

"Hola, Senor Peter. You are better, si?" they called. "You go to see Lupita, si? She save you. Say gracias for us, Senor."

These people lived simple lives. Rusted fifty gallon barrels stood on their homestead to collect rainwater and to be used for washing clothes. They tended their livestock and grew their gardens. They planted seeds that were the ancestors of the seeds their parents and grandparents had brought from their villages. They taught their children. They made candles for light and some used outdoor toilets, others just holes in the ground. They grew their own tobacco and made their own beer. A few lived with the money they made from selling fish or rugs they wove at night. They carved statues out of left over pieces of wood and sold them to boats that happened to, on occasion, stop in their cove. Most of them lived with no money at all. They were poor. They were happy. I was happy to be with them.

As the road rose above the population, it turned rough. I thought about my first visit to Lupita's house and fear welled up in my soul. I remembered the old dog and the crow. I remembered the yard, laden with rusted artifacts, screaming chickens and goats and I remembered Lupita's threats of curses. I wondered if she hadn't made me sick. She had promised to. She had demanded that I save her reputation. She had demanded that she be called to save someone. I wondered if my diagnosis of malaria had been correct. I wondered if it wasn't the dreaded mal puesto that she had promised me. I wondered if Frank had been right about my mental state.

The trees and branches scratched me once again. The road wasn't muddy this time, which made the trek easier. As on my first trip, it took a sharp right and the terrain leveled out at the summit of the mountain. I had arrived.

I wanted to run back down the mountain. I could see the ramshackle house. The front door stood open. The dog still slept on the porch. An identical scene repeated itself. The crow even cawed from the tree.

As I neared the house, Lupita appeared in the doorway. She stared at me and then turned and walked into the house. I followed her and stood in the light of the doorway. She sat at the small table and waved her hand. I sat.

No words were spoken as she roamed her eyes over my face, and then, my body. She smiled, crooked teeth showing under thin, purple lips. She wore her hair tightly wound into a knot at the nape of her neck. Her wrinkled, spiny hand reached across the table and touched my face. She ran her crooked fingers down my cheek and onto my neck.

"You have come to thank Lupita, si? You live because of Lupita's powers, si? Village knows big doctor need Lupita to get well, si?"

"Yes, you saved my life and I am here to say gracias to you. The village knows Lupita's powers are great and given by God. They respect you and your medicine."

Seeming satisfied, she rose from the chair and walked to her clay stove. She poured two cups of hot liquid and placed one in front of me on the table. "Senor Peter, drink this. It is much better than Jesuit's powder. It is not bitter. It is chamomile tea from garden. Much sweeter. Good to make you rest. Good after long hike."

Sometime, long ago in college, I had learned that quinine took the name of Jesuit's powder in its early years of discovery. The Jesuit priests used it for many ailments. How strange to remember how I had scoffed at it in my arrogant years and now I had been saved by it.

I had seen the chamomile bushes on the side of the mountain. "The tea is excellent, Lupita. I have not had a good cup since I left San Diego and you are right. It is much better than the other."

We carefully picked our words, trying to understand one another. We struggled with words often and repeated ourselves many times, but somehow we understood the conversation we were trying to make. I didn't remember ever being patient enough to really listen to people. Unlike my first visit, I felt relaxed and honored to be accepted into this woman's home.

Lupita sipped her tea and her eyes didn't leave my face. "You know of Pancho Villa, Senor Peter. Did Enrique tell you about him?"

"No, I don't think so."

"Do you want Lupita to tell you the story?"

"I would love you to."

"Okay. Many years ago, when I am a young girl, I stood at the bench over in the corner, grinding powders for my mother.

The afternoon is quiet. The sun shines. The birds sing. My mother rocks in her chair, eyes closed.

From behind the house, comes a sound of galloping horses."

She stood and made motions with her body to show me the horses. She jumped up and down, waving her arms, leaning her head forward.

"Grande horses. Hombres slap horses with whips. Dust flies everywhere. Chickens run. Goats run. Cows run. Dog follows. My mother runs to the door. Men are yelling and screaming. The earth shakes with pounding hooves. My mother grabs me and pushes me under the table. She throws blankets all over me."

'Stay,' she says. 'Don't move,' she says.

"Lupita is scared to breathe. I shake with fear." She contorted her face to show fear and shook her wrinkled body.

"I hear my mother go to the porch. I hear horses come to pounding halt in front of the house.

'You have whiskey, old lady?' he says, waving his gun high in the air. 'I am the great Pancho Villa and I am thirsty. So are my hombres.' I hear his gruff voice.

'No, Senor Pancho Villa, I have no whiskey. I have good locoweed. Do you want?' my mother says, voice shaking.

'Go get it, old woman'

My mother comes into the house and fills a bag with special black weed. She whispers, 'Stay down, Lupita. Do not move.'

The men grab the weed and race down the mountain to the village, firing guns into the air.

My mother tells me the story of many men. She says, 'Lupita, these are bad hombres. They kill people. They steal everything from villages, beat men and take women for their own. They are banditos and we must fear them. They must not see or find you.'

Many days later, my mother tells me the hombres are gone. She says hombres go to the village, drink many days, smoke locoweed. They beat up the men; wave their guns in the air. They break up the village and, when they are finished, they jump on their horses. The women tried to run, but the hombres reach down from the galloping horses and pick up the young girls. They ride out of the village, women screaming. The young girls will not be back. The Hombres take them; never let them come back to their home.

Many months later, Juan from our village rode over the mountain in search of the great Pancho Villa and the daughter he had stolen from him.

When he returned, he told the people he found Pancho Villa in a village far north of here and shot him dead in his tent as he slept.

He did not return with his daughter. He could not find her. He again left the village, on his fishing boat, and never returned to his home."

Lupita finished her story with a wide grin. "Many good stories in this village, si, Senor Peter"?

She made dried beef and boiled potatoes for dinner as she told me the story, moving about the room with a rhythmic grace. We ate in silence, as I envisioned Pancho Villa riding up to the front of the house.

Eventually, the chamomile tea produced its time proven purpose and I became sleepy. Lupita insisted I stay the night and arranged a pile of old worn blankets on the floor, next to hers. She fussed over a pillow made of feathers and as the old dog yawned and settled between us, stars twinkled thru the open patches in the roof.

We fell asleep, as would two old friends on a camping expedition. There had been no sign of Isabella all evening, but my mind conjured up images and desires that my body longed for and my thoughts justified.

The morning brought a howling, hungry dog, a baying donkey, clucking chickens and a cawing crow.

I made my way to the front porch, groggy from sleep, only to see Lupita running around throwing food to the hungry animals; cursing them in the same words I had heard the village men use in bar fights. It amused me to hear her threaten them with the curse of mal puesto. As if they understood the curse of sickness from evil spirits, the cows stood motionless, their udders full, watching her every move.

The sun had barely begun to rise.

As I took in the raucous scene, I noticed a small, wooden run-down house about a quarter mile from us. A flickering candlelight shown in a window. Isabella, I thought. Before I could take in any more, Lupita noticed me and hurried to the porch.

"In, in," she demanded, shoving me towards the door. "You will catch cold. You stay in the house."

She followed me inside. "You will eat breakfast and then you will go. You vamos."

"Lupita, I would like to know more about your herbs and your medicine. I would like to know more about your life on the mountain. I would like to tell you more about the hospital and my plans. I mean no harm to you. I want to know you better."

"No. Lupita knows better. Lupita knows you come for her daughter. I see you looking for her house. You have that look in your eyes. The same look a man had for Lupita many years ago. You will not have my daughter. You will not bring shame to Lupita and her daughter. You go."

"Please Lupita, si, your daughter is a lovely young woman, but it is you I want to talk to. It is your medicine I am interested in.

My wife died and I will never get over her. I do not want another woman." My own lies shocked me.

For the first time, in longer than I cared to remember, my body was speaking a language of its own.

Lupita's reaction was immediate. "I am so sorry, Senor Peter. I never have a husband, but I have love. Isabella is all I have left of that love. My mother ran my man off with a broom. When he tried to come back, she shot him. She say he is a disgrace to us and the powers that are given to us by God. He rode his horse over the mountain and I never saw him again. She says he shames me in front of the village. She doesn't love my daughter. She does not allow her in the house.

I built my child a house in the back of my mother's home, and raised her by myself. I give her love and food and I see the man I love in her tiny face. I think she is the child of God, too. My mother never mentions her again.

After my mother died, I brought Isabella to this house to live with me, but she likes the house in back better. It is her home.

When she is older, I took her to the village to meet the people. The village accepted her. They don't know yet that she has the image of God in her eye, too, and will take my place when I die. I will tell them when I am ready.

I don't want any man to ruin her life. No man, you comprende, Senor Peter?"

"Lupita, I promise you, I have only the best intentions in mind for you and me. I will not dishonor you or your daughter.

The men in the village and I have spent a lot of time building a hospital. I want you to be a part of it.

You have so much knowledge that I don't have. We can work together to help this village. We can be friends and we can teach each other. We can learn each other's medicine and you can teach me to make the great beer from your garden and, oh yes, the wonderful tequila from your cacti.

Lupita walked over to a table in the corner of the room, her back facing him.

Yes, I understand your promises, she thought to herself. Yes, I know your hospital cannot be successful without me. And yes, your words belie the longing in your eyes.

She grinned and turned to place two glasses of tequila on the table. Smiling into his eyes, she thought, I can no longer deny the charms of this man and my desire to be part of his hospital. I will just have to curse his life if he touches my daughter.

I accepted the tequila this strange woman offered me and vowed to keep my promise to her. I felt there was too much at stake, my hospital, my newfound respect for Lupita and my love of this village and its people, to risk losing it.

She busied herself preparing breakfast, not uttering another word.

31

Fortunately for him, he had gotten used to rats in his room and the constant swaying of the boat had already made him too sick for the smell of rotten potatoes and carrots to do any further damage. He puked again in the galley sink.

Splashing cold water on his face, he heard the engines fire up and everything in the galley, pots, pans, cooking spoons, dishes and thousands of other things, started to rattle and shake.

The noise pounded in his sick head like a million rockets launched at the same time. He fell to the floor and covered his head with his arms, waiting for his impending death. He heard a loud rolling sound, felt a crushing blow and then, darkness.

"Get up. Get up, you pansy ass. You ain't gonna lay there this whole trip."

Yelling. More yelling. What the hell is going on? Michael felt his eyes open and then a hard kick in his ass. Where the hell am I, he thought, trying to sit up.

"I told you that you were nothing but a pansy ass. What kind of a man passes out on the galley floor? Get up you good for nothing bum before I throw your body overboard and be rid of you for good. And there ain't even nothing cooked. I got rats on this ship that are better than you."

Another hard kick landed on Michael's ass. Stumbling to his feet, he tried to focus his eyes on Crazy Captain Phil Smith.

"Stop kicking me, you son of a bitch," he yelled. Taking a swing at the Captain, he fell back to his knees. "What the hell happened to me, you crazy son of a bitch? What the hell's going on?"

"You drunken bastard. I thought I smelled booze on your breath. I shoulda never taken you on board. That's what I get for being a nice guy. Get up, you son of a bitch."

"Nice friggin' guy? You are crazy you old coot. Something fell on me. I got knocked out when this friggin' old boat started to rock and roll. Look. Look behind you. Look at the sack of potatoes on the floor. They must have hit me in the head. I'm not drunk you old bastard and I'm gonna beat the shit out of you right now."

As he raised his fists, the rest of the crew appeared in the galley and jumped on him like fleas on a dog.

"You no hit the Captain, new man. You back off or we kill you." A man appeared with a huge galley knife and pushed it against his throat.

The Captain stood before him, not speaking, squaring his shoulders; meanness furrowing burrows in his weathered face.

The crew waited.

Finally, the Captain spoke as Michael felt drops of blood running down his neck. "Now, make me something to eat," he spat at Michael, as he turned and left the galley.

The man removed the knife and swatted Michael on his back. The other men laughed. Michael stood in awe watching the scene.

"You are a good man, new man. You stand up to the Captain. He respects that. What's your name?"

"My name? You want to know my friggin' name? You just tried to cut my friggin' throat and you want my name? Well my name is asshole for getting on this ship, that's what my name is."

"No cut throat, man. Just wanted to show the Captain we are loyal. What's your name really?" The men were all laughing and playfully pushing each other around the galley.

A bellowing voice came from above the outrageous scene. "You assholes get back to work. No time for you to be screwing around in the galley. Get to work now or you won't eat for the rest of the crossing or get paid a friggin' dime of my money; you bunch of lazy friggin' bastards."

The men scattered back to their posts without another sound. As he was leaving, the man that had wielded the knife turned, looked at him and said, "Okay, new man, we call you Asshole." He smiled a big, toothless grin and strode off after the other men.

Michael turned to the galley sink, rested his hands on the filthy rim and whispered, "My name is James Shockley and I'm going to the Caymans." He wiped the blood from his neck with a dirty rag. Funny thing, he wasn't sick anymore.

He cut up potatoes and carrots, threw the rotten parts in the corner for the rats and found some salted cod in a filthy icebox. He threw it all in a pot, covered it with water, threw in a hand-full of caked salt and boiled it.

A crusty loaf of bread lay on a counter top. He cut it up with the knife that had been held at his throat and put it on the table. He placed the pot of stew in the center of the table and left the galley, congratulating himself on a job well done and picturing the crazy old coot putting the first spoonful of that concoction in his mouth.

Walking up the companionway, he saw the toothless guy and told him to tell Crazy Captain Phil Smith his friggin' dinner was ready. He followed the narrow passageway to his cabin and fell down on the bed. It only took minutes for him to get sick. He jumped up and climbed the narrow steps to the outside deck. He found his way to the rail and got sick again.

When he could finally look up, he found himself gazing directly into the moon path. The gigantic moon hung so low in the sky that its bottom edge rested on the horizon. It spun its brilliant white light into a path that reached all the way across the ocean and touched the bottom of the ship, precisely below where his feet stood on the deck. It seemed as though he could walk across the light and pick up a rock from its surface.

Never having been on a ship, or the ocean, the sight mesmerized him. Complete and total darkness surrounded him, except for the shimmering white moon path. Silhouetted birds lifted from the water and flew gracefully into the darkness. Warm breezes caressed his sore body. The engines rumbled and the boat moaned. The sound of water being cut by the boat drifted into his mind. Peace and a sense of harmony enveloped him. He realized his body had relaxed and the sickness had disappeared.

He didn't hear anyone come on deck. He heard a gruff voice say, "You wanna play some cards?"

He turned to see Crazy Captain Phil Smith standing behind him, smoking a pipe.

The Captain started to speak in an uncharacteristic tone, almost whispering, but marked with gentleness. "A man falls in love with the sea on a night like this. It seeps into your soul and calls you, like a woman's loins.

You can't live with it and you can't live without it. You think you know it. You think you can predict it. You think it will take care of you, and then, it suddenly turns on you from somewhere in the bowels of its depths and shows you its power.

It rages and rants and swears it'll kill you and then it turns back just as quick as it turned to begin with.

It lets you know you're alive and that your life means nothing to it. It makes you come back. You spend your life willingly giving it everything you have and it caresses and teases you like a woman and when it has you at your weakest point in the love affair, it tries to kill you or, at least, rip your guts out. All the wickedness and whiles of a woman, I say."

"You know you're crazy, right?"

"Yeah. Been that way for a long time. Like a woman, the sea drives you to it. Crazy men are happy. They don't miss nothing and they only care about getting to the sea again. Now, you wanna play some cards? I got twenty bucks says you can't beat me at five card."

"This is gonna be a long trip. Put your money where your mouth is."

In his cabin, he broke out a bottle of dark rum, poured two glasses and threw twenty bucks on a small table.

"Why you headed to the Cays?"

"None of your friggin' business."

"I like the way you think. Ante up."

The night wore on with little talking. Neither man was particularly winning.

"I got an idea," the crazy Captain offered.

"What? I like it best when we don't talk."

"Every time one of us loses a hand, the other one answers a question."

"I thought you didn't care about anything but getting back to the sea?"

"Rum makes me wanna know things. By tomorrow I'll forget anyway, but it makes the night a little less long."

"You're on."

"One rule. If one of us doesn't tell the truth, the asker gets to cut the other ones finger off with this here knife." He slammed a small penknife onto the table.

"You're on, old man."

Michael lost the first hand.

"Why you headed to the Cays?"

"I have money there. Deal. "

He lost the second hand, too.

"Clean or dirty?"

"I cheated some stupid, lonely women out of it. Deal."

"Good man. I knew you had character. Pansy-ass hands, but good character."

Again, Michael lost the hand.

"How do you know I won't kill you after you get it?"

"Because you don't have the balls. Deal."

The Captain lost the fourth hand.

"Wanna play for the ship?"

"Nah, you're right I ain't got any balls. Deal"

"Nah, I'm going to bed. I have to cook for a crazy old fool at sunrise."

"Good night, pansy ass. I want a dozen eggs and a pound of bacon at the suns first ray. By the way, the stew was delicious."

"Right."

Michael walked up to the deck and took another look at the darkness and the now shrunken moon. He began mentally counting his money and planning the rest of his life.

The dollars and cents signs in his head excited him like sexual foreplay and he headed for the galley to start the bacon. Four days to go.

32

The black car wound its way up the steep, winding mountain road. The men drove in silence, chain smoking. A brooding, dark atmosphere prevailed.

The little-traveled dirt road climbed relentlessly higher and higher. No other drivers. No sign of life. Just clouds of brown dust spewing up from the rotating tires. The tension and boredom in the car magnified.

"You're driving too fast around these bends, you idiot."

"You wanna drive this car? If you don't, shut up."

"You're gonna kill us."

"If you don't shut up, I might have to take care of you before my driving does." The driver angrily stubbed out his cigarette in the ashtray.

"What do you thinks up with this guy, Michael?"

"I don't know. I don't know what the girl knows, but he's plenty scared."

"Slow down, you fool. I know our problem is we're running out of money. We better call that lawyer."

Rounding a sharp upward turn, an old gray mule appeared in the middle of the road. The driver swerved. The car skidded to the edge of the deep ravine on the driver's side. It teetered on two wheels for a long moment and plummeted with its passengers, smashing on ragged rock all the way to the valley floor.

Within minutes, black desert vultures smelled the carnage and started circling the car. Within a half hour, the seemingly desolate desert teemed with wildlife heading for the impending feast.

An old man walked down the hill and coaxed his mule off the road. He hurried. He had to deliver some goats milk before it soured. His sweet Maria's visit the night before had outlined a plan laced with promises of a sweet reward for his services. He knew the cheese would be good, too, and quickened his pace.

•••••

Michael stood on the bow of the old ship. Blue water surrounded him. Not another ship had passed them in three days. Sleep eluded him. Hunger did the same.

He cooked slop during the day and took joy in watching the men eat it. Teach them to jump my ass, he mused.

He and the Captain idled away the nights flipping cards down on the table and talking about the years the sea-worn man had spent sailing and the women he had conquered along the way.

Michael said little about himself, which annoyed the Captain.

They warmed their bellies with rum and occasionally threw an empty bottle at a looming rat, sending it scurrying back into the shadows. He beat the old man with ease and lustfully pulled the Captain's money towards him. By morning light, too drunk to walk, the old man didn't know the amount of, or care about, his losses.

He avoided the crew at all costs. He couldn't stand their smell or their incessant singing. The beat of the island songs got under his skin and he wanted to throw one of them overboard. He thought about chumming for sharks with the garbage in the galley.

Feeling the ship make a slight change in course and bringing him out of his reverie, he could now see, in the far distance, a long, low piece of land jutting up from the horizon; a log-like bump in the vast expanse of water. What a glorious sight. He almost jumped out of his skin. Tomorrow night they would land and he would be a rich man, again.

He closed his eyes and breathed in the moist sea air. It filled his nostrils and lungs, leaving the lingering smell of salt in his nose. He had never felt better.

By early afternoon the next day, he could clearly see the island, a flat spoil of sand, laden with palm trees. What he couldn't yet make out were the many private banks, one of them holding his fortune, his future.

One simple numbered bank account that he had been smart enough to hide his money in. One smart guy he was, yes sir, one smart guy!

His plan? A shower, a shave, maybe a sordid encounter with

a sun-bronzed island girl and then, first thing in the morning, a stroll downtown. He was back on top.

Hours later, with the moon hanging over the island and the palm trees swaying, the Captain took the helm. "All hands on deck," he yelled into the night air. He brought the ship up against a long wooden dock with the ease of combing a part in his hair.

The crew jumped from the side of the boat, grabbing lines a half foot in diameter and lashed them down on cleats. The Captain cut the engines and silence prevailed. Michael stood by on watch, an unneeded entity in the proceedings.

The Captain came around from the helm and the men appeared around him. He handed out packets of money, and one by one, they disappeared without a word.

He turned to Michael. "I only took you on board, pansy ass, so I'd have someone to play cards with. You're a lousy cook." He turned, took one step forward and then turned back. "By the way, that money I just paid those men, don't go looking in that bag you're carrying for your winnings. See ya, you pansy ass fool."

He walked across the deck, climbed down off the boat, and swaggered down the dock, his shoulders squared and whistling an island tune.

Michael smiled and followed suit.

He found a small, two story hotel right on the edge of the downtown collection of banks. Hot shower and shave behind him, he left the building to find the sun-bronzed girl.

As he walked, he noticed the men here had their own look. He liked it. Loose fitting white cotton shirts and pants. Open weave leather sandals and white straw hats.

The island people seemed to move slowly, their pace kept in conjunction with the swaying palm trees and the gentle breezes. Oppressive heat formed sweat on his forehead.

He looked for the nearest clothing shop and the shopkeeper dressed him to fit the part. What the hell, he thought. After tomorrow morning, I may stay around here for a while and I should fit in.

He turned onto a narrow cobblestone side street and came upon a dark, smoky bar.

"A bottle of rum and a glass," he said as he sat down on a

stool. His eyes adjusted to the darkness and he could see a small dance floor with entwined couples, their feet unmoving, swaying from their hips up, to the same beat as that damn music the crew sang.

"You want to dance, stranger?"

It was almost a whisper behind him. He turned to see his sun-bronzed island girl. The night belonged to him.

The girl had left hours ago. He was up, showered, dressed and standing on his small balcony with a cup of coffee as the first sun rays fell on the surrounding ocean. Cool air caressed his face and he knew it wouldn't last. The town below him was devoid of human life at this hour.

As the sun rose, it illuminated the sand based surface of the island. A few black roads led into the heart of the town from the outskirts of the island. The contrasting colors of the scene reminded him of a resting tiger's back.

As the early morning wore on, people streamed into the banking area and he joyfully watched men unlock the doors of the banks and step inside. His time had come.

He walked down the one flight of stairs and into the lobby. He tipped his hat to a man lounging in a brightly covered wicker chair, reading a newspaper. The louvered walls of the lobby had been opened, exposing palm trees, flowered bushes and local greenery, giving the room the appearance of a garden.

He strolled among the few streets of banks until he came to the one that held his money. He stopped and looked at the low building, stuccoed in a soft shade of pink. One thin wall stood between him and his fortune. His mood soared upward.

Twenty minutes later, two security guards, carrying him under his arms, cast him back into the street. Two scooters, sirens screaming, brought police, who jumped right into his face. "You got a problem, mister?" the older cop demanded. The younger one grabbed him and led him away from the building out into the street.

"Those bastards stole my money," he screamed, his face wet with sweat and as red as a ripe tomato. "They stole my money. I have a number. I have millions of dollars. They stole my money. Get off of me, you bastard. Let go of my arm." Screaming, out of control, the cops cuffed him.

"You're coming with us," the cop yelled, pulling him down the street. A crowd formed. The bankers locked their front doors.

From somewhere in the medley, a voice demanded to be listened to.

"Officer, this is some kind of mistake. This man is a friend of mine. I'll take responsibility for him. There will be no more trouble."

The policeman looked at the man with immediate recognition. In his wild rage, it took Michael a minute to recognize him.

"You sure you can handle this, Captain Smith? We don't want any trouble from this guy."

"I assure you he will be on my ship and out of here as soon as possible."

He looked at Michael and said, "Come with me."

"Will you uncuff him, Officer?"

The cop looked at Captain Smith, not exactly sure he should let this guy go, but he thought about the troublesome paperwork he'd have to do and the fact that no one on the island would dare refuse a request from the Captain. He uncuffed Michael.

"If I see your face, or hear your voice while you're on this island, I'll get out of bed, if necessary, to throw your ass in jail. Do you understand, Mister?"

"Yeah, yeah," Michael said, rubbing his wrists and walking towards the Captain.

The two men walked away from the crowd. The people dispersed. The cops left the scene and the bankers unlocked their banks.

In a matter of one hour, Michael's fortune had disappeared from his life for the second time.

The Captain led him to a local bar, took a booth in the back of the place and ordered a bottle of rum and two glasses.

"Who the hell are you?" Michael managed to say. His body, racked with shaking, his mind completely frozen; the words surprised him.

"These islands are as corrupt and mean as a New York City cop. Corruption spreads like a cancer. It grows on everything it touches. Requests are made. Money is offered. Things get moved. Jobs get done. Favors get paid back."

Michael downed two tall shots of the dark liquor. He lit a smoke.

"What happened, pansy ass?"

"How the hell do I know? I walked into the bank, gave the teller my number and told her I wanted my money. She went and got the manager, we walked into his office, sat down and he informed me my money was gone. I tried to tell him there was some kind of mistake. He insisted there wasn't. I got crazy and he called the security guards and the cops and now I'm sitting here with you. Oh yeah, I might of punched him."

"Gone where?"

"I don't know. He said someone called and authorized the money to be sent to a San Diego bank."

"Who could do that? Who could have authorized it?"

"Do you think if I knew that answer I'd be sitting here drinking with you, you asshole? I'd be on my way back there to kill someone." Anger raged in his voice and he pounded his fist onto the table.

"Quiet down before the cop hears you, you idiot. You must know someone in San Diego."

The light went on in his head like a bolt of lightning, striking him from a black sky.

"Megan. Megan. How'd she figure it out? I never told her about the money. That bitch. She must know someone on this island." Insane, uncontrollable rage took over his body.

"Who's Megan?" the Captain asked, pouring two more shots.

"An ex-girl friend I conned out of money and a list of art clients whose money I needed for my business."

"She must have some powerful friends to get a favor like that done on this island. Sounds like a woman I'd like to meet. My mama told me when I was just a young mutt to never let my guard down with a woman. She always said, 'Hell hath no fury like a woman scorned.' You really must have done some scorning."

The rum had loosened Michael's tongue and the Captain had every intention of taking advantage of that. "How much money," he asked.

"Millions."

"If you find the woman, you'll find your money. You can put that advice in the bank.

I can take you back to Miami and then you can get to San Diego and find her. Did you get the name of the bank she put the money in?"

"They wouldn't give it to me and I can't go back. The FBI and the SEC are hot on my trail. My passport's been confiscated. I have about fifteen thousand left to my name and nowhere to go and I'm not staying here. Anyway, she's somewhere in Mexico now."

"How'd she end up in Mexico?"

"I had to have a lying, cheating bastard killed in New York and she is the only one with enough pillow talk to convict me. I put two guys on the road to find her and put an end to this mess. They followed her down there. I don't know where the hell they are now."

The two men drank in silence for a while. Pansy ass was turning out to be his kind of guy. His life had been full of unexpected golden opportunities, and this time, he had no doubt that he had unwittingly come across the mother-lode. He always figured, when offered a buffet, eat.

"We could take the ship around, done it before many times. Not much of a trip, clear shot after the Canal. Hire on the crew and play some cards."

Michael thought about this proposal. In his drunken state, it sounded like a good idea. "After we get to the Baja, it'd be a crap-shoot. We don't know where she is."

"We'll find her. I could pick a woman that smart out of millions of them. Know that because I spent a lifetime trying to avoid them. They have a smell that leaves a trail for miles." He chuckled at his memories and the ease of his success.

Michael held up his glass. "To Mexico," he toasted. The sound of the clicking glasses reverberated throughout the bar and would reach far into their lives.

"I got a meeting with some friends in the morning and then we'll pull out," the Captain declared. He got up and walked away from the table.

33

Unaware that they were no longer being followed, the tension in the van remained at a high peak.

Francisco stared out the window, so lost in thought that he did not notice the landscape change from desert to mountain. He had never believed he would see his village again.

His head raced with memories of the day he had left Puerto San Luis. His mind's eye saw his parents standing on the beach and the great white ship anchored in the bay. He pictured the agonizing good-byes to his family and friends; but, the most painful memory remained the look on Enrique's face when he realized the barterer did not want him.

Vivid images of Enrique and Angelina, like snapshots in a photo album, crossed through his mind. He wondered what they would look like with age. He didn't want to tell them how ashamed he was of his life with Consuela. How would he tell his friends what a failure he had been? He would tell them about his son and how proud he was of him. They would ask why he never remarried. He didn't know. They would ask what he did in San Diego. He would have to tell them he had become the best cab driver and the best tour guide in town. Would they think him successful, or a failure?

Lost in his reverie, he tried to picture how his village might have changed in all these years.

He would have stayed in his village his whole life, he thought. He never wanted anything else. He would have built a house on the mountain and been a farmer and a fisherman. He would have taken a wife and had many children.

Carlos ignored his friend's sullenness. Instead he pushed the van to its top speed up and down the mountain. He thought about the black car and what he would do to its inhabitants if they caught up. It amused him to think of them at his hands.

He thought about Amy. His feelings for her scared him. What was he thinking? He knew how to handle emotionless, one-night stands. He had even tried a couple of weekend long trysts, but by Sunday it always grew old.

He'd end up longing for the aloneness of his room. When he thought of himself, and the title 'boyfriend', in the same sentence it muddled his brain. His thoughts never went to marriage, children or forever.

Yet, when the word Amy crossed his mind, he pictured the wedding chapel they'd marry in. Babies came to the forefront of his thoughts.

He had to find a way to stop the madness in his mind. First, he had to get her out of his head. Giving that a try, his nostrils filled with the perfume she wore. The car reeked of it. He loved it. He wanted to stroke her hair. He wanted her in his arms. He wanted her to say she loved him. He wanted to stop being crazy. He didn't even know what boyfriends did. He tried to focus on the black car. He pictured them leaving for their honeymoon. He hadn't noticed that no one was following them.

Tia Juanita slept peacefully, her head thrown back onto the seat, snoring. After the snake incident, she just wanted to ignore the desert and its inhabitants.

Megan spent the seemingly endless journey watching the scenery go by and composing her speech to the FBI and the men in the black car. And she thought about Michael. How she had loved him. How they had made love on the yellow couch. How she had ended up a fool. She wondered if she would ever love anyone again.

Amy enjoyed the same thoughts as Carlos, with a slightly different twist. She envisioned their wedding, their home in the suburbs and their children. They would have a dog named Bear, a big, shaggy dog that would chase their children around the yard.

She loved watching the muscles in his neck twitch and the way he smoked his cigarettes. She admired the manly way he held his hands on the steering wheel. She wondered what Carlos was thinking.

The hours whiled away. The Misfits passed through endless changes in scenery, from flat desert with tall, three or four armed cactus, to treacherous mountain cliffs, to rolling hills. Each lost in their thoughts, silence prevailed.

As the sky changed from a brilliant blue to the soft hues of pink and purple with the setting sun, the van rolled into a small town. A gas station stood on the corner and three or four old buildings lined each side of the road. Dogs and a few goats roamed aimlessly among the buildings.

Carlos pulled the van into a small driveway, its building holding a tattered sign declaring it a motel.

Requesting two rooms and a place to eat, he also asked for a place to put the van so it wouldn't be seen. The proprietor was happy to accommodate him for a price. Carlos cursed him under his breath, but handed him the requested money.

They ate a substantial dinner of fresh fish, refried beans and tortillas and drank a couple of beers, while Carlos kept his eye on the road for the black car.

Settled into their rooms, Carlos didn't have to worry about anyone seeing a light. The generators wouldn't come on until morning. Behind closed curtains, candles dimly lit each room.

Megan and Tia Juanita went to sleep immediately, but Amy lay awake. She heard Carlos's door open and went to the window. He stood by the porch rail, smoking.

"Mind if I join you," she asked, as she walked up next to him.

"No. Why are you out here?" he asked, lighting her cigarette.

"I couldn't sleep. How about you?"

"Same. I like the night." He looked at her and took her into his arms. He kissed her and she returned the kiss. His body burned. He felt the heat in hers.

The moon shined down on them and the cool air caressed their bodies.

"Carlos," Amy breathed, "we can't do this now."

"I want you," he murmured. "I can't be around you. You're driving me crazy."

"We have to wait. This is not our time. We owe it to Megan."

"Screw Megan. She'll be fine. Anyway, we might be dead tomorrow."

His words shocked her into reality and she stepped backwards.

"Don't joke like that, Carlos."

"I'm not joking. Look, Amy, it doesn't matter how I feel about you. I'm no good at this. I've never been in love with anybody. I'm a loner. I'd be no good for a woman like you. You're right; my job is to take care of Megan. That's why I'm here; doing a favor for an old friend. When this is over, I'm going back to New York and be a cop. It's the only thing I'm good at. I don't need any complications. Go back to bed and leave me alone."

"I'm going to go back to bed, but not because I don't want this. And we'll see about you being a loner. I don't believe that for a minute. Lots of cops in New York are married with families and a big dog named…"

Before she could finish her sentence, Carlos saw headlights coming into town. He pushed her to the porch floor and covered her body with his own. As the car passed, he saw that it was not the black car. He didn't tell her right away. He let a minute pass to feel her body under his. When he got up, he helped her to her feet and stood tall, the vulnerable feelings gone. "Good-night, Amy. I'll see you in the morning. That wasn't the right car, but I'm sure the other one is out there somewhere."

"Good-night, Carlos. But don't think for a moment this is over."

He took her face in his hands and brushed her cheek with his fingers. They kissed, a lingering sweet kiss. "I'm not right for a lady like you," he whispered.

"We'll see, Carlos, we'll see".

In the morning, after a breakfast of fresh eggs, refried beans and tortillas, they took the van out of hiding and hurried out of town, but not before noticing the small pharmacy and general store at the far end of the village.

Halfway through the day, in the desolate desert, a man appeared, driving a beat-up tractor along the side of the road. Carlos stopped the van, got out and walked up to the old man. Francisco followed.

They conversed easily in Spanish. After all these years, Carlos found he still could use the local accent.

"Excuse me, Senor; we haven't been here in many years. We used to be from Puerto San Luis. We didn't leave by road, so I am not sure how far we are from the road leading to the village. Can you help us?"

"Are you the boys that left on the great ship?" he asked.

The two men were surprised anyone would remember that day after so many years.

"Yes, we are. How did you know?"

"You speak local Spanish with an American accent. Just figured. Roads about ten miles down, Senor." Without another word, the man tipped his hat and started up his tractor. Rolling away, the old gas can hitched to the back of the tractor swayed with the movement.

As the old van turned onto the rocky, dirt road, the mountain grew taller in front of them. In the distance, they could see passes that looked too narrow for a car to go over. Francisco smiled.

As a young man, he had ridden his horse over this mountain, racing as fast as it could carry him. The sound of the animal's hooves pounding on the hard earth and his own heart beating wildly, echoed from the mountain's cliffs. His young friends and their horses followed him in hot pursuit every time, but he had always won. He was home.

Carlos remembered this road, too. He had killed his first man on these cliffs.

Francisco hadn't raced that day. They were approaching the last switchback, right before the road took a steep turn down. He wanted to win more than he wanted to live.

One horse stood in his way and he decided, in an instant, to move past him, ignoring the sheer drop on the side of the road.

He kicked his horse's flanks with all his strength; the horse reared up from its front legs, landed down, and with fury, forced his way past the front horse.

His friend's horse lost its balance and they fell down the cliff, killing both the horse and rider.

The villagers shunned him for a long time. The only one that stood by him was Francisco. He never forgave himself.

Tia Juanita had her own memories of this road. So many years had gone by. It was on the side of this road, on a cloudless summer day, sitting on a picnic blanket laid out under a tree, that her dear husband had proposed to her.

They realized early into the marriage that she couldn't bear a child. Deep in the throes of despair, he took her to America and bought a ranch.

Riding his ranch one day, he sat under a tree to rest. He looked down at the ground and saw a nugget of gold. A vein ran through his land. He tried to mine it for years, but in his pursuit, he grew old. Another rancher found him at the bottom of his mine, dead.

She sold the ranch and moved to San Diego to be near her nephew and his son, the only family she had left.

Now she was home. It was her turn to die and join her beloved husband. She smiled. She had not felt this content for some time.

Megan knew the minute the van turned onto the road that her life was about to change. A strange feeling she didn't recognize consumed her. She felt a joyous sense of anticipation and a realization that her life would be richer for this trip.

She put Michael and the black car aside and eagerly anticipated every hill the van crawled over. She felt empowered, as though every event in her life had led her here, to this moment, and she was complete. Somehow she knew she would never see San Diego again.

Amy wondered if there was a wedding chapel at the end of this road. She had never really wanted to get married. She certainly had never wanted children. Gazing at the back of Carlos's head, she tried to make the obsession go away. Instead, the thought, we'll name our first son, Carlos, Jr., roamed across her mind.

Carlos pulled the van to a stop and told everyone to get out and stretch their legs. "The road ahead is rough, maybe impassable. Move around. The rest of this trip will be difficult." He knew he was stalling. "Walk with me, Francisco."

Francisco looked at his friend without an idea what was wrong. "You girls be careful of the Cholla."

Megan asked, "What is Cholla?"

"Jumping Cactus. You'll know if you get too close to it, the tiny little burrs jump onto your clothes and burn through to your skin. The only way to get rid of them is to take off your clothes and throw them away."

"Why don't you show us what this cactus looks like," Amy snapped.

"Come with me, child, I'll show them to you," offered Tia Juanita. The girls walked off with the old woman.

Carlos led Francisco in the opposite direction. "Have you

noticed there has been no sign of the black car for two days?"

"Yes, I have. What do you think happened to them? Do you think they gave up?"

"I don't know, but I don't want to get too sure of ourselves. Some memories here, huh?"

"Yeah, some good, some bad. Try to remember the good, Carlos. The past is the past."

"Get the girls, Francisco, let's go"

34

Breakfast finished, I walked outside to the well to get Lupita water for the dishes. I thought about the brass faucets in my own house. Knowing the strange woman was keeping a close eye on me, I deliberately kept my eyes down. I had to convince her that I had no interest in her daughter. I pumped water into a rusted bucket, shooed the chickens and goats away from me and returned to the house.

As Lupita moved about the small room, at her insistence, I sat at the wooden table and drank a strong, hot cup of coffee. I lit a cigarette and turned to the window. I felt peaceful and secure. The smoke from my cigarette curled up into the air and caught the sunrays filtering in the window. The livestock grazed around the hillside and the dog slept. Except for the sound of sloshing dishwater, and an occasional dish clanking against another, silence prevailed.

Chores completed, Lupita led me out of the house and up the hillside to her gardens.

We came upon a small grove of towering cacti. Pulling a large machete from a sheath on her hip, she slashed at the plant, handling the large knife like a Japanese warrior. Several layers into the plant, a large appendage shaped like a pinecone took one strong hit from the knife and fell to the ground with a thud.

Picking up the pinecone, she held it up to my face and with a wide grin declared, "Lupita's tequila trees, Blue Agave."

"I cut out corazon. You know, Senor Peter, the heart. Then cut away hojas punzantes. You know, Senor Peter, sharp leaves. Cook for long time in horno, maybe two days cool off and then grind. Press out pulp and collect juice. You see this leaf from plant, Senor Peter? You scrap this leaf, get yeast, put on pulp, let sit in big wooden vat many days, and then, you have tequila."

Following her to the back of the grove, we came to a large stone oven sitting on the ground, surrounded by wooden vats.

"Horno." She waved her crooked finger at the oven. "Mi madre built it many years ago. She made good tequila for all the hombres in the village. She told me, Lupita, you give man good tequila, he marry you and only come home to you."

Farther up the hillside, we walked through coffee bean plants. "Coffee beans grow best high on mountain. The soil is rich from the ancient volcano. Good water comes from the mountaintops. Lupita uses the same grinding wheel she uses for the tequila plant. Sometimes there is extra good flavor in the coffee." An odd sound escaped from her mouth, a sound that could only be recognized as an attempt at laughter.

In the fresh mountain air and the warm sunshine, her uncanny laughter echoing through the silence, it seemed hard to believe this same woman had threatened me with curses and inevitable mal puesto.

Walking back down the hillside, we passed tight groves of trees. They grew high and appeared covered with a moist bark.

Lupita seemed to sense my curiosity and stopped. She walked up to the trees and put her hand on the bark. Turning to me, she put her head down and spoke in almost a whisper.

"I know you are a smart man, Senor Peter. I know you are a medicine man. I know you do not believe in Lupita's way. I have no school, as you do. I only have my mother and her way.

I only know how to help you with my medicine. I fear you will be angry with Lupita and her way, but this is the bark I saved you with. This is the quinine tree. I sliced bark from the tree and laid it on your body. It drew out the fever, go into your blood and make you live. I know you have a better way. I know Lupita is not as smart as you, but it is all I have. Please forgive me and my way." She lifted her head to look at me, her eyes begging me for forgiveness.

Surprised by her admission of fear, I took her into my arms. "Oh, my God, Lupita," I whispered into her ear. "Oh, my God." I held her for a long minute and then stepped back. "You are the reason that I am alive. What would I have done without you and your medicine? You saved my life. I will be forever grateful to you."

"Then you are not angry with Lupita, Senor Peter?"

"No, I am not angry with you, Lupita. I am glad to be your friend. I will spend my life trying to repay you."

"Then I will show you my tobacco plants and my herbs. Let's go down this mountain."

257

The sun high, birds chirping, we strolled back down the rocky path.

We walked through her small tobacco garden and she showed me her drying racks and taught me how to roll a cigarette in dried tobacco leaves.

Straight rows of plants rose up and down the garden, each one assigned to a different cure.

"You want to sleep well, Senor? You eat cilantro plant. You want to fix bad stomachache? You take Manzanilla. You have worms? You use oregano. You want to be a better lover? You take this big plant over here, damiana. I have so much in the garden because the Mexican man does not need it. I use it for chickenpox in children. You have diabetes? Use this plant, bricklebush. You see, Senor Peter, Lupita has an herb for everything. Villagers know I am a good curandera. My people come here often.

Back inside the house, the shelves of brown bottles I had seen earlier took on new meaning.

She pointed out little bottles of rattlesnake oil to ease the pain of rheumatism, declaring that the snakes can only be captured in June or the oil will not be useful for medicine. She possessed bottles of achiote seed for hemorrhages, hibiscus seeds to cure scorpion bites and countless others.

She refused to tell me the contents of some of the bottles, declaring they were secrets only known to herself and her daughter, taught to her by her mother and not to be passed on to anyone other than their kind.

She took great pride in her ability to apply curses to anyone she pleased, but refused to discuss her know-how in this practice.

She did take on an air of superiority when explaining how she had the power to eliminate a curse if she felt she wanted to. "You know, Senor Peter, the mal puesto invites evil spirits into a body. I am fortunate to have the tree branches to make this curse go away. If I want to, I will rub the branches across the evil spirits in the body and they will go away. This is why I was not worried about cursing you. I have power to fix, but only if I decide." Her crooked lips formed a smile, but a foreboding look on her face compelled me to listen carefully.

"If a man looks at another man's wife or someone's daughter

with a bad eye, I can curse his eyes to blind him, and then, if I choose, use my medicine to take it away. You would laugh, Senor Peter, if I told you what I use to cure this curse. Do you want Lupita to tell you?"

"Please do, Lupita."

"This small bottle has the urine of a black-tailed rat in it. I rub it on the eyes and the curse goes away. Only the curanderas that makes the curse can take it away.

"Have you ever cured anyone of your curses, Lupita?"

"No, Senor Peter, I have not."

The woman had made her point.

Fearing the dark on the mountain, I thanked Lupita for her hospitality.

She reached up and touched my face, looking directly into my eyes. "Buenos Dios, Senor Peter. I have enjoyed your visit, but do not take my warnings without fear. Do not try to see my daughter."

For the second time today, she laughed a wicked, high pitched laugh and turned back to her house."

I felt a desperate need to see if my room at the hospital hid three branches.

I headed down the mountain the same way I came, but not the same man I had been on the way up.

•••••

Several days later, Angelina handed me a white envelope, a look of serious concern on her face.

"A man travelling the road was given this at the Farmacia. They asked him to bring it to you."

My eyes went from Angelina's face to the envelope in my hand.

In his own polished, distinguishable hand-writing, Frank had written "Urgent message, Please Deliver As Soon As Possible".

I opened the letter and read its contents.

Dear Peter,

I am sorry that I could not deliver this information in person. Scheduling prevents it.

As I promised you, I had your blood sample analyzed. Although your symptoms mimic those of malaria, your blood lacked any of the protozoa necessary for that diagnosis.

Instead a parasitic invasion of your intestinal track caused your illness. We have not been able to identify the parasite.

It is strange that no one else in the village has become ill.

I ask that you carefully consider what you ate or drank that no one else did.

I also ask, fearing your wrath, you take the time to consider Lupita's threats of mal puesto. I know the top of your head just blew off, but I remain steadfast in my belief that you are a threat to her.

Please be careful, Peter. Further discussion of this matter will be forthcoming on my next visit.

Your Friend,

Frank

35

Other days brought other pleasures. On an afternoon walk one day, I came upon the narrow brick road that Enrique had introduced me to many weeks before. I climbed the road, following it up and over a hill dotted with cactus. Small desert mice scampered back and forth in front of me, some going right across my shoes.

Enrique showed great pride in this little road. Many generations before him, the village women decided a schoolhouse was needed for the children.

A pile of red brick, no longer needed as ballast, and dropped off by the captains of passing ships, lay on the beach.

A small valley, shaded with eucalyptus trees, snuggled itself behind a hill on the edge of the village.

Soon, the women put together the valley and the brick and decided it was a perfect spot for the children to attend school. The men were put to work. Construction began.

The adobe building, built of mud, clay and straw blocks and then whitewashed with a limestone wash, stood with pride.

The women pounded iron-ore from rocks and mixed it with wild berries and brick-dust creating a rust-colored paint, which the men used to color the wooden window frames and front door.

The women bartered beer, tequila and fish with a friendly captain for part of a European red tile cargo to construct a roof. The men balked at this trade, protesting their now gone beer and tequila. They were ignored.

A winding brick path led to the bottom of the hill, where a little hand-painted sign hung from a wooden post. Escuela de Puerto San Luis, the sign declared. Another brick path led to a small adobe outhouse.

The older village men constructed hand-hewn chairs and desks and their wives carefully penned reading and writing manuals. A wooden Cross graced the wall above the teacher's desk and a clay fire-pit stood in the corner to warm the school in the cool winter months.

Another friendly captain donated his ship's brass bell. The

men built a curved, painted red frame on the roof above the door, to showcase it.

A statue of Our Lady of Guadalupe, adorned with flowers, stood in front of the school, her eyes intended to watch over the children.

As I walked under the now blazing sun, I sat down at the top of the hill and gazed down at this serene little place. I watched as the breeze swayed the leaves on the trees, the eucalyptus fragrance filling my nostrils. Birds drifted on thermals high above the school. Billowing white clouds floated across the sky, their formations changing effortlessly with their journey.

I thought about the grandiose education I had received. I remembered the carefree, naïve time I had shared with my friends. I thought about my professors, the very best in the country. They had taught me everything I knew, but somehow had neglected to teach me anything about life or, for that matter, the real world.

As Enrique had described it, I pictured the jubilant village preparing for the opening day of their new school. A teacher had been selected. The women had made special clothes for the children and prepared food to honor this day.

The men celebrated their own success with beer, tobacco and long nights of grateful thanks from their women.

The day came. The manuals sat ready at every desk. The villagers waited, and then waited some more. Eventually, the mothers and children appeared on top of the hill, where they remained. The children would not come down to the school. The mothers pleaded and begged. They would not move. They clung to their mother's legs and cried.

The children had never been away from their mothers. They had tended the gardens next to their knees. They had played within a few feet of their mothers hanging wet laundry to dry. They had gathered wood for their stoves under mamasita's direction, but they had never been sent away to be by themselves.

Finally, Lupita's grandmother marched to the top of the hill. She summoned the children to gather round her and then turned to face the school. With a wave of her arms, she knelt and the children fell to their knees beside her. She raised her arms to the sky, closed her eyes and began to chant in a tongue. Silence prevailed, except for her language. A crow cawed in the distance. When she opened her eyes and lowered her arms, the children walked down the hill without looking back. The school bell rang across the village.

Enrique had grinned with pride, gold tooth shining in the sunlight, as he told me every child for three generations attended this school and learned to read and write, including himself.

As I sat on the hill, reminiscing, recalling memories, my father crept into my head. I could hear his voice. I could see his face. I could see him caring for the children suffering from cholera in Central America. I began to realize that he had known all along what I was just beginning to understand. He didn't take his position for granted. He didn't take his good fortune and his hard work for granted. He knew about this side of life and appreciated it. He understood it. He had tried to introduce me to it by taking me to see it with my own eyes. He had tried to show me, but I had been suffering from the arrogance of my youth.

I closed my eyes and prayed to him. I tried to say how sorry I was that I had been so arrogant. I begged him for forgiveness and prayed he was listening and would be proud of me.

As I walked down the hill, I looked more closely at the brick beneath my feet. How hard they must have worked. How much they had to love. Were their children ungrateful, just like me? Did they realize this was a labor of love or did they just take their good fortune for granted, like me?

Nearing the end of the road, I became aware of a rumbling sound. I stopped to listen. At first, I didn't recognize the sound and then it dawned on me. It was a car engine. It must be one of the locals from up on the mountain, I thought. Maybe it's the old pick-up I had driven to get the medicine.

From around the bend, a van appeared. I watched it stop in front of me and didn't recognize the five faces looking back at me. Two of its occupants were Mexican men, one a Mexican woman and two very pretty American women completed the group.

I hadn't seen an American face since the last time Frank left.

"Hola," I said to the men. They tipped their hats.

"Hello," I said to the women. They smiled.

As I stood trying to figure out who they were, they opened

the doors and climbed out of the van.

"I am Francisco Gonzalez. I used to live here. We've been on this old road a long time and we needed to stretch. Excuse my manners. This is Carlos Rodriguez. He used to live here, too."

I shook hands with both men. Good, strong handshakes.

He continued. "This is my aunt, Tia Juanita. She used to live here, too. We haven't been here in many years.

I shook Tia Juanita's hand, a soft, feminine, aged hand. She smiled.

"Do you know where we can get a good margarita and a good bathroom?" she said without losing her grin.

"Tia, let me introduce the girls," Francisco chided. She pouted.

"This is Amy Gray and Megan Summerfield. They are from New York, as is Carlos."

The man named Carlos stepped forward. "We are here to visit our families. The girls just wanted to see Mexico." He sounded threatening.

Amy spoke next, stepping in front of Carlos and taking my hand in hers. "Don't mind him, he's tired. It has been a long trip and we all need some rest. Is there a hotel in town?"

"Well, I wouldn't exactly call it a hotel," I responded, feeling a little overwhelmed by the intrusion of these strangers.

The other girl stood in back of everyone else, but started to move forward. She was beautiful, in a tired and traveled sort of way.

"My name is Megan," she said simply, reaching out to shake my hand.

"My name is Peter Brentwood,"

"Do you need a ride the rest of way to town?" Francisco asked.

"No, no thank you," I stammered, not able to take my eyes from Megan's face.

Before I could get a grip on the meeting, they got in the van and, waving good-bye, rode away. Their tires spewed dust in the air and I stood, motionless, pondering the girl I had just met.

I started walking, breathing in the dust, and then, quickened my step. I needed to know who she was. An unnerving sense of excitement cursed through my body. Confusion blurred my thinking. I picked up my pace again.

36

By the time Michael sobered up enough to remember his plan with Captain Phil Smith, the old sailor had finished his meeting and hired a three man crew to work on the boat.

Michael gathered up his belongings in the hotel room and checked out in the Lobby. Frustration, anger and hatred lined his sun-tanned face and his head pounded like a freight train rolling at its highest speed over rocky terrain.

Captain Phil Smith waited, with dizzying excitement, for his passenger to arrive. His ship had come in and he knew it. Michael was his goose and soon the golden egg would be laid.

"Good morning, pansy ass," he yelled, as Michael stepped foot on the gangway.

Michael boarded the boat, throwing his belongings on the deck.

"How's the head this morning, sailor," the Captain asked.

"Shut-up and let's get off this stinking island, you old bastard," Michael shot at him without looking up.

"Whatever you want, pansy ass." He decided he might just kill this guy at the end of the road. Firing a command to the man below decks, the engines roared up. "Drop the lines," he commanded the men on deck. "Shove off," he instructed as he spun the huge helm toward the open sea. In minutes, they were underway.

Michael assumed his role as chief cook, slept on his dirty bunk and played poker all night. Little to no conversation, which was the way he wanted it. Smooth sailing, good water. His hatred intensified.

"We'll be at the Panama Canal tomorrow," the Captain told him one night while they played cards.

"Customs at the canal?" Michael asked.

"Loaded with them," he said, with all the casualness of a woman picking daisies.

"Well, you old fool, that's a problem. The whole frigging world is looking for me. I'll have to hide somewhere on this tub."

"You conceited bastard. Have you looked at yourself? You

look like a bum. You ain't shaved or had a bath in how long? You're filthy. Do you think anyone will recognize you? Do you still think you're some fancy big shot from New York? You're a broke dirt-ball. Best place to hide is right out in the open, as long as you keep your big mouth shut. Let me handle the smart stuff and you just shut-up and do what you're told. I know how to handle this crap."

Michael stared at the old man. His words stung as badly as if he had walked into a hornet's nest. Bile rose up in his throat. He knew the arrogant son-of-a-bitch was right.

The following morning, the sun rose off the stern of the ship. Standing on the bow, alone, Michael found himself gazing out on a peaceful, calm waterway, birds gliding easily from one side to the other, diving for their morning's breakfast. The land on either side appeared undeveloped and jungle-like. He took no solace in the peaceful scene.

He wasn't sure how far the canal was ahead of them, but terror filled his soul. Thoughts of Customs Agents carrying him off in handcuffs to some Federal Prison caused sickness in his stomach and he wretched violently over the bow. The birds came screeching through the air to dine on his offerings.

The Captain's gruff voice bellowed behind him. "Problem, pansy ass? Bit off more than you can chew? We're only a couple of miles out and you better straighten up your sorry ass."

Michael didn't turn around. He heard the Captain's footsteps retreat across the teak decks.

Lost in his terrifying visions of horror, a strange voice broke in. "Hey man, you better get off that bow."

He turned to see one of the crewmembers, his hands on his hips, a red, dirty rag tied around his forehead. The muscles in his heavy black arms bulged out from beneath a dirty, torn T-shirt. I can't deal with another idiot, he thought.

"Shut up and go back to work," he spit at the crewmember.

"Okay, suite yourself, asshole, but when they start throwing those lines off the side of the canal, your ugly head is gonna be rolling down the sea and get to Mexico before you. Suit yourself, though."

He decided to leave the bow. The man walked along side him across the decks.

"My name is Jameel".

"I'm James. Thanks for the tip. Sorry I was a jerk. My head hurts."

"No problem, man. Never been through the canal before, I take it."

"No, I'm afraid not. From New York and we don't have any canals."

"Ain't an easy trip no matter how you do it. I like the canal. Tests a man's skills. Almost killed me three years ago. Got caught up in a line they threw and it bobbed me all the way to the top of the lock, bouncing me back and forth on the wall like a yo-yo. Eighty-five feet. Only broke two bones. One in my shoulder and one in my knee. You got any skills?"

"No." His throat filled with bile again.

"Then my best advice to you is stay out of our way. Those skinny arms of yours don't look like they'll be much help anyway."

The man smiled, a big toothy grin, and punched Michael's arm in a playful swing. Michael lost his balance, swayed to the left and caught himself on a deck line, preventing him from falling head first into the sea.

"Yep, like I said, you better stay away from us," Jameel proclaimed, as he broke into laughter and went below.

Michael went to his quarters to lick his wounds and soothe his ego. He dozed.

"All hands on deck. Get up here. The Captain's commanding voice pierced holes in his brain. Michael jumped from his bunk and raced topside.

Once on deck, he faced, head-on, his worst fears. Three Customs Agents stood squarely in front of the Captain and the crewmembers stood behind the Captain.

"Name your ship and its homeport," the tallest Agent demanded.

"The Crystal Lee, hailing from the Caymans,"

"How many crew on board?" The Agent looked straight into the Captain's eyes and did not appear to count the number of men on deck. Michael took a place next to Jameel.

"Four crew members and myself." Michael kept his eyes down, but he could feel beads of sweat on his forehead.

"Let's see your papers, while we have a look at this ship. Do you believe it is safe to go through this canal, Captain?"

"She's fit as a fiddle, Sir. Made the voyage five times so far, with no incident."

Two of the agents left and went below.

The agent in charge took the stack of paperwork from the Captain and thumbed through it. He lingered over one passport. Michael hoped it wasn't his. The beads of sweat rolled down his cheeks.

The agents returned from below and walked up and down the deck, checking fittings and lines.

Would this hell ever end, Michael thought? The agent with the paperwork was now looking at each of the crewmembers. Up and down. Close inspection of each face. For the third time in one day, the bile returned. His turn was next. In the next instant, the agent stood eye-to-eye with him.

"Ah, you must be James Shockley." The man took a long look, from the top of his head to the soles of his shoes.

His tongue swelling in his mouth, Michael felt his knees go soft. Swallowing the bile in his throat, his nose filled with his own stench.

"You need a bath, sailor." The agent turned and walked away, signaling the other men to follow him.

Michael stood frozen to the deck. The Captain sauntered past him, never throwing a glance in his direction and climbed below. From beneath the decks, he yelled up to his crew to get his ship ready to swing.

Two of the crew moved on command to do their assigned jobs. One held back.

"So what's your story, man? I got a notion something just ain't right about you."

"I think you better go do your job, like the Captain said," Michael spat at him. He turned and walked away from the man, squaring his shoulders, regaining confidence in his mission.

The men worked feverishly. They lashed giant lines onto fittings and then laid them out in straight paths across the decks, turning the end back and running it towards the sides of the ship. They lashed down every unsecured object on the deck. The

Panama sun baked their already leather-like skin.

Sweat poured from every pore of their bodies. The Captain appeared on deck, surveyed the work and grunted at the men. They were ready for the first lock.

The ship glided with ease between the two cement walls. From above, canal workers threw lines, with metal balls, monkey fists, attached to their ends, down to the Crystal Lee's deck. The crew grabbed them and, with the skill of years of experience, attached their own lines to the balls. The lines whipped upwards slapping the wall and became taut between the top of the wall and the deck of the boat.

"Water In." The command came from somewhere above them. From the walls, giant valves below the waterline opened and, with unbelievable force, water poured into the lock. The water below them toiled and turned with the force of a hurricane sea. The ship started to rise as the water filled the lock.

Before Michael could understand what was happening, the ship was even with the top of the wall, the lines were released and the ship started moving forward to the next lock. The men repeated the procedure and the ship rose to the top of the second lock and then again, to the top of the third.

The sixth journey of the Crystal Lee through the Panama Canal ended with an exuberant cheer from her Captain and his crew. A bottle of rum was opened and the successful crew toasted the jungle-clad shores of the Gatun Lake.

The Crystal Lee moved past the shores of jungle growth and towards the lake's small mountaintop islands, ever-lasting icons of the valley filled with water to build the canal.

The sea-worn, weary men, sick with their own stench became drugged with the smell of scarlet hibiscus and passion flowers. The sound of screeching monkeys and the frantic calls of brightly colored Macaws and Toucans lent an air of a festive dance hall to the decks of the ship and the men celebrated with all the fever of drunken sailors.

Long after the sun set on the bow of their ship, four of the men retired to their bunks.

One man remained on deck to guide them across the lake into tomorrow's adventures and the promises of his future. Gently turning the wheel back and forth, staying on course, Michael smiled to himself and remembered his mission.

The starlit night moved effortlessly into the morning sunrise. It had been a long run at the helm of the Crystal Lee all night, but Michael had sent his relief below, preferring to command the ship himself.

Gazing at the stars, a light wind in his face and the soft splashing sound of the water gently peppering the waterline, he thought about the strange turn his life had taken.

Michael realized he didn't miss his three-piece suits or his fast cars. The women? Maybe a little. It dawned on him that other than the poverty he had witnessed in the Philippines as a child, he had known no other life than the fast, expensive lifestyle in Los Angeles and New York.

It occurred to him that he had never had any real feelings; not regret, not sadness, not emotion, but most of all not love. He hadn't even missed his parents after he sent them back. He never thought about the women he had bilked out of millions of dollars. He had only laughed at their stupidity and gullibility.

He looked at his hardened hands and rubbed them over his unshaven face. Yes, he thought, I am a different man. The sleaze balls he knew in New York wouldn't even recognize him, let alone believe the road he had been on. He liked feeling like a man. His ego soared in his head like an eagle in full flight.

He admitted to himself, under a full-moon and a swaying sea, that his whole life had been driven by the almighty dollar and its power to buy respect, no matter who he hurt or destroyed.

This thought reignited his obsession with getting his money back and then was followed quickly by the realization that he did have one feeling that was real, hatred.

He sat, one bare foot resting on the bottom of the wheel, turning it side to side with his toe. Lighting a cigarette and inhaling deeply, he tossed the burning match into Gatun Lake.

Luxuriating in his hatred, he pictured Megan's face when he reappeared in her life, claiming his money and walking out on her again. This time, she wouldn't be standing when he left.

A scruffy voice brought him out of his reverie.

"Get this ship ready for land," the Captain's voice boomed

into the morning air.

The crew appeared and heaved lines. No one needed to be told what to do. The men were eager to put foot on land.

"I'll take the helm. Get out of my way. I'm taking us into Gamboa. Got a pretty little friend there I'm gonna spend some time with," the Captain bragged.

Michael flipped his smoke into the sea and went below.

When he returned, the ship was anchored about a hundred yards offshore.

"Get in the skiff, pansy ass. We're going ashore".

As Captain Smith stood tall on the bow of the skiff and Michael sat off to starboard enjoying one of the Captain's Cuban cigars, the remaining crew rowed the ragtag group of sailors to shore.

A wall of jungle foliage, framed by a narrow strip of white sand beach, was all that Michael could see. A dozen or so other boats dotted the anchorage.

The Gatun Lake rose and fell calmly under their boat and the rhythmic beating of the oars lent background music to the scene.

Once again Michael found himself wondering what his friends would think of him now.

The boat landed hard on the beach, following-waves pushing it the rest of the way to shore.

The Captain stepped onto shore and, as his second foot hit dry land, the crew jumped from the boat and ran into the jungle. Michael remained seated, finishing his cigar and watching the Captain.

The Captain dug deep into his pants pocket, came up with a bar of yellow soap, stripped naked and dove into the sea.

Lathering himself all the way up to his white hair, he dove and jumped around in the water like a playful dolphin.

He walked from the water, re-dressed into his sand-laden clothes and jumped into the water again, agitating himself in his own personal washing machine.

From the beach, glaring at Michael in disgust, he bellowed, "Let's go, pansy ass, we only have two hours to find us a woman. You better find one that has a dead-ass nose."

Michael followed the Captain along a machete-hacked path.

Monkeys jumped from tree to tree. The aroma of tropical flowers blended itself with the scent of monkey and bird excretion. Fist-sized spiders languished on the dense bark of the jungle trees. Rays of sun forced their way through pin-point openings in the canopy, trying unsuccessfully to dry the mist-soaked air.

It seemed to Michael that Mother Nature had taken everything she owned and put it together in this rain forest just to amuse herself.

The bustling town sat poised in the middle of enough cleared land to accommodate a couple of hundred residents. Bars and brothels lined most of the streets. People moved everywhere. Ramshackle huts, tree houses and whatever else suited their jungle lifestyles cluttered the rest of the town.

Sailors and locals hawked tables of fresh-caught fish. Screeching as loudly as the monkeys, seagulls dove down, to gorge on the entrails of the gutted fish. They viciously fought each other midair over their prize.

The oppressive heat overwhelmed Michael. The never-ending cacophony of sounds and the smell of cheap rum and dead fish assaulted his senses. Hoards of mosquitoes sucked the blood from his veins.

Women paraded up and down the street, dressed to leave nothing to a man's imagination.

"A sailors paradise, eh, pansy ass?" The Captain seemed drunk with anticipation.

"I'm being eaten alive by these bugs and you call this a paradise, you miserable fool?"

"Like I said, two hours. You can put up with anything for two hours, unless, of course, you really are a pansy-ass. You'll forget about the little buggers after you have some rum and pick yourself a woman. Now, let's get what we came here for."

Michael kept swatting his arms and face. The bugs were maddening, but didn't seem to bother anyone but him. He ran into the first bar they came to, only to discover the hoards were thicker. He ordered a rum from the grungy bartender and found three dead mosquitoes floating in the glass of murky brown liquid. The Captain had already disappeared into the shadows of the loud, dark room.

In less than a heartbeat Michael decided to forgo the pleasures of this paradise and headed back to the beach. He dove into the water, trying to relieve the unbearable itching.

He waited out the two hours, sitting on the beach, hating the Captain.

The Captain, his drunken crew in tow, appeared, bellowing as usual.

"The 'squitoes here love sweat and stink, pansy ass, almost as much as the woman love sailors with money."

"Go to hell, you hateful bastard."

The crew rowed them back, the same way they had rowed in, only now, they were grinning big, stupid, toothy grins.

Captain Smith stood on the bow, singing some drunken sailor's song. His raspy, rum-laden voice outdid anything the monkeys could come up with. The oars hit the water with perfect rhythm. The only difference was Michael. He spent the return trip scratching his skin raw.

Back on the ship, he went straight to his berth. Minutes later the drunken Captain appeared with a bottle of ugly pink liquid.

"Put this on yourself and try not to bother us with your girly whining." He turned and left.

Michael awoke to darkness and a dull, throbbing in his head. As he became aware of the headache, he realized he was covered in sweat and, at the same time, freezing. His body shook from the chill. Fever, he thought. Great.

He became vaguely aware of someone standing over him. He reached up to touch his head and felt wet towels.

"Are you awake?" a gruff voice demanded.

He recognized the Captain's voice. "What's wrong with me?" His voice seemed to be miles away, in some sort of echo chamber.

"You're probably dying, pansy ass."

"What the hell are you talking about, you son of a bitch?"

"You've been sleeping for a couple of days. Malaria, I think. Damn 'squitoes got you. Already lost one of the crew. We're headed toward a port I know of, Puerto San Luis. They got some crazy, old medicine witch there that cured me of the clap once, a long time ago. Hope she's still alive. I think her name's Lupita. She's mean as a horny bull, but she's got some kind of magic. Got it from her mother, I think."

"I feel like I'm gonna die. I think you're right. How long?"

Michael managed to spit out.

"We'll be there sometime tomorrow. Long run. Didn't plan to stop there. I've got kind of a history with a woman in the village."

"How many of their woman did you ......" his voice trailed off and he fell into a coma-like sleep.

When he awoke again, people were carrying him. He was being lowered over the side of the ship. Burial at sea, he thought. So this is my end. I'm dead. Screwed people out of their money, had people killed, and a mosquito gets me. A damn eighth-inch friggin' insect.

Men hovered over him, wrapping him in something soft. Couldn't possibly be angels. Not me. Maybe they made a mistake. They'll find out who I am and send me the other way.

He expected to hear a splash as they threw him in the water. No splash. He expected fire and brimstone. A hard wooden bottom. Where was he? What was going on? Somebody was saying he'd be alright. Where was the Captain? Blue skies? His mind raced. Do dead people think? Fast, he was moving fast. He recognized the sound of an engine. Sleep befell him.

37

Enrique, self-appointed protector of his dock and his village, dozed in his chair as he had done every day since the big white ship took his friends away.

As families and friends stood on that beach and watched their sons sail away, he instinctively knew what role he would play in his village, and with unspoken words, the village people looked to him for leadership from that day forward.

He took care of his village, his people and his bay. He helped with births and buried the dead. He made sure everyone had enough fish and rice through some of the toughest times. He performed marriages and consoled his people through many moments of despair. He asked for nothing in return.

His burdens had been heavy, but he wouldn't have had it any other way. Fate had left him in charge and he bore his burden with a sense of honor.

He stirred in his chair as a deep voice filled the air above him. He lifted his hat and peered at the man looking down at him. Enrique recognized the voice, but not the face.

"I ask you again, what does it take to get a beer around here?"

Enrique stood up. Tears welled in his eyes. "Francisco, is it really you?" he muttered.

The man opened his arms and embraced him. "I have missed you, my friend."

Enrique pulled away and took a long look at the man he had known so many years ago as a boy. He couldn't find any words to say.

Finally, wiping his clouded eyes with his shirtsleeve, he said, "I never knew what happened to you and Carlos. I thought you were probably dead. I cannot believe you are standing before me after all these years."

"Our lives led us in different directions, which now have led us back to here," Francisco responded.

"Is Carlos here, too?"

"Yes, and Tia Juanita."

The two men embraced again and turned to walk up the pier, joy glowing on their faces.

"You look older," Enrique chided his friend.

"And you look younger?" Francisco chided back. "So, did you ever marry Angelina?"

"She would not have me, Francisco, same as the Captain that took you away. She spent her life in love with another man, a dream. In her heart, she loves me and we both know that, but she would not promise herself to me.

"I am sorry to hear that, my friend. I always hoped you and she would marry and have many children. I, too, had a hard time with love, but I raised a handsome son who is now studying medicine. He is the only good that came from that fateful day so many years ago.

Enrique stopped in his tracks. "Your son is a doctor? We have a hospital now. Our new friend, Peter, built it."

"I think I met him on the road here. He is a handsome American, yes?"

"Yes, he is and smart."

"He could not take his eyes from Megan's face. It didn't look to me like he was too interested in a hospital," Francisco chuckled.

"Who is Megan?" Enrique asked.

"She is the reason we are here, Enrique."

The two men were nearing Angelina's restaurant. "I will fill you in later, my friend. Right now, I want to see Angelina."

Francisco walked to the window of the restaurant and peered in. Carlos sat at a table, a dish of steaming food in front of him, a spoonful headed towards his mouth. Amy and Megan were nowhere to be seen and he could just barely see Angelina and Tia Juanita in the kitchen, bustling around and chatting away.

He opened the door and motioned to Carlos to be quiet. Walking over to the bar, he called out, "Where can I find the most beautiful woman in Puerto San Luis?"

Angelina dropped her spoon and ran to his extended arms.

"I never believed I would see you again," Angelina cried. She took his face in her hands, tears falling down onto her cheeks. "You are still handsome man, eh?"

Enrique made a disapproving sound behind them and she

looked at him with a sigh, wiping her eyes on her sleeve. "Pay no attention to him, Francisco; he still wants me to marry him, even though I am too old to get married now. He never gives up and he is still jealous of every man I talk to. You will see."

"You should have married him long ago, Angelina. He is the best man in town and you are the best woman. You are a match made in heaven. You always were. I thought about you many times over the years and I expected you to have many children running around by now."

Enrique, hat in hand, spoke. "You see, Angelina, this is what I have been trying to tell you all these years. Francisco has a son who is almost a doctor and any man that can make such a great son must be smart. It is not too late to listen to his advice."

"Hush, Enrique, hush right now. A doctor, Francisco? Really, a doctor? I cannot believe this. You must have spent all your money on his education and not on food because you are thin. I must get you something to eat right away".

Embarrassed by Enrique, she hurried towards her kitchen, when another opinion was expressed.

Tia Juanita appeared from behind the bar, a margarita in hand.

"Well, I agree with Francisco and he is a smart man. He found margaritas right here in the middle of this desert, didn't he? I suggest you take his advice, Angelina."

"You hush, too, Tia Juanita." With a wave of her hand, Angelina hurried into the kitchen.

Laughing, walking towards Carlos, Francisco realized his friend had not participated in the conversation. "What's wrong, Carlos? Are you okay?"

"Sure I'm okay. The girls are upstairs cleaning up and taking a nap. You are yakking with Enrique and Angelina about babies, Tia Juanita is getting sloshed on margaritas and I'm just sitting here wondering where the guys are that want to kill us. Everything's fine. That answer your question?"

"Okay, Carlos, I get your point, but when do you want to tell these people that we have led big trouble into their village?

Should we do it without saying hello? Maybe we should just sit on the front porch of this place armed with guns, say nothing to them and just wait for the black car to drive in. Should we eat their food and then tell them to get their guns because they are going to need them?

We haven't been here since the day that ship left this bay. What did you expect us to do when we got here? Neither one of us considered the consequences of what would happen to this village when we brought our trouble to it. Do you have a plan?"

Francisco tried to keep his voice down as he assaulted his friend with unexpected anger. He didn't know Enrique stood within hearing distance.

Carlos sat speechless. He had never known his friend to show any sign of anger. He also knew Francisco was right.

The two men stared at each other and a voice broke the silence.

"Carlos, Francisco, what are you saying? What kind of trouble is coming to us? What is going on? Let's go outside. Right now. You will tell me what you are talking about, but not in here." Red-faced and angry, Enrique stormed towards the door. Carlos and Francisco followed.

As they gathered in the street, Angelina appeared in the doorway carrying a bowl of food for Francisco. "Where are you going? Francisco's food is ready."

"Go back inside, Angelina. The men have to talk. We will eat later," Enrique instructed, feigning calmness.

Angelina put down the bowl and walked into the street. "Don't you dismiss me, Enrique. I will not stay inside. Anyway, I know why Francisco and Carlos have come back here. No one comes back here. One margarita and Tia Juanita spilled her guts. It appears that you are the only one who does not know what's going on. Now, let's figure out how to help Megan."

The three men followed Angelina back inside. She picked up Francisco's bowl and turned to the men. "Sit down, let's talk," she demanded.

The men did as they were told. Enrique looked at Angelina, and turned to his friends. "Do you see why Enrique has always loved this woman?"

As Enrique spoke, the door opened and Carlos and Francisco looked up to see the stranger they had met on the road.

"Peter, come and meet our old friends." Angelina waved him

over to the table and the men stood to shake his hand. "Sit down, Peter. Join us. We are about to have a serious conversation."

Carlos reacted immediately. "No, Angelina. This conversation should only be between us."

"No Carlos, this is not your decision. Your troubles are uninvited visitors in this village and I will decide who sits at the table. He is our friend and has become one of us. I know that if he can, he will help us with this problem. Sit down, Peter. Please excuse my old friend for his rudeness."

No one argued with Angelina. Peter sat, wondering where Megan was. Tia Juanita sat two tables away with her margarita, not saying a word.

"Talk, Francisco," Angelina demanded. Carlos glared at her, but kept his mouth shut.

For the next hour, Francisco told Peter and Angelina the entire story of Megan and Michael. No one interrupted. No one asked questions. They sat in stunned silence.

No one at the table knew they were expecting the wrong enemy.

38

I listened to Megan's story with intense interest. I watched the faces of my friends turn from joy at seeing their old friends, to fear; and then watched these people turn into one family, intent on helping a complete stranger with a very serious problem. No demands to leave their village. No reprisals for bringing this problem to them and dropping it into their laps. No anger, just love and willingness, after all these separated years, to join as one and help their friends.

These people never failed to amaze me and unknowingly guide me to an understanding of what an inadequate life I had led. I needed time. I needed to deal with the feelings of overwhelming love and admiration I felt for them. I needed to deal with the loathing I felt for myself. I rose from my seat and left the building.

I walked to the beach. I marveled at the incoming waves and their rush back to sea. The constant splashing of the water's surface, as jumping fish caught their prey. The warmth of the sand on my feet. All were signs of a God-like peace that calmed my soul.

A dozen or so seagulls circled overhead, riding thermals only they could find. The breeze touched my face with the gentleness of an angel's fingertips. I dug my toes into the sand and gazed across the sea I loved so much, watching lazy, white clouds drift across the horizon.

I pondered the bewildering journey that had brought me to this place. My life had taken strange turns and I wondered if I would ever be able to return home. I wondered if I would ever love anyone again.

God, Sadie. I couldn't remember how long ago I had changed from every waking moment being about her. When did she stop being the sole master of my thoughts?

Images of her wandered around in my head again, but my mind's eye saw a filmy vision of Megan's face.

The snapshot showed tousled, chestnut hair framing a flawless, ivory skin.

Her voice followed the snapshot. 'My name is Megan', she said, and with it came the sound of a soft, sweet musical piece.

Lost in the short moment I had spent in her presence, my hand closed and again I felt her tiny, delicate hand in mine, creating the sensation of a warm embrace.

The brief encounter had reached deep down into my soul and made me feel alive.

As my mind dealt with the thoughts and visions racing around in my head, hitting each other with the impact of cars in a ten car pile-up, a small black spot appeared on the horizon.

The sound of an engine resonated above the sounds of squawking birds and grew louder as the plane got closer.

Frank, I thought. Oh God, thank you for Frank. If anyone could get me on the right track it would be him.

Just before the belly of the plane hit the water, Frank waved from the cockpit, sporting a wide Cheshire cat grin.

I stood as it rode the waves to shore. I knew Frank loved this part of his flight. As the sand and water settled, he jumped from his cockpit, two beers in hand.

"How are you, old man? Good to see you; been awhile."

While still in full stride, he grabbed my hand and shook it. "You look like hell. Your new life finally not agreeing with you?" he laughed.

"You have no idea, Frank. Good to see you, too. Let's have a seat and talk."

I watched Frank remove his flight jacket and throw it into the cockpit. It probably cost enough to feed a small nation. He removed his leather boots and threw them on top of his jacket.

As the plane grumbled and settled itself down into the wet sand, we walked up to the top of a small dune. Rolling up his pants, he plopped down and buried his toes deep into the sand's warmth.

"Remember the leather couches in the club, Peter?"

I ignored him.

After some obligatory small talk and half the beer, he turned to me, that old concerned look crossing his face.

"So what's up? Like I said, you look like hell. Have the stars in your eyes died? Any chance you need a good plastic surgeon or maybe a job?"

"Better get some more beers, Frank. You're going to need them."

As he walked back to the plane, I wondered how he would take this latest news. I laughed to myself, picturing him bounding and gagging me and throwing me onto his plane. The ultimate hero, rescuing his wayward friend. What a story for the Club.

When he returned, I jumped into these thoughts with my first sentence.

"I have a new job, Frank," I stated simply, enjoying the quizzical look on his face. I enjoyed doing that to him. "I have to rescue a princess." I watched for his reaction.

He took a long drink from his bottle. "What's the matter? One of your local pretties been kidnapped by a modern day Pancho Villa?"

Smug. Smug was his reaction. Well, I guess I deserved that. I had put him through a lot.

I told him Megan's story. He had to go get more beers twice, but he didn't say a word.

He sat back in the sand, resting himself on his arms and gazed at his plane. We watched the fish jump and the seagulls circle for awhile. We had another beer.

"You know, Peter, you've had an amazing adventure here.

You've made new friends and discovered a new set of values. You seem to be at a turning point in your life. Your hospital is almost finished and soon Lupita and Enrique, thanks to all your teaching talent, will be able to take over for you."

Anger raged in my head. I interrupted him, as I stood up. "I'm not leaving, Frank. Did you hear anything I said? Why can't you understand what has happened to me here. Why can't you see that I am a part of this place now? I don't want my old life back. For God's sake, Frank, I've told you this so many times before. Why can't you believe it?"

"For once, Peter, shut the hell up and sit down. I wasn't going to suggest you leave. I'm sorry if it sounded that way. It's hard to know where to start after you've been told a story like this.

You didn't let me finish. Why are you so hot-tempered? Talk about not listening. Do you think I don't envy what you have found? Do you think that every time I spend my day catering to some socialite's idea of beauty, my head is not full of thoughts about you and the people here? Why do you think I keep coming back?

I was going to suggest, as much as I can't believe I'm going to say this, that it is probably time for you to start thinking about yourself again."

I sat down. Weariness from the never-ending guilt of the life I had been born into overwhelmed me.

Suddenly, everything made sense. My life had never been about me. The people and the events in my life had defined me. I couldn't escape the shadows. Only here, had I had the opportunity to look inside myself, to not define myself by my father's image, my profession's image and yes, by Sadie's image.

"Peter, we can help our friends save Megan from these idiots. That part is easy. I'm sure Tia Juanita already has some sort of plan.

What interests me more are your feelings for Megan. Do you remember falling in love with Sadie the same way? Do you sometimes wonder if she isn't sitting on one of those clouds pulling your strings?

I have told you before; she would never want you to spend your life alone.

I'm not sure she would have picked this place for you to find love, but who knows? Sadie had a pretty good sense of humor.

Let me ask you this. What strange force of nature would bring this woman all the way down here, presumably escaping from some phantom murderers, accompanied by a stranger bunch of characters than anyone could imagine, if there wasn't a larger scheme of things to play out?"

"You're a romantic fool, Frank. It surprises me you never married."

"Peter, let's go rescue your princess. It may be time for you to love again."

39

The home-coming party could be heard from the beach.

Inside the bar, Francisco took center stage, reliving his adventures in San Diego for his adoring fans.

I found his four friends at a table deep in the room. Angelina found Frank, dragging him into the crowd to introduce him.

"I don't know if you remember me, but I'm Peter. I met you on the road." I stammered.

I stood, unable to take my eyes from Megan. She was lovelier than I remembered. She looked up at me and I felt my face go red.

"Yes, I do. How nice to see you again. Please join us," she said.

"So, Peter. I understand that you know all about my dilemma, why don't you tell us how you ended up here?"

My mind blank, idiotic staring seemed to be the only thing I could muster up.

Amy broke the awkward silence. "Megan is the curator of a fine museum in Greenwich Village. What do you do when you are not enjoying the wonderful sun in Mexico?"

I looked at her. She was lovely, too. A different look than Megan, more impish, cute, spunky. Not goddess-like.

"I am, I mean I was, a plastic surgeon in San Diego." The words came, as long as I was looking at Amy.

"I lost my wife a couple of years ago and couldn't deal with life. I set sail in my boat and, one evening, found myself sitting off the coast of this little village, wanting a beer. I have been here ever since."

As my composure returned, I had no intention of looking at Megan again. "What do you do, Amy?"

"I'm certainly sorry to hear about your wife. She must have been young."

"Thirty-two. A speeding drunk driver hit her from behind.

"I am so sorry."

And there it was. Megan's voice.

"Thank you, but please, tell me about yourselves. I haven't

284

been home in quite awhile. I need to be caught up. I......, never mind, please just tell me about you." I didn't want them to know that my brain had turned to oatmeal.

Amy chatted effortlessly. Carlos sat glumly next to her, watching the door.

Megan only interjected when she thought Amy exaggerated a story.

Satisfied her entire audience had arrived, Angelina stood, with a mallet in hand, banging on the bar-top.

As the crowd silenced, all attention turned to her. Tia Juanita stood behind her, stern and foreboding and more than a little drunk. Enrique stood to her left.

"I know that we are all grateful that our old friends have returned to us. I think you all know by now they have also brought a problem with them, a problem that we all now share.

Our friends have made us proud in their new country, with the lives they have led after leaving our small village. Now they are back and they need our help. I have a plan to help them, but I will need your help."

Cheers erupted. Men slapped Francisco on the back. Women embraced Megan and Amy. Carlos glared at all of them.

When the crowd silenced, one man, hat in hand, said to Angelina, "I think I speak for all of us here. Out of respect and honor for our friends Francisco and Carlos, we will do anything required of us to help Megan. What do you need, Angelina?"

"We have many guns and many strong men in this village. We have good horses and mules. We have only one road leading to us.

I don't believe we need to worry about the sea, the only other way in. I propose that we protect the road and when they arrive, we ambush them.

We know they are in a black car and that there are two of them. We are many. The women and children can bring food and water to the men and we will protect Megan and her friends from here. We will keep her in hiding until this is over".

The men nodded in agreement.

Tia Juanita, standing tall, offered her help. "I would like to organize the women. We can make a kitchen in one of the barns and supply the men from there.

Carlos found himself liking the plan. He hadn't been prepared for the people here. He had forgotten over the years.

"Angelina, I know the road that we came in on like the back of my hand. I, with Enrique, would like to organize the men into a posse.

The crowd started to talk amongst themselves. Carlos balked at the possibility that there would be a question as to his leadership. Amy took his hand in hers.

Angelina raised her hand and the crowd quieted.

The same man that had accepted her proposal stepped forward, his hat still in his hand.

Carlos's body stiffened and the hair stood up on the back of his neck. Megan and Peter sat in silence.

"Angelina," the man began.

Carlos stifled a low growl.

"We, the people of this village, are faced with a great challenge. The lives of our new friends are at stake. We are not fighters, just simple fisherman and farmers. With this humbleness in mind, we are still willing to protect what is ours, as we have for many generations."

As the man spoke, the doors flew open behind him and Lupita appeared in the doorway. The moonlight behind her illuminated her long, hooded white robe creating a surreal, frightful aura.

She carried a gnarled, wooden staff in her left hand, as long as she was tall. Slamming the end of it to the floor, everyone in the room gasped. Lupita raised her arms above her head and silenced every sound in the room. The people stared in awe.

"You dare to make these plans without my presence? I have seen over every one of you since your birth. I have seen over your parents before you. Our old friends bring imminent danger to our village and you do not consult me? Do you have no fear of my wrath? I will curse the earth you walk on, the air you breathe. Your gardens will die and your lungs will explode."

She glared into the crowded room, her black, staring eyes piercing the souls of her listeners.

Megan lost her breath and struggled for air. Amy turned white. Peter expected fire to shoot into the air from her fingertips.

Enrique stepped forward. No other man moved. One

woman did. Angelina placed herself next to Enrique.

Enrique stood before the enraged woman, exuding the confidence of a man that had faced this woman many times before. A man not frightened by her wrath. A man who had also taken care of this village his entire life. He and Lupita both knew the invisible lines of power between the two of them. Neither had ever dared to step over the other's line. Each had learned respect for the other.

"Lupita, your powers have protected us against disease, famine, pestilence and death. This problem cannot be solved with your power.

This is a man's problem. This is a problem about death caused by man. You have dedicated your life to saving people. We may be faced with the possibility of taking a life. No one here would ask you to participate in this kind of decision. Your powers may be needed later if someone should get hurt."

Lupita raised her chin to the ceiling and projected a blood curdling, inhuman sound form the core of her soul.

She lowered her head and looked at them again with her icy black eyes. Local wolves howled in response. The moonlight dimmed, darkening the room. An unexpected chill passed over the villagers.

"This is not the end," she threatened. With one quick move, she turned and disappeared into the night.

Stunned, the crowd remained silent.

Angelina broke the silence. "Please, let's get back to our plan."

The shy man glanced back at the doorway and continued to speak. "Carlos, we would be proud and honored to have you as our leader in this time of trouble. We could ask for no better man than you."

Amy saw Carlos's chest swell with pride. His cockiness returned in the same instant. "Well, then, we better break off from the women and form a plan. The sooner, the better." He stood and moved out to the porch. The men followed him immediately.

The women gathered around Tia Juanita and they spent the rest of the night making plans. Megan and Amy were instructed to go to their room and get a good night's sleep.

As Megan walked up the stairs, she caught herself glancing back at the doorway and realized she was wondering what place

Peter would assume in the newly formed army.

"He's handsome, isn't he?" Amy asked as Megan undressed.

"I didn't notice, Amy. Don't be a silly girl. We are in terrible trouble and have put these people in grave danger. We have a local witch doctor angry with us and we can't keep Tia Juanita sober.

Do you think I have time to think about whether or not a man is handsome? This is not a Jane Eyre novel. This is real life, which, as of now, includes real guns."

"But he is handsome, isn't he?" Amy countered to her little rant.

"Okay, yes he is, and shy, too." Megan gave in.

"Are you scared, Megan?"

"Amy, I am so scared, I can't think. I wake up trembling and crying in the middle of the night. I can't believe all of this is because I fell in love with the wrong man. I can't believe all of these people are willing to die for us. I know that I will never be able to love again."

"I never thought I would be able to love anyone and you get to use the word 'again'. I believe you will be able to love again because you and your soul are composed of love. You cannot deny something that you are. You have always been meant to be loved and to love in return."

"You must be my biggest fan, Amy."

"Would I traipse across the country for anyone else?"

"Megan, do you think Lupita will put a curse on us?"

"Probably, the way things are going, she surely will. What a great story to tell our grand-children.

40

Sweat-soaked sheets chilled the skin on my body, making any form of sleep impossible. The oppressive heat lay heavily over my bed entrenching me in its cover.

The desert generally cooled after dark, but tonight, the only relief came from a cold shower. My hands pressed against the wall, my head down, I let the cool water engulf me, deciding a beer would take care of my insides.

I sat at the only table downstairs that had a fan whirling above it. I couldn't help but think of my most recent patient in the hospital.

He spent most of his time in sleep, battling the malaria raising hell in his body. When he did wake, he mumbled non-understandable sentences, except for the cussing. He didn't seem a pleasant sort and I laughed as I remembered the rich, pampered women cursing the pain from their most recent indulgences in beauty. This guy had nothing over them. He couldn't even come close.

The local men, armed with every gun they owned, stood watch on the mountain road for the black car. The women slept, prepared to deliver their next meal.

My thoughts moved to Frank. I wasn't sure why he left. It had seemed as though he wanted to remain and help see the village through its crisis. One morning, after a long talk with Francisco, he appeared bag and baggage in hand. He bid a farewell to everyone, including me, without offering an explanation to anyone. Francisco would not give up any information.

I heard a sound behind me and turned to see Megan coming down the stairs. In the darkness, she didn't seem to see me. Starlight filtered through corners of the room and illuminated her lithe body as she passed through the gentle light.

God, she's beautiful, I thought. So far, I had managed to avoid her, most of the time, simply not wanting to deal with my attraction for her. It scared me. My devotion to Sadie, Frank's admonitions and all the rest of my demons tormented my mind. I struggled to believe Frank's advice that I should move on; that Sadie would want me to. I also knew that only I could make his advice come to fruition.

As I watched her help herself to a beer, she turned and must have seen my shadow in the dim light. She took a start and then said, "Peter?"

"Yes. Couldn't sleep in this heat either, huh?"

"No," she said as she walked towards me. "This heat is smothering me. I've been tossing and turning for hours. My bed feels like a swimming pool. Does it often get this hot at night?"

She looked as fresh as a summer day.

She touched the back of the chair across from me and said, "Do you mind if I join you?"

Did I mind? Did I mind? My brain bounced around with the ridiculousness of the question, as I said politely, "No, please, sit down. Maybe we can keep each other's minds off of this heat."

"So, I understand you are considered one of the best plastic surgeons in San Diego. You are a humble man."

Well, well, I gloated. How about that? She had asked someone about me. Damn!

"Yes, I am, or used to be. I don't know if I'll go back to it. I kind of like it here."

Settling into her chair, securing her hair into a ponytail from a rubber band stored on her wrist, she said one word, "Interesting."

She moved her beer to her mouth and took a long drink. "Ummmm," she murmured, placing the beer back on the table.

What kind of a response was that? I didn't know whether to pursue the conversation or take it as complete lack of interest. I studied her face to see if it showed any desire for me to go on. I noticed the cuteness of her nose, her perfect lips, her blue eyes and the tip of her chin.

I also realized I wasn't looking at her through a doctor's eyes. No, just a man's, the side of me that somehow always sent shivers of insecurity down my spine. I felt an urge to run my finger along her cheekbone. I tightened my hand into my lap, realizing the one thing I hadn't seen on her face was interest in my answer.

While mulling over my internal battles, she smiled. "Well, I guess you should know. You haven't been around much and some of the locals kind of filled Amy and me in on your business. I hope you are not offended, but I guess because we are all Americans, they thought you would be the most interesting topic of conversation." She paused a minute, apparently to see if I showed any sign of offense.

"No, but I hardly think I am the most interesting thing to talk about. I think your journey running away from killers is much more exciting." I laughed, but she turned pale under the flattering suntan she had already acquired.

"Please, let's keep our conversation devoid of my situation for the time being. I wish this nightmare would end. More and more innocent people seem to get involved every day, but let's talk about you. Tell me all about yourself, your time here and Sadie."

Noticing the expression on my face as the word 'Sadie' crossed her lips, she continued. "Yes, they told me about her and the way you loved her. She must have been a wonderful woman for a man to love her as much as you do.

I, on the other hand, have never been lucky enough to have a love like yours and Sadie's. My relationships have always ended poorly, usually when a wife I was unaware of shows up to reclaim her husband.

This last affair with Michael did take a rather completely, unexpected dramatic turn. As a matter of fact, sometimes I think it warrants a novel. But you know what they say, lucky at cards, unlucky at love." She chuckled. "I guess I'll have to try cards." She lifted her beer again.

The fan whirred above us, crickets' songs of love entered through the open front door. The breeze from the fan moved her ponytail back and forth.

Every breath I took filled my nostrils with her delicate scent. I knew the feeling. It had only happened once in my life and the moment was seared into my brain with a hot branding iron. That time I had fallen in love. God help me from here on in, I thought.

Hours into the quietness of the night, the hot humid air blanketing us, we shared our stories.

"So, here I sit, in a Mexican village, sweating profusely, drinking beer and talking to a handsome man about my saga," her story ended.

Did she say handsome man? Did I dare think that I had heard that? I should say something, but what?

"Another beer?"

"That would be great."

I jumped up from the table and headed for the bar. A handsome man. What am I? A twelve-year old? Collect yourself, man. Turn around and act like an adult.

I hoped my return from the bar did not include a stupid grin on my face.

"Well, you are safe now. We've had no sign of them in four days. Maybe they gave up and went home. The locals are getting restless waiting in the shadows of the road. You haven't been out of this building any further than the front porch. Why don't we take a walk? I'll show you my boat."

"I'd love that. Let's go, although, I must admit, I have already walked down to the dock to take a look at your boat.a I love boats."

Walking up the dusty road, the crickets silenced. The moon shone brightly above us and I reached over to take her hand. It seemed to be waiting for me.

"You know," she said, "I learned to sail at the same time I learned to walk. We lived in Connecticut and my father was an avid sailor. He refused to use an engine on his twenty-eight foot Dory, so it was sail or die. He was a great man."

"I can't believe you are a sailor. Sailing has always been my passion and one day, I'd like to sail the South Pacific".

I admired her sure-footedness as she stepped into the cock-pit and stood behind the helm. I watched as she stepped up onto the decks and walked towards the bow.a Everything felt just right.

"I'll see what I can round up for us to eat."

I sensed, before I heard, her descent into the cabin.

"Nice," she said. "Really nice. I haven't been onboard in a long time."

"Let's take it out into the moon-path. You want to?" I asked.

"Let's do it, Captain. I'll get the lines."

She jumped off the boat, released the forward and aft line, gave us a shove and jumped back on.

"Would you mind if I took the sails?" she asked.

Once out of the small harbor, the ocean's breeze took us directly into the moon path.

She trimmed the sails, moonbeams lighting up the decks, and

then sat down next to me at the helm. Dolphin played in the mirrored water just off the bow, following the light and staying just ahead of us.

"Tell me about your patient at the hospital," she asked.

"The Captain of an old tramp steamer brought him in a couple of days ago. Not a real pleasant guy.

He hasn't left the ship since he dropped the sick guy overboard to us. He told us the guy picked up a bad case of malaria, on some jungle island, coming through the Panama Canal, but that's all we know.

The sick guy barely wakes up and does so only long enough to emit a slew of cusswords and then goes back off into delirium.

Malaria's a wicked disease. It affects everything in your body and stays around as long as it wants. It comes back as often as it wants, too.

I'm treating him with quinine, of which I have an abundant supply, thanks to Lupita and the bark from her wormwood trees.

You remember her from the bar. She's our local curandera; she has the el Don, the healing power.

He'll be lucky if he survives. He didn't get help in time and it has attacked most of his organs."

"What about the Captain? Do you know why he doesn't come off the ship?"

"No idea. He seems to wear a mean streak like a suit. He wasn't open to questions and hasn't tried to check on the sailor. His ship just sits outside the harbor and we haven't seen hide nor hair of them."

Sharing a bottle of wine, the light breeze carrying us along the moon-path, we whiled away the hours, entwined in the sea's magical spell. The night seemed endless.

The moon, having served us well, now rested on the horizon. It looked as though we would run right up on its craters if we kept going.

Megan stood up. "Prepare to come about, Captain. We should head back."

As the boat turned to face shore, the morning sunrise extended graceful pink and blue fingers onto an otherwise purple sky. The mountains hovered beneath the spectacular colors, painted in shades of brown, black and gray.

"Have you ever seen anything so beautiful, Peter?"

I smiled and shook my head. Only you Megan, I thought. Only you.

Her face lit up with a devilish grin. "My goodness, we just spent the night together." We laughed and sailed towards the sunrise in silence.

"May I ask you one more question before we dock?" she asked.

"Just one more."

"Why have you avoided me?"

I thought for a long minute. There wasn't enough time left of the sail to answer such a complicated question. I tried.

"The day I met you on the road, you had a profound effect on me. I felt things inside me I thought were gone. I needed to deal with them." That was it. That was all I had.

The boat touched the dock and she stepped off to secure the lines.

We spoke no words on the walk back to Angelina's, and this time, she kept her hand in her pocket.

I walked with her to the bottom of the stairs, and to my surprise, she turned to me and kissed me lightly on the cheek.

"Thank you for a wonderful evening, Peter."

I watched her walk up the stairs and crossed the room in search of another beer.

Yup, The same feeling.

•••••

I awoke to my name being called.

"Mr. Peter, Mr. Peter, wake up. Wake up".

Enrique stood above me. It never failed to amaze me that I had become immune to these abrupt awakenings by him. It never seemed to occur to him to knock and it crossed my mind that I had never seen a lock in this entire village.

"I'm not going fishing, Enrique. Sorry, not today. I don't care what's running." I rolled over and pulled the cover over my head. I wanted to go back to my dreams.

He reached down and shook me. "Wake up, wake up. An

important thing has happened. Wake up."

I looked at him. Wild eyes glared back at me. He hadn't even removed his hat.

"What is it, Enrique? What's wrong? Is Megan okay?" I shot up from the bed, reaching for my pants, ready to save my princess.

"Megan is okay; but do you remember the man on the tractor who gave us gas on our way to the Farmacia?"

"Yes, I do. What's going on?"

"Yesterday, that man came onto the mountain road to cross over to the ocean and he ran into the posse. They told him about Megan and the men chasing her.

He told them that a black car with two dead men in it were found in a mountain ravine many days ago. Some kind of terrible accident. You think they are Megan's men, Peter?"

"I need to find Carlos and Francisco, Enrique. You stay here with the women, just in case we're wrong."

I headed for the mountain on one of the horses tied up outside. I rode like the wind, a sense of exhilaration that Megan was finally safe.

41

The Captain heaved his last empty rum bottle at the wall in his stateroom. The glass shattered and cascaded to the floor like a meteor shower. Staggering from his drunkenness, he made his way to the upper decks, cussing his crew along the way. He hated the bastards. He hated Michael, that stupid pansy ass.

"Get out of my way, you lowlife," he spit at one of the crew. "I don't need you. I don't need any of you. I'll throw all your sorry asses overboard, just like I did that other jerk. Too bad the malaria got him. I would have enjoyed it more if he was alive."

Climbing the rail, in his quest to go to the village and find more rum, he caught his foot in a line and fell head first into the sea. Scrambling wildly, his mind in a confused state, he managed to board his skiff. Dripping with seawater, he started to laugh, the irony of his situation overtaking him.

•••••

He had sailed so many times to this village in the name of love. Of course, he hadn't been in love, but Angelina, oh God, Angelina. She believed he loved her and she rewarded him with all that a woman had to offer. A few cheap gifts here, a few there and she believed anything he told her. Women were so easy.

Over the years, on lonely nights at sea, without so much as a slight effort, he could conjure up her sweet scent, her soft, dark skin and her young, willing body. She had seen him through many long nights.

As luck would have it, he had to end their relationship with a lie.

There had been an unfortunate incident in a bull-fighting village on the northern coast of the Baja.

With a several-day lay-over due to the ship's Captain's illness and with several bottles of rum under his belt, he wandered up to the bullfight, the only action in town.

Tequila flowed freely and bets on the bulls were flying heavy.

Since he had no money, he got into the action by wagering the Captain's boat.

Unfortunately for him, not only did his chosen bull lose, but its performance was so bad, it became a laughing stock.

As the animal lay dead in the dirt of the arena, after only a two minute fight, he disappeared into the jeering crowd and headed back to the ship, at the quickest pace his drunken state would allow.

It didn't take long for the local men to follow him.

The crew saw the pangas approaching the ship, heard the first gunshots and quickly started the engines. Gunshots crossed the sea, from both sides, as the scared crew maneuvered the ship into deeper waters and escaped any harm.

The Captain appeared on the deck, still sick, and now dumfounded, by the attack on his boat.

When the Captain demanded an explanation from him, he drunkenly laughed about his wager and its results. The Captain fired him. The next day he was thrown off the ship into the waters of another obscure village. He swam to shore with only the clothes on his back.

A pretty, young girl with an ample body sat on the beach, alone.

"Welcome to our village," she said, smiling, as he approached her.

"Well, she's not Angelina, but she'll do," he thought. He could fall in a gutter and come up with a diamond ring.

Sometime later, he went to see the Captain and asked for forgiveness and one small favor. He requested that on the Captain's next visit to the village, he give Angelina a message. Would he please tell her that he had died honorably in a storm at sea? Broke, and at the bottom of his game, he knew he would never return to her.

The Captain, refusing forgiveness and threatening him with death if he ever showed his face again, granted him the favor, for Angelina's sake.

He then pulled a gun from his desk drawer, pointed it at Phillip, and gave him one chance to walk out. He took the offer.

The sad thing was he knew he would miss her, but not being one to languish over life's crazy turns, he proceeded forward, without regret, to leave plenty of other warm bodies, lies and empty rum bottles in his wake.

•••••

Still drunk beyond the limits of an ordinary man, wet and longing for a drink, he now wondered if Angelina still lived in the village.

Her beauty, and her eagerness to please a man beyond his wildest dreams, had qualified her to marry any man she wanted.

Well, he would find out and get a drink at the same time. Maybe no one would recognize him anyway.

His skiff rolled onto shore and buried its bow in the sand. Looks quiet, he thought. Wonder where the pansy ass is? Who cares? I remember where the bar is and that's all I need to know.

Still staggering, he stepped up onto the porch of the familiar bar. Pausing to look through the open door, he saw her. He watched her move around the bar, tending to her chores.

Time had been as kind to her as a man could expect. He grinned, a stupid drunken grin. Maybe he would get lucky.

As she walked to the kitchen, her back to him, he entered the door and strolled up to the bar, trying not to make a sound.

"Can a man get a drink around here?"

Angelina stopped in her tracks, but did not turn around. The voice, she recognized the voice. Not believing her ears, she stood still. It couldn't be, her mind told her. But it was. She knew it was.

Again came the voice.

"Can a man get a drink around here?"

This time she turned and moved towards him. Her mind and body went numb. The room, suddenly spinning like a top, destroyed her balance. She grasped for the bar to steady herself. As she looked past the heavy beard and the weathered skin, her breath left her body.

"Phillip?" she managed. "Phillip? I…I thought you were dead. The… the Captain said you were dead. He said there was an accident, a terrible storm. He said he buried you at sea."

"Well, surprise, I'm not," he laughed. "Pinch me, I'm real." He extended his hand.

Horrified, she stared at him, a thousand questions racing through her mind.

"Why would the Captain tell me you were dead? Where have you been all these years? Why did you never come back for me? Why are you here now?" The questions tumbled non-stop from her brain, down into her mouth and out into the still air of the room.

"Well, that's a funny story, but first, get me a nice big glass of your best rum. Then, how about a big hello kiss for the best lover you ever had?"

Angelina stared at him, unable to continue, unable to move. She looked at him more closely, realizing he was drunk. Anger tore through her mind and body, replacing the numbness.

"You want rum, you bastard? Rum?" She grabbed the closest bottle to her and splattered it in his face. "What are you doing here?" she screamed.

"I stopped by for a drink," he said, wiping his face and licking his fingers.

Her hand rose and connected with his face.

"I always loved your spunk. You know, it was only a little lie. I'm sure you can find it in your heart to forgive me. We had a good time, you and me, didn't we? We can pick up where we left off. How about it?"

"A lie? A little lie? I wasted my life on a little lie? I'll kill you, you bastard." She reached for a bar knife and raised it in the air. "I'll kill you. I'll kill you," she screamed, her arms flailing and missing him as he bounced back and forth, laughing. She started around the bar and he grabbed the bottle of rum and ran towards the door.

"Stupid bitch, just another useless whore," he threw over his shoulder as he shoved by a man at the doorway.

Enrique pushed his leg in front of Phillip. He spiraled into the air, landed face flat on the porch, breaking the bottle of rum as he hit.

Enrique turned to the enraged woman. "Angelina, Angelina. Stop. Stop right now." he ordered. He grabbed her as she tried to pass him. She struggled, fighting his hold on her, kicking and hitting him with all her might. He tightened his grip, grabbing the knife from her hand. "Please Angelina, please settle down. You cannot kill him". Her body went limp and she fell into his arms, sobbing and shaking.

Her pathetic, tear-soaked face looked up at him. "Enrique, did you hear? How long have you been standing there? I have been nothing but a fool. I wasted my life on him. He lied about being dead. He did not love me. How dare he come back here and humiliate me like this?" The shaking subsided and then returned. She pushed away from him, wild with anger again. Enrique held on tight.

"Let me go. I am going to kill him."

"No you are not. I will take care of him. I have always taken care of you, like it or not. Angelina, mi muy bonita, I love you. I have always loved you. This man cannot humiliate you in my eyes or anyone else's. I will take care of him. You are not to leave here. Do you understand me?"

Tia Juanita, joined by Megan and Amy, now stood next to them, having heard the commotion from the top of the stairs.

"Let me stay with her, Enrique," Tia Juanita said as she took Angelina into her arms. "I will quiet her. Go. Now. Do what is necessary."

The women helped Angelina to a chair.

Enrique walked from the bar, out onto the street, murder on his mind. His beautiful Angelina. All the years wasted for the two of them. White hot rage engulfed his soul. He would find revenge for Angelina's honor, even if it cost him his life.

As he reached the beach, he saw Phillip in his skiff, trying to get the engine started.

Picking up a piece of driftwood from the sand, he walked to the boat. With one swift swing, propelled by his raging anger, he hit the Captain across the back of his neck and shoulders. The Captain fell face forward, his face landing on the gearshift. Blood shot into the air and fell in glittering droplets onto the boat.

Enrique grabbed him by the shoulders and threw him into the sand, rage increasing his strength by tenfold. A lifetime of suppressed anger, frustration and unfilled dreams reached out into the open air for the first time. His body convulsed with strength.

He kicked him in the stomach and screamed, "Get up, you bastard. Get up."

As the Captain struggled to get up, Enrique drew back his arm and hit him with all his force in the face, opening another wound.

On his hands and knees, his blood turning the sand red, he managed to smirk at Enrique.

`"What's the matter? She wouldn't have you? You weren't good enough for her after me? You crummy, useless little Mexican scum. She dumped you after she met me, didn't she? Well, you can have her now. You have my permission. I was hoping to get a welcome-home screw, but I'm done with her now."

What happened next, Enrique only vaguely remembered later. He pounded and pounded the Captain in a blind rage.

Even after Phillip lay in the blood-soaked sand, Enrique continued to pound him until, devoid of any more energy, he fell forward onto his knees and burst into tears.

As the spasms of anger and emotion began to subside, he looked at what he had done. The man lay motionless in the sand, covered in blood.

Enrique rose, kicked him one more time in the ribs, lifted his body into the boat and pushed it out to sea.

He turned, walked up the beach and sat on a sand dune. He watched the skiff until it was out of sight.

Staring at the stained sand, he wondered if he had killed him. He hoped so. Time passed. As the sun went down, the evening sky moved from yellows to brilliant shades of orange and bronze, lighting the sky with flame-like fingers. It met its demise melting into the horizon.

A sudden, chilling wind crossed his face and he looked up to see Lupita standing above him.

She wore a long white, hooded garment that swayed eerily in the breeze. The hood framed her wrinkled face and accentuated her mystery. Straggles of gray hair somewhat brighter than the gray of her skin, framed her face from the edges of the hood. He had always liked the way she appeared out of nowhere.

"Hola, my friend," she whispered. "I have come to heal your hands. Angelina must heal your soul". She leaned down and placed his hands in her crooked fingers.

From somewhere unseen by him, she produced a foul smelling

ointment, the same one she had used many times before on his hands.

"I have seen them worse," she said as she lathered on the cream. "In this lifetime of yours, you have fought the strongest and best fish the sea has to offer and won your prize every time, but they have left many scars over the years. No man can hurt these hands any worse."

"How did you know I needed you, Lupita?"

"I do not need to be told what my people need, Enrique. I had that knowledge the day my mother gave birth to me.

I admire your courage and your devotion to Angelina. No man has ever given me that. You have been a good leader in our village. You are a strong man."

"My admiration for you goes as deep, Lupita. We have lived through much together. We have taken care of this village together. We have always depended on each other. I appreciate you coming to me.

I think I have murdered a man with my bare hands and I am ashamed that I do not regret it. I would have said I was not capable of doing this, but now I know that I am."

From one of the folds in her robe, she pulled a bottle of tequila. "Have a drink," she said, handing him the bottle. He accepted and took a long drink. She did the same.

She sat next to him on the dune, a soft white glow from the moon encircling her body. Her gnarled fingers passed the tequila back and forth between them.

"This man you think you have killed. He caused a lifetime of pain and disappointment for you and Angelina, no? Your anger will be justified in the eyes of God.

Your quest will be to save Angelina. To help her heal. I have no medicine to fix your hearts, but you do. You have love. It is the most amazing healer of all, but first, you must heal yourself. You will find the regret. It will live in your heart and make you a stronger man than you are on this day. Only then will you be able to forgive yourself. You will then be able to ask God to forgive you. It will take time."

His head hanging low, his shoulders slumped, Enrique whispered into the night, "Lupita, mi muy bonita Angelina is suffering worse than I could ever imagine.

In her mind, he has shamed her. Her heart is broken and I do not know how to take away her pain.

Please, Lupita, go to her. My actions have caused me too much shame to face her. I am not the man I once was. I need to go to sea. I need the water, the fish. I need the dolphin."

Lupita took Enrique's shoulders in her hands and looked into his eyes. "It is the best place to deal with your inner questions, with your inner agony. Only you can reach into your own depths and search for healing. Go now, my friend. I will explain to the village. Do not stay for more than three days, or I will find you." Do not anger Lupita. Know that everyone is safe in my hands while you are gone."

Enrique walked to the pier and boarded his boat. For the first time ever, he had seen the image of God in her eyes.

Lupita disappeared back into the night.

•••••

At some point, one of the Captain's crew noticed the skiff not far from the ship. They could see the body and recognized their Captain, lying in blood. After some deliberation and a few beers, they decided it would be best to go and see if he was alive.

The strongest of them swam over to the small craft and dragged it back to the ship. They hauled him onboard and put him in his stateroom.

"If in the morning, we find that he is dead, we will take him out to sea and give him the same funeral he gave our friend. His body will be fish food. The fish will probably spit out his devil's blood."

Below, in the stateroom, one eye twitched and the thumb on his right hand jerked.

42

Tia Juanita looked up and smiled at Lupita. She had been waiting for her. No one ever needed to send for her.

Lupita stood in the doorway, her burlap bag strung across her shoulder and neck.

"I am here, Angelina. I will take care of you now." She moved to the bed and placed her fingers on the distraught woman's head. The air turned cool. The sunshine left the room like an obedient slave, replaced by Lupita's presence. The magic of the curandera had entered the room. Stillness prevailed.

Megan and Amy stepped back in unison. Fear, and at the same time admiration, filled their consciousness for this unfamiliar entity. They stared in awe, unable to comprehend the changes in the room.

Tia Juanita left and reappeared with a steaming kettle of water and a cup.

Lupita produced a cross and passed it over Angelina's head, neck and torso, murmuring chants in a tongue neither girl could understand.

"Ven aqui. Estate afuera. Come here, don't stay," Lupita chanted over and over as she passed the blessed cross over Angelina's body, calling the evil spirits out of the woman.

She reached into her bag and placed herbs; a combination of passion flowers, linden flowers and rattlesnake weed into the cup of hot water. She mixed crushed cilantro seeds and dark wine into a small bedside glass. She held Angelina's chin in her hand and offered her the tea.

"Drink, Angelina. Sip the tea. Drink the wine."

Angelina obeyed.

Lupita placed small dried pieces of nasturtium leaves on Angelina's forehead.

She closed her eyes, raised her hands over her head and began chanting. Lowering her arms, she passed her hands back and forth over Angelina, her chants reaching into the hollows of the room.

Wind blew in the window with force and thunder could be heard in the distance.

Opening her eyes, she looked at the women.

"Our friend will be fine now. The spirits are gone. She will sleep and when she wakes, she will see the truth and feel no more pain. Let us go. She needs to sleep."

The room warmed, the sun returned. The women followed Lupita out of the room.

Angelina slept as every moment of her life passed through her mind, in order of event, from her birth to the present. Each one lingered long enough for reflection and consideration. She awoke with a clear sense of what her next mission in life would be.

• • • • •

Enrique fished for two days, his boat drifting at will. For the first time in his sorry life, any fish that he caught, he let go. He couldn't kill again. He didn't want to see the life in the terrified fish's eye die.

Attempted sleep only caused stark visions of blood flying, women crying and fists and arms flying; pounding the air, meeting their target with a willful vengeance.

Being awake proved harder. He searched his soul for regret and found none; only the desire to beat him again and again, and then, again.

On the third day, a small island appeared. The current and wind must have brought him back towards the village. He anchored on the leeward side and tried again to sleep.

The faint sound of an engine awoke him from his fitful state.

He went above and saw his own panga heading towards him. Angelina sat at the tiller.

He helped her board his boat, not that she needed help. She took great pride in being a good boatwoman.

"I have been worried about you, Enrique. Lupita told us what happened on the beach. Many things have happened since that day, but I come to you to talk about what you did for me. I know you are suffering. I know it is not like you to do what you did.

I want you to know that it does not make you a different man in the village's eyes, or my own. You are the hero of every man, woman and child. People have come from the mountain to shake your hand."

"I am not a good man, Angelina. I may have killed a man. I cannot find any regret in my heart. I am no longer the man I used to be. I cannot even kill a fish now. Our people must not consider me a hero. I am a killer."

"We have no law in our village, only the law of our hearts and our consciences. You did what you did to honor one of us, me, and no one considers you a killer.

Enrique, you and I go back a long way. I have shunned your love because of this man. You never married. You never had children. Your dreams were never fulfilled. I was a fool. I ruined your life and mine has been empty.

I cannot hate him because I made my own ignorant choices, but you, do you not have the right to hate him? Did he not provoke you into the beating? Do you not have the right to the uncontrolled rage you feel? The world is better off without him, assuming he is dead."

"I have been married, Angelina, maybe not in a legal way, but in my heart. I have always been married to you. I never wanted another woman, so, one way or another, my life has not been empty. I will always love you, Angelina."

"I have had many hours to think, Enrique. Many hours to see the mistakes I have made. Many hours to admit how I really have felt about you all these years.

I have nothing to offer you. Age has taken its toll. I cannot bear children. I cannot be the young, willing bride you have deserved all these years, but I want you to know that even though I never married you, I have always, in my heart, loved you and wished things had turned out differently. I am sorry for the wasted years, Enrique." Her words caught in her throat and she cried.

No sleep, could this be a dream? Did she say she loved him? In spite of the fish smell on his hands, his salt-caked hair and the slimy, dirty clothes encrusting his unwashed body, he moved to one knee and took her hand.

"Will you marry me, Angelina?" he said simply.

She put her arms around his neck and whispered, "Yes, Enrique, I will."

43

We tethered our horses outside the hospital. We had decided not to take our conversation back to the women, just yet.

As we entered the hospital, I remembered my patient. Isabella stood over the man, sponging his damp forehead.

How is he?" I asked.

"He is fine. He sleeps, he cusses. It seems he sleeps less now, cusses more. I gave him his medicine and bathed him. His bedding is clean. I have tried to keep him comfortable. Can I go home now?"

"Yes, Isabella. You are a wonderful help in the hospital. Please thank Lupita for allowing you to help us. You would be an excellent nurse."

Blushing, she collected her things and left.

I joined Carlos and Francisco in what was now my office. The men had built it for me as a surprise. It even had a window.

"How's the mystery man?" Carlos asked.

"He'll be fine. It'll take awhile for him to recover completely. I don't know if he has much permanent damage, but he's sleeping less and cussing more. Always a good sign."

"Okay, enough of him. Let's go over our options about these other guys. I think these dead guys are probably Michael's hit men. What are the chances of two men in a black car, following us on the same road, being anybody else?

We know they're stupid, so they probably drove off a cliff. You have to wonder if the buzzards that chewed them up died of food poisoning," Carlos laughed apparently amused by himself.

He continued, "I think our next problem is Michael. I would assume he's been in touch with them most of the time, so when he doesn't hear from them, he gets worried. He thinks they gave up the chase and starts to look for Megan himself, or, he sends another couple of jerks to find out what's going on.

From the way Megan talks about him, I don't get the impression he's stupid and therein lies our problem. It wouldn't take him long to pick up their trail.

For all we know, he may be the one that had the first two pushed off the cliff. Maybe he was unhappy with how long it was taking. They also could have wanted more money."

Francisco nodded his head in agreement.

I, also, couldn't disagree with Carlos's assessment.

As we sat mulling over our thoughts, Carlos stared out the window, pensively.

He turned to us, a look of foreboding and darkness on his face.

"Maybe we should change this situation around. Maybe the hunted should become the hunters. We could go to New York and find this punk. Turn the tables on him. If I found the guy, I'd kill him with my bear hands."

Unbeknownst to us, Michael lay in his room listening to our entire conversation.

We heard a woman scream and, at the same time, the sound of breaking glass.

The three of us bolted from the room. I checked out my patient. Broken beer bottles covered the floor in front of his room, but he appeared all right, still in his sleep state. I ran out of the hospital, in hot pursuit of Carlos and Francisco. I knew it was Megan's scream.

We found her, crying hysterically, at Angelina's, cradled in Amy's arms.

"What's wrong, Megan, what's wrong?"

"Peter, Michael is in your hospital. What is he doing there?" she pleaded.

Carlos and Francisco took off running.

My head swam with panic. How could this be? What the hell was going on?

"Calm down, Megan. Take care of her Amy. I'll be right back. Megan go to your room and stay there. Lock the door. Amy go with her. Stay with her. Where the hell are Angelina and Enrique?" I asked, not waiting for an answer.

As I ran out the door, I caught a glimpse of Tia Juanita running towards Amy, waving a shotgun in the air. I heard her ordering everyone upstairs.

By the time I got to the hospital, Francisco and Carlos stood at the door of the hospital room, looking dazed. The room was empty. Michael was gone. The horses remained tethered to the rail.

Before long, the village men appeared, carrying lighted torches. The search lasted long into the night.

Turning over driftwood and beating chaparral bushes with sticks, the men searched the beach and surrounding hillsides. Nothing.

"The bastard disappeared into thin air, like a cockroach into the night," Carlos declared. "I'll find the son-of-a-bitch, if it takes me the rest of my life. You men go home. We'll pick this up at daybreak," he continued. None left.

The night had grown still. The moon hid behind clouds, leaving a starless sky in its absence.

Frustrated and sullen, I sat down next to the campfire and opened a beer. Francisco and Carlos fell into place next to me. Gazing into the fire, dirty, tired and more confused than I had ever been in my life, I asked Carlos what he thought we should do next.

"He's here. We have to find him. The road is still covered. We know he can't get to that ship, except to swim, and we have the beach covered. Let's go back to Angelina's and wait for daylight."

•••••

About a mile down the coast of the small village, Michael propped himself up on a small cluster of rocks, trying to maintain his strength and keep the endless waves from pummeling his face.

He knew he had escaped with his life and shook with glee as he reached the ocean's edge and saw that the Captain's ship had remained at anchor.

Escaping from the hospital, half crawling, half running, towards the sound of the sea, he had tumbled down a steep embankment, just ahead of his pursuers. His fall landed him in a towering pile of boulders imbedded in the sea's floor. He managed to get his twisted body hidden in a slimy, cave-like hole. Sea debris, from the encroaching waves, pounded him.

Michael watched as torches crisscrossed the beach and then moved onto the surrounding hillsides in pursuit of him.

Now, as he realized the search must have ended for the night, his only challenge was to swim out to the ship and avoid being drowned by the rising tide.

He flirted with the idea of hungry sharks, but decided he was out of options. Daylight would ensure his discovery.

He stroked wearily out into the rolling sea. The waves fought him, driving him backwards, with all their might. Weakness overcame him. Waves crashed over his body and water filled his mouth.

Again, as so many times before this night, his hatred for his situation fueled him and his arms began to move powerfully through the water.

His mind cleared. Visions of Megan filled his head. She would not destroy him. No woman would ever destroy him. Rage and fury enveloped his soul.

The anchor rode appeared before him, and, hand over hand, he climbed it. He felt the razor sharp barnacles, clinging to the chain, opening gashes in his flesh.

The water around him turned red with blood. His fear of sharks further empowered him. He reached the deck and swung himself on board. He lay there, bleeding, saltwater choking him, but overwhelmed with the feeling of safety.

From above him, he heard voices. Hateful voices.

"The bastard ain't dead. He's just like the other one. You can't kill the devil, ain't no man that can kill the devil."

One of them spit on him. It hit his face like a stinging bullet.

Michael jumped up, defying his near death state, his body bulging to its largest form. A mad-man's look contorting his face put the fear of the devil himself into the men.

"Get this ship going, you friggin' bastards. Fire up the engines or I'll kill every friggin' one of you with my bare hands. Move your black asses," he screamed, grabbing a metal pole from the deck of the boat and swinging it wildly at the men.

•••••

As I lay on my bed, staring at a black wall of sky, waiting for the impending daybreak, Michael's ship moved out of the harbor and headed north.

44

Daylight crept through the window, extending its fingers onto my face and waking me from a fitful sleep. I lurched to my feet, furious that I had fallen asleep.

Splashing cold water on my face, last night's events raced across my mind. Where the hell did that bastard disappear to? Did he somehow know Megan had come here?

Francisco, Carlos and the women were all seated at a table. A stranger sat with them. They all appeared to be listening intently to him.

Carlos looked up at me and the man stopped talking.

"Peter," Carlos started, "this man has an incredible story to tell us. Sit down."

"This man is Jameel," Carlos continued. "He is from the Cayman Islands and came here on the ship with the Captain and Michael."

Jameel stood to shake my hand.

His demeanor was that of a gentle giant of a man, with the blackest skin I had ever seen. He flashed a sheepish smile exposing crooked, shiny white teeth, contrasting the dark skin and his solemn brown eyes.

I offered my hand and it disappeared into the fold of a scarred hand, one so large it could have killed me with a quick swipe.

Carlos resumed. "The ship is gone, Peter, and Michael is on it."

Stunned, Carlos had my full attention. Angry questions fell from my mouth. "How? How could he get to it? We had men everywhere. Where are they going?"

Carlos continued, interrupting my tirade. "Jameel didn't want to go with them. He jumped overboard as the ship was leaving and swam to shore. We found him sitting on the beach this morning.

Michael and the other men commandeered the ship and the Captain is lying, near death, in his stateroom.

Apparently, they travelled here from the Caymans after finding out someone moved his money to San Diego. They were headed there when Michael got malaria in the Panama Canal. Their stop here was mere coincidence, solely because Michael was sick.

Jameel told us Michael hid for hours in some rocks on the shore. When it looked like the hunt was called off, he swam out to the ship and crawled up the anchor rode. Sick and bleeding, he had a fierce determination to get the ship moving. He raved like a madman about a bitch in a hospital and men wanting to kill him."

Jameel interrupted. "Me and the other guys listened to those two fools talk all the time. Couldn't help but hear them. Played cards and got drunk on rum every night in the Captain's stateroom. Got louder and meaner the more they drank. Carried on about the money and the girl.

Man, your Michael is one mean son-of-a-bitch, and crazy too. Only one person on the face of the earth meaner and that's that Captain.

He's crazier than a crippled wild boar being eaten alive by black flies. Threw one of the crew overboard in the middle of the sea and threatened the rest of us with the same. He ain't right. Man is the devil himself.

Him and Michael got some big plan for that money, but they ain't on the same page. Wouldn't surprise me if the Captain gives him the same end as the other guy once they get their hands on it.

By the way, he don't use the name of Michael, calls himself James. Don't matter though, what they call themselves, they two of the meanest bastards on earth.

Put money and women together in a man's head and bad things happen. Both of them crooked. Neither one trusts the other and ain't nobody can't trust either one of them, but one of them will win. Don't want to know which one. The end ain't gonna be pretty.

Next ship comes by here, I'm gonna hitch a ride back to the Cayman's and forget I knew either one of them."

Megan squared her shoulders and the attention turned to her.

"Michael will never see one dime of his stolen money," she stated, her voice drenched with anger, her eyes on fire.

"Why?" I asked, surprised at the sound of her voice. I had all but forgotten anyone else was at the table except Jameel and Carlos.

"Because before we left San Diego, I called my father's friend in the Caymans, had the money moved to New York and gave explicit instructions that the money was to be released to my lawyer.

I told the banker that if anyone asked for it, they were to be told it was in San Diego. It is waiting to be distributed to Michael's clients, every dime of it.

He can chase its trail until hell freezes over and he won't find it. Neither will the FBI. My father had good friends, all of which would do anything for him. He was very loved."

Everyone stared at Megan, stunned.

"Well, I'll be damned," Carlos said, shaking his head.

"And, when I get home, I'll call the FBI, tell them whatever they want to know and this nightmare will be over."

She turned her attention to me. "Peter, is it possible for you to contact Frank?" I would like you to ask him to contact the Coast Guard in San Diego and have them watch for the ship. I want him to tell them that a wanted criminal is onboard.

I must tell you though, I think Michael is a brilliant con-artist and he will figure this out. I don't believe he'll head for San Diego."

"Well, I'll be damned again", Carlos said. I could get a woman like you a job with the police force in New York."

I looked at her in disbelief. This woman had put wheels in motion, way before she believed she was personally in trouble, to correct a wrong which should have never happened, by a man she loved, proving the truth in the old saying, 'Hell hath no fury like a woman scorned'. Unbelievable!

I will contact Frank immediately, Megan. I sure will."

Footsteps sounded on the porch. We all turned, obviously still a little edgy.

Angelina and Enrique appeared in the doorway. The room fell silent.

Enrique broke the silence. He removed his hat, laid it across his chest and looked at Angelina, and then at us.

"Angelina has agreed to marry me," he stated simply.

Angelina blushed.

45

Michael's disappearance catapulted them into a sense of confusion, anger and disgust. Jameel's revelations had taken them into a mindset of disbelief, confusion, awe and amazement.

Enrique's announcement propelled them to the other end of the spectrum. Joy and happiness surfaced like an eagle soaring out of a great canyon.

By noon, most of the village was celebrating with Enrique and Angelina.

•••••

Meanwhile, out at sea, Michael released the skiff's lines, dropped it into the placid water and jumped overboard.

Rowing to shore, he watched as the ship and its occupants sailed off. He knew it would take no time for that friggin' bunch of idiots to notify the authorities.

Later, he sat on shore smugly fingering the Captain's gun. He was no man's fool, he knew that for sure.

•••••

A thousand bees, searching for their Queen's dinner, would not be as busy as the villagers preparing for the upcoming wedding.

The women formed a commanding force and seized control of the village. They gathered fabrics for dresses, planned food and kept the men in line, instructing and orchestrating their every move.

The men, including Jameel, did whatever they were told, not daring to disagree with one of them. They were rewarded, after their days work, with tequila.

The festive air dominated every breathable inch of space in the once sleepy village.

Due to his stellar ability as a pilot, Frank didn't run over the wedding preparations as he landed his plane.

Ignoring the fear of their women's wrath, the men ran to greet him.

Jumping from the cockpit, he called, "What's going on here."

"A wedding, Senor Frank, a wedding for Enrique and Angelina."

A young man rounded the plane from the other side. The men went silent.

Francisco stepped forward, pulling his son towards the group.

"I would like all of you to meet my son, Antonio," Francisco beamed.

"Frank, thank you for this surprise," Peter said, embracing his friend. "You've missed a lot in your absence."

"Did you save your princess, Peter, or just marry her?"

"You just can't help yourself, can you Frank?"

Today, even the women decided the men should take a day off.

•••••

While they welcomed Antonio into the folds of their life, Michael pushed the skiff onto a rocky outcropping and watched as the breaking waves broke it into pieces.

Following a narrow dirt trail along the coast, a grazing horse greeted him with a sleepy eye. His luck never seemed to fail him; he could always count on that.

"Want to go for a ride, boy?" he said as he mounted the animal.

•••••

Peter and Frank sat in the cockpit of the plane, drinking a beer, hashing over the recent events.

Frank picked up his radio and called the authorities.

"That done, Peter, what's your next plan?"

"I don't know, Frank. I really think Megan and I could have something, but I don't know. She's mighty fragile in the relationship department.

The hospital is finished, Antonio is here and he has Isabella as his nurse. After Enrique and Angelina get married, I may just sail to Tahiti."

"What do you think Megan will do?"

"I don't know. If that Captain survived Enrique's beating, I'm really hoping those two bastards kill each other and end this nightmare for her. I suppose she'll go back to New York and start over."

"You know, Peter, I've told you before that Sadie would want you to be happy. If not now, when? Maybe you should take a shot. Give her a chance to say no. Who knows where it could go? It's not like you have anything to lose."

"I don't know, Frank, I just don't know. Let's go find the others."

•••••

Michael aimed the gun and fired. The coyote fell to its death. Not bad, he thought. I'll eat tonight.

The trail ran high though the mountains of this God-forsaken country, overlooking the fearsome coast. No sign of human life had come into his view for days. No ships could be seen at sea.

He had long ago stopped thinking of his plusher days. Now it was simply a matter of his own survival. He against the forces of nature, starvation and dehydration. One lone force against the world.

Michael's mind played the part of a great, sword-yielding pirate. He, and he alone, would retrieve his gold. Wine, women and song would be his again. Men would fear him. Women would bed him.

His campfire lifted tantalizing flames into the air. The coyote sizzled. His mouth watered. It watered for the flesh of his first kill, for the gold he would reclaim and for the women he would have. Tomorrow would be his day of reclamation.

•••••

Days fled by in Puerto San Luis. The impending wedding grew closer. The people became more excited.

Megan slept peacefully in her bed. She awakened to the sound of her door opening. "Amy, is that you?" Silence, no answer. "Amy?"

In the moonlight, she saw the shadow of a man. She made out the gun in his hands. Panic engulfed her. "Michael?" she screamed.

"Did you think you'd get away with it, you bitch?"

Another body flung itself into the room and landed on top of Michael. They fell to the floor. The gun went off. Megan screamed again. One of the men stood up.

Megan jumped from the bed, falling into Peter's arms. "What happened, Peter? Where did he come from? Are you okay? Oh, Peter, is he dead?"

Carlos and Amy rushed into the room, followed by Francisco and Jameel.

"What happened here?"

"I don't know, Carlos, I heard Megan scream, ran in here, saw Michael and jumped him. He fell, the gun went off and I think he's dead."

"Get the girls out of here, Francisco," Carlos demanded. "And, find Enrique."

"Son of a bitch," Carlos said. "Son of a bitch." The two men stood, looking at his lifeless body.

"How do you think he found her, Carlos?"

"We have to have a look around. Maybe he's been hiding in the village somewhere, watching her."

"Let's get this cleaned up. Jameel, can you get him outta here?" Carlos said with the coldness of a life-long cop. He rolled over the body and spit on him.

Jameel picked up the body and flung it over his shoulder like a sack of potatoes. He headed for the mountain.

"Good riddance to bad rubbish, Carlos spat."

Downstairs, Amy held Megan as she sobbed.

They found his horse the next day. Found his hiding place in the village. Found the left-over meat of his coyote.

The men returned to the village, satisfied that the mystery was solved. At the same time, the mountain willingly accepted another secret into its fold.

46

For generations, the little fishing village, with its pristine bay and towering mountains stood as a stage, encompassing the villagers' lives.

Droughts of both the sea and land caused brutal famine. Marauding bands of criminals burned its buildings and left the people to rebuild from the dirt up, with nothing but their bare hands and determination. Violent hurricanes raced in from the sea and pummeled its earth with floods and raging landslides. Stampeding, infectious diseases attacked its people, leaving death in their wake.

The village came back every time. Its people celebrated the joys of life between each disaster, joining forces and restarting, rebuilding and renewing their faith in God.

Every villager had been born here, almost all of them died here. Only a few ever left. Puerto San Luis stood proud in its history, proud of its joys and sorrows.

Never in the history of this village, would anyone have anticipated the joy of the forthcoming wedding. It would, forever in time, stand out as one of the major events of this village.

•••••

Enrique stood motionless, his unerring eyes fixed on the walkway upon which his bride would come to him. Carlos, Peter and Francisco, his chosen padrinos, stood next to him. Perspiration dampened his guayabera, the traditional wedding shirt men had worn for centuries, the one he had saved from his father's belongings.

Megan stood at the crest of the beach, carrying a silver tray. Upon it, Enrique had placed the same thirteen gold coins, the arreha his father had given to his mother, symbolizing Christ and his twelve apostles. He would hand them to Angelina, placing all his worldly goods into her care and safe-keeping, giving her his unquestionable trust and confidence.

His young niece and nephew stood dressed as a miniature bride and groom.

The boy, his padrino de laso, held two gold wedding bands and a lasso, rosary beads that he would place around the couple as they married, to ensure the Lord's guidance in their union.

Enrique turned his eyes to Lupita. Standing under the flowered arch where he would take his bride, her white robe floating in the ocean breeze, she stood ready to fulfill his lifelong dream.

He had waited for this moment all his life and still, in the hollows of his heart, feared it would not happen.

As the sea lapped gentle waves onto its shore and the seagulls flew overhead, flamenco music filled the air, the love and excitement of the villagers floating on its notes.

As Enrique stood pondering the life that had brought him to this day and the traditions steeped into the history of his village, the music changed.

Megan, followed by Amy and Tia Juanita, Angelina's chosen madrinas, proceeded down the aisle. A serene silence fell over the village.

Illuminated by the sun, Lupita raised her arms above her head, in a wide sweeping move, the sleeves of her robe opening and forming a wing-like appearance. She raised her face to the sky and chanted a prayer to the Lord.

Enrique prayed for the appearance of his bride, his breath caught in his throat, his mind frozen in agonizing fear.

As if by Devine Intervention, Angelina appeared, in glorious beauty, at the head of the walkway.

A tiny girl, the madrina de ramo, dropped flowers at her feet as she walked towards him.

Enrique lost sight of every sound and every person in attendance. Peter took his arm to steady his trembling body.

Taking their places in front of Lupita, their past, their present and their future all blended together into this one moment, this priceless, tiny piece of time.

"Welcome, to this, the most glorious day of our lives," Lupita began. "Welcome to this sacred union of our two most beloved friends. We have waited a long time for this moment.

Welcome to our newest friends to whom we also owe a great

deal, and welcome to our old friends who have returned to us after such a long departure.

Our lives will forever more be enriched by these events. We will go forward stronger, prouder and more loving than we have ever been before.

Please bow your heads and thank our Lord for these unequaled blessings."

The congregation prayed, holding their rosaries to their hearts.

Isabella handed Lupita an ornate cross, which she passed over Enrique's and Angelina's bowed heads. Kissing it symbolized their faithfulness to each other.

The ceremony would begin.

Enrique offered his wrists to Angelina, and she offered hers to him. Lupita tied them together with a pink satin ribbon. Francisco stepped forward to place the lasso around their necks in a figure eight. These traditions symbolized their love, which would bind the couple together every day, as they equally shared the responsibility of marriage, for the rest of their lives.

Enrique listened to Lupita's offerings of prayer. He heard her offer God the presence of her congregation as testimony to their love for each other.

He looked at their bound wrists and realized that they had been bonded all their lives.

Lupita removed the gold coins from Megan's tray and placed them in Enrique's cupped hands. He slid them into Angelina's. She closed her fingers around them, accepting his love and trust. He closed his eyes and prayed his own prayer, his heart bursting with thankfulness.

Lupita, holding the prayer book over their hands, asked "Do you, Enrique, take Angelina for your lawful wedded wife from this day forward?"

Their eyes locked, he responded, "I do."

"Angelina, do you take Enrique for your lawful wedded husband for the rest of your life?"

Angelina gazed into Enrique's eyes, not able to control her own tears.

Enrique waited, his heart pounding in his head.

"I do." She whispered.

"Before God and all witnesses, I now pronounce you man and wife. You may kiss your bride, Enrique."

He leaned forward, placed his lips upon hers, and felt the sweetest passion a man could ever experience.

They turned to face their friends and families as husband and wife.

Amidst tears, laughter and tiny red stones tossed at them for good luck, Enrique led his bride up the aisle to a flowered horse-drawn wooden cart.

This cart, and its golden stallion, would take them to his home, where they would spend the rest of their lives together.

47

As Enrique and Angelina approached the beach, their guests formed a huge heart-shaped circle in the sand. His brothers, now joined by other friends with trumpets and accordions, filled the warm evening air with joyous music.

Enrique, beaming with pride and over-whelmed with the disbelief that his life had finally come to this long prayed-for moment, placed his hand on Angelina's waist and guided her into his arms. He led her into the circle for their first dance as newlyweds.

I stood with Megan and reached for her hand. "Would you do me the honor of this dance?" I asked.

"Yes, Peter, yes I would."

"I have never seen a lovelier bridesmaid in my life."

"Nor I, a more handsome groomsman."

I knew, in that moment, that I wanted to hold her in my arms for the rest of my life.

As the sun set and the moon rose and took its place in a star-filled sky, it created a diamond faceted path across the sand and led to a rocky cliff.

"Walk with me, Megan," I asked.

As we walked towards the path and up onto the cliff, Frank's words reverberated in my head. He had said Sadie would want me to be happy. She would not want me to live my life alone.

I could see him dancing with Tia Juanita from the cliff. I decided to trust my friend. He had been right when he asked, if not now, when?

"Megan, I know I am probably out of line, but I can no longer deny my attraction to you. I think we could have something together. I know you must think I'm crazy and I know, with all that's happened, you are probably not ready for this, but I need you to know how I feel.

Fate brought me to this village, but you, you brought me life. You made me feel again.

Oh hell, Megan, I'm a doctor with a scientist's mind, I'm not a poet, or good at putting feelings into words".

I paused to take a breath, staring out into the moon-path, suddenly hating Frank for talking me into this and feeling foolish.

Megan remained silent by my side, adding to my embarrassment. Going against my own common sense, I continued.

"Megan, I've only been in love once in my life and never expected to be again. The people and the love in this village have given me back the desire to live and made me realize that I will be able to love again.

I've known hundreds of women. I've spent my life indulging them in their idea of beauty. I had no interest in any of them.

But you, from the moment I met you on the road, I haven't been the same".

Wishing again I had never brought the subject up, I waited for her rejection.

She moved away from me, her hands suddenly trembling.

"Peter, out of millions of men, in the largest city in the world, I managed to become involved with the three biggest losers to ever walk the face of the earth.

That being said, I don't know if I am ready to try again."

"Okay, Megan. I'm sorry. I over-stepped my bounds. Please forgive me." I dug my feet into the sand like a school-boy.

"Peter, please hear me out. I didn't say no. I said I didn't know if I was ready. I have been attracted to you, too. I just can't trust my feelings, or yours, for that matter. Maybe it's not you I don't trust. Maybe it's love I don't trust.

I do know one thing for sure. I have nothing but time and if you're willing to give me time, I'm willing to give you a chance."

I took her into my arms and kissed her. She returned my kiss with a passion I never thought I'd feel again.

"My dream has always been to sail to Tahiti, Meg. Come with me," I whispered into her hair.

"Only if I can Captain the ship," she giggled into my ear.

I knew, in that moment, I had finally heard the human voice I so desperately needed to hear.

•••••

Michael's breath on Jameel's back would change the course of the village's history again.

Made in the USA
Columbia, SC
29 May 2019